Arkhangel

Arkhangel

JAMES BRABAZON

MICHAEL JOSEPH
an imprint of
PENGUIN BOOKS

MICHAEL JOSEPH

UK | USA | Canada | Ireland | Australia
India | New Zealand | South Africa

Michael Joseph is part of the Penguin Random House group of companies
whose addresses can be found at global.penguinrandomhouse.com

First published in the UK by Michael Joseph, 2020
002

Set in 13.5/16 pt Garamond MT Std
Typeset by Jouve (UK), Milton Keynes
Printed and bound in Great Britain by Clays Ltd, Elcograf S.p.A.

A CIP catalogue record for this book is available from the British Library

ISBN: 978–0–241–34925–0
TPB ISBN: 978–0–241–34926–7

www.greenpenguin.co.uk

For Bella

This is only a foretaste of what is to come, and only the shadow of what is going to be.

Alan Turing

Prologue: Appointment in Arkhangel

Sunday 27 January 1991

'So, tell me,' she said. 'How does it start?'

'Where all stories do,' I said. 'At the beginning.'

'And where's that?'

'In Moscow. A long time ago. There was a merchant there, you see, very rich and very powerful. And one morning this merchant, he sent his servant to the market to buy food. In a little while the servant came back, empty handed. The master was about to punish him, but he saw that the man was terrified. He was white and trembling, and could hardly talk. So, once he'd calmed his nerves . . .'

'With vodka?'

'Of course! It's Russia. Always with vodka. So, once he'd calmed his nerves, the merchant asked him what was wrong. And he said, "Master, just now, when I was in the marketplace, I was jostled by a woman in the crowd. I turned around to look at her, and when I did, I saw it was Death who jostled me."'

'What did she say, Max?'

'Nothing. She just looked at him and raised her old, bony finger, like this.' I unfolded my right index finger and beckoned her with it. She shuddered, and pulled herself closer to me. 'The servant was scared out of his wits, of course,' I continued, 'and asked the merchant to lend him his horse so he could ride away from the city and avoid his fate.

I

"I'll ride all day and all night and go to your house in Arkhangel," he said. "Death will not find me there."'

'So, what happened?'

'Well, the merchant lent him his horse and the servant climbed up into the saddle.'

'What kind of horse was it? You have to tell me all the details. Was it a stallion, or a gelding?'

'No, it was a mare. A pale mare, sleek and beautiful and fast as an arrow.'

'Could it have jumped the old fence at O'Byrne's farm?'

I smiled and wrapped her fingers in mine.

'Oh, yes. And then some. She'd have taken the Aughrim River at Woodenbridge with a single stride.'

'That's some horse he has there, Max Mac Ghill'ean.'

'Do you want to hear the story, or what do you want?'

'Well I would if you'd ever get on with it,' she laughed.

'So,' I said, 'the servant got up on her and dug his spurs in the mare's flanks and they lit off at a gallop, as fast as they could. The merchant watched them go and he was well pleased because he liked the servant and wanted him to be safe. But now he had no food in the house, so he went to the marketplace himself and sure enough he saw Death standing in the crowd. He went over to her, bold as you like, and said, "Why did you threaten my servant this morning?" But Death said to the merchant, "I didn't threaten him. He startled me. You see, I was surprised to see him here in Moscow." "And why is that?" asked the merchant. "Because," Death replied, "I have an appointment with him tonight in Arkhangel."'

I

Monday 8 January 2018

It was an easy kill.

He was trapped, hemmed in by the Atlantic and the wild country of Donegal. No road. No telephone. Nowhere to run.

On the seventh night I pulled the plug on the skiff tied up on the beach by his cottage. I settled into a gully a hundred and fifty metres from the front door and waited: a black shadow dripping rainwater in a muddy ditch. The moon was hidden by banks of cloud that rolled in across the ocean from Iceland. Thick, fast squalls cut visibility and drowned out everything except the waves ripping up the bay.

The tide had turned. Conditions were perfect.

He was alone. He went nowhere, did nothing, saw no one. He was scared. Or stupid. Or both. I didn't know who he was, or what he'd done – but, at seventy-five, he'd either forgotten how to run, or didn't think he had to any more. Maybe he just wasn't thinking at all. Desperate men live only in the present. That much I did know. For ten months I'd anticipated nothing beyond sunset. Since I was sixteen I'd seen no further than the end of a barrel. The future was another country explored one day at a time. Interred in his thatched stone casket, he was waiting for someone or something. But whatever he was expecting, he wasn't expecting me.

*

He'd already been inside for two days before I arrived. I watched the house for a week from a holiday park across the bay. Our lives ground down to the same rhythm.

Each morning he rose at seven thirty.

He lit an oil lamp and kept the windows covered. Candle grease smeared the panes. Only the faintest of shadows cast on the age-browned curtains allowed me to track him from the living room to the bedroom and back again. No smoke leaked from the chimney. The rooms would be damp and cold and half-heated by Calor gas. There was no electricity. If he cooked at all, it would have been in the living room. There *were* only two proper rooms, and a wooden washhouse tacked on the back – an ancient extension, perhaps once an elderly relative's bedroom. Maybe it covered a well head. Maybe he drank his whiskey neat. Either way, he'd need to resupply before long.

At dusk he lit the lamp again.

He extinguished it at ten.

And rose at seven thirty.

Moss grew in the roof. Weeds tangled the kitchen garden. Garden trash was piled against the back door. The cottage was desolate, but not derelict – one of the few surviving remnants of a lost landscape of thatched poverty. Americans thought they were quaint. I thought they were more like millstones than monuments, tying us to a past that had got us where, exactly?

Here. *Exactly*.

I flexed my palm around the grip of the semi-automatic and focused on the rain-roar berating the headland.

The nearest house was five hundred metres to the north-east. It had been empty for a year – an unwanted holiday home languishing in negative equity. The track to its front door wound off to the main road four hundred metres further on. Seven hundred metres to the south-east a couple from Birmingham gazed out over Ulster in the midst of their retirement. Good luck with that. Drongawn Lough lay due south. Everywhere else was just rough sea or sodden turf.

I spent twelve hours in the gully. Out of habit I clicked a little pebble I'd picked off the beach against the back of my teeth. I didn't need it: the rainwater kept my throat moist and my head clear.

It was a two-man job. But, as usual, I was flying solo: the details – and the consequences – were on me alone. While I'd snatched moments of sleep a night vision camera picked out in electric green the whitewashed walls of his self-imposed prison.

A week-long reconnaissance was just enough to establish a pattern of life, and short enough not to cause suspicion by hanging around: the target was secluded – no bystanders in the way and none to threaten the operation; the holiday park owners were glad to take a week's rent out of season and asked no questions. If it blew up, there were only two people at risk: me and him.

Colonel Ellard – who'd drilled me hard as a new recruit – had been fond of reminding me that the enemy has a vote. 'He won't do what you expect him to just because you want him to.' That was day two of training and a lifetime ago. But Ellard would have agreed there was no point figuring out what this target's plan was. He'd made a choice, and he was going to have to live with it, however briefly. The fact that he'd chosen to come here, now, was the only certainty, the only fact to consider. I assumed he was armed, and that the doors might be rigged. But only one of us was going to leave the cottage, and on the current balance of probabilities that was going to be me. 'Surprise,' concluded the colonel, 'neutralizes ignorance. Briefly.'

But Ellard didn't send me on jobs. Commander Frank Knight did. And Frank had been clear about two things: the kill had to be verified and the cottage had to be swept. I didn't know what, exactly, I was looking for. And neither, I suspected, did Frank.

This was a rare target of opportunity – the sort I hardly ever dealt with. No prep, no briefing, no one in Whitehall pretending they couldn't remember my name – just another bloody love letter from Frank to his dagger man. Maybe it was personal. Maybe I should have asked. But questions had got me into a lot of trouble in the past. For better or worse, if I was in it again, I was in it for good.

No ifs. No buts. No questions.

Zero six thirty.

Dirt fouled my black kit; my face filthy with bog grime. I left the balaclava rolled in my pocket. There was only a dead man to see me, after all. The inside edges of the tiny window frames, which in an hour would glow gold with lamplight, were still solid black: ancient beams as tough as prison bars. I could no more get in through them than he could get out of them.

I press-checked the SIG – a silenced .45. Ten rounds in the magazine and one up the spout. I'd chosen custom-made semi-wadcutters: thick lead rounds with a flat nose and no jacket, hand-loaded into spent brass picked up in Derry twenty years ago. Whoever got the blame for this would already be enjoying his Good Friday amnesty.

*

6

Zero seven hundred.

The sky lightened over the limestone ridges that cut between the cottage and the village at Cashel Glebe. People would be stirring: children dressing for school; farmers already at their herds. The glare of car headlights flickered on the low cloud over the lough.

In the past I'd liked these last moments; cherished them, even, for their clarity, their sense of purpose: before the green light the world drew into focus. At first I had imagined it a trick of the rifle scope. But I found the same simplicity of vision glinted off a knife blade, too, or gleamed on the tight wire of a garrotte.

Now I just went over the exfil details step by step, over and over. I turned the job around and upside down and shook it until it shed its secrets. Any idiot can get in anywhere on earth. The trick is getting out again.

He might have trapped himself – but he'd given me an exit. It was two and a half klicks to the jetty at Altaheeran on the west side of the lough mouth. I'd run the skiff down on the flood tide and then pull hard across to the opposite shore. No need for an outboard. If she sank, I'd swim to the quay. I'd left a Kia rental and a change of clothes there and was wearing a base layer of neoprene skins. It was too risky to head towards Belfast and the barracks at Raven Hill; and, as old man Ellard said, 'A rabbit never bolts straight for the burrow.' Frank would let me know where and when we'd debrief. Knowing Frank it would be in a pub in Mayo. And if not in Mayo, then in a pub for sure.

I rolled my shoulders and turned my face to the west. The squall blew through and a little of the old clarity seeped back.

*

Zero seven thirty.

H-hour.

The lamp lit up the window. I cocked the hammer and spat out the stone.

Good to go.

I made my way along the gully and emerged at an oblique angle to the front of the cottage. If he bolted out the back I'd hear him first and then see him run. Then he'd have to choose between me and the sea. It was just light enough to step foot safely, briskly. The soles of my boots trampled the ragged winter grass, cutting a trail to his door. I covered the distance gun up, ready.

Nothing, no one moved. So far, so good.

I put the silenced muzzle of the .45 to the keyhole. The slugs could take the lock out of a door, and the heart out of a man. I held my breath and squeezed the old latch with my thumb and pushed gently. Unlocked. No wires. Exhaling, I pushed harder. Nothing went bang. The door opened and inched into the gloom.

And then, immediately, the stench of rotting meat. I stepped in, the door still opening. He was there in his hearth chair, sitting with his back to me, the unthatched pate of his skull cresting the antimacassar. I fired immediately. The top of his head vaporized. A shower of brain and bone went up as the slow, heavy bullet tore on unchecked, shearing a lump of masonry from the fireplace.

I circled around him quickly, taking in the room. Oil paintings dotted the walls: above the mantelpiece a pale mare galloped across the fields; on the opposite wall the sun set in oils over Drongawn Lough. By the window a stopped clock hung above a stuffed and mounted woodcock. It was bitterly

8

cold and my breath fogged the foul, stinking air. A hurricane lamp by the window raked the room with thick, juddering shadows. The door to the bedroom was closed. Bolt upright, the target had hardly moved. Only his head had slumped forward. There was an open leather bag between his feet. I kept the SIG on him and kept moving. The front door banged to, muffling the rush of wind and waves. I faced him then.

I hadn't killed him.

But he was dead all right.

Six-four, a hundred and seventy pounds and in good shape. The top of his head was missing, but his face was intact, eyes open, staring down into the hearth. His skin was blackening, cadaverous. And in the middle of his chest a dark ring alive with maggots spread out from the bullet to the heart that had finished him.

Held loosely between the fingers of his left hand was a folded slip of paper. I bent down and pulled at it, keeping the SIG at the ready. His hand fell away and left me clutching a hundred-dollar bill. As the body moved, I gagged. The smell was almost overpowering. He hadn't lit the lamp that morning. He'd been dead for at least a week.

For the last seven days it was not his shadow I'd tracked from room to room, dawn to dusk, but his killer's.

And then all hell broke loose.

2

'So what happened?'

Commander Frank Knight sipped his Guinness and pinched the foam from his lip. Then he settled his glass and looked directly at me, evaluating the clues staring at him from across the table. I looked away and sank into the chair.

'What didn't happen?'

No matter how much I bit down on it, I was obviously in pain. I'd rubbed just enough fentanyl into my gums to make the drive bearable. As it wore off I could feel my muscles going into spasm.

'Have a drink,' Frank urged, and pushed my untouched pint towards me. His tone was encouraging and relaxed – which was a warning, because Frank was never relaxed. He was either for you or against you, and there was no neutral ground. His anxieties – rages, sometimes – kept mine in check: two sides of the same bad penny that cropped up in the pocket change of every off-the-books job the Brits had cashed in for over two decades. Since we'd first met on the firing line at Raven Hill back in the mid-nineties, he'd engaged me in nearly every kind of killing there was to be done, nearly everywhere on earth. In the process we'd propped each other up as guarantors of our mutual survival.

But things had changed. My perspective on his hall of mirrors had shifted.

The last job Frank sent me on – a virtual suicide mission

in Sierra Leone – had unravelled badly enough for him to question the appetite of his once willing executioner. Groping for an exit that wasn't there, I'd come back from West Africa and gone into hiding: at first in self-imposed exile as my body purged itself of the memory of the jungle; and then wherever a day's walk would take me. I'd surfaced in the only place I could call home: the base at Raven Hill outside Belfast. Old Colonel Ellard was still running the place – his retirement postponed indefinitely after I'd declined to fill his shoes. He took me back in and put me to work on the ranges to keep me busy.

Two months later and there I was being debriefed in a pub with Frank.

It was a relief of sorts to be sitting at that table in the front room of Doherty's – a locals' boozer on the main drag in Ballina, a stone-skip from the salmon-torn waters of the River Moy. Behind us rows of blue and yellow flies with faded price tags gathered dust alongside unsold reels and old cane rods. The windows were half-shuttered in precaution against the prying eyes of passing wives. We both faced the door. Old habits die hard.

I'd come full circle – except that now I looked to my own defence, and, as a result, Frank to his. Sierra Leone had proved what every job had always promised: that one man is always expendable. To know that – to have *lived* it – and to have decided to keep at it, anyway, was neither normal nor reasonable. We both knew it. And I guessed in Frank's eyes that made me as useful as it did dangerous. It was a fine balance, too, because no matter how dedicated the disciple, disillusionment breeds disloyalty – and Frank didn't allow his gamekeepers to turn poacher.

When I was nineteen, he'd told me I'd been selected

because I'd fulfilled his search for 'a legally sane psychopath'. But you reap what you sow. So now we met in public. Neither of us was likely to shoot the other in broad daylight.

His eyes flitted across the room and scanned the bar. He was unsettled. Anxious.

'We don't have much time,' he pressed me. 'Your check-in was incomprehensible and you look like shit.' He smiled and took another swallow of stout. The Dublin in his accent thickened, taking the edge off his officer's clip – the only clue he ever gave that his temper was about to blow. 'So what the fuck happened?'

'You never were one for small talk, I'll give you that.'

Frank sized me up and went to speak again, but thought better of it. I'd stretched my left forearm across the table. A trickle of blood had run down it and smudged the back of my hand red where it rubbed against my jacket cuff. I licked my right thumb and worried away at the stain. Beneath my sweater unsealed wounds leaked into my shirt.

The first bullet to hit me – an armour-piercing 5.7 round – had grazed my left bicep. The shot that followed it had been slowed by the thick wooden chair I'd dived behind – burrowing into my left shoulder, and not through it. The lump of steel-tipped aluminium ground against my clavicle. Of the blood and mud that had fouled my face and clothes during the flight from the cottage, nothing remained. The hard, cold swim to the far shore had seen to that. I'd patched myself up as well as I could with the trauma kit in the Kia.

As far as ambushes went, it had been spectacular. If I hadn't bent over to pluck the note from the corpse's fingers I'd have been shot dead then and there. The first rounds zipped over my neck. I'd launched myself over the cadaver and come up firing behind his chair, shooting directly into the flares of burning gas erupting from the end of the enemy pistol. I sent three massive lead slugs into . . . nothing.

As I'd dived, my arm had been grazed. But it was as I came up again that I'd been hit in the shoulder – through the chair. I'd put my miss down to my wounds and kept firing. Shards of wood exploded from the frame and panels of the bedroom door. I'd fired again, high, low and wide, cutting a triangle of certain death in the darkness.

But through the holes the SIG tore into the gloom of the other room had come a bright, deafening volley in reply. One round buzzed my ear. The other clipped my watch. Four more peppered the edges of my jacket. The bullets were streaking out of the holes I'd blasted. I'd turned side-on and fired again, trying to anticipate the movement of an assassin I couldn't see but was almost close enough to touch. Yet the shots had kept coming.

In the end I'd hurled myself towards the front door of the cottage, rolling and tumbling back on to the sodden turf, all the while pursued by a stream of armour-piercing pistol rounds.

I'd made it to the car. But the drive from Donegal to County Mayo had not been a pleasant one – six hours at the wheel, changing cars first in Strabane and again in Monaghan. Of the other half-dozen rounds from the shooter's little pistol that had drawn blood, only one had checked me at the time: a ricochet that had torn a neat furrow in my right thigh. Mercifully it hadn't kneecapped me, or severed an artery.

It was in Strabane, too, that I'd first looked properly at the banknote I'd pulled from the dead man's fingers. The shock of unfolding it had been so unexpected that I'd sat and stared at it for a full five minutes before driving on. Crouched in the rain-soaked gully I'd imagined that, whatever the target might have been expecting, it wouldn't have been me. But perhaps I was *exactly* whom they'd been expecting.

I shivered at the thought of it.

Frank couldn't see the wounds, but I knew he'd already be calculating the blowback in London, and how to deal with it. I summoned my strength to play the game and lifted my glass.

'*Sláinte*,' I said. I drank deeply, gulping down the bitter-sweet black. As the alcohol relaxed me, I remembered I was exhausted. 'Before "what happened" how about "who was he"?'

Frank shifted in his chair.

'You didn't want to know who he was when you took the job.' He picked up his pint again deliberately, holding it in front of his mouth. 'So why do you want to know now?'

'Cut the crap, can we? When I agreed, I didn't know there'd be a one-man army waiting for me.' *Or a message*, I thought. But I kept my mouth shut.

Frank just shook his head like the ever-disappointed parent he pretended to be. It was a role he both loved and loathed in turn, mixing affection and admonishment as my father had done before he died.

'Max,' he hissed, 'it's your fucking *job* to know that. At least to anticipate that there might be. Anyway, he was hardly an army, was he? For Christ's sake, what did you do – walk in whistling "Danny Boy"?'

I took another slug of the stout.

'Pretty much.'

The barman topped off a pint for a tourist dripping in blue

waterproofs at the bar. Outside it was, inevitably, still pouring down. There was no radio playing, but the rain and the
river made their own music which filled the pub with a steady
murmur. We could talk without being overheard or the fear
of audio surveillance – which was why, I guessed, Frank had
chosen it.

He shifted in his seat – preparing, I knew, to give as many
excuses as he was given.

'OK,' I conceded. 'What happened is that I didn't kill
him.' Frank put his glass down and leaned fractionally
towards me. 'I tried, but I couldn't kill him.' His eyes narrowed, as if by concentrating on my face he might discern
the truth of what he was being told.

'This is becoming somewhat of a speciality of yours,
McLean.'

'Oh, right. So it's surnames now, is it, *sir*?'

'Jesus, Max,' he snapped, '*you* wanted the bloody job. *You*
took the bloody job. And *you* agreed to do it on the information you had *at the time*. You turned down the command at
Raven Hill. So, let me remind you what that means.' He drew
breath, reminding himself, perhaps, what it really did mean –
for both of us. 'You are *given* orders. By me. And you *follow*
them. You aren't a fucking boy scout. You've killed more
people than most other operators have had hot dinners. So
why is that piece of shit not dead?' He breathed out hard and
rolled his shoulders.

I looked at him and smiled.

'Oh, for fuck's sake.' He just about held on to his temper.
'OK. His name was Chappie Connor. He was an Old IRA
man. Pretty senior. Joined the Provos after Aldershot. He
dropped off the radar in eighty-eight.' Frank sat back in his
chair and shook his head. 'Max McLean getting his arse

whipped by old fella like that. You daft cunt. Get you that desk to fly after all, shall I?'

I didn't rise to it. As messed up as the job looked, there was no way that Frank had sent me to kill a pensioner for something he did when I was still in short trousers. Almost no one even mentioned Operation Banner any more, no matter how hard it had been fought. Besides, half of PIRA's commanders had been British agents. In the end we'd practically been fighting ourselves. I also knew Frank didn't believe for a moment it was Connor who'd shot me. So the debrief game unfolds.

'*I'm* the cunt? Jesus, what did *he* do – fuck your wife?'

'What he did is need to know.'

'And I don't need to know.'

'Bravo, Max. You're getting the hang of this. And before you ask, it's got nothing to do with the Troubles. He's been out of that game as long as you've been in ours. He hasn't even been back in the country for five fucking minutes.'

I looked at Frank, but Frank was looking at the bar. The tourist sat and sipped his pint, lost in his phone.

'Why me? Why task UKN? Why not give it to Grumpy Jock and the Wing?' Frank turned his attention back to me and hesitated for a second. And then the bad penny dropped. 'Because you couldn't. No one knows, do they? Whitehall didn't sanction it. And neither did DSF.' Frank cocked his head to one side, which he always did when he was about to change the subject. When faced with anything he didn't like, Frank either stepped on it or over it. True to form, he ignored me and ploughed on.

'What do you mean that you tried to kill him but couldn't? Stop enjoying yourself for a moment and explain to me why it is that Chappie Connor's brains are not decorating a cottage in Cashel Glebe.'

'They are,' I said. 'He's dead.'

'But . . .' Frank stopped short of demonstrating his ignorance. The nerves at the base of my skull tingled. I was getting the better of him, and it felt good. It almost made up for the grinding pain in my shoulder.

'He was already dead, Frank. Someone had shot him through the heart, in the cottage at least a week ago.' I put my right hand under my sweater; Frank's jerked reflexively towards his open sports jacket. In this respect he'd never changed: threatened or confused, he reached, unfailingly, for his pistol. I removed my hand, slowly, and held it up. My index finger was bright red with blood. 'There was another shooter. A very good shooter; probably the best I've gone up against. *Ever* gone up against.'

Frank sat upright and put his hands where I could see them.

'Go on.'

I told him what had happened.

'As I made it out the door, I threw in a Willy Pete. The thatch went up like a rocket.'

'Jesus,' Frank sighed. 'You let off a phosphorus grenade? In the Republic? DSF is going to fucking love this. And outside?'

'I made it to the skiff. The whole place was in flames but I was still taking fire from the side room.'

'Second shooter?'

'No. I don't think so. Whoever it was shot out the window and then shot up the skiff. Shredded it. I made it to the surf and swam from there.'

Frank considered what I'd told him and fiddled with his pint glass.

'Max, please tell me this shooter is dead and not about to join us for a drink.'

'If he got out of that cottage, he's a fucking magician. Check the sat feed. You'd see a runner clear as day. There's no decent cover for miles. He fried.'

'Huh,' Frank grunted, and glanced towards the door. He looked suddenly defeated.

'He had me pinned, Frank. Either I got in the water, or he got me. That simple.'

'The hundred-dollar bill. You still got it?' I'd been waiting for him to ask. My orders had been to terminate the target with extreme prejudice – and, specifically, to search the cottage – though for what, exactly, hadn't been specified.

'No,' I answered immediately, putting my hands on the table and my eyes on Frank. 'Lost it in the surf.'

He wrinkled his nose and took the lie at face value. At Raven Hill we'd been taught subterfuge and sabotage in equal measure. We were all professional liars – though some of us forgot to remember we were no longer telling the truth.

'OK. The bag. What was in the bag?'

'Notes. Loose notes. US dollars. I only saw them for a second, but if they were all hundreds like the one in his hand? Ten grand? More, maybe.'

'Well, there's your answer,' he said. '*An* answer, anyway. We . . . rather, *I* . . .' he corrected himself, 'have been following the money. *That* money.'

'Yeah, well it looks like you weren't the only one.'

Frank ignored me and pressed on.

'He arrived in the country nine days ago from Moscow,

via Heathrow, and made a run for the cottage straight from Belfast City.'

'Round and round the money goes, but where it starts only a Russian knows.'

'That's it. And now, thanks to you and Willy Pete, the only piece of evidence not burned to a crisp is currently floating to Iceland. So figuring out *which* Russian just got a whole lot harder.'

'You know me,' I said. 'Always happy to help. Anyway, what's special about it, the money?' My stomach tightened.

'It's not the money that's special. It's what it's being used for that's special.'

'I see,' I said, though I didn't. 'What is it being used for?'

'I don't know.'

'Ah,' I said. 'That makes it very special indeed, doesn't it?'

He cleared his throat and lowered his voice so that I could barely make out his words above the hiss of the rain.

'All *I* know is that there's rather a lot of it.'

'How much is "a lot"?'

'Well, if my calculations are correct, and this is back of a fag packet mathematics, you understand?'

'Yeah, go on.'

'It could be up to a billion dollars.'

'Fuck.'

'To be honest, "fuck" doesn't quite cover it.'

'And no one knows what it's for?'

'Don't be a bloody idiot. Of course *someone* knows.'

'Best guess?'

Frank shifted in his chair.

'The money's being handled by the Russians, but I don't know where it's from or who's laundering it. Too big for the *bratva*.' Frank took another sip of his drink. He was right: even if the Russian mafia's ranks had been swollen by an oligarch, a billion dollars was out of their reach. 'Could be a private bank. Could be a national bank, a government. All I know is that it's being kept in cash and kept on the move.'

Commander Frank Knight had talked himself into a brief, stunned silence. At the bar the tourist finished his drink and braved the rain. The chill of the downpour outside fanned into the saloon as the door banged shut behind him. The barman cleared away his empty glass and came over to ask if we'd be interested in something to eat. Frank smiled and shook his head, and ordered me a whiskey instead.

'For the road. And make it a Jameson. I'm not wasting money on your Johnnie Walker rubbish.' Then: 'Get yourself sewn up and keep your bloody head down.' Frank checked his phone and buttoned his jacket. 'Seriously, Max, do what you're best at. Go dark and stay dark. I mean it. No comms whatsoever. I'll be in touch when I've worked out who Goldilocks is.'

I touched my temple in a mock salute.

'I'd concentrate on the bears if I were you, sir.'

He snorted and stood up and shrugged himself into his trench coat. He made to leave, and then stopped.

'Oh, and Max?'

'Yeah?'

'I don't have a wife to fuck. The only people getting screwed here are you and me.' And then he, too, disappeared through the door and into the deluge.

I limped to the bar and drank the whiskey neat. It burned my throat but tasted good enough. There were a lot of questions to answer. Sure, I wanted to know about the cash. I wanted to know who the shooter was, too – and why he'd left the hundred-dollar bill behind. But, right then, there was only one question worth worrying about. If he was fast enough to sidestep every round I fired, and good enough to hit me through the holes my own bullets had opened up, why the fuck was I not already dead?

3

'You're a bloody mess all right, Mac Ghill'ean.'

I inhaled hard as Doc leaned across me and prodded the wound in my shoulder with a long metal grip.

'What have you got yourself into this time?' His tone was both concerned and offhand, talking to me as he always had done, with personal affection tempered by professional detachment. He was the only person I knew who could be simultaneously disdainful and caring. Maybe that went with the job. Or maybe he was just anticipating my lies.

'Fishing accident,' I said. I tried to smile as he probed further and ended up grimacing instead.

'I see. Deep breaths now. That's good . . .' He trailed off – uninterested in my bullshit, distracted by the hunt for the little bullet still inside me.

He'd been patching me up for more than half of his eighty years. My father, a military doctor, resolutely refused ever to treat me himself, though whether out of uncertainty at his own ability or in awe of Doc's, I never knew. Either way, every sprained ankle, broken bone or bloodied nose was treated by Doctor Jacob Levy.

I'd never called him anything but 'Doc'.

His hands were neither as strong nor as steady as they'd once been, and the unruly mane of black hair that he'd once swept aside to wink at the officers' wives had receded to a brilliant white fuzz cresting what was otherwise now a brown, bald pate. But his green eyes still flashed wickedly in the lamplight, and when he smiled you still could see why he'd left half a century of broken hearts behind him.

And one inside him.

He'd carried a torch for my mother until the day she died. The flame still burned, too, and all the more brightly now that time had erased the certainty of who she really was and blunted the truth of what he'd become. When she waded into the lake behind our house with stones in her pockets, he'd dived into the depths of the whiskey bottle. It was too much for his wife. After she left him, he'd retired from Wicklow to a Victorian pile teetering on the shores of Lough Conn. No phone, no electricity – but plenty of *eau de vie*. I'd been lucky to find him sober after sunset.

I hadn't seen him for three years. It had never been safe to visit and it wasn't safe to be there, then – for either of us. But I could no more check myself into St Joseph's Hospital in Ballina than I could leave the wounds I'd sustained in the cottage untreated. Just as he always had done, he helped me unconditionally. I supposed that keeping me alive kept the memory of my mother alive, too.

'Nearly there, now. Tricky little beggar this one. Tiny, isn't it?' Doc probed deeper. I breathed out, hard.

He knew I was putting us both at risk. All those years and my mother still ruled his heart. One day it would be at the cost of his head. I couldn't decide if that was admirable or absurd – but the weakness it created worked to my own advantage: if anyone came looking for me, Doc would deny knowing me on pain of death.

'Fishing, you say? I'll remember that next time I'm casting on the lough. It's bad enough the Americans taking all the best salmon without the ones that are left shooting at us.' He twisted the steel in my shoulder. I gasped with the shock of it.

'And I'll remember to bring my own anaesthetic next time.' The fentanyl had worn off. For the pain Doc had nothing more than a glass of Paddy – one for him, and one for me. I swallowed what was left in my tumbler. Doc motioned for me to keep still.

'I'll be honest with you now, Mac Ghill'ean, anaesthetic would have been grand.' He looked at me and smiled a quick, tight-lipped smile. 'Because this is going to be some dose all right.' He turned his wrist as if springing a lock with the forceps, and then drew them slowly towards him, working the bullet clear. I tried to breathe through it. One final tug and he produced the mangled round before my eyes with a flourish. He smiled again, triumphant. I grinned back weakly.

'Five-seven,' he concluded, correctly. 'Nasty. Ricochet?'

'No,' I said. 'It went through a chair.'

He wiped the spent round on a swab and then dropped it on to the bedside table. It clattered to a halt beside his own, half-empty glass.

'The wound isn't pretty but it's not that deep,' he said. 'Damned thing got wedged by the bone. If it had hit you properly it could have taken your shoulder out.'

He cleaned fragments of wood and clothing from the wound and made especially sure there were no shards of bone that could threaten my lung. Then he packed it with disinfectant-soaked wadding and wrapped it with a bandage. I was propped up on a captain's bed in an attic room – lit only by an oil lamp – which within minutes of my arrival had been transformed into a makeshift dressing station. Like the rest of the house, it was an echo chamber of a life lived on the road: Indian cloth paintings lined the walls, depicting improbable intercourse in impossible profile, their blue silk and gold leaf shimmering in the half-light; a battle-worn Martini–Henry hung above the mantel; an assegai leaned against a Victorian tallboy. And beneath a glossy canvas of a black stallion standing alone in a field, a silver menorah competed for space on top of a dusty antique dresser overflowing with brand-new, newly empty bottles of whiskey.

He drained the last of the peat-coloured liquor from his own glass and ran through the inventory of my other injuries.

'Your thigh's a bit ragged, too, but it's not serious, either. The butterfly stitch should hold it. Another ricochet, or what-have-you, by the look of it. Surprisingly clean. The bicep's just a graze. And you,' he concluded, putting his empty tumbler down, 'are one lucky bastard.'

'I've felt luckier.' I winced again as I shifted my weight on to my right elbow. He removed the extra pillows from behind my back so I could lie flat on the mattress.

'I'm sorry I've nothing else for the pain,' Doc said. 'Used up all the local I had left on myself last week. Riding accident. Too much wire in the hedges.' Too much whiskey in the saddle, more like. He patted his thigh. 'I should have been off shooting for a week by now. Bloody old, that's my problem. But you'll be in good hands with Paddy here.' He poured a large slug of the amber liquid into my empty glass and refilled his own. 'Knowing you, I doubt you'll be staying for breakfast. I'll leave fresh dressings by the letter rack on the sideboard downstairs.'

Then, stooping next to me, Doc opened a drawer beneath the bedside table. Out of it he produced a Browning Hi-Power semi-automatic pistol. He placed it carefully next to the bloodied metal souvenir he'd just dug out of my shoulder.

'That should help you sleep easy.'

I nodded my thanks and caught a whiff of the gun oil that made the blueing shine.

'It's loaded,' he said. 'Full clip. And the safety's off. In case you need to go fishing again.'

He limped his way carefully across the Persian rug – an ornate blue island that spread out under the bed – and pulled the attic door open.

'Doc?' He stopped and looked at me from the other side of the room. He knew what I wanted to ask but let me find the courage to say it for myself. Three years had passed since I had last spoken his daughter's name. I still struggled to, even then. 'How is she?'

'Rachel?' he helped me out. 'She's in London now and happy.'

'*Má fheiceann tú í . . .*' I stumbled on in Irish. But it was no easier to find the words.

'If I see her, what exactly? Hmm? I'll be sure to say nothing to her. Nothing at all. You wanted to vanish, remember? And so you did. Whereabouts unknown. Presumed dead. And as much as he'd like to, not even this doctor can bring you back.'

He raised his glass in a toast. '*She'tamut.*' I shrugged. He smiled. '*To death.* One day I'll teach you Hebrew.'

'And I'll teach you Russian.'

'I'm assimilated,' he said, and winked at me.

I nodded and smiled back. There was nothing more to say. And come morning I'd be gone. The door clicked shut behind him. I waited for his footsteps to fade on the stairs.

'Rachel Levy.' I said her name out loud. The force of it in the silence of the empty room startled me. It was easy to pretend to want something I knew I couldn't have. But you don't forget your first love – even if I struggled at times to bring her face into focus. No matter how futile it was to pretend anything could have gone differently than it did, the feeling for her was still there – though whether what I felt was for her, or the *idea* of her, was impossible to untangle at that distance. Whatever it was, it still felt real: as real as the bullet wound in my shoulder, or the scars that ran down her wrists like tramlines – a journey that never reached its destination. It was a relief of sorts to know that I could still feel anything at all. I saw her as if from the wrong end of a telescope. I'd fantasized about bringing her back from the brink. Maybe it hadn't been her that needed saving. As a teenager I'd thought she'd blown my world apart. And then it was – for real.

'Forget it,' I said out loud. 'Forget *her*.' But I'd become as bad at taking orders from myself as I was from other people.

I reached over and picked up the Browning, dropped the magazine and checked the breech: one 9mm ball in the chamber, twelve in the box. The familiarity of the moving parts was reassuring. I ejected the round and checked the safety, the trigger pull, the hammer drop. I peered inside, worked the slide and reloaded. Definite actions with definite outcomes. Concentrating on the details helped me weigh anchor. The pistol was in immaculate condition. Most likely Doc's old personal protection weapon; most probably never fired in anger. Shootouts weren't his style. But he'd been deadly in his day, about that there was no dispute. I gulped down the refill of Paddy and thought about the hundred-dollar bill. But then, still trying to remember what Rachel looked like, I lapsed into deep, exhausted sleep – one hand on the whiskey glass, the other on the Browning.

Zero three hundred.

The rain stopped. The timbre of the room had changed.

Doc's house was south-west of Ballina town, on the north-east shore of Lough Conn. I could hear lake water lapping limestone outside and nothing else. County Mayo spread out around us in silence. Frank couldn't have chosen a better place for a debrief; Doc couldn't have chosen a better place to retire. The wick in the lamp still burned bright. I sat up and put the loaded pistol and empty glass on the bedside table, and examined my dressings.

The wounds hurt, but they weren't disabling. I'd managed the twenty klicks on foot from Ballina via Knockmore to Doc's place OK – all of it in the dark, most of it across country. I'd stopped only to buy a change of clothes and then pulled them on in a hedgerow. To the bullet holes and grazes I'd added a slash from a strand of razor wire hidden in a culvert and a mass of scratches on my left hand from a blackthorn bush. Doc was right, I was a mess – but I could walk, swim, run. My right hand and arm were uninjured. Besides, it wasn't my wounds that concerned me, but time. Frank had told me to go dark. That meant no contact with the barracks at Raven Hill, or with London, until Frank figured out who'd been waiting for me at the cottage – and how they'd known that's where Connor and I would collide.

He'd need to make sure he was in the clear with the Head Shed in Whitehall, too. It would take some deft footwork to explain why a job that no one had sanctioned had gone bang, and why I was no longer available to clean up any human mess that Her Majesty's Government wanted rid of. DSF – Director Special Forces – an old-school major general called Sir Kristóf King, was not well disposed towards Frank's bullshit at the best of times. Or mine.

No wonder Frank was pissed off. It could be weeks, months even, before I was back in business. And if I wasn't in business, I was up shit creek. The unpalatable truth, when I cared to swallow it, was that I wasn't Frank's close protection detail. He was mine.

I took a crumpled packet of Marlboros from my jeans pocket, lit one of the bent white sticks and sucked down the blue smoke. My shoulder burned. My left arm throbbed. I exhaled. I felt OK. I smoked the cigarette slowly, carefully. And when I'd finished it, dropped the stub in the empty glass. I couldn't put it off any longer.

Out of the ticket pocket in my jeans I took the hundred-dollar bill I'd plucked from Chappie Connor's dead fingers. As I unfolded it my heart rate climbed. I took a deep breath, and opened it fully, half expecting that my eyes had deceived me.

They hadn't.

Written in the thick, imprecise strokes of a permanent marker on the back of the note was a single Russian word:

Архангел.

If you twist the Russian Cyrillic letters into the Roman alphabet – like my mother taught me to do when I was a child – it becomes *Arkhangel*, and means the same in Russian as it sounds in English: Archangel. But in a country whose culture is rooted in the traditions of the Eastern Orthodox Church, the word also refers to something other than the angels themselves: the places named after them – or, more accurately, named after the Archangel Michael.

But although there is a city and parks and streets – and even an entire oblast – that borrow from the title of the divine warrior, in all of Russia there are only two places simply called 'Arkhangel' and they are both as ignorable as they are unknown to the outside world.

One of them is so small it barely registers on maps: a tiny hamlet two hundred and twenty klicks north-east of Moscow, buried deep in the countryside of the Komsomolsk district of the Ivanovo oblast. A clutch of houses dotted around St Michael's church and surrounded by miles of fields and forests, it's neither on the way to anywhere, nor a destination anyone who didn't live there would seek out.

Anyone but me.

I'd never been, but every stone of the road that ran through it; every bough that bore blossom at the back of the churchyard; every face framed by the windows of the wooden shacks dotted between stands of birch trees – they were scored into my mind as if I'd lived and breathed the experience of it all for myself.

Arkhangel was not a ragged corner of an unread map. For me it was home.

A home.

My grandmother had been born there. She had died there, too – after pushing my mother into the world cloaked in the thick slick of blood that haemorrhaged freely from between her thighs. She had survived Stalingrad. But there were no miracles in 1950s Russia – not even in Arkhangel. My mother's first screams had filled the room as the last light guttered out of my grandmother's eyes. And she a nurse, too. So it goes.

I examined the note in the glow of the lamplight. My father had told me once that there were no coincidences. He believed in synchronicity – the idea that things, events, could be connected across time and space without cause. I believed that I made my own luck. The paper was a bit dog-eared, and still slightly damp, but a defaced hundred-dollar bill was all it was. If it was a message, it had been delivered all right. If it wasn't, then I'd lied for no good reason about stealing the only piece of evidence that might unlock Frank's mystery for him.

One thing was clear, though – I'd told Frank not one but two lies: that I didn't have the note, and that the shooter was dead. But I didn't, couldn't, know that for sure and Frank knew it, too. He'd let it go. But *I* shouldn't have.

My first job in nearly a year and not only did I let someone get the drop on me, I didn't go back to finish it off. Finish *him* off. I knew as I hit the surf that I was saving myself and not the mission. That didn't bother me: dead men can't save anything. What did bother me was that from one angle it looked like the shooter didn't *want* me dead – he wanted me to run. And I'd obliged.

I looked at the hundred-dollar bill again. Benjamin Franklin looked back at me. Neither robbers nor assassins sit in a room they've turned over, with a bag full of cash and a rotting cadaver, for a week. Not the ones I'd met, anyway. I refolded the note up as small as I could and put it back in my pocket.

I got to my feet and walked over to the dresser to see if any of the empties weren't quite, but I was out of luck.

Max, I said to myself, *you don't know anything.*

But I did know I was glad I'd ended up at Doc's. He always insisted on using my Irish name – a name I never used. It belonged to another time. Another person. When my father was shot down over Angola in ninety-one and reported dead, I made a break for it. Sixteen and on the run. No mother. No father. Nothing to do but keep moving. When I called Doc from a phone box in Liverpool and told him I was enlisting in the Parachute Regiment 'as Max McLean', he'd reminded me there wasn't an English bone in my body. I'd reminded him

31

that *both* of his parents had been Russian, émigrés from the Communist shitshow that my maternal grandfather had fought to defend. 'But we've Irish hearts, you and me,' he'd said. 'We both became proper Irishmen' – and not, he'd meant, an *im*proper Irishman like my father. Although we both knew that I had always been my father's son, seduced and repelled in turn as he had been by the false idols of duty and honour.

Doc tried to talk me out of joining up, of course, but in the end he'd given in and faked a letter of consent for me. Thanks to the eminent Doctor Jacob Levy, the British were satisfied that my application was kosher. It most certainly wasn't.

Legitimate or not, it was the greatest gift anyone could have given me. From the ashes of my father's plane wreck, and the depths of my mother's grave, rose Private Max McLean. A new life. Unidentified. Untraceable. Undetectable. Or so I'd thought.

At Raven Hill, Colonel Ellard didn't care what you were called. He cared what you did. And what I did was learn to kill. When I said hello to Ellard I said goodbye to the army. Officially, I ceased to exist. I surfaced into the Unknown – a special operations kill team called by its army acronym: UKN.

But whereas, once upon a time, I'd been motivated by the idea of service, now I was prepared to kill without illusion. Quite what that made me, exactly, I wasn't yet ready to speak out loud. It's hard to accept yourself as someone you don't admire. At forty-two years old I was pushing it in the self-awareness stakes. But even old soldiers have to look in the mirror sometimes – if only to see who's standing behind them.

All I saw was a ghost.

Every story has a beginning. The trick is knowing where

to find it. I'd always thought my first kill was a long shot I'd taken across the roofs of West Belfast. It wasn't. The first life I'd ended was mine: Maximilian Ivan Drax Pierpoint Mac Ghill'ean was dead and buried.

Chasing his memory at Doc Levy's – or mooning over his daughter – wasn't going to bring him back. I sat on the bed and closed my eyes. *She'tamut*. I could choose to celebrate my death, or to regret it – but, either way, the last threads of my past were at breaking point.

Downstairs the front door banged to. The noise brought me to my senses. I turned the oil lamp down low and moved to the window. The curtains were open enough that I could see on to the driveway without disturbing them further. A figure darted across the gravel below, face hidden by a hooded top. Five-eleven, a hundred and fifty pounds. He stopped for a moment and turned towards me, looking up. I couldn't see him clearly. I stepped back into the room and made for the stairs. But I was too slow. I opened the front door of the house on to the red glow of his tail lights, disappearing on the road to Rathduff church. A breeze picked up, carrying with it the high-pitched hum of fast tyres on tarmac. I stared hard into the night and saw above the rise of the fields the juddering flash of halogen headlights.

I closed and locked the door and turned back into the hallway. No movement in the house. I twisted the handle to the drawing room and stepped inside. Doc's chair was pulled up by the fireplace, back towards me. The smell of peat and whiskey mingled with the smell of iron. I skirted the chair, eyes fixed on the floor, heart banging in my chest.

Face it, damn you. Face him.

I looked up and into Doc's eyes. He'd been shot. A single silenced bullet to the heart. I reached out to him and my phone rang. I knew who it was. Only Frank had that number. It wasn't until I went to answer him that I realized I was still holding the Browning and my breath. I put the phone to my ear. The line clicked and buzzed. And then a voice distorted by the failing signal said simply:

'Run.'

4

The first car arrived as I pulled my boots on.

I'd taken the stairs two at a time, the tear in my thigh burning with the effort. I stood at the bedroom window. Half a dozen more sets of tyres bit into the gravel below – unmarked, armoured BMW X5s of the Garda Emergency Response Unit. An ambulance followed them in, too close. Above, the fast *chop-chop-chop* of an inbound helicopter reverberated around the old pile – carrying, most likely, a Special Forces sniper looking for runners. *A* runner. I watched the police debus. Twenty-four operators in full, black battledress, assault rifles up, respirators on, combing the front of Doc's country house. Within seconds a shotgun was taking the front door off its hinges. Classic fortress assault. Capture or kill: I wasn't planning on finding out which.

In any combat situation there are only two choices: do something, or do nothing. I didn't want to start shooting cops. But convincing them we were on the same side before they shot me looked unlikely. And if I broke cover or got on to the roof while a sniper was airborne, I was a dead man. The house was laid out like a wide, grey horseshoe: the front of the main building ran north–south, with the front door opening east; there was a converted stable block at the north end; and, to the south, a newer wing – and my bedroom. The buildings enclosed the wide expanse of the driveway and lawn on three sides. There was no vehicular access to the back of the house, and the entire demesne was encompassed by a high stone wall.

There was only one way out – and that was the way we'd all come in: the front gate. And once I was out, I didn't want anyone following – wherever I ended up. As for Frank, it looked like he knew where I was, all right – and we both knew that, as far as the British government was concerned, Max McLean didn't exist. The cavalry wasn't coming to rescue me: it was coming to ride me down.

I was on my own. As usual.

I brightened the oil lamp a fraction, rechecked the Browning and scanned the room. Doc's Martini–Henry drew a flat, dark smile over the fireplace. I tucked the pistol into the back of my jeans and took the antique rifle down and turned it over in my hands. The weight was reassuring, an ancient anchor steadying me against the gathering storm. I lowered the cocking lever. The wood might have been scarred, but, like the pistol, the working parts were clean and oiled. Spread out along the mantel a row of Kynoch drawn-brass cartridges rested in the leather pouches of an outstretched bandolier. I slung the wide belt over my bandaged shoulder and extracted one of the monster Victorian bullets. Doc and his obsessions. He'd always taken them too far. I slid the cartridge into the breech, clicked the lever home and slipped the sights to a hundred yards.

By the sound of it they'd been clearing each room downstairs as they went, prepping them with stun grenades. Now the men coming for me fell silent. Most likely they'd discovered Doc's dead body.

Doc's dead body. The adrenaline dissipated. In my mind's eye I saw the old man shot in his chair, and for an instant the world shrunk to the horror of what I had done; had caused.

My throat tightened. And then a blast from downstairs brought me back to my senses. I moved to the window. The assault team's BMWs were drawn up in a semi-circle on the drive. The ambulance that had followed them in had stopped behind them, just in front of the gates that formed the only break in the old boundary wall. The crew were civilians, drafted in at the last moment I supposed, and certainly not briefed on how best to park up. The driver and paramedic crouched behind their ride, nervously looking up and down as the chopper came in, as if watching a game of vertical tennis.

I stepped three feet back from the curtains and rolled my shoulder forward to compensate for the old infantry rifle's short stock. Through the open crack of the bedroom window I could see the ambulance lit up clearly enough by the flickering light of the porch lamp. I drew a bead on the crook of the backward *L* stencilled on the bonnet – and fired. The butt bit into my shoulder; my ears rang with the big, bold *bang* of the shot; and the room was engulfed in gunpowder smoke. The crew flattened themselves. Whatever the Gardaí had been expecting, it wasn't an ounce of Victorian lead. The round smashed through the front panel and into the engine block. Oil spurted from the gash it tore and spread out under the ambulance, seeping on to the pea gravel beneath in a wide, dirty slick.

If I was trapped, so were they.

I worked the lever. Pain flared down my arm. The spent brass tumbled out of the breech. I loaded another of the soft lead rounds from the bandolier, snapped the lever home and listened. Boots on the stairs. I put down the rifle and stripped a pillowslip off the bed. I dropped half a dozen of the rifle rounds into it and then wrapped the improvised cotton cartridge bag around the fat etched-glass font of the oil lamp. God bless Doc Levy and his fetish for Victoriana.

Crouching down to the side of the bedroom door, I listened again. They were still on the stairs. Stun grenades and smoke would follow. Tear gas maybe. And then a lot of modern, accurate, high-velocity lead and copper. I had seconds left. I turned the lamp flame up as high as it would go and opened the door, lobbing the makeshift bomb into the air over the stairwell. It came down hard with a satisfying *crack*. The oil splashed and caught, igniting a thick tapestry hanging on the far wall. Shouting erupted from the unseen policemen. Lamp oil burns hot. The old wooden stairs would go up in no time. The house had survived the War of Independence. But it wouldn't outlast the night. If I was lucky, the rounds would start to cook off. Anything to buy time.

The bedroom was in almost complete darkness now – the only light from the fingers of flame licking up the banister. I stayed at a crouch and watched the glowing stairs. Two Guards emerged on to the landing, burning. They'd been above the strike point, and both were alight. They dropped and rolled and beat the flames on their fatigues with gloved palms, and then together they recovered themselves, inching their way towards me – assault rifles up, the beams of the LED torches under their barrels cutting through the smoke like bright white lasers. They should have waited for the rest of their stick before clearing any more rooms. But everyone wants to be a hero. Once.

I moved fast. One foot up on the door handle, hauling myself up on to the top of the tallboy. As the door flung open and their searchlights cut through the gloom of the bedroom, the corridor echoed with the *pop-pop-pop* of exploding Martini–Henry rounds. The lead Guard had stepped

38

across the threshold and pulled the pin on a stun grenade but hesitated as the cartridges behind banged and whistled. His comrade turned fully, Heckler & Koch in his shoulder, firing into the smoke.

Blink and you miss.

I came down hard, boots into the leader's back. He sprawled beneath me, the stun grenade fell free. I recovered in time to shield my ears and eyes. The metal cylinder bounced off the skirting board and exploded in a blinding white flash. I reeled from the blast – eardrums singing. The fallen Guard stayed on the floor – down, but not dead. I turned to face the second Guard. The barrel of his Heckler & Koch caught on the door jamb. Elbow in. Right shoulder low. I struck below his left ear, clear of the helmet. My knuckle hit home. He staggered. Alternating strikes. Weapon dropped, hanging from its sling. He lurched backwards, recovered, and then lunged, both arms up. I blocked from the inside, arms crossed and then opening in front of him. Straight kick to the left knee, pushing forward, my leg between his. His right arm in my left hand. My right hand pushed across his face, grabbing his respirator. Pivot. My weight down, right knee on his chest, his head immobilized. Short punch below the left ear. I reached behind him and tore a set of flexicuffs free from his webbing. One hand tied, then the other, immobilized behind his back.

Torchlight and orders barked from below. I rolled him over and took two canisters from the front of his battledress. One stun. One CS. No frag. Over the stairs they went.

Bang. Pop. Hiss.

I dragged him into the room, pursued by the assault team who'd made it on to the landing. The old oak door would stop a few dozen rounds of 5.56 – but they wouldn't risk hitting their own men. I pulled the tallboy down in front of it

39

and breathed out hard. The room was illuminated with a single beam of light from the fallen leader's rifle LED. I unhooked the tactical sling from his shoulder and gave him the once-over. He was out for the count but still breathing. His trussed-up companion thrashed around on the floor.

'*Téigh in ainm an diabhail!*' he swore at me.

Fair enough. Fucking off with the Devil was pretty much what I had in mind, anyway. I pointed the recovered Heckler & Koch at him.

'You shout, you die. OK?' I took the bodycams off his ballistic vest and the leader's and crushed them both under my boot heel. Next I threw a blanket from the bed over his head; like a black canary he stopped cursing. Outside, his team would be lining up for a fresh assault, assessing whether I'd taken hostages or not. If they stormed the bedroom, the oak door and the tallboy would hold them only so long once they got that Benelli twelve-gauge working on the hinges.

It was time to play chicken.

I stripped the vest off the team leader still sprawled on the floor and strapped it across my own chest, covering it with my shirt, before rolling him into the recovery position. Then I plucked the radio headset from his ear.

'Man down! Man down!' I bellowed into the transmitter. 'Target exiting upper floor window. Weapons free. Repeat weapons free.' And then for good measure in Irish: '*Leag é!*' *Take him down!*

I picked up the old rifle from the bed. Then, as thick shotgun slugs ripped into the door frame, I drew the curtains back and flung open the window. The rush of winter air sharpened my senses, brought me back into contact with the world outside. The police Eurocopter flared into the night breeze, coming in low and loud above the roof of the north wing. A searchlight swept the upstairs windows and rested on mine, bleaching the room white. Two hundred metres away the two-tone hull of the little chopper swung starboard, drifting towards me, doors locked back.

I couldn't see him, but I knew he was in there, strapped in, staring at me through the scope of a .308. The bird lurched. I gambled on him doing what he'd been trained to do: aim centre mass. Few professionals would risk a headshot, even at that range – myself included. I was relying on him taking his time, too. His unit was in danger. Two were already out of action. The building was on fire. He needed to knock me out. And certainty takes time. I waited, drawing a deep breath into my lungs. The pilot brought the nose further around starboard and held the chopper as it levelled off above the driveway. For both me and the sniper on board the aircraft had to be side-on. He'd be on the gun, waiting for me to settle in his sights. Exhale. I put the short rifle stock into my shoulder. Inhale. From shooting up the ambulance, I knew how the bullet would fall. I half-emptied my lungs. I needed the chopper to be as still as he did. My point of aim settled, just, I hoped, as the aim of the unseen shooter would be settling, too. Our fingers squeezed the trigger steels. And together we fired.

Lighter, faster, flatter: his round hit first. The shock of it took me off my feet as my own slow, heavy shot streaked out towards the hovering bird. I let the Martini–Henry fall away and rolled clear of the window, winded. I was on my back, struggling to breathe. Everything hurt – my old wounds from the cottage, my head from the stun grenade and now my ribs from the .308. I put my right hand up and under the flak vest: thumping, bruising pain – but no blood. I sat up, gulping air back into my lungs. His bullet had struck high and left. It had been caught by the vest's ballistic plate with an inch to spare, a neat black hole drilled through the white shirt I'd pulled over it.

Through the impossibly bright arc of the spotlight my own bullet had hit home, too. I didn't hear it, couldn't see it. But the ball of soft lead once used to cut down the enemies of the British Empire now did its job for me. The arc light juddered and leapt and swept away from the window, plunging the room back into darkness. I went back to the window. I'd hit the enclosed tail rotor dead centre, sending the huge rifle round directly into its pitch-control mechanism. As I knew from personal, frightening experience, once the tail rotor fails, you can't pull power. The pilot had gone immediately into autorotation, trying desperately to get his spinning ship down on to the lawn that flanked the driveway. It was a bumpy ride. The main rotor blades clipped a branch and then the front of the house. Huge lengths of metal sheared off. The ambulance crew took to their heels. And then, just as the bird went over on its side, the bedroom door was blown off its hinges. The tallboy still covered half the entrance but immediately the beams of the assault squad's torches combed through the room. I picked up the discarded Heckler & Koch, clicked the fire selector to semi-auto and fired high and wide.

Keep your heads down, boys.

I emptied the magazine around the doorway. Plaster and wood vaporized under the stream of lead. In reply: CS gas. I dropped the assault rifle, touch-checked the Browning in the back of my jeans and pushed myself out of the window followed by shouts and shots. My right hand caught the limb of a wisteria branch that curled below the windowsill, but my weight snapped it as I fell. Fifteen feet down into a thick laurel hedge. I landed on my back, stunned by the fall, but cushioned enough by the evergreen not to break my spine.

Above me, black-masked faces at the window. More shouts; first one, then a dozen rifle reports. But I was already up and running, hugging the wall of the house, sprinting east towards the old stone boundary wall and the bunged-up gateway. The wall itself was too high to vault and a dash through the gate close to suicide if the sniper wasn't definitely out of action. I scanned the crash site. Figures were moving in the wreckage. The medical crew had recovered themselves and were freeing a grab bag from the back of their truck. Fire poured out of the upstairs windows of the house. Reaching up into the black winter sky, the flames lit everything a deep, dirty orange. The angle of fire from the bedroom window to the end of the south wing was too oblique for a clear shot. But if anyone was at the front door I was in trouble.

Do something or do nothing.

Fuck it.

I took off for the iron gates as fast as my wounded knee would let me. The ambulance crew passed to my left, the gate post to my right. I stepped foot outside Doc's threshold and then . . . nothing. I rolled into the dead ground the wall afforded. I'd sprung the trap. Now I needed speed, not protection.

I ripped off my shirt and then the vest. Blue jeans and a black T-shirt were as good a night-time camouflage as any in County Mayo. It was a half-klick straight shot to Rathduff church, and another three to the main Ballina road beyond. Too easy. Too obvious. I'd already worked my way up from

43

Knockmore on the way to Doc's and knew the country better than they did. If they didn't already have eyes in the sky, they would before I made the nearest town.

I ran hard, head down, tight to hedges and ditches, bearing south-east towards the village of Newtown Cloghans. I'd seen cars there, and trucks. I could hotwire an old farm banger. Or hijack a night driver. Anything was better than being in the open. My lungs heaved. My wounds burned. To my right I could hear the waves of Lough Conn slapping the shore. To my left, nothing. And then, behind me, the unmistakable barking of German shepherd dogs. Two of them – three hundred metres and gaining. I could outrun the heavily laden ERU. But their dogs would be on me in seconds. I made it to the edge of the next field and took a stand on the far side of a low hedge.

One hundred metres.

I drew the Browning from the back of my jeans, dropped the safety and cocked the hammer.

Fifty metres.

I could hear them but not see them.

Twenty-five metres.

Two black shadows flitting across black turf.

Ten metres.

So fast now it was hard to see them at all.

And then they were over the scrub in tandem, leaping, snarling, closing. I shot the dog on the right in the centre of its ribcage and swung left. But the second dog was on me. The force of impact twisted the pistol out of my hand.

I put both hands up. The dog's teeth bit into the right sleeve of my T-shirt. Don't run. But never stop moving. I turned in a tight circle and swung my left leg over the dog, purposely falling across its body and then twisting on to my back. I

44

folded my arms around its neck and held its muzzle to my chest as I rolled on the ground, wrestling eighty pounds of compressed power. I got my arms up higher under its neck and spun both of us on to our fronts. Its head was trapped hard against the ground. I rolled further and felt its spine snap under me.

And then I was up again. There was no time to look for the Browning. I kept running. Rifle rounds zipped overhead. A ditch running to my left snaked in front of me, looming up out of the dark. I heard Colonel Ellard's voice in my head.

'That's not a ditch. That's cover. Now get in it.'

And so I did. I squirmed down into the reeds and wild water mint and waited.

They came soon enough.

LEDs combed the fields, hedges, ditch. Boots in the air over me. Heavy footfall running ahead. And then quiet. I looked up at the low cloud scudding against the waning moon. My oldest friend was dead. I'd been shot twice and killed no one. So far everything was going to plan.

But whose?

I lay on my back and dug my phone out of my jeans' pocket. Frank had said no comms. But Frank had warned me to get clear. I dialled his number through the waterproof cover. Three notes beeped, and then a woman's recorded voice told me that the number I had dialled was unavailable. It was the first time he'd ever failed to pick up, the first time he'd ever been unresponsive. I switched off.

Up and moving again, slowly, deliberately. Once an operation like that starts, it doesn't stop. The Gardaí would double back soon enough, and get another bird up, too. I turned hard left and made straight for the little hamlet.

45

Dripping, bleeding, stinking, I came out on to the road and two parked cars: a brand-new Cherokee and a rusting Mondeo. I tried the door of the old Ford. It was unlocked. I climbed in and reached down for the ignition column.

And then the lights went out.

5

Motion.

I saw nothing. Felt nothing. Suspended in darkness. Floating. I moved. Air moved. The world moved. I was suspended in darkness. Falling, maybe. Flying. Spinning.

I was moving. But I could not move.

My hands were fixed, legs pinned. I could feel the flesh of my arms against my body. I swung. Swam. Spun. I could *feel*.

Pain.

I woke up to it, the power of it unplugging the comfort of unconsciousness. Pain in my head: deep, throbbing, uncompromising pain that beat my skull from the inside, pushing brain against bone. My head felt full, as if it were filled with blood. As if it would burst. Pain in my back. A long, searing, tearing along my spine, flaring out across my ribs, gripping my stomach. My shins, calves, thighs burned. Pain so bright it had colour. Pain so hard I could see it.

Light.

Swinging, reeling in stark, brilliant white light – orbiting a blinding sun. Out of the light, colour. Infinity. Swirls of brilliant shapes merging, locking, shifting. The colours deepened with the thud-throb in my brain.

Thud. Thud. Thud.

I could hear.

Sound.

The anvil-song of metal striking metal, an undifferentiated, resonating peal that rang with the monstrous timbre of tolling sunken bells.

But with echo, distance. And with distance, time. I was in the world.

I was.

Sweat crept up my torso, dripped into my nose, ran up my legs. My carotid artery bulged in my neck. The sound of blood roared in my ears. My tongue lolled on the roof of my mouth.

I came to with a rush of realization and nausea and opened my eyes. My hands were tied behind my back. My legs were bound at the ankles. My ankles were fastened to a twist of rope. Back and forth, back and forth: my body swung upside down between two metal walls like a bleeding, lurching pendulum.

With a start I crunched my abdomen and brought my head up towards my legs. The effort was crippling. I couldn't hold myself up for more than a few seconds, but it was enough to see how well fixed my feet were. I collapsed again, the abrupt jolt on the rope jerked my head back and pulled at my spine. The movement interrupted the flow of my swing and twisted the rope. I relaxed and let myself go limp and looked around, spinning and swaying on my own axis.

At their closest point the walls were four feet away on either side. As I spun, they receded and then lurched back towards me. I looked up again, and then craned my neck backwards to look down. Corrugated lines of infinity separated and converged around me. The ceiling was close, a foot above the soles of my bare feet; the plywood floor so near I wondered that my head did not scrape on it as I moved about. Twenty feet distant a bright white halogen lamp shone into my face. The jagged black lines of my own shadow leapt across the grey metal tunnel. The light picked out four air vents and no obvious cameras . . . but hid the exit behind its blinding halo. At the opposite end was a metal wall. Dead centre, stencilled on a red oblong, white Cyrillic letters spelled out the acronym *РЖД*: *RZD* – the name of the Russian state railway. I was, without doubt, inside a shipping container. And I was, without doubt, moving. 'Where to?' was the sixty-four thousand dollar question.

My throat was parched. I licked the sweat from my lips and tried to swallow. My stomach was empty and racked with cramp. The bullet wounds in my thigh and shoulder burned, though separating the pain of one injury from another was almost impossible. But I couldn't have been hung like that for long. The human body isn't meant to be inverted – and the consequences are ultimately, inevitably, fatal. At around the twenty-four-hour mark death from asphyxiation becomes imminent. Stroke was a possibility, too, as was heart failure. I knew: I'd seen the CIA string enough people up during black site debriefs to be intimately familiar with the consequences of not cutting people down in time.

I wasn't a fan of torture. Especially not when I was the subject. You can make anyone confess to anything – eventually. If your captive doesn't fear death and you have nothing to trade – their family, usually – then you may as well quit while you're ahead and save yourself the bruised knuckles and, if you're that sort, the guilty conscience. I just hoped that whoever had strung me up was as well versed in the medical implications of enhanced interrogation techniques as I was.

I gave myself a once-over as best I could. No boots, no T-shirt. The dressings Doc had patched me up with were loose and dirty, but still in place. I was wearing the same jeans I'd made my run in. My wrists felt as if they were bound with a cable tie. I peered up towards the ceiling. My ankles looked like they were gaffer-taped together under the rope that held me to the ceiling. How, exactly, I was fixed in place I couldn't see, but there was no pulley, no guide rope, to lower me.

I tried to get my head above my heart again. It was pointless. I relaxed and hung there in a grotesque parody of a dirty-blond bat. Outside, metal banged and creaked. The air throbbed with the drone of a powerful engine. Once or twice I thought I could hear the muffled shouts of orders being given – but in what language or to what end I couldn't tell. I continued to sway. I was definitely moving forward. Not fast, but the container was in perpetual, deliberate motion.

I closed my eyes and tried to add up what I knew – which wasn't much. Doc Levy, dead; the figure of his assassin, fleet-footed, making good his escape; the phone call from Frank – if it had been him who'd called. I felt the knot of revenge tighten in my gut, and chided myself.

No, Max. Concentrate on what you know – not what you think you saw or heard.

But my focus wandered. In my mind's eye I drew a bead with the old Martini–Henry on that little man running away and . . . and then came back to reality with a start.

Never make it personal.

It was one of Colonel Ellard's rules that I'd never learned to obey. *Personal* was exactly what the job had become.

I didn't know if the man I'd seen leaving that night had killed Doc. But whoever did murder him had left a deliberate calling card: another bullet to the heart – and not the head, as you'd expect from a professional. On the face of it, whoever had shot me up in Donegal had done for Doc, too. If that was true, then perhaps the gunman hadn't fried. He'd survived.

Frank had sent me on a job to kill an old terrorist. Why,

exactly, he wanted him dead I didn't know – and Frank wasn't saying. But he'd expected me to find something important in the cottage. Perhaps I had.

It wasn't unusual, either, for Frank to act outside DSF's chain of command – except for one defining fact: the kill was on home ground. Frank could run his shitshow wherever and whenever he liked, but absolutely not, as General King would say, 'in bloody Blighty'. The job might have been across the border, but it didn't matter. Ireland is Ireland, and different rules applied now that the war was over – for Whitehall, at least. Breaking them would have consequences.

The metal room spun around me. Shooting pains ran through my calves, thighs. It was hard to think straight. There had to have been a security breach. That much seemed obvious. But if the message on the banknote had anything to do with me, then it wasn't a leak: it was a tsunami. UKN was an entirely black outfit. And Max McLean didn't exist. I was a creation with no birth certificate, no queen's commission and no past. A nowhere man with no way of being traced. If London really was out of the loop, then the only way that either Connor or the shooter could have been waiting for me, specifically, was if they knew that Frank would send me. If that was true, if *Arkhangel* was meant *for* me because it meant something *to* me, then UKN had been blown wide open. There was only one possible source for a breach that bad: Commander Frank Knight himself.

So, Max, I asked myself as the metal box spun around me, *how well* do *you know Frank?*

He'd apparently never let anything slip. Not once. But Frank knew me better than I knew myself. That much I'd learned in the twenty-four years we'd worked together. I considered the last word he'd said to me at Doc's.

Run.

But if he was setting me up, why tip me off? As warped by digital encryption as the voice had been, only Frank had that number. Only Frank had *ever* had my number. It didn't sound like him. But it had to have been him.

It wasn't just me who'd been tipped off, though. The Gardaí had known exactly where I was and had come prepared: they knew what they were going up against.

The most palatable explanation was not treachery but technology – though separating the two was nigh on impossible. I'd been very careful with my communications. If the shooter had followed me to Doc's by tracking my cell phone – or if Frank's phone had been hacked – they would have needed serious help to do it. Our comms were so protected that even the geeks at Cheltenham weren't supposed to be able to tail me or monitor our conversations – and purposefully so. UKN is supported by MI6 but operates outside its control – a failsafe that keeps us protected, and them in check. If the shooter – or whoever he worked for – had managed it, they must either have been helped from inside our firewall, or have been unnaturally brilliant. Neither prospect filled me with joy.

And anyway, who's that good?

I opened my eyes as the logo of the Russian railway swept past.

Maybe the Russians were behind it.

Or the Americans. Or the Israelis. Old alliances were stretched to breaking point; new ones untested, unreliable. Anyone could be bought with a billion bucks. The CIA stood Janus-like at the dawn of a new era: one face looking down on the legacy of Joe Stalin, the other looking forward to the opportunities a frenemy in the Kremlin might afford. Even MI6 – *especially* MI6 – didn't know whether to shake the hand of the resurgent Russian devil, or cut it off. The motivations of monsters like Philby and Burgess no longer seemed archaic and irrelevant. Anyone could work for anyone. Everyone was expendable. No one was above suspicion.

My face pivoted into the beam of the halogen spotlight at the end of the container. The rope contracted, fully wound, and held me still for a moment, frozen in the bright white light. Behind it, steel scraped against steel. A rush of cold air. The smell of diesel. The continual pulse of a heavy engine. And then the sound of footsteps striking plywood.

Here we go.

Three pairs of feet. Two in boots. One in shoes.

'*Bystro! Shevelites'!*' Someone was being begged to get a move on in Russian. '*Esli ego tak ostavit', on dolgo ne protyanet.*' Whoever was speaking did so with the calm but urgent authority of a professional – telling the others in no uncertain terms that, tied up like that, I didn't have much longer to live. He was right. I guessed he was the person wearing the shoes – and that he was wearing the trousers, too.

The guards hesitated.

'We should leave him. Please,' a second voice pleaded in Russian. They were scared of me. It was almost flattering.

The man in charge spoke again.

'Just do it.'

I spun back around; as I twisted past the men, I squinted at them through upside-down, sweat-clogged eyes. Three upturned figures emerged from the light, clinging to a wooden ceiling like thin black spiders. The two in boots stayed near the door, cradling AKS-74 carbines. Six-two, six-four, a couple of hundred pounds apiece, kitted out in vests and combat fatigues. The man in shoes stepped forward, floating above me. He was lighter, smaller, carrying a tan portmanteau, not an assault rifle. A doctor. Most likely he'd check my vital signs first and then, all else being equal, sedate me and cut me down. I had to convince him there wasn't time for that, that I had to be untied immediately. Staying conscious was the only hope of escape I had.

Snipers learn a lot of tricks. Most of them don't require a rifle. Keeping still keeps you off your target's score sheet. At Raven Hill, Colonel Ellard kept us on the gun for an hour at first. Then two. After a month we could lie prone for a day. By the time he'd finished with us, we'd all pushed ourselves beyond what the human body is supposed to endure: seventy-two hours without moving more than a whisker. Snipers eat, shit, piss and curse where they lie – very, very quietly. Being immobilized wasn't out of the ordinary; it was commonplace.

But no matter how still you are outside, inside there's always over half a pound of muscle thumping in your chest – beating up to a hundred and thirty times a minute in combat. Slowing your heart down secures the shot. Shooting between the beats is unbeatable. We could slow it quickly, too, like pulling the handbrake on a joyride.

My blood pressure was already low. No matter who they were, or what they were planning, if the doctor was going to cut me down *before* he knocked me out, he'd have to be sure I was in immediate danger of death. There were only three things he could measure easily: my heart rate, my breathing and my blood pressure.

I could control them all with my lungs. They were the only weapons I had left.

6

I kept my right eye open just enough to see shape, judge distance. The area beyond the container door was too dimly lit to pick out detail. My only light source was the halogen which, in turn, blinded me with brightness and then plunged me into darkness as I swung on the rope. But I was guided by smell more than by sight. Above the reek of diesel fuel rose the scent of aftershave and clean laundry. The sweet-smelling doctor – if that's what he was – came close. I rotated slowly on the rope and saw him squat down on his haunches next to me.

'Be careful,' his chaperones implored him in Russian. 'He's fucking dangerous.' But the doctor seemed unflustered. He was wrapped up in a long black coat and was only now removing his gloves. It was January, and cold outside – wherever outside was.

'*Byl opasnim.*' He muttered to himself. *Was* dangerous. And then so they could hear, also in Russian: 'You should have kept him in the room, like we agreed. He's not fucking Houdini.'

No response.

From the intact state of Doc Levy's dressings it didn't look like the bullet wound in my left shoulder had been properly investigated. If I could convince this Russian doctor that my lung was punctured and collapsing, he'd be forced to take action. It didn't have to be perfect. Even the mere *possibility* that I had a tension pneumothorax would, for any doctor worth their salt, elevate me immediately to the category of medical emergency.

He produced a stethoscope from inside his bag and hooked it into his ears. At arm's length he pressed the diaphragm to my chest. On cue I breathed rapid laboured breaths – forcing my heart rate up as high as I could manage. He moved the diaphragm, listened to my heart for a further fifteen seconds and then unhooked the stethoscope's eartips. The noise of the engines reverberating through the metal cavern was so loud I doubted he could make out anything at all.

'Can you hear me?' He spoke in faultless English.

He turned immediately to his chaperones.

'*Privedite kapitana*,' he ordered. No one moved to fetch the captain. '*Nemedlenno!*' he yelled at them in Russian. *Now!*

One of the men backed out of the metal tunnel, swallowed by the glare of the halogen. I heard his boots break into a sprint. The other guard walked towards us.

'*Idioty*,' the doctor said under his breath as he produced a blood pressure meter from the portmanteau. I took a deep breath, shut my mouth and blew out as hard as I could against my lips, straining as forcefully as possible. My heart rate fell. Moving quickly now, my examiner stood and fixed the rubber cuff around my grazed bicep and began pumping the bulb in his fist.

I felt the bladder contract around my muscle. I kept trying to drop my heart rate. Forty beats per minute was the lowest I could manage. That wasn't unusually low – but I hoped he'd think the sudden change was serious enough to take action. I couldn't see him. Most likely he was checking the gauge. Then he slipped the stethoscope's diaphragm under the tight cuff and listened again. The bladder deflated.

'*Snimite ego!*' *Get him down.*

'*Vrach* . . .' The guard began to remonstrate. The rope contracted. I saw the doctor straighten up and square off at him.

'Listen to me very carefully. His lung is collapsing. And
the reason his lung is collapsing is because you and your
mudak colleague hung him upside down.'

'If he escapes, we're all dead men.'

'He has minutes. Seconds, maybe, before he goes into car-
diac arrest.' The doctor turned his palms out towards me.
'And if he dies, you're going to wish you were dead, too.'

'But our orders were to keep the prisoner secure.'

'I am in command of this operation now, soldier. Your
orders are to get him down. Immediately.'

The guard shifted his weight from one foot to the other
and then grunted his consent. The doctor unwound the
blood pressure meter and then, taking a pair of rescue shears
from the leather bag, cut through the cable ties behind my
back. My arms fell and struck the ground. Blood forced its
way back along my brachial arteries. I couldn't move my
arms, but I could feel them. And that was a start – even
though all I could feel was pain. A cannula had been taped
in place on the back of my left hand – through which they'd
probably delivered a sedative and saline before we'd set off. I
remembered nothing after getting in the car – the pain in my
head possibly from the blow that had knocked me out.

The guard put his shoulder into my back and lifted me up
lengthways along the container, facing away from the light.
The doctor reached up and severed the rope above my ankles.

I needed them to move fast. Once the captain and the other
guard arrived, the chances of the container becoming my cof-
fin would rise dramatically. In the movies the hero takes
everyone by surprise and kills them all. In reality the bad guys
watch you on CCTV and then shoot you in the back.

They laid me down. The doctor passed the scissors to the guard. While he cut through the gaffer tape binding my ankles, the doctor tipped my forehead back, lifted my chin and opened my mouth. Airway clear. He lifted my right forearm, palm out, and rested it beside my head, like a policeman stopping traffic. My left hand he held to my right cheek, palm in. As the guard cut the final binding that pinned my legs, the doctor grabbed my jeans above my left knee and rolled me towards him, swivelling me into the recovery position.

I was free.

I kept my left leg moving, pitching it upwards, driving my foot as hard as I could into the back of the guard's legs. He crumpled at the knees. I pushed myself up on to my feet . . . and then crumpled, too – my own legs unresponsive lumps of flesh beneath me. I staggered and reached out for the metal wall to steady myself. The doctor backed off, his right hand disappearing into the now open front of his coat.

Weapon.

The guard should have done the same, but instead recovered himself and tried to land a clumsy left hook.

I could barely stand. But I could lead this lamb to the slaughter.

I twisted right and caught his arm above the cuff. His left wrist in my left hand. I pulled his forearm into my chest. I slid backwards. The whole weight of my body pulled him across me. I twisted his arm and pushed downwards. He stretched out in front of me, doubled over, neck extended. My right hand came down hard. The side of my palm bit into his spine. The vertebrae beneath the base of his skull fractured with a *crack*. Beneath the skin his spinal canal imploded, severing the delicate cord within. He dropped, dead. I went down with him, close to the wall, diving headlong towards his feet. The

AKS was strapped across his chest, trapped between his body and the floor. The doctor had drawn, and began shooting around me – not at me. Pistol rounds sparked off the metal walls. He was trying to keep me down, not kill me.

But opening fire in a massive metal box guarantees two things: deafening noise – and ricochets. One nicked my left elbow, the others took off every which way but loose on a 9mm pinball game from hell. Rounds bounced off the ceiling, the walls, even the guard's flak vest. I got my head down, squirming myself small against the lifeless barricade, facing the door. His shots went nowhere near me, but they were potentially lethal nonetheless – if only accidentally. Spent brass cascaded to the floor as the lead swarm screeched through the forty-foot cavity. Halfway through the tirade the second guard arrived back on the scene, carbine up, followed closely by another man, pistol drawn. The guard stepped into the open container at precisely the right moment to stop one of the doctor's pistol rounds from leaving it. His nose exploded in a thick red spray as the mangled bullet blew lead and cartilage back through his brain. He fell instantly, lights out. The man behind recoiled out of sight.

My ears rang with a flat, high-pitched whine. My limbs throbbed as blood surged back into them. I'd counted eighteen shots.

On your feet, sunshine.

I got my head up. The doctor stood six feet in front of me, deafened, disorientated, staring in mute disbelief at the empty Grach in his hand – though whether at the fact that every bullet had missed me, or him, I couldn't say.

I stepped over the dead guard who'd shielded me and twisted the Russian pistol out of the doctor's hand. No resistance. I hit him with it, hard across the right temple. His skin split across his skull with a wide, red tear. He fell with a grunt, clutching his head, blood spilling through his fingers.

Movement at the door.

Bang. Crack. Zip. More shots. More ricochets.

Whoever the second guard had gone to fetch was firing high and wild into the container, emboldened by the doctor's decision to start shooting. Out of sight, hidden behind the halogen glare and the lip of the steel door, only his gun arm was visible – firing pistol rounds into the roof and walls around me. I stuffed the Grach into my jeans and hit the deck again. I rolled the dead guard over. Working fast, I unhooked his carbine's tactical sling, and freed the assault rifle. The fire selector was set to single. There was probably a round in the chamber – but I wasn't taking any chances. I snapped back the charging lever with my left hand as I brought the muzzle up. An unspent round spun out to my right.

Ready to go.

As the butt went into my shoulder and my cheek made contact with the stock, I fired. Out of the doorway the bullet ripped the guard's hand off at the wrist. Arterial blood arced out across the opening. Another one gone.

I turned to the doctor on the floor, rifle still in my shoulder. He was sitting on the floor, face smeared with blood.

'No, don't!' he said, the look of disbelief on his face morphing into a horror-mask of understanding, red hands held out in supplication. 'Please. I'm just ... I tried to save you ...' My shot-blasted eardrums distorted his voice like an over-modulating microphone. He sounded more machine than man.

'Where am I?'

'Please. I tried to save you.'

'Save me? You tried to shoot me!'

I took a step towards him, and fired a shot close enough to his ear to nick it and draw blood. The round bounced off the floor and hit the rear wall with a spark. He screamed a deep, guttural yell.

'Who are you?' I shouted at him. I glanced at the dead guard. 'Who are they?'

His right hand moved from his ear to his bleeding temple and back again. Tears welled in his eyes, snot bubbled under his nose. I settled the front sight post between his eyes.

'Please! Please don't. The guard. I tried to shoot the guard. Not you. Please . . .'

But he was right: he had saved me, or at least had allowed me to save myself. And the last thing I needed was another dead doctor on my conscience. The microsecond it takes to pull the trigger is the same hair's breadth of time you have to decide not to. Instead of drilling a neat hole just below where his eyebrows joined, the little steel-core bullet stayed in the breech. He was breathing hard, covering his bloody face with his bloody hands.

Stressed, shocked – he wasn't going to give me anything coherent. Depending what I found outside, I could come back for him. At least getting shot by him didn't seem likely. I took another step towards him, delved into his coat pocket and removed his cell phone. I stuck it into my jeans, frisked him quickly and looked inside the portmanteau. No weapons. I moved out of the container. Immediately to my right the man whose hand I'd blown off was sitting up in a pool of his own gore clutching his wrist. I shot him twice in the chest. He toppled sideways and I shot him again, at point blank, in the left ear.

I looked around. Wall-mounted tungsten lights illuminated the interior of an almost-empty green-painted steel hall, twice as long and three times as wide as the container itself. A row of metal drums – of diesel, most likely – sat along the near wall, two deep, one high. At either end heavy bulkhead doors covered the exits. Steep metal ladders climbed to a gallery twenty foot above, running the length of the wall. Realization dawned. My gut tightened. I was in the hold of a ship.

Fuck.

Down the passageways, heavy footsteps were coming for me.

I slung the assault rifle across my back and made for the nearest companionway, lurching sideways, my bare feet slipping in a pool of oil. I caught hold of the rail before I fell and hauled myself up, climbing as fast as I could. But as I clambered on to the narrow ledge of the gallery, three men in tactical vests and combat boots stomped into view thirty feet to my left, cutting me off. I rolled, bringing the rifle around again, looking over the iron sights with both eyes open. I fired low. The rounds tore through the leader's thigh, groin. He made a half-turn, arms flailing, blocking the men behind him, who swore in Russian. I kept firing. The leader staggered backwards and fell over the guard rail on to the metal deck below. The other two were exposed now. I shot centre mass. Two rounds each. Their vests caught the bullets, but the shock of the impact gave me enough time to get to my feet.

Neither returned fire. I closed on them, firing rapid single shots. Both were dead by the time I'd covered the distance to where they lay. I reloaded my AKS from theirs and took a pistol from a thigh holster strapped to the nearest body – a 9mm Grach, like the doctor's: standard Russian military sidearm. I stuck it in the back of my jeans.

I stopped and listened, straining to hear above the rounds still ringing in my ears. Metal creaked against metal. Buried deep in the warren of passageways, an engine pulsed on. No shouts. No shots. Blood seeped through the metal grate of the gallery deck, dripping into the chasm beneath. I stepped around the bodies and over the lip of the metal door leading off the walkway and emerged on to the freezing upper deck of a cargo ship.

Waves detonated against the hull beneath me. Everywhere was darkness. Black sky above. Black water below. A point of light flashed above the waves – a single star glinting in a firmament of one. And then behind, above and closing in on each side of me, the thundering of boot heels. I dropped the carbine. I could hear orders in Russian amplified above the drone of the ship's engines by a loudspeaker.

'*Ostanovite ego!*' *Stop him.*

I flexed my shoulders. Death by drowning: my mother had chosen water as her way out. Now it was mine. But I had no intention of following her all the way. At least not yet.

And then they were on me.

Tic. Tic. Tic.

Contact left.

I stepped up on to the handrail as the first rounds of my pursuers skipped and skidded off the ship's metalwork. Braced, bent at the knees, arms out, I pushed forward and fell through the pitch black down into the waves.

7

A deep, penetrating chill wrapped around me, went through me, sent spikes of pain shooting through my fingers, between my temples, down my legs. What bits of me didn't hurt were numb, unresponsive. Spray soaked me. Wind lashed me. The tearing sea-song of water slapping shingle ripped across me and filled my head with the roar of the flood tide.

Water.

I was still in the water.

I opened my mouth, my eyes, gasping, gulping in air and brine under the grey sky and the gulls wheeling beneath low, rain-heavy clouds.

Still alive.

I got my head up and sat and coughed hard into the white-tipped waves that ran up my legs and broke against my chest. I put my right palm down on to the stones, turned over and forced myself up on my knees. I tried to stand, but I could feel neither my hands nor my feet. Instead I lay prone, face down, propped up on my forearms, still rinsed by the rising water. Hand over hand, elbows down, legs dragging, I hauled myself out of the surf. The beach rose steeply. Stones tumbled past me as I clawed my way above the tide line. Seaweed clung to me. The skin on my chest, arms, feet, chafed on chalk-smeared shards of flint. The dressings Doc Levy had wrapped me up in worked free, exposing raw, bloody flesh.

I looked left and right, casting about for any landmark, any sign of where I'd come ashore. But my eyes stung and my vision blurred, and I was shaking uncontrollably. I forced my hand behind my back and touched my jeans at the base of my spine. The Russian doctor's cell phone was gone, the Grach too. Half-blind and desperate I ran my hands over the pebbles, searching for it.

'It's here,' I chattered to myself. 'Damn you, McLean. It's here.'

But the pistol wasn't there, and I collapsed back on to the stones. I stopped fighting then, and the light ebbed out of my eyes, colouring the world solid, silent black.

Beep. Beep. Beep.

The patient lay still. No fluids. No plasma. She faced away from me, hidden, partly covered by a blanket.

'Rachel?'

She didn't move, but I knew she could hear me.

Beep. Beep. Beep.

'You can hear me, can't you? Rachel?'

I wanted to touch her, but she was so far away I couldn't reach. The more I stretched out to her, the further away she seemed.

'Rachel, it's me. It's Max.' I pulled back my hand and then she turned towards me. But something wasn't right. It wasn't Rachel. The woman turned and looked at me. Wet blonde hair clung to her face, pale blue eyes stared at me, unblinking. She was gaunt. Drawn. Changed but unmistakable. *'Mamka?'*

I put my hands out towards her again, but she smiled and shook her head. My mouth opened to shout, scream her name, to beg her to come back to me, but she put her fingers to her lips and whispered.

'Bayu-bayushki-bayu, nye lozhisya na krayu . . .' Rock-a-bye baby, don't lie on the edge . . .

65

I looked down and saw I was standing waist deep in water. My mother wasn't lying down. She was floating, drifting away, murmuring the lullaby that soothed me as a child.

'Pridyot serenkiy volchok I ukusit za bochok . . .' Or the little grey wolf will bite your side . . .

She slipped beneath the surface. And then blackness again.

Beep. Beep. Beep.

'So what have we got?'

Bare skin on dry sheets. I kept my eyes shut and my ears open.

'Dover uniform brought him in this morning. Dog walker found him on the beach near Kingsdown. No ID, no nothing.' Male junior doctor. Mid-twenties. Smoker. Biddable. 'Superficial scratches on his forearms and knees. Bruising on the wrists and ankles.'

'So there are.' A woman's voice. 'Restraints of some kind? Unusual, anyway. Looks like his hands were bound. Penetrating trauma to his left shoulder and right thigh. Gunshot wounds, possibly.' Consultant. Forty something. 'That would explain why there's a copper outside. Never a dull moment at the William Harvey.' I squinted into the low light of the isolation room. Brunette. Five-ten. Hardcase. And handsome with it. I dozed off and came back mid-sentence.

'. . . bear with me, I . . .' While young buck struggled with his notes, I struggled to stay conscious. 'Right, OK. Yes . . . this is *really* interesting because – sorry, hold that for a sec, would you? – his wounds have already been treated. You see here, just below the clavicle, and here, above the knee.'

'Pretty tidy.'

'Whoever patched him up changed his clothes, too.' He

66

pointed to a plastic bag on a chair by the bed. 'There was no bullet hole in his jeans.'

'Quite the sleuth, aren't we, David?' I felt the hands of the consultant on my chest, right arm, lower legs. 'Whoever he is, he's been in the wars, all right.' She was talking to herself more than her sidekick. 'Scar tissue all over him.' She pressed her thumb into a depression in my left calf. 'I bet that one tells a story.' And then to me: 'Soldier, are you?'

I wanted to tell her that, if I'd been a soldier, someone would have been looking out for me. As it was, General King and whichever queen bee was now running MI6's hive at Vauxhall Cross wouldn't even bother to disown me: you can't deny knowing someone that doesn't exist. I said, did, nothing, except pretend to sleep.

'X-ray?'

'Came up clean – no drugs, no bullets, nothing up his bum.'

'Thank God for small mercies. Bloods?'

'Normal.'

'Lucky us. GCS?'

'Thirteen. Spark out since he got here. The paramedic said he came to briefly en route. Fought like hell when they tried to cut his jeans off. Kept muttering a woman's name. "Rachel", he thought. Next of kin, maybe?'

My heart jumped involuntarily. Pause. They were both distracted by the ECG trace.

'Right, well, while the inestimable intelligence that is Kent Police untangles that little riddle, let's make sure Mr Mystery here doesn't shuffle off this mortal coil on our watch, shall we? Though, given everything, he's in good shape. Let's keep him that way.' She dropped her voice. 'And keep those vultures out of here. I don't want anyone questioning him till he's fit to talk.'

'Yes, Rose.'

There was a long pause.

'What are we missing here?' She spoke quietly, distract-edly almost.

'Sorry?'

'I said, "What are we missing?" Head, abdo and pelvis CT, please. Let's make double sure there are no bullets in him. Admit him under the medical team until he's less drowsy.' I heard her heels make for the door. 'Oh, and David?'

'Yes?'

'The monitor. Switch that bloody beep off.'

I closed my eyes completely and their voices morphed and merged into a blur of undifferentiated data. The room pres-sure shifted as nurses came and went. I realized in a passing moment of lucidity that I'd been asleep for hours and then drifted back in and out of consciousness, clinging only to one certainty: it wasn't a question of if they would come for me, but when.

The room was dark.

Above and behind me, the medical monitor hummed and clicked. A crack of green fluorescent light escaped from the bathroom and picked out a jug of water and a plastic beaker on a trolley by the bed. Apart from that the room was bare. It looked like I'd been moved to a new ward. I closed and opened my eyes. The beaker disappeared and reappeared. It was definitely there. I was definitely awake. And I was alone – inside the room, at least. Outside, a policeman would be sitting in the corridor trying not to doze off, no doubt curs-ing his luck to his mates at being put on a babysitting detail while secretly being relieved at the warmth it offered.

I untangled the observations in my dreams from the

observations of my doctors and began to weave myself back into reality. Thread by thread I knitted myself into Frank's knot garden. The container. The doctor. The killing. I couldn't recall hitting the water, but memories of the swim washed over me: head down; front crawl; lifting my face just enough to suck in the black air before the next wave broke across my back. The beacon I'd been aiming for had been ripped out of view within seconds, torn away from me by the running tide.

I was in hospital in Kent. The ship could have sailed south through the Irish Sea and through St George's Channel, or cut out into the Atlantic before moving east along the English Channel. In my condition, in that water, there was no way I could have swum more than a thousand metres – which meant that when I'd dived we'd been coming into Dover or looking for anchorage in the Downs. There was no other way we would, *could*, have been that close to shore, heading in that direction, in a ship that size. If I'd embarked at Dublin Port – or anywhere on the east coast of Ireland – it would mean I'd been at sea for two or three days, and then possibly in hospital for a day more. And *that* meant that whoever was on that ship was likely only a day behind me.

I sat up in bed fully awake. I'd been disconnected from the drip, but the three pads of the ECG trace were still stuck to my chest and abdomen, and the sats probe was still attached to my left middle finger. I couldn't move away from the bed without triggering an alarm: where it would sound was a risk I wasn't yet prepared to take. I rolled my shoulders and stretched my legs out. The consultant was right: although I *looked* a mess, I was in reasonable shape. My thigh was stitched; my left shoulder packed and wrapped. If I wanted, I could get up and run, albeit painfully. But to, or from, whom? Kent wasn't exactly home turf, either, although a decade earlier I'd spent a week at the Shorncliffe base outside Folkestone with the Gurkhas. The William Harvey hospital was in Ashford – which was twenty miles from the barracks, and two miles from the Eurostar station to Paris.

Frank had told me to go dark. UKN was already dark. What he meant was 'go darker'. And the only way I could do that was to vanish again – and so completely that not even my own side could find me. I could do that. But if I did, I asked myself, what incentive would there be for me to come back? The work would never have any closure, except death. The only way out was to force an ending. If I could make it across the Channel, I would be free. Even if I just stayed put in France, the options were almost endless. Never mind a few months or weeks – up in the Pyrenees or the Massif Central the odds were that I could survive indefinitely: undetected, untraceable, unknown. I had nothing to lose. My mind ran away with itself. If I could stomach it, there was even the Marseilles mafia. As every mercenary knows, warriors aren't trained to retire.

I thought about that for a moment – that kind of killing.

But I couldn't do it. In twenty-four years I'd never even drawn a salary – much less murdered for money. I owned, and owed, nothing. The person I saw looking back at me in the bathroom mirrors of the hotels I called home was not a sicario, as Frank had once called me. I carried out hits. But I wasn't a hitman. True, I'd never sold out. But I'd had nothing to sell, and I had no pockets for pieces of silver, either.

My eyes grew accustomed to the dimly lit room. I reached out with my right hand and felt for the plastic bag I'd seen earlier in A & E. It had travelled to the new room with me – tucked away under the bedside trolley. I removed the damp denim jeans inside one-handed, and then wormed my right index finger down into the ticket pocket. I might have been close to moral bankruptcy – but I wasn't quite penniless. Soaked, squashed, but still there: I left the hundred-dollar bill where it was and pinched the sleep out of my eyes.

I needed to see clearly.

Maybe I didn't have to vanish. Maybe Frank would come back online with all the answers. Maybe the mission would become clear. Never mind a hitman, Frank had conjured me up out of Raven Hill as his Irish avenging angel – visiting death upon all those who threatened the idea of the Crown we served. Even if we no longer quite trusted one another, we still needed each other to fight the forever war. Although I had accepted death long ago, I wasn't ready to quit. Not today.

I swung my legs around and sat on the edge of the bed, facing the bathroom door. The ECG leads were long enough to let me move. I put my feet on the floor and flexed my toes. I stood up. The surgical gown they'd wrapped me up in clung to me like a winding sheet. That was me, all right: a dead man walking. No matter who was after me, this was the point of maximum vulnerability – not just on this job, but since the very moment I joined UKN. For the first time I was not only outside the system that supported me but trapped in the world that supported the system – the real and ultra-visible world of doctors and police and processes and procedures. If I could be seen, I could be identified. And if I could be identified, I could be eliminated: without investigation, without interrogation, without trace. You cannot be held accountable for killing a dead man.

I put the jeans on carefully. Damp, but not torn. They'd evidently peeled and not cut them off me in the ambulance. Good to go.

'I'm glad you're not ready to quit.'

I turned around. The consultant was standing in the door-way, lab coat bleached bright white by the harsh light of the ward beyond. She turned her head towards the policeman outside. I spread my hands wide and caught her eye. She startled and looked at me.

'Please,' I said.

8

I sat down again and she stepped into the room.

'I was talking to myself, wasn't I?' She nodded. 'Bad habit. Sorry. I can't think straight if I don't talk things through.'

'And now?' she asked. 'Are you thinking straight now?'

'Yeah, I guess.' I looked at the half-open door. Eyes on me, she reached behind with her left hand and pushed it to so that it was only ajar. 'Thanks. How long was I out for?'

'All day. You were admitted early this morning. It's Friday night now.' She checked her watch, adjusted her lab coat. She was nervous, working out what to say next. 'It's bloody mayhem out there. And I'm not even supposed to be on call tonight.'

Neither of us spoke for a moment. The sounds and shouts of frenetic work being done further down the ward percolated into the room. I calculated how quickly, quietly, I could incapacitate her. She stepped closer. Taking out the police guard would be easy, too. But that was a last resort – and, as yet, as unnecessary as it was undesirable. If I made it past the exit – which was a big 'if' – getting any further in the south-east of England with no support and no kit would make outrunning the Gardaí look like a walk in the park. No: if I was going to jump, it had to be clean. Doctor Rose was the perfect springboard. I relaxed and let my shoulders slump.

'So,' she asked, 'the "avenging angel". What's that all about?'

'I really was gabbling.' I rubbed my face with my hands.

'I'm guessing you reckon you should have got me a head shrink, not a head CT?'

'I'm not guessing anything. I *know* you've had a very traumatic experience.' She sized me up and clicked her tongue, considering, perhaps, how much of her bedside chat I'd heard earlier. 'You might feel all right in yourself, but a shock like that – falling into cold water, or exposure – that can make your mind play tricks on you.' She paused, casting around for the right words. 'Your wrists . . . I mean . . .' She paused again and then asked what she really wanted to know. 'What should I call you? What's your name?'

'It doesn't matter what my name is,' I said.

'Well,' she replied, 'it matters to me. And I'll bet it matters to whoever it was you were asking for in the ambulance, too.' She was hyper-alert. Night after night of dealing with junkies and drunks kept her on her toes. But she was softening. 'And for the record, I don't think you need a shrink. I think you need rest, and plenty of it.'

Her pager went off and she apologized as she checked it, all the while keeping one eye on me. 'You know, if nothing else, you'd do yourself a favour by telling me who you are . . . or at least what happened. We can look after you better, and you'll recover faster. Which means you can leave sooner.' She took her hand off the pager. 'The police would like to ask you some questions.' I snorted and shook my head. 'Yeah, OK, I know . . . But you mustn't worry. It's just that they think you're a migrant and they've had the bloody coast guard out all day looking for wreckage or other survivors. The sooner you tell them you're not, the sooner they'll leave you alone. I'm not going to let anyone question you until you're fit to talk.'

I pursed my lips and shook my head again.

'I'm not under arrest, am I?' She agreed that I wasn't. 'So then I don't have to say anything to them. And in case they ask, I don't want my photograph taken, either. Is that clear?'

'OK,' she shrugged. 'But you *are* going to have to talk to them. Eventually. You have no clothes, no money, no ID. I *can* help you, you know.'

'How?' I said.

'Well . . .' She hesitated. 'Apart from getting you well again, we, I mean *they*, can help protect you, if that's what you need.'

An edge of exasperation crept into her voice. She was moving between *caring* and *irritated*. That was a good sign. People are rarely scared by someone who annoys them.

'No,' I said. 'You can't. Protect me, I mean. That policeman outside? What was it you called him, a "vulture"?' She cleared her throat and dropped her eyes. 'You know, I'm sure he's a very decent vulture. But when his boss finds out I'm not a migrant, helping to protect me isn't going to be top of his to-do list. Believe me. You're very well meaning and all that, Rose, but this isn't just a hospital now. It's a prison.'

'You wouldn't be the first patient here to think that, I can tell you. But you *were* awake, eh? You had me *and* Doctor Mann fooled, that's for sure. Well . . .' she sighed, 'God knows you need something. Everyone in here does. But no one's going to hurt you. Not on my watch. I can give you my word on that.' She hesitated for a moment, and then decided to ask again. 'Tell me who you are. Or at least . . . At least tell me what your name is.' She looked at the monitor and checked her pager again. 'I can hardly call you "angel", can I?'

'If I tell you my name . . .' I struggled to find words that would inspire trust, not instil terror. 'Oh man, this is going to sound nuts.'

'Try me.'

'Right, well . . . I'm going to tell you straight, and you can take it or leave it.'

'OK. Go on.'

'If I tell you my name, I can't guarantee your safety.'

As I spoke, her pager beeped again. She looked at it, distracted. I raised my voice a fraction. '*Listen* to me.' She looked up and backed away abruptly. Harmless eccentric or dangerous madman? I'd asked myself the same question many times before – though not often of myself. 'I'm sorry,' I said quickly, and swung my left leg up on to the bed, rolling up the cuff of my jeans. 'Look.'

The scar on my calf that she'd pressed her thumb into earlier appeared deeper than usual, picked out by the slanted light from the bathroom.

'Colombia,' I said. 'You're right, there is a story behind it. I only wish I had time to tell you.' I pointed to my left ear, the top of which had been torn off ten months before. 'Sierra Leone. You could write a whole book about that one.' Then I pointed to a long-since healed laceration on my right bicep. 'Afghanistan. I lost three friends that night.' Finally I pointed to my left wrist, ringed with bruises fresh from my ordeal on the ship. 'English Channel. Last night.' I rolled the jeans leg down again. 'I'm not mad, and I'm not dangerous,' I said. 'Not to you, anyway.'

'So what are you, then?' she asked.

'Unless you help me to get out of here? A dead man.'

She said, did, nothing. I was winning. Slowly.

'It's just . . .' I cleared my throat. 'It's just that I've spent my whole life convincing people I'm someone I'm not. Now I need to convince you I am what I am, and I don't know what to say.'

76

'The truth,' she said. 'Tell me the truth. The truth will set you free.'

'No,' I said, 'it won't. The last time I heard someone say that was during an interrogation. They executed the prisoner in the morning. And anyway, I can't tell you the truth. You wouldn't believe it. But if I can *show* you the truth,' I continued, 'will you help me?'

'You don't have to show me anything. I believe that you're a soldier,' she said. 'And I believe that you're in trouble, and that you need help. What I don't believe is that running away or holding back vital information – from me, or the police, from *anyone*, frankly – is ultimately going to do you any good. There are probably people out there, right now, risking their lives searching the sea on your account. Think about that, about them, for a moment.'

'You see, that's the problem,' I said. 'I'm not a soldier. Not in the way you mean. Please. Let me show you.'

She didn't say no – which was a good start. I looked at her and showed my palms in supplication. The muscles in her jaw worked, and she sucked the inside of her cheeks. Any decision she was going to make would be as much personal as it would be professional. I'd clearly been through the wringer. The question for her, perhaps, was whether or not I'd deserved it. But despite the sheer weight of her misgivings, her evident ambivalence towards the police, mixed up with a high dose of good old-fashioned curiosity, was getting the better of her.

She nodded.

'OK, take out your phone and google the FCO.'

'The what?'

'The Foreign and Commonwealth Office.'

'Are you serious?'

'Yup. Go on. It's not going to blow up or anything.'

'No, I mean about my being at risk?'

'Uh-huh.' Another pause. 'But look at it this way: if I am delusional, then all this will add up to,' I nodded towards her wedding ring, 'is a good story to tell your husband tonight. Five minutes. That's all. And then we can all go home,' I lied.

She shook her head as if being petitioned by a child – or an idiot. 'Wife,' she said. 'I'm married to a woman.'

Nearly two and a half decades of professional people-watching, upon which dozens of life and death decisions had been made, and I still couldn't work out if women were flirting with me – or just fucking with me.

She fidgeted and tugged at her sleeve, wrestling with her reservations. Then: 'Oh, sod it!' She exhaled the words hard. 'Five minutes, OK. Deal?'

'Deal.'

Her phone was tucked away in a trouser pocket, hidden beneath her lab coat. She fished it out and unlocked it. 'I must be bloody mad.'

I kept looking at her phone. She tapped the three letters in with her right thumb, her eyes now flitting between mine and the screen.

'OK, good,' I smiled. 'Click on their website and then scroll down, all the way to the bottom, to the main switchboard number, the one that ends with fifteen hundred.' She went to speak but stopped herself. 'You're going to dial the number,' I said slowly.

'Anyone could have memorized that number. That doesn't prove anything.'

'Of course,' I agreed. '*When* you dial it, you're going to get a recorded message with a menu asking what extension or department you want. Ignore them all and key in star, followed by one-nine-zero-nine and then the hash key. That's going to put you through to an operator who's going to be bloody rude. She'll say, "Embankment", and then ask you what extension you require. Tell her, "Stirling Lines".'

'You've got it all worked out, haven't you? What is this — some special code to sucker unsuspecting civvy girls?'

'No,' I said. 'This is an absolutely spectacular breach of MI6's security protocols that's going to land me in even deeper shit than I'm in already. But it's all I've got right now. So, you know, how about it?'

She gave a deep sigh and carried on despite herself, determined, perhaps, to find out where this would take her.

'So, I ask to be put through to extension "Stirling Lines"?'

'No. Just say, "Stirling Lines". Nothing else. There'll be a delay.' I relaxed and spoke calmly, deliberately. My smile was gone. There would be consequences to making the call that I couldn't explain. I hoped my demeanour would prepare her for what might happen next. 'You'll be put through to another number. Someone else is going to answer the phone. Probably a man. More relaxed. Tell them you want to speak to Grumpy Jock. That's it.'

She looked at me, uncomprehending. 'That's it?'

'Yeah. That's it. They're going to put you through to a *very* grumpy Glaswegian.'

'Of course they are. And what do I say to this charming Scotsman?'

'Describe what you can see. Describe me. Describe what's happened, where I am. Tell him anything you like. If he wants you to positively identify me, tell him I won't give you my name.' I thought for a moment. 'But, uh, tell him about the scars. Tell him about the scar on my calf, and say I'd told you it was from Colombia and that I never got any thanks for it. Then just take his lead. And if you still don't believe me, well . . .' Well, then my luck would have run out like I always knew it would some day.

'Why don't you do it?' Her voice was rising. 'Why don't you make the call on the speaker? I have to leave in thirty minutes.' She offered me the phone. She was rattled now and obviously so. 'Look, to be honest it's more fun talking shit with you than playing mum to the junkies downstairs in ED, but why don't you just do it, eh? You've convinced me you need to make a call. So make it.' Fear crept into her speech, edging into the gaps between the syllables. Fear that she had made, was making, the wrong decision; but fear, too, that it was already too late to row back. She breathed out through her nose, and looked first at her shoes and then at me, remaking her decision anew, qualifying it as she went. 'I don't want to speak to anyone.' She held the phone out further towards me. 'You make the call. You speak and I'll listen.'

I've watched people play at roulette like that, their hand hovering over their stack on red or black, odd or even, twitching to get it back until the wheel stops spinning.

'I can't make the call, Rose. I wish I could, but I can't. They have the most sophisticated voice recognition software this side of Langley on that line. I say one word and all hell will break loose. They'll tear the fucking roof off this building to get me, kill anyone who gets in their way. Trust me. I know.' I held up my wrists. 'You think I did this to myself?' Then I pointed to my ankles. 'And that? You think I shot myself in the shoulder and then strung myself up? As everyone keeps reminding me, I'm not fucking Houdini.'

She let the hand holding the phone fall to her side. She looked scared now – but in dread of the situation, not of me.

80

That fear was good: it meant that she believed me. As long as her fear didn't turn into panic, it meant I could control her.

'Who is "they"?' she asked. Scared, but not stupid. She was taking nothing for granted.

'I don't know, Rose.' She raised her eyebrows. 'Honestly. I don't know. That's why I'm in here, why I'm asking you for help.' And that, finally, was the truth. If my comms with Frank – or his with Vauxhall – had been compromised, then no call I made was safe – and anyone or everyone could have been hunting me.

She braced herself and held her phone at the ready. Her voice steadied.

'What else will Grumpy Jock ask me?'

'Very little,' I replied. 'Except, perhaps, whether I'm still playing chess.'

'What should I tell him?' she asked.

I wrinkled my nose and sniffed the air, and decided – against a lifetime of experience to the contrary – to stick to the truth.

'Tell him,' I said, 'that I resigned.'

9

'Passport, please.'

I handed the Eurostar security guard the junior doctor's brand-new maroon passport. I yawned and looked down, covering my mouth as I did so. 'Sorry,' I apologized from behind my palm. 'Late night.'

David Peter Mann was sixteen years younger than me, black-eyed and brown-haired, with a jaw square enough to play liar dice with. A grey beanie covered my head. A disposable razor had smoothed my chin. I pinched the sleep out of my blue eyes, feigning a hangover headache. While he scanned the photo page, I busied myself with the contents of my coat pocket.

Rose had played her part well. An hour earlier I'd stalked across the freezing parking lot at Ashford International in a shirt, shoes and coat she'd filched from a cupboard downstairs in the Emergency Department. In the back pocket of my jeans, the passport and driver's licence she'd lifted – albeit reluctantly – from the bag she allowed the eager junior doctor who'd done my initial assessment to keep in her office. I had no phone, and didn't want one. As for money, I had a hundred-dollar bill – and five hundred pounds in cash courtesy of Rose's bank card. She had a promise of repayment from a terse Glaswegian.

And Grumpy Jock – Regimental Sergeant Major Jack Nazzar – was as terse, and as tough, as they came. Legendary Special Forces old-timer, he was the founding father of the

Wing – or the SAS's Revolutionary Warfare Wing – a Dirty Dozen of Hereford's most experienced operators. MI6 called them 'the Increment'. I called them when I was in trouble. I'd relied on them for overwatch on dozens of UKN operations, and spent more weeks in the field with Nazzar than I could remember. I wasn't sure if I was still operational or not. And with Frank out of the picture, there was no one to report to, or receive orders from. I couldn't call Whitehall even if I wanted to. As far as the Establishment was concerned, I didn't exist: Director Special Forces didn't take phone calls from a ghost. Frank was my only link to the offices of state and backchannels of diplomacy that ultimately determined every operator's fate; Jack Nazzar was my only remaining connection to the off-the-books world of warcraft that supported them. I'd counted on him being a friend. He hadn't let me down.

And neither had Doctor Mann.

'Thank you, sir. Have a nice trip.'

I took back the passport and stood in line for the X-ray at security, wondering how outlandish my appearance would have to be before someone questioned my identity. I filtered my way through French customs – who barely looked at the photograph – picked up a cup of coffee and a croissant and crossed over the steel and glass footbridge that dropped me down on to the platform. I'd booked myself on to the 0655 to Paris, Gare du Nord. A small clutch of other passengers braved the icy morning as if by their perseverance they might conjure the train from St Pancras a few minutes early. A stiff breeze picked up from the south-east. Anyone with any sense clung to the warmth of the waiting room upstairs for as long as possible. It was an hour before sunrise. My wounds ached, and I remembered that I wanted to smoke. I tried not to think about either and watched the clock instead. My breath steamed in the frigid air.

Ten minutes to departure.

The call to Nazzar had achieved its single objective: to persuade Rose to assist me by proving I was on the side that deserved her help. She'd stayed at the hospital overnight, eventually distracting the policeman and the nurses on my ward with a dropped cup of coffee just long enough for me to bolt. The wires weren't, it turned out, linked to a central bank: the room monitor bleeped feebly as Rose said it would when I peeled the pads off and then stopped abruptly as the unit's machine-brain realized it was no longer hooked up to a human.

As I stood on the platform, the ward sister would have been cursing my accomplice for having ordered my transfer to another ward without filling out the proper paperwork. She could fret about finding me as the irate policeman jabbered into his radio; or, more likely, she would throw her hands up and tell him she had better things to do than unpick a consultant's cock-up. But whatever she chose to do next, I would be lost in the system for a precious hour: a man who didn't exist, nowhere to be found, in a bed that hadn't been assigned.

When the police finally discovered that I'd flown the coop, they would issue a missing persons report. But with no photo, and limited manpower for migrant-hunting, the chances of them sweeping the station before departure were minimal. By the time they'd pulled my image from the hospital's CCTV – if they even bothered to do that – I'd be in Paris.

What Nazzar chose to do next was anyone's guess. The call would have been logged and recorded but not monitored – so there was no reason why any wires would have been tripped at his end unless he chose to raise the alarm himself. It could take days – weeks, even – for the call to be reviewed. Nazzar had taken chances on me before. Whether I made it on to the train or not would tell me whether he had again. I guessed he'd hold off until I'd fired a flare. As much as he was a an ally forged from the furnace of old times' sake, he was a friend out of necessity, too. His necessity. If there was a problem with UKN, there was a problem for the Wing. And Jack Nazzar didn't like problems. I knew he'd always vote for the most effective solution to deal with them – sanctioned or otherwise. He didn't like politicians either.

Rose would be safe. I'd take the rap for the stolen passport; if asked, she'd say I forced her to make the call. But her guilt by association in the eyes of whoever was hunting me was not so easily solved, not even by Nazzar. I knew he'd send an operator to keep tabs on her and her wife – and in all likelihood take them into unofficial military protective custody. That was as much an insurance policy for him as it was for them. If – when – that happened, it would feel like they'd been kidnapped at first, and I was sorry for it. Depending on how things worked out, a new identity, home, job, life were all potentially coming down the line at them. I'd told Rose to take her wife on a surprise holiday, immediately, though I doubted Nazzar would let them leave the country. The brutal fact of the matter was that, irrespective of what ultimately transpired, both of their lives would be changed irrevocably by Rose's chance meeting with me. She would be protected by the Wing – but at a cost she'd not calculated.

Five minutes to departure.

I revisited the plans I'd made from the hospital bed. In Paris I'd catch a connection to Toulouse. From there I'd

85

hitchhike and walk into the Pyrenees. The winter would be tough, but there would be isolated chalets and retreats abandoned till spring. Breaking into second homes owned by foreigners was a national pastime in France; so much so that the thinly stretched rural gendarmerie were mostly unconcerned as long as no violence was employed. I tried to shake off the cold of the platform and imagined the warm spring sun that would follow the vernal equinox. In my mind's eye I saw the mountains' snow caps melting into the streams and lakes where I'd drop a hook at dawn. There was no question that I could sustain myself. Special Forces selection, followed by years of training in a succession of increasingly harsh environments, would see to that. In comparison to Nunavut's Arctic tundra, surviving the Pyrenees would be a cinch. What would happen when – *if* – I re-emerged was a question I would have plenty of time to consider.

Three minutes.

The train pulled into the station. Metal ground against metal. Hydraulics wheezed. Doors opened. A guard wrapped up in a blue-black fleece stalked along the platform. I stepped over the yellow line, jostled by the backs and bags of a disorganized family eager to be in the warmth of the carriage.

Of course I could survive. But to what end?

I'd persisted in the pursuit of death because I had been persuaded by my soldier-scientist father that it mattered who pulled the trigger. And so it also mattered to me – if not to Frank – that even if what I'd become was a killer, at least I wasn't a murderer. But the reality was that Doc was dead because – and only because – I'd gone to him; and gone to him in the full knowledge it might kill him. I may as well have pulled the trigger myself. If that wasn't murder, what was?

Worse still, the consequence of his death could be another

fatality as unconscionable as it seemed inescapable: if Doc had been killed somehow because of his connection to me, then there was every possibility that Rachel Levy could follow her father to the grave. No loose ends. God knew I'd tied off enough myself. *Arkhangel* didn't just read like a message: it felt like a death warrant.

If she died, I would lose the last person who knew me when I was Mac Ghill'ean, and not McLean. I thought of Frank and of the tide of blood we had loosed upon our enemies. His enemies. And suddenly, for the first time in a long time, it felt like who I'd been mattered more than what I'd become. Doc had said Rachel was in London. Stop running and start thinking.

Stay.

Find her.

Save her.

I checked myself. I could dress it up all I liked, but a killer wasn't what I had become; it was what I had chosen to be. I screwed up my eyes. The fact was, I hadn't pulled the trigger on Doc. Someone else had. I was sorry, but there it was: a single tragedy written in the unending roll call of the dead. Rachel: a woman whose face I tried not to remember, and could hardly recall when I did; a woman whose name I struggled to speak out loud. Aged forty-two, and I was still acting like a cunt-struck teenager.

No.

Fuck her.

And fuck Frank and his circular firing squad.

I stepped up towards the open carriage door and stopped there, one foot on the platform and the other foot on the train.

And yet Frank might still keep faith. Maybe he had never lost it.

87

You made a choice, I told myself. *You're still a soldier. So wait for orders. And then follow them.*

Still I hesitated. Move forward or step back. The past was a foreign country, too, and one I had much less idea how to navigate than France. I thought of my father, who for stretches of my childhood I very rarely saw; and I thought of Doc, too, who perhaps saw more of my mother than either my father or I had wanted to admit. If love for her had bewildered him until he died, then he would have died for me, too. Maybe my mother murmured his name with mine as she swept her tired child's limbs into bed.

I'd never thought too much about love. Every man I'd killed had been some mother's son. To dwell on that could make a strong man lose his mind. Or his soul. Even now – *especially* now – thinking about my mother and father, about Doc and Rachel, was like standing too close to a wall. All I could see were bricks and mortar, not what they encompassed. But there were no walls I had not scaled in the past. I would survive. And yet what was the point of survival if there was no one, least of all myself, left *to* love?

Get a grip on yourself, Max. You're a fighter. So fight.

One minute.

I stepped down off the running board and put both feet on the ground. I paused and turned around, smacking into the frantic father of the family that had boarded before me, busy with a folded stroller. As his hand went out to steady himself, a rolled-up copy of *The Times* unfurled itself from under his arm and tumbled to the platform. I stared down at the wrinkled pages curling in the brittle air, straight into my own eyes.

The portrait was reproduced twice its original size, captioned with my name. I looked passively at the camera. No smile. Short haircut. Shave. The tip of my left ear missing. A bright, perfect print against a white background. It was my passport photograph, and it had been taken three weeks before at Raven Hill barracks. The headline above it: *'Lone wolf' sought over terror attack*. Below the fold, in lurid colour, was a photograph of Chappie Connor's burned-out cottage. Thatch gone, glass gone, door gone: it sat, still smoking, like a charred skull sinking into the sodden headland.

Fifteen seconds.

I stooped to pick the paper up, and the man said 'Thank you'; but grappling with the baby carriage, he had no hands to take it. I stood and watched as he clambered on, received through the open door by his panicked wife. The last whistle blew. The platform had emptied of everyone except the guard and myself. In a moment the doors would lock. I looked at the paper up close. There was only one person who could have released that photograph. Commander Frank Knight had vaporized my most valuable asset in the creases of tomorrow's fish-and-chip wrapping. My face would be everywhere. My name, too. Movement would become impossible. Helping me would be suicide. I was beyond the pale.

Time was up.

If I stayed, it would get bloody, quickly. If I left, it might be impossible to return.

All bets were off.

I stepped on to the train.

10

'*Monsieur?*'

'*S'il vous plaît, un café et un verre d'eau.*' My eyes scanned the menu chalked up on a thin blackboard hung near the door. '*Et un croque-madame,*' I smiled. '*J'ai faim.*' The waiter nodded and cleared the cups and plates left by the couple whose table I'd taken. The *bistrot* was set to the side of a small square dominated by a large church, a short walk from the Gare du Nord. In the summer tables and chairs must have spilled out of the concertinaed wood and glass doors on to the flag-stones outside. But on that cold morning the panes had fogged over, creating a damp, grey curtain that cut off the city beyond. It was good to be inside.

When I'd arrived, I'd exchanged the sterling left over from getting to Paris and then used some of those euros to buy a train ticket to Berlin, via Düsseldorf. I'd walked the cavernous concourse cautiously but casually. In Ashford there'd been no point in hiding my face from the station's security cameras: Mann's passport would have given my route away immediately. But in Paris I was careful not to show my face to the lenses that pivoted on gantries above me. This was where I needed my trail to go cold – or at least cool.

The station seethed with passengers and tourists, watched by patrols of maroon-bereted paratroopers from the 3rd Marine Infantry Regiment. The troops moved slowly, purposefully,

Famas assault rifles cradled across their chests, eyes looking for a fight – and, if and when they got word, for me.

The Thalys fast train to Düsseldorf departed in less than two hours from the platform adjacent to the Eurostar arrivals. I'd double-checked the departures board and cooled my heels for a minute. When the video of the station CCTV was played and replayed, I'd be spotted, eventually, exactly where I wanted them to find me: scoping out another international train, but one I had no intention of boarding. If whoever was looking for me concluded Germany was my next stop, it would buy me time. And time, as always, was golden. Head down, I'd scuttled off and buried myself in a crowd of Dutch students making for the Métro. I'd descended with them. At the bottom of the stairs I'd peeled off and ducked into a photobooth. After putting five euros in the slot, I'd sat there impassively, waiting, counting my breaths, listening to the weekend bustle beyond the curtain.

A few minutes later I'd emerged again on to street level by the Buffalo Grill, opposite the main entrance, ditching my bundled-up coat into a litter bin. Walking back into the station by the taxi rank, I'd lifted an unguarded Yankees ball cap sitting on top of a careless American's rucksack.

I'd considered stealing his phone, too, but unlocking it would have been impossible. I could have bought a burner, but I needed to stay as low profile as possible. Unregistered phones don't stay active for long in France – and authenticating the SIM card would require identification. Showing Doctor Mann's stolen passport wouldn't just alert London – it would ring an alarm bell loud enough to be heard as far away as Washington and Moscow.

I hadn't thrown the passport away with my coat, though. Doctor Mann's ID wouldn't get me through immigration again – but his identity might still come in handy. The steps I'd taken to get to Paris would be revealing themselves behind me, pace by pace, hour by hour. The most I could do was give anyone in pursuit the runaround while I made my own best guess at what to do next.

The world had shrunk to the radius of my vision. I had to assume that any attempt to reach out would see my hand severed. Whatever had been written about me in the papers would have multiplied a hundredfold or more online. Searching the web at an internet café was a possibility – but even if I could connect via a VPN, the shop itself would have cameras to watch its customers. Besides, any searches of any value were so specific that, if I was being tracked online, entering the search terms that interested me would be like waving a red flag above the parapet of whatever anonymity I had left. Nothing was certain, but if the people hunting me enlisted the help of French internal security, it would be a matter of hours, not days, before I ended up in the papers again. The DGSI didn't mess about. And once Interpol got its act together, all of Europe – and beyond – would be on the lookout for me.

Old media: it was the best and only option. Paper and ink were untraceable. I'd grabbed a copy of *Le Monde* and the international edition of *The New York Times* from a Relay news-stand and headed out to the *bistrot* I had in mind, tossing the stolen cap into a rubbish cart as I went.

The waiter returned with the coffee and a glass of water. I grunted my thanks. He grunted his acknowledgement of it. I tried to concentrate on the facts, or what passed for them on an operation this messed up.

I didn't know if Frank was – or ever had been – managing

the Connor job solo, as he'd let me believe, or if instead he'd been working with Whitehall and Vauxhall Cross all along. I didn't know if General King – Director Special Forces – was involved or not. I didn't know if Jack Nazzar had let me get away because he wanted to, or because he'd been ordered to. And I sure as hell didn't know how the Russians – if they were Russians – fitted into the picture, or how they'd found me in Mayo. They'd done their damnedest *not* to kill me, despite every opportunity to do so.

I didn't know why Frank had ordered the hit, or if it was definitely Chappie Connor, and not me, he'd hoped to eliminate. But it didn't take faith in archangels to see that I, personally, was of interest to someone – and not in a good way: I'd been ambushed, and then tracked and kidnapped.

I did know this: MI6 was in turmoil. The same thoughts came back to me that had spun around my head as I pivoted upside down in the ship's hold: *no one was above suspicion.* That was the truth of it. The fact that Frank had kept Whitehall out of the loop was proof, if ever it was needed, that the men in charge – and men, to a man, they were – ran their own shows, for their own reasons. And even if the bad apple could be singled out, the rot rarely stopped where you could see it. I'd always been too focused on the job in hand, too occupied with tactics to consider strategy, let alone embroil myself in intrigue. If MI6 was rotten, I had no idea how far the contagion might have spread – if indeed it had at all.

Sure, the chairs around the national security poker table at Vauxhall Cross were rearranged every so often. And when the music stopped, some of those men in charge were amazed to discover they no longer had a seat at the game – even, recently 'C' himself, the Chief of the Secret Intelligence Service. But when the stakes are as high as national survival, shuffling the players doesn't clean up the game if men like Frank make sure the hands are only ever dealt from a stacked deck. Do what thou wilt had become the whole of their law, as it had mine when I ran to Doc.

I reread the story in the paper I'd picked up in Ashford. It was illuminating, in so far as it was inaccurate in almost every detail. You could always rely on journalists to get everything wrong. Which was nothing if not alarming, given that MI6, MI5 and GCHQ counted on them for an astonishing amount of their information. The piece asked the usual simplistic questions. 'Are the Troubles going to blow up again?' (Answer: 'It's Ireland; you never can tell.') And, 'Is this the work of a dissident lone wolf?' (Answer: 'It's Ireland; you never can tell.') Over the following eight hundred words the reporter supposed the attack part of an obscure Irish Republican feud – which, because it wasn't, rendered the entire write-up extravagantly absurd. The article attributed the release of my name and photograph to unnamed 'security sources', while simultaneously stating that 'British and Irish intelligence services had declined to comment'.

I bet they had.

But I did learn something from the newspapers: Doc Levy had lied to me. Rachel was not in London. She was in Tel Aviv. I didn't blame him. He must have been desperate to keep his daughter out of the messed-up world of Max McLean. And fair play to him. Hitmen don't take lovers; they take hostages. My copy of *The New York Times* cited a story originally run by the Israeli paper *Haaretz*. The combined reporting tentatively connected the 'firebombing' of Chappie Connor's cottage with another violent attack the following day: the shootout at Doc's. While no named deaths were attributed to the former, the latter was illustrated with an old photo of Jacob Levy from his army days. It was illuminated, too, by a quote from 'his daughter Rachel, 44, the Azriel Jacobs research fellow at the Kolymsky School of Computer Sciences at Tel Aviv University' – who, the report said, had 'made *aliyah* to Israel in 1991'. She praised the Irish authorities for attempting to apprehend the attacker and hoped that 'the coward who murdered her father' would meet a similar fate. After the inquest, his body would be flown to Israel for burial.

I folded the pages and massaged my temples.

Fuck.

Twenty-seven years, and the first words I heard from Rachel were that she wished me dead. The waiter set the ham, egg and cheese sandwich down wordlessly on the crumpled paper. My appetite had dissolved into the newsprint. I forced myself to eat.

Maybe one day the Pyrenees, or wherever those mountains on the horizon turned out to be, would be an option – but not now. On the station platform in England I'd decided *what* to do, but didn't know *how* to do it. Now the world had shifted on its axis. Not only was Rachel plausibly in danger *because* of me, but in all likelihood she'd believe she was in danger *from* me.

Getting into Israel on a hot passport to convince her otherwise was not possible. Nor was buying a clean one from the mafia in nearby Montreuil. I had three hundred euros left, not three thousand, and the gangsters in the *banlieue* didn't give credit. Jack Nazzar had been my last lifeline in the UK: there was no one left in Britain or Ireland I could call on for a favour, not even in UKN – which was impenetrable, and purposefully so.

UKN personnel had half a dozen aliases to choose

95

from – all backed up, where necessary, by social media profiles, school reports, employment references, criminal records ... whatever it took to create a robust, three-dimensional, deniable avatar. Each avatar was firewalled from the others, and from the operator's real identity. Although MI6 and the Special Forces mob all knew me as 'Max McLean', I had no official documents issued in that name. And in my case, it was a double bluff: 'Max McLean' was, itself, an invention – but my own, not UKN's.

The real identities of UKN operators at Raven Hill were a mystery even to Colonel Ellard. Only Frank knew who we were. He hand-picked potential recruits. No one was told what they were training for until they passed – and less than one per cent did. Some of the failures went to MI6, most went to pieces. Anyone selected for UKN went out into the world to join the unsung Three Hundred who stood alone at whichever Hot Gates Commander Frank Knight sent us to.

And there was no commander more loyal than Frank. He was accountable directly to the Crown. And his job was to watch the watchmen. Under him we formed an analogue, off-grid failsafe – an impenetrable fifth column carrying out discreet, deniable operations abroad, and a supposedly incorruptible praetorian guard keeping a weather eye on the security services at home. We might have enjoyed overwatch from the Wing and briefings by MI6, but we were fundamentally separate from them – civilians, not soldiers, who had no existence outside the frame of a passport photo. We could be captured, tortured and broken and all we could give anyone was the handful of magic beans that were Frank's name, rank and tailor.

Everyone except me.

Although I didn't know a single other UKN operative's

true identity – or even if 'Frank' was Knight's real name – I knew enough to unmask him. Over the years I'd become embedded at Raven Hill, groomed to take over the barracks from Colonel Ellard. I knew where the bodies were buried. Maybe Frank figured that, sooner or later, I'd turn my hand to grave digging. Maybe releasing my photo was his way of breaking my shovel.

Fucking maybes.

The photograph in *The Times* had been taken for an as yet unused British passport issued in the name of Gordon Sim – a fictional car mechanic from south London. *Suspect*, the caption underneath the picture read: *Irish Police want to question Max McLean, a British citizen named in connection with the attack.*

Looking at it made me feel sick.

Whoever released the photo knew how to link it to me, personally. To do that, they'd have needed to know my name, my assigned alias, recognize my face, have the security clearance to access the server the image was stored on and the motive to go public with it all in the press. That *specific* photograph captioned with the name of Max McLean narrowed down the usual suspects to a line-up of one.

Only Commander Frank Knight knew that Gordon Sim was one of my covers; and only he knew where to look for him: on the servers at Her Majesty's Passport Office. That was the sole place where any trace of Gordon Sim could be found. Mr Sim was just another innocuous citizen, his details filed alongside those of millions upon millions of other innocuous citizens. There was nowhere else *to* look. But now, short of announcing my arrival from the top of the Eiffel Tower, I was about as exposed as it was possible to be.

I wiped up the last of the egg yolk with the last of the fried

97

bread and swallowed it down with the last of the coffee. I left the price of the meal on the table and found the blue-tiled pissoir at the back of the *bistrot* and washed my face. Outside, I got rid of *The Times*, dropping my printed paper face into the trash, and bought a cheap tan overcoat and a box of Marlboro Reds from the row of shops opposite. Then I struck out into the city with Chappie Connor's hundred-dollar bill burning a hole in my pocket.

I turned right, off the square and on to Boulevard de Magenta for three hundred metres, before bearing right again on Boulevard de Strasbourg. From there it was a half-hour straight shot south to the Île de la Cité and the cathedral of Notre-Dame. It was eleven a.m. I walked against the flow of the traffic. I kept my head down and clung to the scant protection afforded by shop awnings and the tangled cover of winter-bare trees from the prying eyes of CCTV cameras.

Low on the skyline to my left the sun broke free of the clouds on the horizon, picking out the ivory buildings on the west side of the boulevard with long shafts of mellow winter light. But as I walked on, the long perspective of the street gave the impression that the walls were closing in. Rising up on either side of the road like an urban canyon, the monumental architecture was purposefully wide enough to carry cannon and cavalry to the heart of the city in case of rebellion. Getaway drivers in Paris needed to know their shit. The cops could lock down the centre in minutes.

But there were no revolutionaries on the march that morning, just an endless parade of people braced against the chill. Aimless tourists in Gore-Tex meandering across black and white striped crosswalks; haughty women in belted coats; men sporting trimmed beards and half-smiles. And me. On the outside I was just on the right side of ignorable. But

98

inside, my bullet wounds chafed, my ankles burned from the rope that had held me up two days before, and the scratches I'd sustained on the beach shed their scabs under my clothes. Above all, though, I felt sick to my stomach: 'coward' was a bitter pill to swallow.

I continued to wind my way south, past the Pompidou Centre and deeper into the heart of the city. It felt safer turning on to the little streets but I had no idea who, if anyone, was tracking me – or how. The Pont Notre-Dame carried me over the Seine, and before I knew it the twin towers of the cathedral reared up above me. I stood and stared at the famous edifice, at the massive rose window, at the angels and demons beneath whose wings the city spread. Statues of the damned and the saved stood sealed in their stone fates above the west door, presided over by an Eternal King who'd encouraged his followers to turn the other cheek and then thrashed the money-changers in the Temple with a whip.

I lit a Marlboro and dragged on it, hard. I hadn't walked here by accident. When I was fifteen, my father and I had explored what felt like every inch of those streets. I dived with him into the underground soul of the City of Light, flexing my French, learning how to drink and how to smoke. It was the last trip we made together before I was told that his plane had come down over the African savannah. The avenues and cobbled lanes were etched into my memory. Twenty-five years later I'd been operational there, protecting an asset – and buying myself some credit in the process.

Beneath my feet was *Point Zéro* – a stone disc set with a metal sun-like compass from which all distances in France were measured, the point to which all roads led. Fifteen minutes' walk across the Pont de l'Archevêché and into the Latin Quarter and I'd find my way to Rue Rollin. I wasn't supposed to know the address, much less who lived there. But there were a lot of things I wasn't supposed to know. I wasn't sure precisely how I was going to get to Rachel. But I knew which way to turn. I crushed out the half-smoked cigarette under the sole of my shoe and turned my back on the church.

It was time to sell my cloak and buy a sword.

11

'Max McLean? Are you out of your fucking *mind*?'

Sergei Lukov was a bad Bulgarian. Five-eight, a hundred and forty pounds, trussed up in an old leather jacket as black as his heart. He must have been pushing sixty but looked a decade younger – his face all angles and suntan, eyes gleaming like two black marbles. He sized me up, and his expression turned from incredulity to horror. I looked, and felt, awful. I gave him a tight-lipped smile and shrugged, showing him my empty palms. It was inconceivable he didn't know my picture was in the papers. He shook his head.

'OK. Come in.'

He stepped behind the street door, which he'd opened just enough that I could squeeze past without revealing him to the world outside.

'Quickly. This way. *Barzo!*'

I didn't speak. He ushered me through into his apartment on the left-hand side of a little courtyard area around which other flats were arranged.

The door to the apartment closed behind him. For a brief instant we were sealed in darkness. And then, one flash at a time, a strip light overhead sputtered to life, revealing the room in fluorescent bursts. The apartment was tiny – a fifteen-foot square, freezing cold pied-à-terre in which a round table, a sofa and bar jostled for space with a kitchenette. A mezzanine spread out above a third of the floor space; beneath it a shower and toilet. The cistern rushed with water.

There were no windows, and the room smelled of shit. We turned to face each other. His right hand hadn't left his jacket pocket. Both of mine had remained in the clear.

'So? You are not here to kill me, because Sergei would already be buried in Père Lachaise. No?' His accent rang with all the charm of a Russian–Bulgarian car crash colliding somewhere in the Balkans. Abrupt. Sparse. Swerving always between murderous and mischievous. 'And besides, Sergei would have known that you were coming. *Da?*'

'Sergei knows everything.' I said. 'That's why I'm here.'

'Yes. Good. Maybe. So, if we are not killing each other, Sergei will take his jacket off. OK?'

'Sure,' I said. 'Make yourself at home.' He snorted and purposefully turned his narrow back on me while he hung the jacket from a brass hook by the front door. I didn't move. 'Trust me,' I said. 'I'm here to do business. Just business. OK?' He turned around, a Makarov pistol clutched in his fist. The muzzle pointed at my chest. There were only five feet between us. I moved my hands up, slowly, palms out. 'But if you're going to kill me, you'd better do it right, and do it right now.'

Lukov burst instantly into a deep peal of laughter, weirdly resonant given his weasel frame. He flicked the barrel up and held the pistol side-on, unthreatening, grinning widely. He paused, and then jerked his hands as a boxer might if feinting a punch, and then laughed again.

'OK,' he said. 'Just business,' and tucked the semi-automatic into his jeans, under the hem of a thickly knitted sweater. 'You are lucky to find Sergei. He has an appointment. A beautiful woman.' He cupped his hands, and held them up in front of his chest. 'Like *dini*. How do you say?' He scratched his chin. 'Watermelons!'

102

Everyone has a weakness. Lukov's was women. Enslaved to his cock – to which he proved himself a devoted and unaccountably successful servant – he was an internationally notorious skirt-chaser. He roared with laughter again and then as quickly as it flared up his face dropped.

'Are you buying, or selling?' I went to answer but he cut me off. 'And don't think Sergei is going to be cheap. You, here – this is a problem, my friend. A big fucking problem. You understand?'

I told him I did and lowered my hands, looking around for somewhere to sit. He pointed to the table and I drew up a chair. I sat down and folded the tan overcoat I'd bought on the way tightly across my chest. Lukov reached up to a cupboard over the sink and produced a bottle and two little Duralex glasses, into each of which he poured an ounce or so of clear liquid.

'*Rakia*,' he said. 'For the cold.' I hesitated. 'Relax,' he smiled. 'Guaranteed one hundred per cent Bulgarian grape poison.' We lifted our glasses and banged the rims together loudly. Lukov looked me straight in the eye. '*Nazdrave.*'

'*Sláinte*,' I replied, holding his stare.

I took the grappa at a gulp and clenched my throat before breathing out. My guts burned. Lukov sat down and lit a Gauloise and then pushed the packet and a lighter towards me. I lit one too, and held the smoke down. It tasted good. We both exhaled into the room. The tobacco smoke smothered the tang of shit, the grappa, the biting cold.

'Selling,' I said.

'Bad luck for you,' he smiled. 'Buyer's market. Seems like everyone has something to sell these days.' I took another drag on the Gauloise and he fixed his marble eyes on me through the smoke. No smiles now. We stared at each other for a moment over the empty glasses. 'What are you offering?'

I dropped my cigarette into the ashtray. Then, slowly, so as not to incite his trigger finger, I removed the hundred-dollar bill from my ticket pocket, careful all the while to keep his gaze. I unfolded the note and placed it face up on the table between us.

'Benjamin Franklin,' I replied.

The laughter erupted again. Lukov's face warped into a mass of unshaven creases. His body rocked; his left hand slammed the table like a tag-wrestler desperate to climb out of the ring. But his right hand never strayed more than a second from the pistol in his belt. It was a talent of his that you never knew if he was genuinely amused or just hamming it up; likewise, his bouts of gravity were equally inscrutable. But Lukov's real talent was not as an actor, but as a broker.

Neither buying nor selling anything personally, he was merely a key – albeit an expensive one – who unlocked the doors through which clients that could otherwise never be seen to meet could do business: the Americans and the Russians; the Russians and the Chinese; the Chinese and the Iranians; the Iranians and the Saudis; the Saudis and the Israelis; the Israelis and the North Koreans; the North Koreans and the Americans. The list was infinite; the cycle unending.

His stock in trade was not intelligence but information. What other people did with it, how they assessed it, categorized it, classified it, was apparently of no interest to him. Whether he took pleasure in pimping his wares, thrills from driving up or down the price, remained unclear. What was clear was that he took ten per cent of every transaction, in cryptocurrency, in advance. A multi-millionaire who lived and laughed like a hyena, he was, in his soul, a mirthless motherfucker, both loved and loathed by Vauxhall Cross,

Langley and Moscow in turn. Though they all despised him, they all protected him, for the simple reason that they all needed him.

His world revolved around percentages, but his business was built on trust – and favours. Two years ago I'd saved him from a Chechen hit squad on his own doorstep and he'd been resentful ever since: he owed me, big time. He dug his left hand into his pocket and tossed a crumpled fifty-euro note on the table.

'For you, Max McLean,' he snorted, 'and only for you, my friend, Sergei will wash your C-note at fifty cents on the dollar.' He slapped his thigh. 'Buyer's market! *Super!*'

'Yeah,' I smiled. 'Incredible. Really incredible. You know why?'

'No, my friend. Sergei absolutely promises you he does not know why.' He was still laughing. Tears formed at the edge of his eyes and moistened his cheeks. 'Tell me, please.'

'Because . . .' I paused and reminded myself to be patient with him, tempting though it was to throttle him. 'Because this isn't a hundred-dollar bill.'

'Ah, really, Max McLean, what is it then?' His smile was slipping again.

'It's a death warrant.'

Lukov stubbed out his cigarette and dried his eyes and poured two more glasses of *rakia*. He lifted his high, and then with great and sudden solemnity proposed a toast.

'To death.' We clinked glasses again and swallowed the grape distillate. 'But whose?'

'Mine, nearly,' I said truthfully. 'The Brits want the bill, and so do the Russians. And they aren't choosy about how they get it.'

'My friend, there are a hundred and forty million Russians.

Sergei knows. He's met all of them.' He licked the last of the *rakia* from the rim of his glass and lit another Gauloise. 'Which Russian?'

I raised my eyebrows.

'OK. And the British, they are trying to kill you, too? For this?' Lukov rarely asked questions to which he didn't already have the answer. His interrogations were intended to corroborate what he already thought he knew.

I shrugged. He shook his head.

'But . . . why?' He sounded genuinely, uncharacteristically confused.

'I don't know, Sergei. Truly. Maybe it's me. Maybe it's the note. Maybe it was the hit.' *There isn't one damned straight line in any of this*, I thought to myself, and I wasn't about to lay out everything I knew for Sergei Lukov. 'The last week has been, uh, *unpleasant*. The note, *that* note, is the only thing that links a series of very unfortunate events.' I picked up the cigarette and drew on it again. 'That note, and me.'

'So . . .' He picked his words carefully. 'The golden boy of MI6 is here to see Sergei, how shall we say, in a personal capacity?' I nodded again, and pushed the note towards him. He laughed and picked up the bill, turning it over in his hands – and flinched. Not even Lukov could mask his surprise at seeing the single Russian word scrawled across the back of the note. '*Ebah mu maikata*,' he swore. 'What is this?'

He held the note up so I could see what I already knew was written on it.

'It's what makes it personal,' I said.

'What, Max McLean is on the side of the angels now?'

I smiled at that.

'Maybe. Maybe not. You've seen the photo?' I asked him. 'In the press?' Lukov choked on his cigarette smoke and held his hands up – Gauloise in one, hundred-dollar bill in the other – as if to say, *Of course*. 'So? What do you hear?'

Lukov dropped his hands and his expression and pushed the note back across the table towards me.

'Sergei hears,' he said, 'that you tried to do the Russians a favour.'

'How so?'

'By completing their contract for them.' He stubbed his cigarette out. 'But he also hears they lost something very valuable in the process.' He pointed to the hundred-dollar bill on the table. 'Maybe that is half the mystery solved, *nali*?'

'Their contract? I don't understand.'

'Max McLean,' he said, pausing to drag hard on his cigarette, 'are you just talking or are you buying now, too?'

'Buying. Fifteen per cent on the note.'

'Twenty.'

'Fuck.' I rubbed my face. 'OK. Twenty. Which contract?'

'The old man.'

'What *old man*, exactly?' I said, choosing my words carefully.

'The old man in the, uh, *v kashtata*?' He fished for the right words in English. 'In the cottage?'

'Got it,' I said, though I hadn't. 'The Russians and the Brits both wanted Chappic Connor dead?'

Connor hadn't been named in the newspaper reports. Throwing it at Lukov was like trying to land a spotting round on a fire mission when you couldn't see the target. Sometimes you overshoot. Sometimes you get lucky.

'Chappie Connor?' Lukov spluttered. 'That piece of shit?'

'Uh-huh.'

It was always amusing when Lukov thought someone else was deplorable. The Lord only knew what he thought other people said about him. He pressed his lips together into a tight smile and nodded, processing the information.

'Connor worked for the Russians. No question. But he worked for the British, too.'

'How do you mean?'

'Simple. Like I said. He worked for the British.'

'When?'

'When he was in the Irish Republican Army.'

'And how would you . . . ?' Then the veil lifted. 'Because you brokered his defection. You sold him back to the Russians.' I looked at the note, and the empty glass of *rakia*, and into Lukov's beady black eyes. 'Wow.' Lukov finished his cigarette. 'And when he, uh, *died*, who was he working for then?' I asked.

'My friend,' he said patiently, 'now only the angels know who Chappie Connor really worked for, and when he worked for them.' I could do nothing but accept the infuriating truth of that. 'Sergei,' he continued, 'is not an angel.'

'You got that right.'

'But Sergei does know that the man you were sent to kill was not Chappie Connor.'

'How so?' It was uncomfortable being perplexed in his presence. He cocked his head to one side and grinned widely, relishing my ignorance.

'OK. But first, Sergei has a question for you.' His nose twitched and he fiddled with the cigarette packet. 'When did Chappie Connor die?'

'You know that,' I said, wondering if in fact he *did* know that Connor had been dead at least a week before I got to him. There was every reason not to tell him anything; but once bargaining began, it was difficult not to tell him everything.

'*Da*,' Lukov agreed. 'I do. But does Max McLean? Sergei Lukov doesn't think he does.'

'Sergei Lukov,' I replied, 'is very close to pissing me off.' I caught hold of my temper and smiled again. 'All right. You can have this for your twenty per cent. Connor was already dead when I got to the cottage. So, if there was another contract on him, they got there first.'

'That,' said Lukov, 'is correct.' He plucked another Gauloise from the packet and lit it carefully. 'Chappie Connor was already dead. *Da*. Bravo. He was killed by the KGB.'

'The FSB, Sergei.' It was hard not to laugh at his slip-up. 'The Cold War is long gone, my friend.'

'Not in 1988 it wasn't.' His face was set, serious. Lukov wasn't joking.

'What, *exactly*,' I asked him carefully, 'do you mean?'

'Sergei means,' he said, 'exactly what Sergei has said.'

'That Chappie Connor was killed thirty years ago? By the KGB? That's what you're telling me?'

'*Da*. That is what Sergei is telling you.'

'And how would you know that?'

My mind raced. It didn't matter that Lukov had brokered his defection. Connor would have been given a new identity, a new life, a fireproof exit into the new Russia emerging in the thaw of *Glasnost*.

'He was hit by a truck. In Sofia,' he said with evident pride, patting his chest with his free hand. 'Sergei's home town. The driver of the truck,' he continued, 'was Sergei's *priyatel*.'

'Careless driver, your friend.'

'That is the only problem with Bulgarians. They are very bad drivers. Very bad indeed.' I felt a line of sweat break across my back. My mouth went dry. 'Sergei has a better question for you. There are sixty million British. Which one ordered the hit? That is the *real* question, *nali*?'

'Yes, Sergei. That is the question.'

'And what is the answer?'

'Are you buying now, too?'

'*Da*.' He scratched his head. 'Why not?'

'Ten per cent on the note.' I smiled. Lukov sighed and raised his eyebrows.

'Fifteen?' he countered.

'Done. King. General King. Director Special Forces. Off the books, of course.'

Lying to Lukov was a hard card to play. His face remained expressionless. Not even a flicker.

'Of course.'

'Though whether he knew it was Chappie Connor, I have no idea.'

'And now you are in shit?'

'No offence, but I wouldn't be here if I wasn't.'

'*Da*. OK. That is the truth. So . . . You are sure you want to do this?'

'Yeah. Sure. Just put the note on the market. See who bites.'

Lukov dragged on the Gauloise and blew his smile away for good with the smoke.

'Let me be very clear with you. Sergei is a broker. He makes sales. And the way he makes them is to guarantee them. You put that note on the market, then you sell it. It's merchandise, not bait. Sergei does not do your reconnaissance for you. You know the rules. If you want to sell, then *you* guarantee the sale, so I can.' He dragged on the cigarette. The moment he stopped calling himself 'Sergei', I knew he was serious. 'And what, Max McLean, do you have for collateral?'

I showed him my empty hands again and pulled the left-hand side of my overcoat away from my chest. With my right thumb and forefinger I produced Doctor David Mann's passport from my inside pocket and dropped it on the table in front of him.

'Me,' I said. 'I'm your collateral.'

Lukov picked up the passport. I picked up the hundred-dollar bill and put it back in my pocket.

'It's not you,' he said. 'It's not your cover. Who is David Peter Mann?'

'A sap,' I said. 'It's stolen and it's how I got here. Like I said, the job was off the books. And like you said, I'm in deep shit. Whoever pays the most gets the note. If you give them this, they'll believe you, believe it's really me selling.'

'And the note? I can keep it?'

'I like you, Sergei. But I don't want to fuck you. So don't try to fuck me. I keep the note. You keep the passport.'

'OK.' He slipped Doctor Mann's identity into his back pocket. 'And the price?'

'Five million.'

'Dollars?'

'Pounds.'

He inhaled sharply across his teeth.

'That is a very expensive hunch, Max McLean. It will make them take notice. Of that we can be sure. You want it in crypto, *da*?'

'Yes. It has to be anonymous.'

'Sergei will drink to anonymous.' He filled the glasses for a third time. But I stopped him before he drank.

'One more thing.' His eyes narrowed and he nodded. 'When this blows up, I'll need a way out.'

I dipped my hand back into my coat pocket and put the

strip of instant photos I'd had taken earlier that morning at the Gare du Nord on the table between us.

'A passport?'

'Yeah. Canadian.'

'Canadian will take one week. Greek, Sergei can have tomorrow.'

'*Yamas*,' I toasted him in Greek.

Lukov raised his glass, too. '*Yamas*,' he replied. 'Finally those Hellenic sons-of-bitches are good for something.' We drank down the *rakia* and both stood up. He extended his hand, and I took and shook it. 'Noon, tomorrow. There's a bar in the *onzième*. La Fée Verte.' He winked at me. 'The waitress there. *Sochni dini*.' I shook my head and walked to the door. He pressed my hand again, serious this time, with a wad of folded euros. 'In case you get hungry. I don't want my collateral to get damaged.'

I thanked him and he showed me out, carefully, on to the street. A trickle of light crept into the courtyard through the open door. My temples felt tight from the alcohol and the intel.

'You know, Max McLean,' he said as I pulled up the collar of my overcoat, 'you Irish have the same problem as us Bulgarians.'

'Oh yeah,' I said, 'what's that?'

'Nobody ever knows which side we're on.'

12

Goddamned Lukov. He was either an idiot or a genius.

La Fée Verte – an absinthe joint north-east of the city centre on the corner of Rue de la Roquette and Rue Basfroi – had about as much cover as a greenhouse. Along each street tall wooden-framed French windows, shut against the cold, stretched the full length of the building. Shooting fish in a barrel would, by comparison, have been challenging. Outside, a couple of smokers sat at one of the small tables heated from above by electric burners. Inside, it was already buzzing with brunch customers. Blending in as a solo diner is an unenviable task. There was no immediate sign of the fabled barmaid through the windows, which remained worryingly clear. And there was no sign of Lukov, either.

I resisted the temptation to circle the block and instead made for the bakery on the corner opposite. The entrance was set well back under the overhang of the first floor, shielded from the street by a masonry pier. I bought a croissant and loitered plausibly in the doorway while I ate it.

After leaving Lukov's cell the day before, I'd ditched the tan overcoat and bought a decent black waterproof jacket with deep pockets and a down liner, new jeans and hiking boots – plus neoprene gloves, a sweater and a baseball cap. I'd reupped on painkillers, too. And a toothbrush. Man cannot live by Gore-Tex alone. In my jacket pocket: one hundred millilitres of legal pepper spray and a Pozidriv screwdriver with a six-inch shank. Knives were illegal to carry, and if I got stopped and searched I needed to be as clean as possible: a screwdriver would be easier to explain away than a blade, and would stab and throw just as well. On my wrist: the cheapest waterproof watch I could find. On my mind: nothing except the angles and arcs of fire around La Fée Verte that a sniper might use.

The Senegalese guesthouse I'd stayed in three blocks north of our RV demanded double the rack rate when I asked to pay cash with no ID. My shopping spree hadn't left me with enough change to cover that and dinner – but the night porter took pity on me and brought me up a bowl of *chere* couscous and seasoned meat with tomatoes: '*Un cadeau de ma femme.*' He brought me a beer – '*Un cadeau de moi*' – too, and told me just to open the window if I wanted to smoke in the room – which I did.

Twelve fifteen.

Lukov was late. While I tried to work out where he was watching me from, a motorcycle cop pulled up. He killed the engine and dismounted, nodding at me as he flicked his visor up and moved past me into the bakery. Six-two, a hundred and eighty-five pounds. He wore the two-tone blue uniform of the gendarmerie, combat boots and a Glock pistol on his hip. I nodded back, waited a beat, and moved out across the road to the bar. The junction was ringed with six-storey buildings, mostly apartment blocks, all covered with dozens of windows. The crossroads could have been circled with snipers, but I was out of options. I breathed steadily as the grey pavement gave way to the white and green tiled floor of the bar. No shot rang out. The door creaked closed behind.

Safe.

I looked around and drew up a bar stool at the centre-sweep of the curved counter. At the far end the barmaid emerged from a narrow doorway that I guessed led to the kitchen. Lukov had been right about one thing: she was quite a creature – all teeth and tits and blonde tresses. I ordered a whisky.

'*Tu bois pas l'absinthe?*'

I asked her if, frankly speaking, I looked like Ernest Hemingway.

'*Franchement?*' she laughed. '*Non.*'

She turned her back on me and I watched her pour the Johnnie Walker Black into a tumbler and then took in the scene properly. The whole place teetered between nineteenth-century chic and, judging by the clientele, tourist trap. But it was hard not to get caught up in the Parisian vibe: flower baskets hanging from the high white ceiling between *fin-de-siècle* lampshades, simple wooden tables and plenty of strong drink. It was the kind of place you might come to impress a certain sort of woman. Or to forget one.

It was busy, but not loud, as plates of food found their way to the brunch crowd. A solid murmur of conversation and the click-clack of cutlery on plates and no recorded music. Couples sat by the windows, looking on to Ruc de la Roquette. A solitary drinker nursed a beer at the end of the bar near the door to the kitchen – out of which a teenager in cook's whites – whom I took to be the *plongeur* – stuck his head out to see how many covers he might be washing up. He made a wisecrack as the barmaid bent over behind the bar and she caught him on the ear with a drying-up cloth as she straightened, sending him whooping back through the narrow doorway. A group of men in body warmers and maroon and mustard trousers – Italians or Spaniards by the look of them – rocked up outside the glazed main door, finishing their cigarettes before diving in for lunch.

I lifted a newspaper pinned by its spine to a wooden baton hanging from a hook under the bar. When I looked up, Lukov was sitting next to me, grinning.

'You see?' he said, directing his pitch-black stare at the bosomy beauty behind the bar. 'Incredible.'

'You're late.'

'And you,' he said, reaching into his coat pocket, 'are a free man.' He slipped me the Greek passport. I covered it with the newspaper and thumbed the pages. It was masterful: worn, but not battered; old, but well within date; clean, but with holiday stamps.

'Thank you,' I said. 'I appreciate it.'

I looked at the photo page. He'd taken two years off me, too. Maximilianos Ioannides was born in 1977.

Lukov ordered a *demi pression*.

'Over there,' he said, pointing to a table by the entrance I'd just come in through. 'More comfortable for lunch.'

I followed him to the table and sat with my back to the wall. Lukov faced me. Neither of us spoke until the waitress had put his beer down in front of him and retreated behind the bar.

'So?' I said.

'So, you asked Sergei to sell for five million. *Da?* To be honest, Sergei thought that was a bit, uh, *trop*. But, my friend, you are going to get more than you bargained for. Of that I am sure. The world and his wife and his whore and her lover want your Benjamin.' I sipped the whisky and said nothing. 'They *all* want it.'

I looked around the bar. The tourists were still smoking outside. The lone drinker still nursed his *demi*.

'Who's *they*?' I asked him. It was a question I'd been asking myself a lot, recently.

'*Every*body. The Americans want it because the Israelis do; the British, because it's you. Even the fucking *Lebanese* want it because they're shit-scared of being screwed by the Israelis.'

'What about the Russians?'

'Not yet,' he grinned. 'But not *nyet*. There is an auction.' His black eyes flashed at the thought of it. 'I think they will offer big money, Max McLean. Maybe double.' He fiddled with his beer glass. 'But they want to see it.'

'No way, Sergei. They have the serial number and they've seen Mann's passport, right? That's enough.'

'Relax,' he countered. 'It's no big deal.' He removed his phone from his coat pocket. 'Just a photograph. That's all. You keep the note. They see the note. They see the, how do you say, *inscription*? Everyone is happy. *Nali?*' I shook my head. 'Please.' His shoulders slumped. 'Sergei is trying to do you a favour.' Lukov blew out hard and rubbed his scalp.

'Is that a fact?'

'OK,' he conceded. 'Sergei is trying to do himself a favour. They see the photograph, the price doubles.' He took a long pull on his beer. 'Fifteen per cent of ten million. They'll close tonight. And then, my friend, we are both rich.'

'You're already rich, Sergei. And besides, I thought the Russians loved you.' I tried not to sound irritated, but I should have known that Lukov would want to milk this for all it was worth.

'*Da*. They love me. All of them. But they don't trust you, my friend. Not one of them. One day Max McLean is sending Russians to their grave; the next he wants to do business with them. That is strange, if you are a Russian.' He looked

117

up at me again, and waved his phone towards me. 'It is strange if you are Sergei, too.'

I rolled my shoulders and steadied my breathing. Suddenly he looked old and worn out, a black-eyed weasel washed up in a Parisian bar. Maybe women just took pity on him. Or maybe there were some things I'd just never understand. I leaned in.

'What's strange, Sergei, is that my picture is in the fucking newspaper.' I took another sip of whisky. 'And anyway, I don't have it on me,' I lied. 'So you can't take a photograph now.'

As I sat back, Lukov shuffled his chair closer to the table as if we were connected to each other by an invisible cord. 'But you could get it,' he said, leaning closer to me. 'Think of the money.'

'Don't fucking play me.'

'Please,' he begged. I scanned the bar. The tourists outside trooped in and filled the remaining table by the window. The barmaid laughed. The *plongeur* reappeared and cracked a dirty joke. 'One more day. The Russians are *serious*. But they want a photograph. That's all.' His demeanour had changed. Happy-go-lucky Lukov sounded like the one thing he never was: desperate.

'You promised them a photo, didn't you?' He hesitated, and then nodded. 'And they've threatened you, haven't they?' He nodded again. That was serious. Only people who didn't need Lukov threatened him. And everybody needed Lukov. 'Who are they going to pay double for, eh?' I leaned in again and brought my face close to his. 'Benjamin Franklin or Max McLean?'

'No,' he swallowed hard. 'I swear. The bill. Only the bill.'

Shielded from the rest of the bar by the bulk of his coat,

our exchange went unnoticed by the other customers. He smiled and tried to reassure me the deal, *his* deal, was legit. But something wasn't right. Lukov wasn't right. I finished the whisky.

'Which Russian is it,' I asked him, 'that wants to play ball?'

'Sergei cannot tell you that. There are rules.'

'Twenty-five per cent on the note.'

'Please, do not ask me this.'

'Fifty per cent. A name. A description. Anything.'

Nothing. Lukov tried not to look at me. But we were so close now our noses were almost touching.

'Do you know what I think, Sergei?' I carried on. Lukov stared past me and chewed his lip. 'I don't think you know. In fact, I don't think you have the first fucking clue who you're really dealing with. So let me help you out. Small guy, nicely turned out. Black wool coat. Black gloves. Expensive aftershave.' Then he looked at me, unblinking. 'Nasty cut on his right temple, which I gave him three days ago.'

Lukov rocked back abruptly in his chair, but my right hand caught him round the windpipe. I dragged him back across the table towards me, my thumb and fingers closing around his trachea. He attempted a scream, but I squeezed harder and felt the cartilage in his throat begin to collapse. He nodded and I relaxed my grip and he slumped back in the chair, hands to his throat. Eyes wild, he sat there staring at me, sweat breaking across his brow, teeth gritted against the pain.

'Keep your hands where I can see them,' I warned. 'Did you negotiate using this phone?'

He paused, and then dropped his chin to his chest.

'*Da.*'

Careless prick. I picked up his phone and dropped it into his beer.

'Do they know about the Greek passport?'

'No. Sergei's scout did it.' He glanced over his left shoulder towards the bar. 'He works here.'

Fuck.

'OK, Sergei. Time to go. The deal's off.'

'No,' he said, rising to his feet. 'Please.'

I shook my head and he backed away from the table, staring at me. He was standing by the window where the light was strongest, silhouetted against the winter sky. The sound of lead licking glass filtered above the lunchtime banter. A fragment of the shattered pane twisted like a jagged diamond in the bar-light. Frozen to the spot, black eyes fixed on mine. The bullet entered the back of his head and severed his tongue at the root before exiting out of his jaw. Teeth, bone and brain blew out on to the table. His head jerked forward from the force of the shot, unbalancing him, so that he fell lengthways in front of me.

He was dead before he hit the ground.

13

Pandemonium.

The shot came from high left. I dived right, over the table towards the bar. Lukov's beer glass, my whisky glass, shattered on the tile floor. The diners turned in their chairs. The barmaid saw Lukov laid out, the thick crimson bloom spreading on to the tiles beneath his head.

Screaming. Someone shouted, 'Sergei! *Non!*'

I stood. Left hand on the bar. Vault. On the countertop. Over the edge. I fell on to the floor, trapped between the bar and the wall behind it. Out of sight, chairs scraped on tiles; tables overturned; heels clicked, men shouted in French, Spanish, English. The blonde barmaid crouched beside me, blocking the way to the kitchen, hands over her head, sobbing insensibly. My left hand on the back of her neck.

'Move! *Allez! Vite!*' I shoved her forward. Head down. Back stooped. She stumbled, fell. My eyes on the floor. In front of her: black clogs, white trousers. I looked up. Lukov's scout, no doubt. His hand emerged from behind his back. Makarov pistol.

I leapt forward over the fallen waitress and tackled the boy around the waist. He hit the wall, but held on to the pistol. We fell together. He was on top of me, over my back. I pivoted and he spun with me. His gun hand arced over us and he loosed a shot at the ceiling.

Falling plaster. More screams. People running.

I sat up. He scrabbled backwards, trying to recover himself, and raised the pistol to my chest. Too close. I lunged, knocking his arm aside with my right hand and grabbing the underside of the little semi-auto with my left. I twisted the barrel up hard as I bore down on him, turning the muzzle away from my chest. The weapon discharged under his chin, and he was finished.

I got on to my knees and turned about, peering round the side of the bar. Boot to my temple. *Fuck*. I rolled back and looked up. The lone drinker at the bar was on his feet, a taser in his hand. I grabbed at his ankle, but he sidestepped. The oversized black barrel aimed at my chest. I rolled, but was blocked by the end of the bar. I heard a shot, a flat, deafening pistol report. The lone drinker flinched and grunted and turned away from me. Blood stained his upper arm. Dropping the taser he produced a machine pistol from under his trench coat and began firing towards the open street door. The motorcycle cop I'd brushed past outside earlier was in the fight. From his position by the entrance he dived for cover behind a tangle of upturned tables, firing into the room as he fell. He'd winged the man trying to kill me, and was being shot at in reply.

I levelled the Makarov and drew a bead on the middle of the lone drinker's back. A have-a-go-hero diner went for me. Hard kick to my arm. The Makarov spun out of my hand. I lay prone and he went at my head. I dodged. His foot hit the wood of the bar with enough force to break his toes. He buckled. I swept his legs from under him and he crashed down on to a bar stool face first, hitting his head with a crack. He didn't get up.

I crouched. The cop and the lone drinker couldn't get a clear shot at each other. One of the Spaniards broke cover from under the table where he'd been hiding. The cop brought his Glock round and dropped him with a bullet to the thigh. He fell, screaming.

Glock.

Glock.

That wasn't right. French motorcycle cops use SIGs. And they don't wear combat boots. *Fuck.* The lone drinker fired behind himself, blind, trying to hit me. A rack of absinthe bottles above the bar exploded into a shower of emerald fragments. The air filled with the reek of wormwood.

More shots. Rifle rounds, coming from outside. The plaster, paintings, shelves began to disintegrate. I got back behind the bar and threw myself headlong through the doorway into the kitchen and looked up in time to see a silver flash of steel. Right arm up. Block. My forearm swept aside the deep flat blade of a meat cleaver thrown from across the room.

The chef stood there, switching a long-bladed Sabatier from his left hand to his right. I scrambled to my feet and he sized me up, left foot forward, knife drawn up behind his head.

'You've got to be kidding me.'

He wasn't. It was a good throw. But not good enough.

The blade embedded in a bag of flour on a shelf to my left, close enough to my ear to hear it slice through the paper. The chef froze. His timing was split-second perfect. I reached around, grabbed the handle and tugged the blade free, keeping it moving in a semi-circle across myself as I spun the blade around. I brought the point to bear behind me into the stomach of the lone drinker who'd followed me through the door into the kitchen. He buckled, a foot of steel in his guts.

I turned and twisted the blade around and up and pushed it harder into him, through him, so that the point stuck fast

123

in the door frame. We stood close, touching, locked in a final embrace, like blood-sodden lovers fucking in a doorway. The machine pistol clattered to the floor. His fingers scrabbled at my face, seeking but not finding eyes to gouge. His own collapsing weight drove the cutting edge up. His belly split. His guts unravelled into the room and fouled the air with the stench of bile. His arms went limp, and as the light guttered out of his eyes he hissed in Russian.

'*Yob tvoiu mat*', McLean.'

'No. Fuck *your* mother.'

I wrenched the knife free. He fell, covered in his own gore, with a snarl on his lips. I drove the blade into the back of his neck. Whoever he was, he died like a dog.

The chef was cowering against the back wall. There were no windows, no doors to be seen; no visible exit at all – though there must have been one in the kitchen somewhere. The jet-engine drone of industrial extractor fans filled the room. Back in the bar the fusillade continued, muffled by the kitchen walls. Pistol rounds, rifle rounds, and then the erratic *rat-a-tat-tat* of an assault rifle, like corn popping in a pan. I bent down to pick up the machine pistol – a Russian SR-3MP – and checked the mag. Empty. I dropped it. The barmaid stumbled through the doorway and tripped over the disembowelled assassin, collapsing like a heavy-headed ear of wheat. I dragged her to one side and rolled her into the recovery position. She was still breathing, but her hair was matted with blood. Whether it was hers or one of her customers', there was no time to check.

A dozen frantic, shouting civilians followed her into the kitchen. I considered who among them might be harbouring a grudge or a weapon, but they were too wrapped up in their own private hell to worry about anything other than themselves. No one broke ranks; no one confronted me. But the fact they'd made it safely through the doorway meant I could, too. I dropped my shoulders, braced myself and headed back into the maelstrom.

La Fée Verte had been transformed from a classic Parisian café into a shitshow of a close-contact firefight. Who was shooting at whom was hard to unravel; but why they were shooting each other was, I suspected, folded up in my jeans pocket. The Russians, and God only knew who else, had tracked Lukov to the bar.

The phoney cop had got himself behind the crook of the counter and was busy firing at two sets of new arrivals. In the sheltered doorway of the bakery on Rue de la Roquette three men in headscarves emptied AKs through what remained of the French windows into the dining area. Erupting in the air: shards of glass, chips of floor tile, splinters from tables and chairs and window frames. Screaming on the floor: trapped civilians marooned between islands of broken glass and half-eaten *steak-frites*. There were casualties, too, but, as was often the case, fewer than seemed likely given the volume of fire raking the building. Down the side of the restaurant, on Rue Basfroi, another gunman crouched behind a parked car, respirator over his face, suppressed M4 carbine in his shoulder, taking single, aimed shots at the phoney cop – who'd ducked to reload his Glock.

I pivoted around the kitchen doorway, keeping low as rounds from the assault rifles opposite stripped the render off the wall above me. The cop looked up and I came down on him as he dropped the slide on the reloaded pistol. The force of the dive winded me, and brought his head down hard on to the tile floor. We grappled, dazed. He tried to point the Glock into my ribs. But he was too slow. Thirty-six years of Shaolin kung fu and the best I could manage was a Glasgow kiss. It worked. My forehead split the cartilage in his nose. Blood splattered his face and mine. His eyes automatically filled with tears, blinding him in an instant.

All fights are improvised. And your own skill is always relative to your opponent's strength. I reached left, pinning his gun arm to the floor. My right hand found the broken top of a blasted absinthe bottle. I drove it into his neck, grinding it against the jugular. Gouts of arterial blood spurted against my hand and chest. I prised the pistol away from him and pushed the muzzle into his left eye. As he raised his hand, I turned my head away, and fired.

I checked the magazine. A Glock 19. Beloved of US Special Forces, and a lot of bad guys, too. I pressed the clip back home and looked in the breech. Fourteen shots remaining. I rifled through his pockets. No wallet; no phone; no ID – just the keys to the motorbike he'd ridden in on. I snatched them and pressed my eye to the fractured wood in front of me.

Through the holes blasted in the side of the bar I could see the gunman in Rue Basfroi leaning around the cover the parked car afforded him, engaging the shooters by the bakery with sustained, aimed fire. Then his left arm snapped forward, sending a grenade up and over the twenty metres between them. I heard the distinctive *ping* of the detonation lever flying free even over the crack and thump of the AKs it was sailing towards. I got my head between my knees. The blast bounced back off the concrete pier by the doorway, which made it sound louder than it really was. I snatched a glimpse over the bar top. Two men lay motionless in the road, heads wrapped in bloodstained keffiyehs. Smoke seeped from the doorway of the bakery. The third man made a break towards La Fée Verte, AK at his hip, black and white scarf

126

across his face. He was floored instantly by a sniper round from above.

The grenade-throwing gunman on Rue Basfroi wasn't taking any chances. He walked forward slowly at a crouch, alternating his shots between my position – which went high above my head – and the gang by the bakery. No one returned fire. No one shot at him from above – though whether that was because they were on the same side, or because the sniper was relocating to a fall-back position, I couldn't tell. He stepped out of the street and into the restaurant. I sat still, back braced against the wall, knees drawn up to my chest. Through the gunshot spy hole in the bar I watched him fire a double-tap into Lukov's body, then stop and sniff the air. I could hear someone whining and the scuffle of shoes on tiles as the surviving customers squirmed under the tables. The gunman cradled his M4 and produced another grenade from under his coat. The wooden bar was too thick for me to shoot through accurately with the Glock, and his rifle rounds would shred it. I was only going to get one chance.

I looked to either side of me, and then up. Tendrils of ivy hung above the gunman's head, twisting down from a hanging basket suspended over the dining area. As I shifted my weight a patch of blasted plaster fell free of the wall behind me, crashing into what remained of the bottles behind the bar. He swept the M4 around towards me single-handed. I braced my forearms on my knees, the Glock's rear sight six inches from my face – and fired. The 9mm ball cut the chain of the hanging basket where it joined the ceiling. Damocles ducked but didn't dive. It was all I needed. In the second he was distracted, I came up firing.

Boom. Boom. Boom.

The shots hit him in the chest. He staggered backwards and

127

dropped the grenade, but raised his rifle. *Body armour.* I fired again. A single shot to the head. He fell on to his knees and then keeled over. I stepped around the remains of the bar and stooped over his body, keeping the Glock on him until I was certain he wasn't getting back up. I tucked the pistol in my jeans and picked up the discarded M4. The rig mimicked classic US Special Forces specification: suppressor, holographic sight, magnifier, laser–torch combo and a forward grip. His arms splayed out, cruciform. On the inside of his right wrist a line of gothic script read: *The only easy day was yesterday.* If I'd have stripped his shirt off, I'd most likely have found an ink trident, too – both tattoos beloved by US Navy SEALs.

The tactical vest under his coat was lined with spare magazines and hung with grenades: one frag, two smoke and another that matched the canister he'd just dropped: a non-lethal sting-ball grenade, which exploded with rubber balls and CS, not shrapnel. I loaded my jacket pockets with the lot. I dropped the used magazine out of the M4 and reloaded with a fresh one, stuffing two more inside my jacket for good measure. Finally, I plucked a pair of Oakleys off his vest and hung them off the neck of my pullover. For an instant: silence.

And then, far off, the old-fashioned *nee-naw* of French police sirens filtered into the blasted cavern of the little bar. The distorting effect of the maze of city centre streets meant it was hard to tell where they were. I thought of the young squaddies I'd seen patrolling the Gare du Nord. There were ten thousand troops deployed across France, protecting against terrorist attack – two-thirds of them in Paris alone. Of the many ways I thought I might go out over the years, being cornered *à la* Butch Cassidy by the Foreign Legion wasn't one of them.

I edged around the bodies on the floor. Glass cracked

underfoot. I caught a glimpse of my face in a shard of mirror and did a double take: blood-smeared, tired, hollow-eyed. I barely recognized myself. Voices came through the kitchen door behind me. Distressed, frantic, the trapped customers were arguing among themselves about how best to escape. Enough people had been hit in the crossfire already. I racked the charging handle on the M4 and fired a shot at the door-way to keep them inside. They fell silent instantly. I squatted down next to Lukov and quickly went through his pockets, extracting a tightly rolled wad of fifty-euro notes, a calfskin wallet and an unopened packet of Gauloises. I crammed everything into my overloaded jacket, with the grenades.

Time to run.

Judging by the angle of the shot that killed Lukov, the sniper had most likely been working in one of the apart-ments on Rue Basfroi. In the time it had taken me to kill the phoney cop and the SEAL gunman, he could have relocated anywhere. I pulled the pin on one of the smoke grenades and took a chance, lobbing it through the shattered windows upwind and into the middle of the crossroads outside. A thick grey plume billowed in its wake, an expanding snake filling the junction with an impenetrable dirty haze.

As I emerged into the street, the sound of the police sirens grew immediately louder. To my left the smoke had temporar-ily cut off the south-eastern stretch of Rue de la Roquette and Rue Basfroi. To my right the rest of Rue de la Roquette was clear for three blocks. But what I needed was parked dead ahead. The phoney motorcycle cop's Yamaha stood propped up on its side-stand outside the bakery, nose pointing north-west out of the crossroads.

I hovered in the café doorway with the M4 in my shoulder — right index finger on the trigger, left hand around the forward grip on the Picatinny rail. I scanned sight lines and door-ways, shopfronts and rooftops. Nothing moved. No civilians, no cops, no shooters. Not even a cat. But the window panes around me flashed with the blue lights of approaching police cars. And above the windows came the drone-whine of an inbound chopper. I combed the bodies of the three men wearing keffiyehs through the magnified sight. No move-ment. I edged out further into the street.

And then, a couple of hundred metres to the east, a swarm of blue and white police motorbikes and vans led by unmarked saloon cars – single blue lights flashing inside their windscreens – poured into the wide traffic circle where Rue de la Roquette met Boulevard Voltaire. I crouched and looked in the opposite direction. A red laser sight strobed through the swirling smokescreen. Then another, fragment-ing and strengthening and dying back again as the beam formed and dissipated in the billowing, choking cloud. And then a dozen electric-vermilion death-fingers clawed at the fog – probing, reaching, searching for a solid human target.

I pulled the pin on the second smoke grenade and flung the canister towards the police fleet approaching to the right. It bounced along the middle of the street, a fresh spiral of dense smoke expanding in its wake. The cops ground to a halt, dismounted immediately, and fired a salvo of shots dir-ectly at me as the grey cloud expanded between us. I pressed myself to the pavement. Bullets snapped past my head, shoulders, smacking against the brickwork further down the street behind me.

I balled up in the gutter and the buildings, street, sky van-ished. Visibility was close to zero. But as soon as the chopper came overhead, the downdraft would leave me exposed. I dragged myself on my elbows across the street. The bullet wound in my shoulder tore and burned. The tear in my thigh pulled and pulsed, sending hot flashes of pain down into my knee and up into my groin. The smokescreen twisted sound. The guns behind the lasers to the left began firing in reply to the police rounds coming from my right. It looked like the opening salvo of a horrific blue on blue tirade.

Stray bullets ricocheted off the shutters and street lamps. Window glass imploded. Shouted orders in French bounced off the buildings. Radios crackled. Distance, time, perspective – everything was confused in the swirling mist until, stretching out my hand, I gripped the back wheel of the police motorbike. I slung the carbine over my shoulder and climbed on, head low, hugging the chassis. Key in. I pinched the clutch, revved the throttle. The four-cylinder engine roared to life. I kicked the stand away and shifted down into first. I had no idea what was in front of me. But it had to be better than whatever was behind.

I gunned the bike and dropped the clutch and leapt out of the fog into the unknown.

14

For an instant the cloud clung to my shoulders and limbs –
the ragged wings of a dirty grey angel curling out into the
slipstream behind me. And then I cleared the smoke in a
rush of grey-white winter light, pushing a quarter-tonne of
Japanese metal out of the kill zone. A police van had stopped
dead centre in the street. Thirty metres and closing. Fast.

Ten.

Five.

Two.

One.

Brake.

Officers in tactical gear spilled out, weapons up. I pulled a
hard right, jumping the kerb on to the pavement between a
row of metal bollards, ploughing through a brace of parked
scooters.

Shouts.

Shots.

Blue-black uniforms scattering behind me in my wing
mirrors.

I broke contact, gulping lungfuls of ice-cold air, adrenaline surging, raging. I turned left on to Rue Sedaine. The rear
wheel of the heavy bike slipped right, but I held it and came
around on top. I slowed down. Ahead: more blue lights.
Above: the chopper closing in. I needed to get out of the
chokehold of the side streets and find space and speed. The
Yamaha was built for touring, not racing. But it had guts. I

hoped it had balls, too. I pinched the clutch and opened the throttle. The tachometer touched red. A hundred metres ahead, patrol cars pulled up side-on, blocking the little lane by a car park entrance to my right. Uniformed cops swarmed up steps. Roofs came alive with sharpshooters. Paris in lockdown. On the left a rubbish skip blocked the pavement, fed rubble by two long wooden planks from the building site adjacent.

I was cornered, but not trapped. But if I didn't get over the river before they cut the bridges, I was fucked.

I revved harder. And then I let it go. I felt the pull in my chest as I took off. I kicked up through neutral into second and up again. I hit sixty in three seconds and dropped my head low, just like I had done hacking horses under woodland branches with Rachel back home.

The *pop* and *snap* of incoming rounds barely registered above the rush of air and growl of the engine. But come they did. Three punched through the windshield. One sparked off the engine block. Another scraped the toe of my right boot. But I was too fast, too close. My front wheel hit the improvised ramp dead straight, pushing seventy. I held hard and kept the revs high and felt the ground slip away. The plank came up behind me, flying up with tatters of cardboard and sheets of old newspaper caught in the draft.

Airborne.

I held my breath and counted slow.

One thousand.

The police passed to my right, the barrels of their assault rifles tracing my arc in the air, unable to shoot for the faces in the apartment windows opposite.

Two thousand.

I cleared the skip and a police Yamaha identical to the

one I was jumping. A flash-bang went off behind me, ineffectual.

Three thousand.

The pavement raced up to meet me. I kept the front fork steady; its wheel lifted higher.

Four thousand.

The back tyre hit the tarmac, squashed by the impact. The fork twisted an inch to the right. The rear wheel slid sideways a fraction and reformed. I corrected the front wheel and brought it down straight. I braked, released, and took a left past a Carrefour supermarket and punched on, dog-legging back over Rue de la Roquette and then due south against the traffic to Rue de Charonne. The chopper was as low as it was safe to fly, banking overhead, shadowing my movements. Police motorcycles roared in pursuit. I snapped my right wrist down. The LCD speedometer raced like a stopwatch. Eighty. Ninety. One hundred klicks per hour. French police 1300s are limited to a hundred brake horse-power. Not this one. Wherever the rider with the Glock had come from, he knew where he was at with his bike. And if he'd fitted it with a tracker, his handler would know where I was at, too.

Fancy shopfronts, chic cafés, parked cars . . . all reduced to a smudge of sound and colour. Faces blinked past, pressed to plate glass. No one was on the street. I kept my face behind the peppered windshield and carried on – straight, steady. Speeding. My jacket billowed in the slipstream. Freezing cold air whirled around me. My ears stung; my knuckles went white on the grips. The rifle magazines I'd stashed in my jacket worked free of the overfilled pockets, clattering to the ground behind me.

I swung right but came off the brake too late and felt the

rear wheel drifting me into a lowside crash. I held my nerve and the rubber held the asphalt. Just. I sat upright and pulled a left, skirting bicycles and bollards, and rolled under a garret into a cobbled alleyway. I thundered through a courtyard, hooked left under a wide, bare tree, then roared under another building and out into a wider passage. I put on the sunglasses I'd taken from the dead SEAL. There was no time to put my gloves on, too. My eyes were already streaming. I blinked and checked my mirrors. Four uniformed cops followed on Yamahas, and, behind them, a plainclothes rider on a BMW rig. Pistol shots blew lumps out of the walls, shattered my left mirror. Two children dived for cover, their father shouting, colouring the air blue in my wake. I pushed right. Then right again, nosing out on to Avenue Ledru-Rollin.

Make or break. Five engines growled behind me. The chopper circled around in front. I touch-checked the Glock in my jeans and the M4 across my back. All good. As my mate Roberts in Freetown would have said: *Come on, old girl. Let's be 'avin' ya.*

Revs up. Clutch out. Rock and roll.

I kicked through the gears, keeping the throttle wide open and my head down, counting the seconds as the speedo climbed again. The chopper banked to my left. I checked my right mirror. The five bikes were hot in pursuit. The avenue curved a kilometre south-west all the way to the River Seine.

The city strobed past. Trees. Lamp posts. People. I leaned left and right with my shoulders, weaving through the Sunday-chicane of cars and tourists. Car horns and police sirens screeched past, harmonics distorting, mutating, whining, whizzing, fusing as I rode faster into one long wailing corridor of noise. Cortisol coursed through my brain, shutting down everything unnecessary to surviving that moment,

135

blanking out everything behind me. One hundred kilometres per hour down an unknown Parisian street. The slightest miscalculation will kill you, or stay with you for ever. I saw the river ahead, the bridge, and the main road across me.

The drive down Ledru-Rollin had taken thirty seconds. I braked and kicked down into second and looked fully over my shoulder. The pursuit bikes had kept pace behind me, one hundred metres, slowing but closing – the rider of the BMW hung back, sun glinting off his visor, no weapon visible. I faced front again. The junction ahead was open, but a military unit from the Gare d'Austerlitz on the left bank had made it over the river and cut the bridge at its summit. Legionnaires sprinted to take up covering positions, green berets bobbing in the winter light. The chopper caught up with me. The sirens grew louder.

Think.

If I ran the roadblock it was a short blast south-west through to where I needed to get. But they'd cut me to ribbons before I cleared the first fifty metres. I could try the Pont Charles de Gaulle, one over to the east, though the chances were they'd make it there before me, too – and I'd be driving against the traffic. West was best. I risked getting lost in the maze of city centre streets, but if you're in a tight squeeze, the thing to do is get smaller. As long as I had room to ride, the more people around me the better. Colonel Ellard would have approved. Use everything to your advantage – human shields included. I accelerated right and buzzed on north-west, river to my left, police bikes on my tail. They appeared to hold all the cards. But I had an ace up my sleeve: they didn't know where I was going. If I could get over the river, I could disappear.

I took off right along the Quai de la Rapée and over the

Arsenal Basin. The window glass of the van to my right exploded into tiny crystal cubes. A squaddie had opened up from the bridge. On a busy street in London they'd shoot you only at point blank. Hit and you're a hero; miss and maybe you're a murderer. I'd been there myself. In France they didn't fuck about. More lead skidded off the asphalt around the tyres and I felt the *tic-tic-tic* of bullets hitting the panniers. But I was away and out of range in a couple of seconds, dodging round to the right before he could line up on my back. The river forked around Île Saint-Louis. Pont de Sully slipped past to my left, a blur of blue flashing lights through a gap in the bare winter trees. I tipped to my left and opened up harder, the quayside flitting past in a mess of booksellers and tourist-trappers selling everything from peanuts to Picassos.

Then I was on it. Pont Louis Philippe. No room for error driving against the one-way system. I came in as tight as I could to the kerb on the left and let the brake go, left knee skimming stone. The back wheel held. A patrol car handbrake-turned parallel to me, the officers inside shouting, weapons drawn. But they were too slow and I outpaced their pistols as they fought with windows and door frames. I checked over my shoulder as I straightened up. The motorcycle cops were still on me, but one of them oversteered. Another gave it too much front brake and their bikes collided – fibreglass frag-menting as the frames skidded side-on into the patrol car. One rider hopped clear; the other catapulted over the handle-bars, walking first on air and then turning somersaults into the windshield of the stricken patrol car. Two cops and the plainclothes pursuer stayed on me.

My tyres hit cobbles and the timbre of the road changed to a fast rip as the little square stones shook the Yamaha's suspension. Either side of the road the bridge's stone balustrade was punctuated with apertures, capturing the *bateaux mouches* plying the river in dozens of frozen images juddering past like a reel from an old movie camera. Ahead and close, the red awning of a café on the south-west corner of the bridge; far distant, the colonnaded dome of the Panthéon crowning the urban horizon.

I twisted the throttle, leaning right and low, cutting the corner off the little island and burning over the pedestrianized Pont Saint-Louis on to the Île de la Cité. The M4's suppressor hung down behind me, scraping for an instant on the road as I stooped into the turn. Water flashed to the left of me and I was beside Notre-Dame, rising above the winter-dead gardens that spread out beyond the cathedral's iconic east end. In seconds I was back on to Pont de l'Archevêché, which I'd crossed the day before on the way to Lukov's apartment.

I was far enough away now from the gunfight in La Fée Verte for pedestrians to be ignorant of the shootout. People fell back. Couples grabbed each other. Near-misses swore and flipped me out – but I heard nothing except the rattle-roar of the engine on cobbles and stone and asphalt; that, and the *thump-thump*, *thump-thump* of my own heart pounding a metronomic pulse in my ears. From the moment the Bulgarian had bitten the dust until I crossed Boulevard Saint-Germain and came screaming out on to Rue Monge, less than ten minutes had passed. I got my face down behind the Perspex that remained intact in the battered bike's windshield and gritted my teeth, eyes half-closed, squinting through the sunglasses against the hurricane breeze blown back by the surge forward.

The two bikes were still with me, a steady pistol shot behind; the visored BMW rider let them keep pace, a constant twenty metres further back. Another kilometre. South-east. Due south. And then, in seconds, on to Avenue des Gobelins. From there it was a direct, wide run south-east to Place d'Italie, along a street I'd first walked with my father as a teenager. Now I gunned it at ninety, straight towards the 13*e* *arrondissement*. Past a supermarket, over a broad junction – weaving through unsuspecting traffic crisscrossing me on their green light. A blacked-out police van, a blue light flashing on the dashboard, swerved to hit me but missed, T-boning a garbage truck exiting Rue Le Brun with a bone-cracking *bang*.

And all the while the chopper shadowed me. I jumped the kerb, dropped the revs and zapped down the pavement. At my three o'clock one of the police bikes shadowed me along Avenue de Gobelins. I dodged Sunday strollers who unfailingly dived in the wrong direction, and zoomed over the zebra crossing at Rue du Banquier, sticking to the sidewalk.

Rue du Banquier. Shit.

It was too tight to turn. I pulled out into the street, over the crossing that cut Gobelins, straight into the motorcycle cop who'd been on my right. SIG drawn, arm out. But my sudden move had wrong-footed him. I veered left, towards him. He fired. The round snapped across my face. As our bikes closed, I leaned out with a straight right. I caught him under the chin, into his neck. His pistol discharged again, high this time; as he toppled backwards, his Yamaha slid out from under him. I looped around him. His stray shot had shattered a pharmacy window. Passers-by lay flattened on the street.

And then the rev-roar of the second police bike coming at me from the south-east. I'd not seen him pass me. As I doubled back on myself to leave him behind me, the plainclothes rider pulled up ahead. I stopped. He stopped. Blue jeans, black biker's jacket, mirrored full-face visor. Five-eleven, maybe, and wiry with it. I watched his hands. Tactical Kevlar gloves. Behind, the police Yamaha closed in. I flattened myself against the tank, right hand opening up the revs, left hand on the clutch lever. As I ducked down, I looked around. The motorcycle cop was on me, SIG up. I was stuck there on the street, sandwiched between two would-be killers. I was finished.

I stared into the cop's eyes and read the rapt concentration etched across his face that was keeping pistol and pistons moving together. I blinked and saw for a fraction of a second Rachel staring out of the void. And then the policeman's face folded in on itself, distorting surprise into disgust. His nose, cheek, eye vanished into an eruption of thick, meaty gore as the round ricocheted inside his skull, trapped by his helmet. I hugged the Yamaha hard and snatched the clutch. The BMW rider's arm swung down. The tip of his suppressed pistol arced across me, but there was no second shot. I pressed on, looking over my left shoulder just long enough to see the policeman I'd punched out spin sideways from a single shot to the side of the head.

I rode the stolen police bike as hard as the cylinders would let me, plunging along Rue du Banquier, lying flat against the body of the bike, estimating the turn from the space in the buildings and trees above me. I flew past the first right and then down the second; it was flanked by high-rise apartment blocks, and I realized the chopper had banked away, out of sight, looking for a new angle on me. If there was a sniper on board, he was out of luck. I raised my head and checked the mirror. The cop-killing BMW rider was still on me, matching me move for move.

140

But I was close now, seconds from my destination. I kicked up into third and ran the intersection at Boulevard de l'Hôpital, swerving a baby buggy. The trees of Rue Pinel loomed up on either side. I asked the stolen Yamaha for everything it'd give me. As the bike growled, I sat up straight, put my hands down on to the saddle and leapfrogged backwards. The heavy police machine sped away from me between my legs. I found the road feet first – then with my left shoulder, back and right shoulder. I spun head over heels, twisted face down, braced with my forearms – and stopped. I pushed up. Hands bleeding. The elbows of my jacket ragged, knees of my jeans scuffed. Nothing broken. I stood, staggered, righted myself, and brought the M4 up as the BMW behind me hit the crossroads.

Inhale. Exhale. Settle. Fire.

As my finger squeezed the trigger, the rider pulled up on the handlebars, rearing into a roaring wheelie. Instead of shedding his sternum, the suppressed 5.56 round tore the front tyre apart. The handlebars jerked. The fork twisted. The bike was too heavy to hold. The BMW jackknifed and went over, the plainclothes rider with it, pitching him out of sight behind a delivery van. Meanwhile my bike had carried on to the next, wide junction, smashing into a row of parked cars, triggering a slew of alarms. The chopper buzzed above them, out of sight, zooming in on the crash site, not on me. I turned to get my bearings and ducked right, under the trees and scaffolding at the back of the ParisTech engineering college.

The street was deserted.

It had been nearly twenty-eight years since I'd stood in front of that white panelled door and old stone wall. It had been dark then – exactly three a.m. on a warm summer night.

I didn't know who lived there in 1990, and I didn't now. It wasn't what was *in* the house I needed. I dropped to my knees to the right of the door, kneeling in front of three adjacent manhole covers. I took the screwdriver from my coat pocket and quickly put the tip under the wide lip of the cover furthest to the left . . . and took the longest shot of my life.

15

Sparks of light erupted across the emptiness. Deep greens and reds brightened, swirled and died. Yellow flares twisted into nothingness. All I could see was a patchwork of fractals spinning away from me.

I closed my eyes.

Nothing changed.

I blinked hard and waited for my eyes to accustom to the dark. Eventually the crazy patterns dancing across my retinas spun themselves into oblivion. As they faded, my heartbeat steadied. And then there was nothing except darkness. No shapes, no depth, no shadows. No light at all. I was engulfed in perfect pitch blackness.

I stood at a half-crouch, stock-still, and cocked my head and listened – but there was nothing to hear. No sirens. No alarms. No helicopter. Silence so profound I could feel it on the edge of my teeth. The fast buzzing of the road had evaporated. All that was left was the high-pitched whine that the firefight in the café had scored into my eardrums.

But then, close, very close: the unmistakable sound of breathing.

I tensed, right hand on the pistol grip of the rifle. I held my own breath and strained into the void. The rasping stopped. I waited – and then exhaled in a rush of relief. It was my own lungs I could hear. There was no one nearby, no one in pursuit. I laughed out loud – just as I'd done when I first stood there.

But an entire lifetime had elapsed since then. This time I was alone.

My voice went nowhere, bouncing back at me in a flat, close echo. I checked with my thumb that the fire selector was still on semi-auto, brought the rifle up, pressed my back against stone and went white.

The LED torch beam stretched out from under the barrel of the M4 along thirty metres of low, limestone tunnel – illuminating, at its furthest point, what looked like a dog-leg in the passage. There was just enough clearance for the barrel to traverse the hundred and eighty degrees to light up the other direction. As I whipped the rifle round to my left, the wall directly in front of me flared up in a bright white hot-spot. In the middle of it a circle of slack-jawed skulls stared back at me – empty eye sockets filled with deep, moving shadows; teeth missing, broken, discoloured by cave-slime; craniums cracked and mouldy. Around the skulls a ragged circle of femurs set them off like a shield on the passage wall. As I moved the LED beam across them, the shadows made the dead eyes flit this way and that, as if they were following the rifle, examining me.

It was exactly as I remembered. I jumped, anyway.

I was neither in the sewers, nor in the shafts servicing the Métro. I hadn't ended up in a basement or a siege tunnel. The manhole I'd slipped through wasn't a door so much as a portal, because it wasn't just an entrance to an underground passageway; it was a gateway into a parallel Paris.

Beneath the capital's pavements limestone quarries mined centuries ago to build the houses and churches above spread out in a network of caverns and wells, galleries and caves – all connected by three hundred kilometres of pitch-black passages. But all that, my father had told me as we sank into

144

the darkness together that first time twenty-eight years ago, wasn't what made Paris unique.

It was what happened *after* the quarries were dug, he said, that was truly remarkable. The basements and cellars of huge swathes of the city south of the Seine sat on top of – and in many cases, were connected to – more than just an ancient mining complex. In the eighteenth century the abandoned chambers were used as the perfect solution to an unspeakable problem: what to do with the horror show of the capital's overflowing cemeteries. Into those acres upon acres of suburban caverns had been interred the bones of six million bodies.

It was not a journey to be undertaken without maps – though maps alone, my father had impressed upon me, were not enough to save anyone down there. Most of the tunnels were hardly tall enough to stand up in; some shrank to barely a foot high. Seemingly bottomless wells that plumbed the black abyss of underground aquifers; cave-ins; flooded tunnels; eye-gouging metal spikes; ankle-breaking holes; and deep, dark pits that could swallow a man all lay in wait. The fresh corpses of careless explorers were easily added to the ancient, unnamed remains.

All those years ago we'd emerged from that vast, random city of the dead in Montrouge Cemetery, south of the centre near the Périphérique – the busy highway that ringed Paris. If I could escape the city, I could escape – period.

The stretch of tunnel where I stood formed the elbow of a bend. Right led south-east; left, north-west – where, barely two metres further on, the continuation of the tunnel was also masked by a crook in the stone passage. I straightened carefully from my crouch, turned about face – and looked up. The footholds I'd used to drop down the shaft disappeared into the blackness above. I killed the torch, and kept staring up, listening, squinting into the darkness.

Still nothing.

If anyone had followed me underground, they'd used a different entrance. I switched the torch on again and played the beam across the rock around the crude ladder. The name of the street above was chiselled into the stone in mid-nineteenth-century letters, along with the date the passage was reinforced: 1865. But in between these signposted con-vergences, the routes of the tunnels and the city streets diverged wildly. I looked carefully around the inscription, putting my hand on the cool stone as if that would guide my eyes. I found what I was looking for almost immediately: two small sets of letters carved at head height.

MMG JMG

Max and John Mac Ghill'ean. The initials were scratched deeper than I remembered; and although covered with fine green moss-like mould, they were as clear as the night we'd cut them, if you knew where to look. I traced my fingers over my father's initials and slipped into a kind of shock. It was the only physical trace of him that remained. Beneath the letters we'd carved a St Patrick's Saltire. To the left of where the two arms of the cross joined, a dot, bored into the stone with the punch of a Swiss Army knife.

Turn left.

And in the *V* that made the top of the cross, another.

Climb up.

It was an adaptation of the same simple system of way-points he'd first taught me as a child. Together we'd marked the tree trunks in the plantation that stretched out behind

146

our house in County Wicklow so that I could find my way home again if I lost my compass. Alone, I'd mapped on to the bark of the trees themselves vast tracts of the woodland that swallowed me for hours. My wanderings were stopped abruptly when my mother had realized how far from home her nine-year-old was venturing.

'If you did this where *mamka* and *babushka* grew up, you would have been eaten by wolves,' she told me firmly in Russian – which meant there was no arguing with her. I never looked at the forest in the same way again.

I snapped out of the reverie and willed myself to concentrate. The calm of being underground was deceptive. Only a couple of minutes before I'd been running a full-scale escape and evasion. Just because I'd paused didn't mean my pursuers would, too. The gunfight was bound to trigger a manhunt on an epic scale. The helicopter, the police vans, the army and the Foreign Legion would all still be up there – but that was just for starters. They'd already been joined by the mystery bike rider and whoever else had been stirred up by Benjamin Franklin.

The Navy SEAL, if that's what he was, could have still been working for the Americans if he was out, or he could have been working freelance. The guys in keffiyehs, the phoney cop – all of them could have been on anyone's payroll, from the Brits to the Bulgarians, the CIA to the FSB. In a strange twist of irony probably the only people *not* after me were the IRA – although I wasn't ruling them out, either.

But sting-ball grenades and tasers weren't what I usually went up against. And if I'd been on the other end of that sniper rifle, I'd have shot me dead vaulting that bar. The only firm conclusion I could draw was that the people actually trying to kill me were the French. And fair enough.

147

I steadied myself against the wall, and slowed my breathing. Clarity in darkness.

I'd dropped twelve metres under the city streets – if not out of mind, then at least, for the moment, out of sight. But the city wasn't simply hiding me now, it had buried me: no satellites, no thermal imaging, no cell phone signal – and no CCTV. It was as if modern technology had never happened. Above all, my one advantage persisted: they didn't know where I was going, or why. The fact that I didn't either was, I tried to convince myself, neither here nor there. All I had to do was stay the one step ahead that I'd kept up since diving into the Channel, and hope that I might find some answers before I was tripped up for good.

I turned my back on the crook of the passage. So many of the tunnels around the Place d'Italie were blocked off that travelling in a straight line was impossible. It had been years since I'd been down there, too – and although the tunnels had been hewn out over two centuries before, they'd never stayed the same for long. An organic, ever-changing net-work, it was more like the intestines of the city than its foundations. Ultimately, I needed to be going south-west, but to take that bearing I'd first have to head south-east and then loop round.

I set off into the world's largest catacombs still guided by my father's helping hand. But the sheer immensity of the labyrinth was almost overwhelming. The rough earth floor was strewn with small loose stones; the walls were mined rock, patched with brick and injections of cement. I walked slowly, head down. After twenty metres a short passage opened up on the left, which terminated in a T-junction after only a few paces. On the wall to the right of the entrance, another cross, with another marker.

Keep going, it said.

Ten metres more and the tunnel made the dog-leg I'd seen from the foot of the ladder. The passage sloped downwards; the earth underfoot gave way to mud; the ceiling height fell rapidly. I stopped and listened and went dark again. There was a decision to make. Keep the torch on and move faster – but risk being seen. Or go dark and rely on only the M4's laser sight – that would allow me to see basic changes in the tunnel terrain, like a blind man sweeping a stick in front of him, but it would slow my progress to a crawl.

Slow and steady wins the race.

I killed the light and switched on the red laser, dropped to a walking crouch, and carried on, one short step at a time. The wound in my thigh burned from the strain. I moved the rifle barrel from the roof to the floor, the left wall the right wall, cutting a bright crimson sign of the cross in the passageway ahead of me over and over again. It was tiring, disorientating. The laser marker danced in front of my eyes in duplicate, triplicate, so that I had to stop and blink to reduce it to one clear signal. And all the while the roof got lower, and the floor wetter. After barely any distance at all I was ankle deep in water, and getting deeper.

I carried on. The floor began to slope down steeply. Since I'd last been there, nearly three decades before, the muddy puddles my father and I had splashed and waded through had expanded into a full-scale flood. The water reached waist level – which meant, bent over to keep clear of the tunnel roof, I would soon be completely submerged. I combed the surface of the water with the beam of red light. It was crystal clear and smelled slightly of sulphur. The laser cut through it perfectly. There were no ripples ahead of me, and not even a mote of dirt suspended in the stone-filtered deluge. It would be different behind, though. Each step would have stirred up the chalky clay on the still-sloping tunnel floor. I ran the red light down the ceiling until it found the surface. Five metres, after which the passage was completely inundated.

'Fuck!' I swore under my breath. 'What is it with fucking tunnels?'

I'm frequently scared – anyone who tells you they are not afraid in a firefight is either an idiot or a liar. But I have no phobias: no entrenched dread of snakes or spiders, water or flying; no terror in the daytime of the horrors that haunt my dreams at night. But death by drowning was different.

'Be careful when you go under, Max,' my father had said to me that night in Paris, suspecting, perhaps, that one day I'd want to try it alone. 'The surface can be hard to find.'

How I wished it had been my mother he had warned instead.

Drown.

It was a word to gulp down, to choke on; a word it felt like I had been born with under my tongue – tethered to, like my mother had been to the stones in her pockets. I scanned the water for her face, but there's no use in looking for the dead. I backed up.

Find another way, I told myself.

But I knew there wasn't – neither in the tunnel nor back in the world. I remembered Colonel Ellard's mantra, repeated endlessly to any trooper who asked what to do when their officer or their radio died: 'Always follow the last order.'

I considered that for a moment.

For whatever reason, Frank was unresponsive. He'd either cut me off or been disconnected himself. His last order was to go dark. And releasing my photograph had forced me to go about as dark as it was possible to get. He might have turned me into a fugitive in the process, but depending on who had been sent to kill me, and why, I had to accept the wild possibility that Frank had actually done me a favour.

But I wasn't going to get far working out who was after me, and what skin they had in the Benjamin game, while I was buried in a pitch-black grave with the whole city piled up on top of me. In any case, supposing Lukov was telling the truth, there were only three conclusions to be drawn: Frank had set me up; Frank had been set up himself; or, for whatever reason, Frank couldn't trust me with the target's real name. Working blind wasn't unusual: turning up to find my target already dead and his killer lying in wait to ambush me was. Any way I looked at it, going on the run had either been the smartest thing I'd ever done, or the stupidest.

If Lukov had been lying, though, it meant someone had got to the bad Bulgarian first – someone who wanted to throw me off track. But for all his faults – which were legion – Lukov had been loyal to the deal. His deal. He owed me, and he'd known it; and despite his bravado he'd also known I could have – *would* have – killed him there and then if I'd thought he'd been trying to fuck me. He was good; but not that good. Nothing about his body language had suggested fear: if he'd been playing me, his eyes would have betrayed him. The same could not be said for Frank, always every bit the smiling executioner.

I blinked into the void.

I had no clear memory of this part of the tunnel, other than it ran with water and took a sharp bend to the right. After that the specifics of the route I'd trodden as a teenager faded from mind. As well as the unknown length of the tunnel ahead, there was another, logistical problem with pressing on: as soon as I submerged myself, I would also submerge my Greek passport and cash. They would dry, but the passport would be damaged. Using it was already dangerous enough. The more reason anyone had to check it, the more likely I was to fail check-in. I ran my hands through my pockets. No bags, no liner that would keep it dry. Then I found Lukov's wallet.

I flicked the torch on again and combed through it. Cash; credit cards; French ID; a slip of paper with a woman's name – Karolina – and a French cell phone number scrawled on it.

'Lukov, you fucker,' I whispered as I ran my fingers under the card inserts. 'Help me out.'

And so he did: my fingers closed around a soft, square, pale blue plastic packet marked *Soft RIDER*. The horny old bastard never went anywhere without a condom. I tore open the wrapper, put the foil in my pocket and stuffed the wallet, passport and roll of cash into the French letter. I stowed it inside my jacket, checked that all the pockets were zipped shut, and that the Glock was firmly in my waistband. The fire selector of the M4 was set to semi-auto; there was a round in the breech; the laser was on. I took a last, deep, sulphurous breath, and then my head was under. I gave the tunnel one last look with the torch beam, and went dark again.

There was no question of actually swimming. Weighed down with sodden clothes, never mind the grenades and rifle, the best I could manage was an unsteady walk. I counted out the seconds. On a good day I could free dive for five minutes. This was not a good day. Injuries, exhaustion, kit and clothing all reduced the time I'd have under water. I gave myself four minutes maximum: two minutes out and, crucially, two minutes to get back if there was no exit at the other end – and that was pushing it to the absolute limit. Once I was underwater, the most important thing was to keep moving. If I pressed on, I'd have almost perfect visibility; turn back, and I'd be blinded by my own wake. God help me if I got stuck on the return trip. When I did get out, I'd be operating in soaking wet clothes. That wasn't ideal – but the catacombs weren't cold. In fact, it was warmer underground than it was at the surface. The entire complex maintained a steady fifteen degrees Celsius – the perfect temperature for storing wine and for swimming assassins.

Wet blackness engulfed me. The last pockets of air in my clothing bubbled out. I trod gingerly, left hand in constant contact with the wall, M4 braced into my right hip, barrel forward, describing the same hypnotic red cross on the passage ahead. Progress was painfully slow. I stubbed my toes on hidden rocks, scraped my skull on the invisible ceiling. One minute in and I'd covered less than ten metres. After a minute and a half I reached another T-junction. To the left the red beam vanished into the clear black water. To the right the route curved around. I followed it, left arm out, steadying myself in the weird weightlessness of the submerged passage. The route divided again. I kept right, completing a hundred-and-thirty-degree turn back on my original direction. If I'd worked it out correctly, I'd be facing south-west. I stood still in the blackness. My two minutes were up. I began to feel the tightness in my chest. The straining at my throat.

If I went back now, I'd have to risk going *all* the way back, and that risked a lot. There could have been five metres or fifty metres of flooded tunnel still left to navigate – all with unknown height and access. There was only one thing to do: go white again. The tactical LED on the M4 would illuminate the water like a floodlit swimming pool. I'd be able to see if there was a way out. But anyone on the other side would see me coming out of the dark long before I saw them.

Lungs pulling in my chest, I weighed up the pros and cons and decided to go white. Sometimes you doubt if you're making the right decision. But whenever there's doubt, there is no doubt. I let a little air out of my lungs, and found the *on* switch for the torch with my left thumb. As I felt the pad begin to depress, the water ahead of me glowed with a stream of bright white light.

I could see, immediately, that I was standing in a tangle of femurs and cracked skulls, washed into the passage with the floodwater. Their jagged shadows leapt towards me. But my thumb hadn't made full contact with the switch. The light wasn't coming *from* me. It was coming *at* me. I could see, too, that the floor of the still completely submerged passage ahead began to rise, ending in a pool only a few metres away, where the tunnel climbed up sharply over a rockfall out of the water. I resisted the strong urge to exhale and sank down into the bones, trying to make out what was happening beyond the waterline.

First one, then two beams of light arced across the width of the passage above and in front of me. They moved erratically, in different directions, lighting the walls, roof, water as if at random. And then one of the shafts of light silhouetted the outlines of three people in the dry part of the tunnel, juddering, shimmering through the distorting optic of the water. They were moving closer, much closer, and fast.

I killed the laser immediately and moved, crab-like, to the side of the flooded passageway. The bullet wounds in my thigh and shoulder throbbed. I was in bad shape for diving. I had overestimated the length of time I could stay submerged and had much less than a minute of air left. It was too late to turn back. I edged forward, disturbing the ancient human remains. My chest was screaming. My ears rang. My throat pulled down hard, desperately seeking oxygen that wasn't there. As I moved closer to the surface of the pool, the lights and shadows cast by the people in the tunnel loomed above me. I kept my head down, so that my pale face would be both the first and last thing they saw. Between two thick, torch-wielding shadows on either side, a smaller, slighter figure was squirming, fighting, struggling to break free.

I steadied myself at the edge of the rockfall and prepared to surface into the dry tunnel. And then the water exploded above me, erupting in a whoosh of air bubbles and swirling current. Finger on the trigger, I lifted the muzzle of the M4, and looked up into the bulging eyes of a frantic, drowning boy.

Our faces nearly touched. The oblique sweep of a torch beam lit the water long enough for him to see me while blocking my face from whoever was holding him under. Then the light arced away from us and we were both plunged back into darkness. His head was held under long enough for him to take in water. He screamed, filling the tunnel with a strange, muted howl, drawing water in through his nose. He was hoisted out again, coughing and spluttering in silhouette. Mud kicked up off the tunnel floor billowed around me, masking my outline, clouding my vision. Down the boy came again, held by a single hand to the back of his head. Bubbles leached from his mouth, and then from mine. He stopped struggling.

We were both out of air. Out of time.

16

I came up fast.

Left hand open wide, fingers spread across the boy's chest. I lifted him clear of the water. His torso slipped sideways, caught in a push-me-pull-you with his faceless attacker. Breath roared in the boy's lungs and mine, as if we were breathing as one. My chest heaved. Adrenaline surged.

Head-lamped and silhouetted, rifle hanging by his side, the boy's assailant reared up as I emerged from the water. I thrust the barrel of the carbine past the boy's head and into the man's throat. I fired. The first round blew his windpipe out. The second emptied his brainpan into the void of the tunnel. The boy hit the floor to my left with a thud, rasping.

I turned. The dry tunnel was less than two metres wide. A torch blinded me. Then two rifle reports deafened me. The first round skimmed my chest. The second ricocheted off the brickwork behind me, bouncing back to clip the upper receiver of the M4. I dropped into the water. I swept the suppressor across the attacker; he moved his barrel across me. We aligned. I fired first. His head jerked back. His rifle went down. I got up and out of the water. He was braced against the wall, left hand on his stomach, screeching through gritted teeth. I crouched. Gun up, breathing hard. I'd gut-shot him. I tensed on the trigger again, but wanted – needed – to get something, anything, from him before he died.

I switched the LED torch on next to my forward grip and blinked the water out of my eyes. He wasn't feeling his stomach for an entry wound; he was struggling to free the cotter pin on a grenade hanging from his webbing.

I squeezed the trigger, but it would not pull.

Stoppage.

His legs went out from under him. As he fell, the grenade rolled clear, the ring hooked in the crook of his finger. I dropped the rifle and twisted right. I hit the half-drowned boy in the lower back as he struggled to stand, wrapping my arms around him, rolling us into the depths of the flood. I pushed us under. My ears rang from the shots. I felt my heartbeat.

And then: *boom.*

The blast wave pulsed through the water, through us, as we spun thrashing in the darkness. The expanse of the tunnel absorbed the force of the explosion, but still I felt it. I held the boy fast, getting his head above the water and then levering us both over the lip of the pool we'd tumbled back down into.

I sat up on the floor, coughing, while the boy crawled on all fours over the body of the first man I'd shot seconds earlier. He vomited water, and then whatever else was in his stomach. I retrieved my M4, its torch still on, and travelled the beam around the tunnel. I saw the boy properly for the first time. He wasn't a teenager but a young man. Five-ten; a hundred and thirty-five pounds; hair covered completely by tightly wound black cloth. He was wearing blue jeans tucked into wellington boots, and a green T-shirt. He tried to stand, but collapsed back to his knees.

The air hung heavy with dust from the blast, so thick in parts that the light from the LED whited out the passage, like car headlamps shining into dense fog. The assailant I'd shot in the stomach lay lifeless on the ground, torn by shrapnel. I looked ahead.

No lights; no lasers – at least none that I could see.

I listened as hard as I could, but above the gunshot-whine in my ears nothing registered. I moved towards the shredded body. A piece of brick fell beside me, narrowly missing my shoulder. And then another. And another. I covered my head and dodged, looking up as I skirted first a handful and then a rush of rubble from above. The grenade had weakened further the already unsound tunnel.

'Cave-in!' I yelled. 'Run!' And then in French, *'Cours!'*

Clothes steaming, I rushed forward, rifle in my right hand, and gripped the young man by the scruff of the neck as he clambered to his feet. I pushed him, screaming at him to move, as the sickening rumble-roar of tumbling masonry thundered around us. He staggered, slipped, but did not fall. Propelled as much by terror as by me, he lit off down the tunnel, both of us sprinting to outpace the brick and limestone avalanche that lapped at our boot heels. Ten metres. Twenty. A small boulder struck me between the shoulder blades. And then a larger one, which sent me sprawling. I let go of the young man and found my feet, pushing myself off the walls, dodging the limestone downpour. Dust billowed in front of us. The air thickened. The light on the rifle barrel barely lit the way. Thirty metres. I ploughed on. Massive slabs of ceiling rock shattered with terrific crashes only inches behind me. In the torchlight I saw the roof ahead open in a sickening, black crack.

And then the young man, sprinting despite his awkward boots, dived left mid-stride . . . and vanished. It was as if he'd ducked behind an invisible wall and slipped out of the rubble-strewn tunnel. The LED beam found only a feature-less void where he'd disappeared.

You can't outrun the Reaper.

Fuck it.

I shouldered left into the black hole that had swallowed the young man and found myself falling, spinning in infinity. I thrust my arm out into nothing. Saw only the crazy arc of the white rifle light whirling around me. The roar of the cave-in muted. The dust dissipated. And I hit the ground hard, landing straight on top of the disappearing man.

We disentangled ourselves, cursing, and sat facing each other, slumped against opposite walls of the new tunnel we'd ended up in. I aimed the torch up and saw the edges of the hole we'd dived through, and then looked around us. We'd fallen another three metres deeper into the catacombs, tumbling into a short linking passage no more than a dozen metres long. I crawled to the far end of it. Back in the direction we'd come from – beneath our old tunnel – was a seventy-metre straight section that ended in a T-junction. To the right the passageway carried on for what looked like more than two hundred metres. There was no sign in either direction of the collapse on the level above. Once I was sure that we were alone, I turned the torch on the young man. He put his hands up to shield his face from the brightness and I adjusted the barrel of the M4 so that the muzzle wasn't pointing at him or the torch blinding him.

'*Ça va?*' I asked him, though he didn't look OK. His clothes were sodden; the fine dust from the crumbling cave had stuck to him and turned into a milky white paste that coated his face, jacket, boots; and his hands were trembling and bloodied, his elbows and knees grazed and bleeding. But his breathing was calm, and his eyes were focused. I'd been clobbered myself, but neither of us had been badly injured.

'*Oui*,' he replied. '*Qu'est ce* . . .' His French faltered. 'What happened?' he tried again in English. His accent was soft, educated, the vowels stretched and flattened in turn. Indian, maybe. Or Pakistani. Via England.

'Two men tried to drown you,' I replied. 'I killed them and then the roof collapsed.'

He opened his mouth to speak, thought better of it, but then asked, anyway.

'Are you a cop?'

'No,' I said. 'I'm not.' He stared involuntarily at the rifle in my hand. 'It's complicated,' I said. Which was true. 'I'm not going to hurt you. But we're in deep shit.'

'Really?' he said, closing his eyes as he rubbed at the grime covering his face. His tone was sarcastic. But his hands were still shaking.

'"Really" I'm not going to hurt you, or "really" we're in deep shit?'

'Really . . .' He screwed up his eyes harder, trying not to cry. 'Really, just . . . who are you?' His tone was plaintive now. The self-defence of sarcasm was too much effort to maintain.

'I'm Max,' I said. I reached out to shake his hand. He pinched the tears out of his eyes with his thumb and forefinger across the bridge of his nose and looked up at me. He hesitated for a moment, and then we clasped our palms together. He was beautiful, and by the look of him hardly out of his teens. His chin was fuzzed over with straggly, grimy bumfluff that looked like it had never seen a razor. He was lucky to be alive. We both were.

'Bhavneet,' he said. And then, awkwardly formal, 'Bhavneet

Singh.' He took his hand back, but didn't stop staring at me. 'People call me "Baaz", though,' he added.

'OK, Baaz,' I said; and then, half-laughing at his earnestness, 'How d'y'do?'

He lifted his palms and breathed out through his nose as if to say: *How does it look as if I'm doing?*

'Before they tried to . . .' I thought better of the question and cleared my throat, shifting up on to my haunches. 'You're Punjabi, right?'

'Right.'

'From India?'

He nodded. 'From Chandigarh. I . . .' He stared at me. 'Those men,' he said. 'They were looking for you, weren't they?'

It was my turn to nod. 'What were they asking you?'

'I don't know. They weren't speaking English.' He tentatively touched the black cotton binding his hair, making sure it was still tied securely. I wondered if he'd lost his turban in the water. 'Maybe they were asking which way you'd gone?'

'OK,' I said. 'Try to remember. What did it sound like, what they said? The words?'

'I don't know. *Kuda*-something, maybe. I think they were Russian.' The sarcasm flared up. 'I wasn't, you know, really paying *attention*.'

'Could have been *Kuda on devalsya*,' I replied. 'It's Russian for "Where did he disappear to?"'

'Right,' he said. 'Are you Russian? You sound Irish.'

'I am,' I said. 'Irish, I mean. Well, mostly. That's complicated, too.'

'I see,' he said. 'Well, I tried to get free, and, ah . . .' He paused for a moment. The adrenaline of a succession of near-misses had begun to abate and tears welled in his eyes again. 'And then the bastards tried to do me in.'

161

'OK, that's good,' I said.

'Good?' He wiped his eyes again. 'How is any of this bull-shit *good*?'

'Because if they asked you where I was, it meant they weren't tracking me. At least not down here. Which means now they're not tracking you. And believe me,' I added, 'that's good.'

I supposed that once they'd realized he couldn't help them, they'd tried to drown him. When – *if* – his body had been found, he'd have looked like just another unlucky explorer fallen foul of the catacombs. He breathed out hard. He was trying to keep himself together. For a kid who'd just sur-vived his first firefight, he was doing well.

'OK,' he conceded, 'that *is* good. But they're ... you know . . .' He looked down. 'They're dead, aren't they?'

'Yup,' I replied. 'As doornails. But there'll be more of them. A lot more. And nearby. Trust me.' He kept looking at the patch of muddy chalk between his feet. 'Can you stand? We need to move. The more distance between us and them the better.' No reply. 'Do you know the tunnels? Properly, I mean.' He was zoned out now, unresponsive. I raised my voice. '*Baaz?*'

'Ah, yeah.' He came to with a jolt, tilted his head back, blinked and looked at me again. 'Yeah, I know the tunnels.'

'So, let's go.'

I pushed up off my haunches, and held out my hand again. We grabbed each other's wrists, and I hauled him to his feet. I felt the bullet wound in my shoulder, and winced. We stood in front of each other and he sized me up, nervously.

'Are *you* OK?'

I'd seen that look before, and given it myself a few times,

too. However screwed he was *because* of me, it was dawning on him that he needed me, too.

'I'm good,' I nodded. 'Really.' I forced a smile over the top of the deep, throbbing pain spreading inside my shoulder. That seemed to relax him and he started to look around the tunnel, getting his bearings.

I checked that the grenades were secure in my pockets, that the Glock was in my jeans – and that the condom bundle was still intact. Then I remembered with a jolt that I'd forgotten to seal up the hundred-dollar bill with the passport. I slipped my finger into the ticket pocket of my Levi's, and felt the damp bump with relief. Finally I freed the torch from the Picatinny rail and clamped it between my teeth, examining where the ricochet had hit the M4. I dropped the magazine and worked the charging handle with the rifle turned on its side. A spent cartridge case fell out into my hand – its lead in the guts of the attacker who'd brought the roof down. I looked inside the breech, and examined the upper receiver. Then I saw the problem. The gas return tube had been ruptured forward of the chamber, which meant there was not enough pressure to cycle the bolt. It would still fire – but I'd have to recock it manually after every shot. Effectively, the rifle was as much use as Doc Levy's old Martini–Henry – which was to say, good enough. I checked the integrity of the barrel and the suppressor, put the magazine on, and chambered a round. I hesitated for a moment, then gave the flashlight to Baaz.

'Thanks.' He flicked it on. If you need someone on side, show them you have faith in them. It's reassuring to be trusted. 'Cool. You don't need it for your . . .' he tailed off and pointed to the M4.

'For the rifle? No. You know your way around. So you're

going to need it. Because you're going first.' He smiled. 'Besides,' I added, 'if anyone shoots at us, they'll aim at the torch.'

'What?'

'OK, let's go.' We shuffled into the main tunnel. I slung the M4 over my shoulder and drew the Glock.

'No, but seriously.'

'Yes, but seriously. Let's *go*.'

'Go fucking *where*?'

'Montrouge,' I said. 'The cemetery.'

He turned around to face me again, staring in disbelief. 'No way.'

'Listen.' My voice was stressed, too forceful. He recoiled. 'Listen, Baaz,' I tried again, softening. 'I need to get out of the city, out of France. I can't explain more than that. If you can get me west of Place d'Italie, I can get myself out. I'll find the way.'

'How?' he asked, incredulous.

'I cut waypoints down here when I was a kid. I know what I'm doing.'

'No,' he said, 'you don't. No offence, but that must have been, like, *years* ago?' I shrugged. 'Montrouge is messed up,' he added excitedly. 'A hundred metres of tunnel came down before Christmas. What didn't collapse, flooded.'

'There's no way?' I asked, thinking, *There's always a way*.

He shook his head emphatically.

'It can't be done. Trying to get out there would be suicide.'

'Staying down *here* is suicide. As soon as those two dead guys fail to check in with the rest of their team, a tsunami of shite is going to flood these tunnels.' I looked around at the passage walls, pointlessly. 'Fuck!' I could feel my temper fraying in exasperation. I breathed deeply and composed myself. 'Can they seal the catacombs? I mean, completely cut them off?'

'No,' Baaz replied. 'Impossible. For a start there could be dozens of cataphiles down here right now, maybe even hundreds.'

'Who?'

'You know, people who come exploring at the weekends, like me. Tourists, students.' He paused for a moment. 'All sorts of weirdos.'

'So what?'

'So, if you sealed the entrances, we'd die. There are always people down here, so the cops always have to leave exits open. They'd be done for murder otherwise.'

I decided not to press the point that the people after me – after *us* – weren't overly concerned about their rap sheet.

'OK. If not Montrouge, where? We can't use an exit the police know about.' He thought for a moment, twitching the fingers of his left hand as if tapping an invisible keyboard. 'Baaz,' I urged him, 'we *really* need to move.'

I started to pace up and down, hanging on to the coat-tails of my temper.

'Montparnasse,' he said eventually. 'There's an exit there, but, ah . . .'

'But what?'

'But it's going to be *mushkul*.'

17

'*Mushkul*' sounded OK until Baaz explained, as we kept up a steady jog south-west through the tunnels, that it was Punjabi for 'about as extreme as it gets'.

While I tried and failed to imagine what he might think was worse than nearly being drowned, he also explained that more of the tunnels south of the Place d'Italie had been walled off since my teenage excursions, so we couldn't simply loop around it. We had two options: take a long detour south, or cut straight under the great traffic junction – and risk another confrontation. The men who'd found him, he thought, had most likely entered via the Place d'Italie Métro station.

Surviving another shootout underground would be not so much a matter of skill and training as chance. As soon as we went up against someone with night vision, we couldn't hide. If we were caught in a long stretch of tunnel, we'd be mown down before we could turn around. I didn't even want to think about the damage another grenade strike might do.

We headed south.

As the possibility of using my father's waypoints receded into fantasy, the reality of my reliance on Baaz grew sharper. He twisted around fragile columns, slithered under low passes, directed me left and right – pointing out where flooded tunnels breached at ankle height and where to jump the metal-spiked shafts that yawned wide in the passage floor. He was fit and fast, but, like most people who don't train for it, had little upper body strength and struggled to pull himself up where there was no foothold to boost him. He was alert, though – stopping constantly, listening, picking out the distant murmur of voices. At one junction he just stood still and sniffed the air. I asked what he was doing.

'You can smell the cops before you can see them,' he said. 'Their aftershave.' Here and there throughout the old quarries police he called the 'catacops' patrolled looking for trespassers. All entry to the catacombs was forbidden. And although the consequence of being caught was ordinarily only a small fine, the implications for us of being seen by the patrols were potentially fatal – for everyone. But the cat and mouse game the cataphiles played with the cops, he said, gave us one massive advantage. Although the people who explored that vast random city of the dead didn't like strangers, they hated the police – and the system they thought they stood for – even more: no one who saw us would ask us who we were, or what we were doing. Anarchists, ravers, students, dreamers, lovers, potholers, cave divers, misfits, thieves and simply the downright curious – anyone and everyone could be found underground. Illegal bars hosting massive parties, Baaz told me, and even a fully functional cinema had been carved out in the inverted utopia that ran wild deep below the chic boulevards above. Graffiti, sculptures and elaborate shrines marked the waypoints of a world that I'd imagined I could navigate but that would have swallowed me without trace. I considered this, too: my father's route map might not have led me out of the catacombs, but it had led me to Baaz – which, right then, seemed like the next best thing.

Several times a light at the end of a cross tunnel saw me

raise the Glock in expectation of trouble. But each time Baaz waved my hand down.

'Carbide,' he explained. 'They're explorers. The cops use LEDs like yours. It's cool.'

The challenge of getting us to the ancient necropolis of Montparnasse gripped him obsessively. He didn't ask me about myself; I asked nothing more about him. The fact that our clothes were soaked and steaming, that we were filthy and scuffed and only alive by the thinnest of margins, weren't things he was ready to talk about, now or maybe ever. If he was in shock, he was still functioning; if he wasn't in shock, he was, frankly, a freak. *I* was in shock. But Baaz, he just turned and turned again, until the level of the floor started first to ascend and then climb sharply. We were getting nearer to the surface. We branched away from the main tunnel, clambered through an antechamber furnished with a wax-smeared stone table, and then made a hunched thirty-metre walk to what looked like a dead end.

In fact, we'd reached a low arch in the tunnel wall. He killed the light. I tensed. We stood next to each other in deep, impenetrable darkness.

'What is it?' I whispered, pushing the pistol up and out with both hands into the pitch black. 'Where?'

'Forward,' he replied, voice tense with expectation. 'Crouch. Slowly.'

We inched onwards. I felt the stone of the arch brush the length of my spine. I kept the Glock's barrel half an arm's length in front of me and felt above my head with my left hand. Stone. And then void. I swept the same hand down and left, making contact with Baaz's right arm. I held it fast and took another step.

'Listen,' he said, almost inaudibly.

But I could hear nothing. It was the most profound silence I'd ever experienced. Quieter than the jungle before dawn; quieter than the caves in Sierra Leone; quieter than the lake water that lapped at the edges of my dreams. We stood for a few seconds like that, me clutching his arm, engulfed in nothingness.

'Don't shoot,' he said at last. 'Just look.' And with that he flicked on the torch. I lurched forward, finger tensed on the trigger. But no shot sounded. We were completely surrounded – encircled by hundreds, thousands of people. But Baaz was right: there was no one to shoot at.

Skeletons piled up around us. Femurs and tibias; humeri and ribs; and row upon row of uncounted skulls stacked high. The chamber must have been twenty metres across, but so densely packed with bones that the circle clear enough to stand in was less than five metres wide. Baaz looked at me, for my reaction, and then played the LED slowly across the ancient faces staring at us.

Here we were, fighting for our lives, standing in the centre of a mass grave. For an instant I thought of the dead I'd left behind me, the piles of bodies that marked the waypoints in my journey from orphan to assassin. How much space would they take up? I didn't know. I didn't want to know. The only thing I knew for sure was that I wasn't ready to join them. Not yet.

'Just for kicks,' he said. 'If you come in with the light on, it's not the same.'

I said nothing. The shadows cast by the blue-white beam had the curious effect of making the mandibles of the skulls appear to work, grinding jaws which had not tasted meat for centuries. Coated with fur and mould and cavern slime, long bones stuck through smashed pelves. Finger joints crunched underfoot like pea gravel on the Devil's driveway. Cave-slime ringed the eye sockets – glistening emerald irises winking back in the torchlight.

I spun around the illuminated epicentre of that empire of the dead, avoiding their gaze, searching for the exit Baaz had promised.

'Here it is,' he said, lighting up the far corner. 'I told you. It's crazy, isn't it?' He'd lit the tiniest of apertures, a one-foot by two-foot opening where the sweep of decaying bones curved up to meet the ceiling. 'No one has ever been up it,' he said.

And I could see why.

It was the chute down which the cemetery above had been emptied into the limestone cavern below. Like a macabre calcified waterfall, the remnants of the long dead spewed out from its mouth, engulfing the room with the mortal remains of generation upon generation of Parisians. At first the bones had been sorted and stacked, filling the charnel house with concentric rings of partial skeletons. At the end, though, it looked like the last deposits of upwards of a thousand bodies must have just been tipped into the gallery below.

I unslung the M4, stuck the pistol back into my waistband and then scrambled up the bone scree to investigate. Skulls click-clacked like castanets. I squirmed around on to my back and found myself taking a deep breath as I pushed my head up into the hole. I could see nothing.

'Baaz, are you sure this goes through? It's pitch black. Not even a speck of sunshine.'

'Look at your watch,' he replied. I wriggled out and did a double take. It was seven o'clock in the evening. We'd been walking for more than five hours. 'Everyone loses track of time down here,' he said with a smile. 'It's unreal.'

I was still on my back, suspended by that massive bed of bones, staring at the ceiling.

'How do you do it?' I asked him. 'Navigate, I mean. No maps. No waypoints.' I pushed myself up on to my elbows and looked down at him. 'It's not normal,' I said. The Glock pressed into my spine. *It's not possible*, I thought.

He looked up at me and cocked his head to one side.

'My brain,' he said. 'It's different. It works differently.'

'Different how? To what?'

'To yours. To everyone's.' He smiled again. '*Chust chalak*, my mother says. He put on a strong Punjabi accent, mimicking her pronunciation. '*Clever clogs*. I remember things. Patterns. Numbers. Once I've seen them, I can't forget them.' He tapped his right temple. 'It's bloody crowded in there.'

I looked back into the hole.

'Well, it's going to be bloody crowded up there, too.' I waved my right hand. 'Pass me the torch, will you?'

He did. I wanted to stay dark during the climb, for when we emerged. But I needed to see what I was getting into first. I took the black barrel of the LED from Baaz's fingers and angled the beam into the shaft so that as little glare as possible would leak out. Immediately above my face the outline of a skull leapt out, mouth grimacing in the slanting torchlight. I swept the beam out at first by a foot, and then another. As the light climbed higher, I understood more clearly the true horror ahead. No wonder no one used this exit. Even if the cops did know about it, no one would ever be stupid – or desperate – enough to try it.

Bodies had caught down the sides of the chute, so that the length of it was lined with the detritus of the dead. There were no footholds except upturned skulls; no handholds except the unreliable levers of femurs. A ribcage jutted out here; a scapula there. Looking up and seeing the bones cascading down in frozen motion was like seeing a freeze-frame of being sucked into hell.

'I'll have to remind Grumpy Jock to add this to selection,' I said under my breath. And then aloud, as I worked my way out again, 'There was one thing you *did* forget, Baaz.'

'What's that?'

'I'm nearly twice your size.'

'Oh,' he said, at first dumbfounded and then dejected. 'Oh *no*. Can we do it?'

'No idea,' I said truthfully. 'Can't see the top. It curves around after four metres or so. Maybe I'll get through, maybe not. You're going first, anyway.' He looked at me, nervous, left hand drumming away at the air again. 'You have to. I can get through what I've seen, but I'll bring everything I brush past crashing down as I go.' He reached for the torch. I held it back. 'It's better you don't see what you're holding on to.' He wriggled his way into the hole, coughing and swearing in Punjabi as he went. I held on to his ankle to slow him down, and bent round so he could hear me better. 'Baaz?'

'What?'

'Two things. First – if we get separated, don't go straight home, and definitely don't go to the cops.'

'OK. And what's the second thing?'

'This was your idea.'

I let go of his ankle and slapped his calf through his wellingtons and he vanished up the chute – the fine shower of bone splinters that fell back into the cavern the only trace anyone was up there at all. I turned around to do a final sweep of the chamber. I slung the M4 tight to my chest and killed the torch. I waited for Baaz to get a couple of metres ahead of me, and then forced my weight up behind him,

172

pulling myself up the rungs of the bone ladder one femur at a time, snaking my way through the shaft.

Everything I touched, snapped. In the pitch black it was impossible to tell the bones apart. My shoulders scraped the sides clean, sending a shower of osseous matter down into the cavern below. I wedged my back against the wall and pushed up with my feet, bracing, scrabbling, pulling with my fingertips where I could. Unknown lumps of skeleton fell from Baaz's own scramble out, hitting my head, shoulders. I was at the bend now. The chimney constricted. My eyes clogged with dirt and dust. My nails bled; my face was scratched red raw. I paused to catch my breath, and tasted for the first time in hours the cool sweetness of fresh air.

I was nearly there.

'OK, I've done it. Bloody hell.' It was Baaz calling from above. By the sound of it he was out. 'It's tight, but I think you can make it.'

'Good,' I yelled up. 'Run. You hear me? Run, and don't look back.'

If he got busted, he'd be screwed. If he got busted with me, he'd be dead. I rested my right hand on the pistol grip of the M4 and cursed the stupidity of carrying it up with me. But as I looked down and braced myself for the last push up and out, the air filled with the pulsating boom-roar of a grenade blast. I looked down. A rifle-mounted torch probed the bone-pipe. The chute flooded with light.

Shit.

The white faces of the dead pressed in on me. If you're going through hell ... keep going. So I breathed in and pushed for all I was worth against the walls. But my shoulders would not move.

I was a dead man.

Do something. Or do nothing.

I tucked my chin in, squeezed my legs together, folded my arms across my chest. And dropped.

The frozen faces fell away in a helter-skelter frenzy of bone-blurred descent. The minutes taken to inch my way up took seconds to reverse. As I landed hard, a man's head poked into the opening. My feet found his shoulders, pushing him back and out, exiting at speed in a slimy skull-wave of broken bones that plunged us back into the charnel house together. I picked myself up. He was heavyset, black combats, tactical vest. Two twenty, two thirty pounds. And out cold. His body was half buried by the skull-slide, partly lit by the rifle light wedged tight beneath him. His face was covered by a military respirator. Could have been a cop. Could have been whoever the fuck else was after me.

I got the M4 in my shoulder, laser on. The rest of the cave was clear. The blast had been a flash-bang, not frag. Pound to a penny they'd try and gas me out. I pulled the respirator off his face and on to mine and then I scraped a heap of bones over his rifle's flashlight. The ossuary went darker, but not black. The lip of the arch under which we'd first entered the room threw a shadow back towards me. Then the whole edge of the roughly hewn doorway juddered as more light fell on it. It was being lit from the other side. I knelt and squinted down the passageway. Torches, not carbide lamps. Half a dozen of them, closing in.

French GIGN assault team or Russian death squad? The motopsycho nightmare ride across the capital had floored a lot of policemen – but none had died by my hand. I intended to keep it that way for as long as possible. Fifteen metres. I took the sting-ball grenade out of my jacket pocket, and stepped back from the low archway. Ten metres. I pulled the pin, let the lever fly clear, and flung the little black ball down the passageway.

A loud bang. Exploding rubber and CS gas. I heard a man fall. One screamed. They all stopped. I backed away, M4 up, facing the gateway, treading the hill of bones in reverse back to the escape hole. I imagined my shoulders grinding bone against bone as I tried to work my way up again. But there was no time to get clear.

The men in the tunnel were already up and running, boots pounding on the passage floor. I squatted down, the stock of the damaged rifle braced to my right hip by my right elbow. In the half-dark I hooked the index and middle fingers of my left hand around the T-bar of the M4's charging handle. A metal cylinder bounded through the archway, billowing white smoke. CS gas, most likely. Then another. There was a pause as the room filled with vapour, and then the first man came in at a crouch. I landed my red dot on the shooter's left shoulder and followed it with a single 5.56 round. I was glad of the suppressor.

'Blyat!' he swore in Russian as he went down, twisting away from me. French cops got a second chance; Russian gunmen got no mercy. I put the next round through his back, the one that followed it in his ribs, racking the charging handle of the broken M4 to recock it after every shot like an old movie cowboy fanning a six-gun. The light on his dropped rifle fell away from me, illuminating an inverted skull by the foot of the door in a blazing halo. Despite the glare from the torch I could make out only shapes, not details, in the shadows it raked up around the door. The ossuary was entirely filled with gas. If they decided to play rough and lobbed in a hand grenade, the first I'd know about it was when it went off.

I threw myself headlong down the pile of bones, landing

175

hard on the floor three metres in front of the stone arch entrance. The M4's laser reached through it, probing the shins, boots, thighs, of the men on the other side. There could have been a hundred men in that tunnel; a thousand. So narrow was the doorway that, as long as there were bullets to shoot with, it didn't matter: they could only fight me one to one. So fought the Spartans at Thermopylae.

I opened up before they could get into position. Bone shattered; muscle tore; ligaments sheered and snapped. I fired until first one and then another of the rounds from the M4 streaked out strontium red. The shooter in the bar had loaded tracer for his last three rounds. It was an old trick, and I wasn't a fan: as well as telling you when you were about to run out of ammunition, it let the people who you were shooting at know it, too. It also let them know exactly where you were – although that was currently the least of my problems. I pulled the trigger for the last time on the M4 and sent a final crimson-glowing slug into the solid black mass of the nearest fallen man.

In the silence following the shots, the deep, tearing screams of the wounded rang out.

And then orders shouted in Russian: '*Vyrubite svet!*' – *Kill the light!*

They were down, but most – maybe even all – of them would still be alive. I've seen a man lose his leg at the knee and keep engaging the enemy until a medic prised the weapon from his hands. It was too dangerous to retrieve the rifle by the door. I still had the Glock and one grenade left – but an explosion in the tunnel risked another cave-in. I dropped the spent carbine, drew the pistol, and flicked on my own torch with my left thumb, covering the lens with my thigh. I got to my feet and stayed low, sending the lit LED arcing out through the entrance, above and beyond the bodies of the men I'd cut down: shots followed the swooping, spinning beam as it sailed past like an erratic lighthouse. Rifle reports thundered along the passage – their muzzle flashes giving their positions away as surely as the tracer had done mine. The torch landed on the floor, pointing down the tunnel. Its flight had distracted them for a second.

And a second was all I needed.

I came through the archway firing. The fallen torch cut the gloom enough to see to kill. I aimed shots into the out-lines of the three men from whom points of light had flared a moment before. I worked smoothly, accurately, enjoying the feeling of the Glock, the precision of it. All the time Colonel Ellard's words in my mind.

If you want to win a gunfight, take your time.

Some of the rounds connected with a dull, wet thud. Others crunched as copper clipped bone. Up close, bursts of light from the Glock illuminated faces on the floor, hands clutching wounds, mouths open, screaming, in split-second freeze-frame. Movement to the left. I dropped on my haunches as a bullet licked the air above me, scoring the stone wall behind. I fired two shots in return. The rifle fell silent.

The four men I'd shot lay face down, unmoving – lower limbs wrecked, chests opened up with copper-coated lead. Among them, three wounded shuffled on the ground. Dying among the dying, they snaked around their wounds, darken-ing the chalk-slime of the passage floor with thick clots of blood. The taste of iron mingled with the bitter tang of cordite.

I leaned over and shot the nearest survivor in the head. I stepped over him and moved to the next, shooting him in the same way. The third man was further off. He lay on his back, hands up and out towards me. There was enough light from the discarded torch to see that his face was bloodied, neck lacerated. His leg lay at right angles to his body – torn out of place by the M4. I aimed into his one, dying eye. His hands came together as if in prayer.

'*Ne ubivai menya!*' he begged, choking on the blood collecting in his throat. *Don't kill me.* But when the killing starts, it doesn't stop until the job is done.

No one moved. I checked the magazine in the Glock. Empty. One round left in the breech. I looked around for a weapon to take – and then, at the far end of the tunnel, a long black shadow spread across the tunnel ceiling. I straightened up, raised the pistol and brought my left hand across to steady the grip. Picked out by the beam of the torch at my feet, a slight man in a long black coat emerged into the tunnel. He took a step towards me, head back, hands raised and empty. One shot, one kill. The crease beneath the pad of my index finger flattened across the trigger.

'McLean,' he shouted. I steadied my breathing. 'You are a very hard man to help.'

The clipped vowels of his perfect English echoed off the stone corridor. It was the doctor from the ship. And he'd been reading the newspapers. Once upon a time no one knew my name unless I told them. Now it was on everyone's lips. I settled the sight post of the Glock in the centre of his chest and exhaled slowly. But I wanted to talk to him. Not kill him. At thirty metres I could put him down. But I couldn't guarantee he'd survive. A hair's breadth of steel stopped the hammer from dropping, kept his heart beating.

'I don't need your kind of help.'

'I think you do, Mr McLean. Look around you. Your own side has betrayed you.'

'Keep walking,' I said, louder than I expected. 'And keep talking.' He took another step forward. I lowered my aim a fraction, into his stomach. Whoever he was, he had guts.

'General King hasn't just left you out in the cold. He's buried you.' He'd most likely got King's name from Lukov. But he was right. It was open season on Max McLean.

'Step closer,' I said. He did.

'You have something that belongs to me,' he said. 'I'd like it back.'

'Sure. Come and get it.'

I might have been disowned. But I hadn't been disarmed. The trigger crept a fraction of a millimetre. And then movement to my right. One of the gunmen was still alive. In his hand the hard lines of a Grach 9mm. The shot went wide of my leg. I returned fire reflexively. He dropped the pistol and breathed out a last, long death rattle. I looked up again as the shadow cast by the doctor slipped from sight along the passage.

I dropped the Glock and took the pistol from the dead man's hand, checking the magazine. Then I removed the remaining grenade from my jacket pocket and waited for the onslaught.

But none came.

So I picked up my torch and ducked back into the ancient ossuary, leaving the assault squad's carbines where they'd fallen. They were too visible, their ammunition too hard to come by. But NATO 9mm – which the Grach's magazine was loaded with – could be scavenged from any policeman's belt. Why it wasn't charged with the Russian armour-piercing rounds it was designed for could have been due to operational security or expediency – or because they weren't serving military.

I crouched and listened but my hearing was shot. There was nothing to do but get out while I still could. I stretched out on my back and craned my head into the bone-pipe. I flicked on the flashlight, checked the integrity of the boot-damaged walls, and started the ascent – forcing myself up, clinging on to the crumbling foot- and handholds that I'd already half-destroyed in my first attempted surge to safety. I pushed and braced and squeezed and kicked, and emerged back into the world choking on bone dust, spitting out fragments of femur on to the damp cemetery ground at the base of an elaborate stone tomb. I rolled clear and lay flat, swallowing deep breaths of clean, crisp, night air.

The remaining grenade was the last thing that went down the chute after I came out – ensuring I'd be the last person to use it. Going off five metres underground, the blast hardly registered between the densely packed gravestones and mausolea around me. But I felt the vibration of bones and earth collapsing beneath me, and I knew that the entrance would be sealed.

I sat up and got my bearings. Low cloud. No moon. And no movement. The soft sodium light thrown by the street lamps that ringed the graveyard settled on the ancient stonework like an orange blanket. It made everything look unreal, insubstantial. But at least I could see. I needed to head south. How, exactly, I'd be able to keep moving, where, exactly, I'd go – I just didn't know. But then, as I got to my feet, one of the alabaster angels presiding over the tomb I'd emerged next to lurched forward, arms thrust out at me. I jumped back and raised the Grach reflexively, not knowing whether I was under attack or whether the grenade had caused a cave-in. Then I saw. Smeared with tunnel slime, clothes torn, eyes bright in the darkness, the figure reaching out for me wasn't an angel – but it was a saviour nonetheless.

I lowered the pistol and reached out, too, and clasped the muddy hand of Bhavneet Singh.

18

Zero eight thirty.

I parted the blinds a fraction. The wind was picking up. Grey clouds piled up on the horizon. There would be rain later. I pressed the back of my fingers to the window glass. It was cold, too. Not far off freezing. The sun hadn't yet risen, but the city was already seething. Monday morning and everyone was back to work. Me included. I'd been awake for hours. Waiting. Listening. Just because I couldn't see them didn't mean I wasn't surrounded. The French army and the police, Russian hitman and random gunmen, snipers and bike riders, and, of course, the Russian doctor: they were all out there. Somewhere.

I withdrew my hand and let the slats snick shut.

The room was spacious and well heated, with high white walls that rose to a lofty, corniced ceiling. At either end stood a tall window covered with blinds. Beneath each window sat an iron radiator, adorned with my drip-drying socks, gloves and jacket. In between them, pushed up against the front wall, was a massive wooden table laden with three large flat-panel displays, a wireless keyboard, two laptop computers and sheaves of paper printed with what looked like equations and calculations.

I picked up the nearest set of notes. They'd been crossed out with deep slashes of a blue biro. At the top of the page, written in the same blue ink: *Shor is God.*

I pushed the papers to one side and made space among the mess to set out the remainder of my kit:

Grach MP-443 pistol and fifteen rounds of ammo.

Pepper spray.

Pozidriv screwdriver.

Lukov's wallet, driver's licence, credit cards and French identity card.

Greek passport in the name of Maximilianos Ioannides.

Waterproof watch.

Two thousand euros in fifty-euro notes and a couple of hundred in smaller notes — courtesy of Lukov.

A lighter and unopened packet of French smokes — also from Lukov.

From the ticket pocket in my jeans I produced the tightly folded, damp hundred-dollar bill. A little battered and worn along the creases, but it was still in one piece. The scrawled Russian letters on the reverse that spelled out *Arkhangel* hadn't faded, either. I spread it out to dry on one of the pages of equations.

'Miraculous,' I said out loud.

'There are no such things as miracles.'

I turned around to see Baaz backing in through the swing-door to the kitchen, which wafted a rich smell of fried onions and spices into the living room as it fanned shut. In one hand he carried a bowl of steaming beans, and in the other a plate laden with a stack of parathas, hot out of the pan.

'Although my auntie's *tarka* beans *are* pretty close to divine.'

He went to set the food on the table, saw my things spread out, and motioned for me to move the laptops to one side. I did, and he put the food down, returning to the kitchen to fetch two mugs of hot tea and two squares of kitchen towel. We sat down on wooden stools that were tucked beneath the table and ate ferociously with our fingers.

It was the first time I'd seen him clearly. He looked more

substantial than he had done in the gloom of the tunnels – more like five-eleven, and a hundred and fifty pounds. It was the sniper's curse to assess everyone as a potential target; mentally adjust every breeze for windage; scope every distance for elevation. His hair was bound up in a simple, neat black turban. Washed clean, his beard was still wispy, but at least looked a little more dignified. I hadn't shaved. And my bullet wounds burned continuously.

'That,' I said, mopping the last of the spicy bean sauce from the bowl with the last of the parathas, 'was grand. Thank you.'

'They're *literally* the only things I can cook. My mum's sister taught me how to make them the day before I left the UK. She was worried I would starve. She was completely correct.'

I took a slug of the tea. It was sweet enough to put my teeth on edge.

'I thought you were from Chandigarh?' I asked him.

He nodded. 'I came to London first, to see my auntie and finish school. Then I came to France. To Saclay. The university,' he clarified, gesturing towards the piles of notes and the bank of screens. 'I'm doing an MA. Computer stuff. But the campus is miles away.'

He looked around the living room as if to say, *So here I am.* I looked around, too. The apartment was large for Paris, never mind student digs.

'Rich parents?'

He looked taken aback, and slightly sheepish. 'Oh, no. Not at all. I . . . the course is OK, but, ah . . .'

'But what? It's OK, Baaz, I'm not going to call your auntie.'

'OK.' He drew a breath as deep as I had done before my

first confession. 'I trade crypto. Digital coins. It's going quite well.'

'So I see.'

There was a plain three-seater sofa in the room – which I'd slept on – with matching armchairs. The décor was simple, neutral: the walls were peppered with bland abstract art, the bookshelves lined with most likely unread classics. It felt more like a hotel room than a home – and would've had a rent to match. There were few, if any, personal belongings to be seen: hardware and notepads consumed his entire attention.

The living room, bathroom, kitchen and Baaz's bedroom were all connected to an L-shaped hallway, at the long end of which a bolted, double-locked door led on to a landing that fell away down a steep twisting staircase to the main, intercom-operated street door one floor below. Rue du Texel was a narrow road in Montparnasse with no visible CCTV cameras, south-west of the graveyard, sandwiched between an imposing police station and the church of Notre-Dame-du-Travail – though as things stood, I doubted either of them would respond positively to a call to save our souls.

Downstairs there was a red-fronted café selling crêpes and sandwiches; opposite, half a city block had been levelled for development – affording a clear view from the living room of a swathe of dead ground. I'd rather have been higher – there were three floors above us – but otherwise it was as good a place to be holed up as any. Baaz wiped his fingers on the kitchen towel.

'And you,' he said, looking at me intently, as if making his mind up about something, 'you're the guy in the news, aren't you? The one Interpol is after.'

'I didn't know they'd issued a Red Notice. But yes, I am.'

I sipped my tea. If he tried to run for it, he'd be on the

floor before he crossed the room; if he went for the Grach, his arm would be broken before his fingers closed on the grip. I blinked and smiled.

'You shot up that bar yesterday, too, didn't you?'

'No. I was the one being shot up. The bar got in the way.'

'Well, the whole joint is messed up. There are pictures online.'

'How many dead?'

'Eight. Plus two more in intensive care.'

'My photo in the papers, and the attack in the bar. Who's connecting them? The press or the police?'

'Neither,' he said. 'But I'm right, aren't I, Max McLean?'

I nodded and put down my mug.

'And the bike chase across town? I expect you looked that up, too. Has anyone released CCTV footage of that?'

'I don't think so. There's some phone footage on the internet. Mostly rubbish. I didn't know that was definitely you, though.' He smiled, too. 'You can't see it clearly enough. Your face, I mean.'

I felt dangerously close to being played. But the truth was that, unlike Doctor Rose, in Ashford, Baaz didn't need convincing of anything. He'd lived it. And he appeared, unaccountably, to be enjoying it – whatever *it* was.

'Baaz,' I said. 'I need to ask you something.' He slurped his tea and shrugged. 'Last night I told you to run. But you didn't. You were waiting for me when I came out. And this . . .' I looked around the room again, and gestured to the empty breakfast platter, choosing my words carefully, 'this, *hospitality*. Don't get me wrong. I'm very grateful, but . . .'

'But I'm in deep shit, aren't I?'

'Yes, you are. And I'm not sure I can help you, the way you've helped me. There's nothing, I mean, I can't . . .'

'You saved my life,' Baaz cut me off. 'That's why I didn't run. And this,' he said, lifting up his cup of tea, 'is the least I can do. And besides, my auntie would kill me if she thought I wasn't showing my friends proper hospitality. She takes that very seriously.' I nodded. Baaz knitted his eyebrows, as if concentrating on solving a puzzle. 'I know those men did what they did to me because of you. But I was breaking the law by being down there in the first place. So maybe that was my just deserts.'

I had to laugh at that.

'I don't think even the Russians have the death penalty for trespassing. What were you doing down there, anyway?'

'Mapping,' he replied. 'To be honest with you, it's a bit of an obsession.' He looked away from me, at the table, and began drumming the fingers of his left hand as he'd done in the tunnels. 'You see, I can recall the routes very well.' He tapped his temple with his index finger. 'Bloody crowded, remember?'

'Yeah, I remember.'

'But there are no maps. Not proper ones. The last decent one was made in 2011; but there are so many floods and collapses, that it was out of date as soon as it was printed.'

'So?'

'So that's my challenge. For my dissertation. To come up with an algorithm that works with a map of the catacombs across all the levels – just like a map on a phone *finds* you the safest, most efficient route between multiple points, and doesn't simply tell you if the one you've found is correct. It's basically a three-dimensional, subterranean, travelling salesman problem. Only I'm plotting between tunnel junctions, not cities.'

'And that's hard, is it? To solve, I mean.'

He looked at me as if I was an idiot.

'OK. Imagine you are a travelling salesman and you want to visit a certain number of cities before returning to the place you started. But you only have a limited amount of fuel for your car, so you need to find the shortest route.'

'OK.'

'If, say, there were, seventy cities.'

'Right.'

'Well, then the number of routes you would have to consider is more than the total number of atoms in the universe.'

'You're not wrong,' I smiled. 'That *is* hard.'

'But not,' he said, 'if you're using a quantum computer. That's what I'm writing my algorithm for.'

'A what?'

'A quantum computer – one that uses qubits and not, you know, just *bits*.' I shook my head. 'Am I speaking Punjabi?' He looked at me, earnestly.

'No, we're still in English. I think.'

'OK, it's just sometimes I forget. It drives my teachers *crazy, huna?*'

'Quite.'

'OK, well a, classical, er, *normal* computer uses binary digits. It doesn't matter how big the computer is or how powerful, everything comes down to ones and zeros. You can have a very fast machine, but it can only do one task after another – sequentially. Never mind the travelling salesman problem – a ten-character password would take even a supercomputer three years to crack. But a quantum computer is completely different. It uses qubits. They're, like, subatomic. They can be *either* ones, *or* zeros, *or* a simultaneous superposition of the two.'

I held my hands up. 'In English, please.'

'Ah, sorry. I mean they can be both one and zero at the same time.' He scratched his beard. 'Mystical, really.'

'That's one word for it.'

'So,' he continued, 'two qubits can be in *any* quantum superposition of four states; three qubits, eight states. But a normal computer can only ever be in one of those states at any one time.'

'And what does that mean?'

'It means you can do every step in a big calculation simultaneously.'

'Like your travelling salesman . . . thing?'

'Yes, although there are already algorithms exactly for . . .'

'OK,' I cut him off. 'I get it. With enough qubits you could solve really hard problems really fast.' He nodded. 'Like adding up on a calculator rather than your fingers.'

'Yes,' he agreed. 'It's the difference between illuminating a room with a candle and a stadium with a floodlight.'

I didn't understand anything about the physics, or the maths, of what he was saying. But the implications were obvious. 'So, cracking the ten-digit password?'

'With a quantum computer? Instantaneous,' he grinned.

'And they exist, these computers?'

He snorted and gulped down the last of his tea.

'No way! That's just sci-fi. Last month IBM revealed a working fifty-qubit quantum computer. But get this: it can only maintain its quantum state for ninety *micro*seconds. There are loads of issues to resolve. Decoherence, scalability, noise . . .'

I held my hand up to stop him.

'The main issue to resolve right now, Baaz, is that I have literally no idea what any of those things mean, OK?'

'OK.'

'So, let's keep it simple. If anyone *could* resolve those issues and build a working machine . . .'

'If anyone could demonstrate quantum supremacy, and build a proper machine – with, say, ten thousand qubits?'

'They'd break all known cryptography. Right?' Confusing as it was, I felt I was at least beginning to understand the basics.

'Wrong. They'd break *most* known cryptography. Some algorithms would be resistant, though. But if you could solve the dihedral hidden subgroup problem, you could use quantum to break lattice-based cryptosystems.'

'That's not Punjabi, Baaz.' I looked at my passport on the table. 'It's not even Greek to me. Give it to me in simple terms.' I rolled my shoulders. 'Please.'

'Well,' he said, scratching his head, 'with the right algorithm, you could say that quantum isn't *the* bomb – it's *all* the bombs. Imagine. You could empty every bank account everywhere in the world; crack all security, access anything online, anywhere, anytime. You'd have unrestricted access to everything – from the thermostat on the fridge to the thermonuclear arsenal.'

'Just like that? With one machine?'

'Yes. With one machine that doesn't exist and an algorithm that hasn't been developed. A computer is just hardware. It won't work without software. Like buying a PC without installing an operating system. You know, like Windows. Useless.'

'So that's what you're doing? Writing an algorithm for a computer that doesn't exist?'

He nodded again.

'I get a grant, too. Absolute con job.'

I smiled. But rather than smiling back, Baaz suddenly looked serious again.

'Max,' he said, lowering his voice. 'I have a question for you, too.' He paused. 'Don't take this the wrong way . . . but . . . er, it's just that you've been accused of murder and there's a gun on my table and a bunch of commandos are after us and, well . . .'

'It's OK. Fire away.'

'Who the fuck *are* you?'

I finished my tea, too, and drew breath. Under normal circumstances I wouldn't tell him – or anyone – anything at all. Nothing true, anyway. But these were not normal circumstances.

'I work for the British government,' I told him. 'Or at least, I think I still do. I was sent to do a job. It went wrong. And now, apparently, the world and his wife are after me.'

'And "the world" is the Russians and "the wife" is your boss?'

For a twenty-something-year-old kid, he was remarkably perceptive. I pursed my lips and stared at him.

'And?' he asked.

'And that's pretty much it.'

'No,' said Baaz, excitement building in his voice, 'I meant *why* are they after you?'

'Good fucking question, Baaz. Good fucking question. I don't know why.' The billion dollars, the bad deal with Lukov . . . those were things definitely not to share. 'Actually,' I said, having an immediate half-change of heart, 'that's not completely true.'

I reached over and plucked the soggy hundred-dollar bill off the table and laid it out in front of him. Baaz gestured to me for permission. I nodded and he picked it up.

'That is why,' I continued. '*Part* of why. The note. It's special. It's from a cache of notes the bad guys have; and it's the only one we have. *I* have. A lot of people have died because of it. You and me both, too, nearly.'

'So we're the good guys, then?' Baaz was grinning. He was refreshingly straightforward.

'Yes, Baaz,' I reassured him. 'We're the good guys. Scout's honour. But it's more than that. This note is valuable in some way that I don't really understand.' He turned the bill over.

'What does it say?' he asked.

'*Arkhangel*. It means "Archangel" in English. Like St Michael, you know?'

'I know as much about archangels,' he said, 'as you do about Guru Gobind Singh.'

'Fair play,' I admitted. 'But Arkhangel is also the name of a village in Russia.'

'I see.'

'No, you don't. It's not just any village. It's the village where my mother was born.'

He scrutinized the bill up close.

'Oh my God,' he exclaimed, 'I don't *believe* it!'

His shining eyes darted between Benjamin Franklin's gaze and mine. It was as if a Eureka moment had lit him up from the inside. My heart leapt. The thought half formed that maybe he'd seen, understood, something I'd missed, that he understood what the note meant.

'What?' I asked. 'What is it?'

'This whole thing,' he said, fizzing with excitement, 'is so *totally* James Bond.'

My shoulders slumped. 'All right then, Q. Tell me this. All this kit you have for trading . . .'

'And studying,' he said quickly.

'And studying. Can you use it to make calls, too? Encrypted calls.'

'Of course.' I raised my eyebrows. 'The actual call can't be hacked. Not at all. Even if someone captured the data stream, it would be useless to them. Unless the person you want to call has malware on their system that records the audio of the call separately from the call itself, it's completely safe.'

'And how likely is that?'

'It entirely depends,' he said, 'on who you want to call.'

It was a chance I was willing to take.

'OK then,' I said. 'Set it up while I go to the bathroom.' I stood up and retrieved the banknote, feeling the tear in my thigh again. 'When you need a lifeline, there's only one thing to do.'

'What's that?' he asked, clearing away the breakfast things.

'Phone a friend.'

19

'*Hal-lo?*'

'Ezra?' The line sounded dead. Not even a hiss. It was the fifth time I'd tried his number. I adjusted the headset. 'Ezra, it's Max.' There was a long pause. 'Max McLean,' I added, uncertain how solid the connection was.

The call from Paris to Sierra Leone had been relayed through three separate servers – all of which had been changed for each new attempt to get through. Then the line came alive with what sounded like the fumbling of a hands-free set being connected.

'Good to hear from you, my friend. I thought maybe you were dead.'

I breathed out a sigh of relief. 'Almost,' I said. 'But not quite.'

'*Al tid'ag,* there's plenty of time yet.'

Ezra Black's voice was unmistakable. He peppered his English with Hebrew, and his English accent sounded at times more French than Israeli. But when any Israeli told me not to worry, I wondered immediately what was wrong. There was another awkward pause.

'So, what's up, buddy?' he continued. 'Did you find my plane yet, or what?'

'Oh, come on man, you were paid for that.' Baaz looked at me, uncomprehending. He could only hear one half of our conversation. 'Paid more than it was worth, too. A *lot* more.'

At the other end of the line, the faintest suggestion of laughter – or the closest Ezra got to it.

'OK, but I liked *that* plane.'

'Seriously, Ezra. I'm in shit. I need a favour.'

'OK.' The lightness in his voice evaporated immediately. 'Tell me what you need, then. *Seriously.*' He rolled the *r* and protracted the *ou* in such a way that, if I didn't know better, I'd have guessed he was from the Jura, not Jerusalem. 'One day you can do something for me, eh?'

I didn't doubt that he was serious about that, either. Ezra ran a private security company in Sierra Leone, headquartered in the capital Freetown. And although he'd been out of the Israel Defence Forces for nearly two decades, his paramilitary police training operation in West Africa was still very much bankrolled by the Israelis. The last favour he'd done me had nearly killed me. Baaz set down more tea and switched on the table lamp. It was overcast outside and half-dark indoors. The blinds were still drawn.

'I'm in France. There's an Interpol Red Notice on me and . . .'

'Interpol?' Ezra cut me off. 'What do those *tembelim* want with you?'

'It's a long story.'

'It always is, eh?'

'The Russians are after me. Possibly the Brits, too. And the Yanks. Not even Grumpy Jock can help. So, I came to see Lukov, but . . .'

'Lukov?' he spat down the phone. 'That *aluka*? I swear to you one day I will kill him. No, I won't kill him. I'll just fuck him up. Death is too good for that *ben zona*!'

'You're too late,' I said. 'The leech bled to death yesterday while we were having a drink. In Paris. In public. Sniper. Pro job. Tricky headshot. Russians, most likely. Or the Brits. Or, you know, literally *anyone*.'

'*Ken*, or one of his *kalat da'at* women.' Ezra cleared his throat. 'But that is serious, my friend. That piece of shit was untouchable.' He thought for a moment. 'You are sure,' he added, 'the bullet was meant for him, and not you?'

'No,' I said truthfully, 'I'm not.'

'So. This favour. I sense it's going to be a good one.'

He was right about that.

'I need to get out of France and into Israel on a hot Greek passport.'

'You should work for the Mossad, my friend. It would be so much nicer. They give you proper passports. And they don't shoot their own operators, eh?'

'Eh.'

'From the Israeli side it's OK. Send me a picture of the passport. Say nothing to no one. Just show them your passport. That's it. *Barur?*'

I told him it was crystal clear.

The four-and-a-half-hour flight, he said – a private charter from Paris to Tel Aviv – would take twenty-four hours and cost sixty thousand US dollars to arrange, including ground transportation. He would send a car to me in Paris tomorrow that would take me straight to the aircraft at Le Bourget – a business airfield seventeen klicks north-east of where I was holed up. As with most other private flights, the paperwork would be handled prior to boarding. At Ben Gurion I would be met airside by Ezra's man – who would navigate Israeli immigration for me, and take me to a hotel.

'But, Max,' he cautioned me, 'about the French, I can do nothing.'

In the background I could hear the sounds of Ezra's world breaking into the call — hard, high cricket-song and the chatter of monkeys. It brought back memories of the heat, the unceasing sweat, the smell of exhaust fumes and rotting vegetation. I imagined Ezra's eyes, unreadable beneath heavy, drooping lids.

'It's very, very unlikely the French will interfere,' he went on. 'It's a private place, Le Bourget. Only businessmen and air shows. They never check flights like this. Never, never. But if this Interpol *shtut* blows up and they *do*, then you'd better pray that Bulgarian fuck did his job with that passport, my friend. It's a risk you take. About this I have to be absolutely clear.'

'Got it.'

'Over and out, buddy.'

I signalled to Baaz and he cut the connection.

'Who was that?' he asked.

'Let's just say it was a friend of mine. He helped me out on a job last year. He's going to send a plane. Tomorrow. I need to message him with a pick-up point.'

'A plane? What, you mean like a private jet?' he said excitedly. 'He's going to send a private jet for us?' As soon as he'd said it, he regretted it, and he looked down, blushing.

'No, Baaz. He's sending a private jet for *me*.'

'But . . .' He looked up, crestfallen, through the black wells of his eyes. 'But we're in this together, right? You helped me and I helped you.' He looked at the screens, and around the room. '*Am* helping you. Max and Baaz. Sounds good, doesn't it?'

'No, Baaz. It doesn't. I know everything feels OK now, safe and warm up here — no one fucking with us, no one trying to kick the door in. No one trying to kill us. Last night already seems like a crazy dream, right? A great story to tell your mates about one day.'

His shoulders sagged again. There was something about him I couldn't put my finger on. It was the same feeling I'd had in the catacombs, something not quite right about him. His responses weren't . . . *normal*. No one rational survives a firefight only to turn around once it's over and beg to get stuck in again – no one except the Paras and the legally sane psychos that swelled the ranks of Special Forces. And he was neither a red beret nor a psychopath, of that much I was sure.

'But it's not some story,' I continued. 'It's really fucking serious. We got out of those tunnels by the skin of our teeth. Believe me, I've been in the shit before. Deep in it. But no matter how bad it gets, it can always get worse.'

My voice had got louder, imploring him to listen. But I wasn't telling him anything he didn't know. Young men infected with romantic notions about adventure can do wildly dangerous things. I knew. I'd been one myself. We were both standing up now. He looked away, struggling to find the words he wanted.

'I don't want to tell my mates,' he said quietly, staring first at the ceiling and then at the floor. 'I don't have any mates to tell, anyway. I am twenty-two years old. My father is in prison in Chandigarh, and my mother never leaves the house – which is worse than being in bloody prison. My cousins think I'm a freak because I can do *maths*, and my brothers think I'm . . .' he summoned the word with difficulty, 'a *traitor* because I'm not interested in any of their nationalist Khalistan nonsense. I'm supposed to be doing this bloody master's degree, but my professor is *actually* retarded, I can hardly speak enough French to order a meal, never mind get laid, and the only person I've had to stay is a bloody Irish spook, or whatever the hell you are.'

'OK,' I said. It was hard not to smile. 'You've been very brave, and I'm very grateful, but . . .'

'But I thought we were friends,' he cut in. The fingers on both his hands were drumming the air now, as if typing reams of unseen digits on an invisible keyboard. 'We are friends, aren't we?'

'Yes,' I said. 'We are. And friends look out for each other, right?'

'Right.'

'We looked out for each other in the tunnels. And you've looked after me up here. But I can't look out for you where I'm going . . . Man, I don't even *know* where I'm going, never mind what I'm going to do when I get there. But you have to get away. Lie low, have a holiday. Right now, no one knows you're involved in any of this. And believe me, that's a really, *really* good thing.'

'How much is it?' he said, still refusing to look me in the eye. Even though we were standing a foot apart, I wasn't sure he'd heard a word I'd said.

'How much is what?'

'The jet. How much does it cost? Expensive, I bet.'

'Yes. It's expensive. Where are you going with this?'

'How much? Ten thousand dollars? Twenty?'

'Sixty,' I admitted. 'It will cost sixty grand.'

Under the circumstances that was both exorbitant – I had no way of getting the fare that didn't involve robbery – and supremely reasonable: how much is anyone prepared to pay for their freedom? In my case, right then, right there, the answer was, *Everything.*

'OK. So, Mr Max, how are you going to pay your Israeli

friend sixty thousand dollars when you have . . .' he glanced at the money spread out on the table, '2,245 euros, and, ah, 100 dollars?' He looked me straight in the eye then. 'Tricky, *huna*?'

He bent down and leaned across me and opened a secure web browser on one of the laptops between us. Left-handed, he typed in a few strokes and turned the screen towards me, angling it back so I could read it standing up. It was an Ethereum cryptocurrency trading account. His holdings showed as 1,225.5 coins.

'And?'

'And I can pay for your flight. Our flight.'

I felt my estimation of his mental stability slipping. I needed to appease him. Carefully. As much as he could be a risk to himself, his fantasies posed a threat to me, too. But I also needed to find a way of financing the flight. Ezra wouldn't press me for the money, but eventually the debt would have to be settled. And this time I couldn't rely on Her Majesty's Government to pick up the tab.

'But,' I said, pointing at the screen, 'you only have twelve hundred coins.' He grinned. And then it dawned on me. 'Baaz . . . how many dollars are there to one of these Ethereum coins?'

'Today, 1,389 dollars and 18 cents. Yesterday, 1,377 dollars and 72 cents.' He closed the browser. 'While we were sleeping, I made 14,044 dollars and 23 cents.'

'What? But . . . twelve hundred and . . .' I struggled with the multiplication.

'OK, 1,225.5 coins are worth 1,702,440 US dollars and 9 cents.' I opened my mouth, goldfish-like, but Baaz ploughed on. 'On the second of January last year I invested 10,000 dollars in Ether. One Ether was worth 8 dollars and 16 cents then.'

'I . . . I don't know where to begin. I mean, for a start, where on earth did you get 10,000 dollars from?'

'From my auntie. "Living expenses", *huna*?'

'Wow, that's . . .' I started to laugh. 'That's crazy.' Baaz started to laugh, too. 'You're a millionaire. And your auntie . . . she has no idea, does she?'

'No,' he said, shaking his head, grinning from ear to ear. 'I think today would be a good day to cash in, don't you?'

'Yeah,' I said. 'I think it would.'

The Challenger 300 banked hard to the south-east. The dark lines of the boulevards cut the city into what looked like slabs of stone, paving the Île-de-France white in the weak morning sun. The little streets I'd raced along two days before merged into a web of fine black lines between them, knitting the capital together. Of the underworld that stretched out south of the Seine, there was no sign: no ripple in the lanes and highways, no hint of what lay beneath. Not even from that unique perspective hundreds of feet above the ground, it seemed, could the whole of the city be seen. The big, bright, imperial capital was as lost to the catacombs as the dead they concealed were lost to the world above.

But as we climbed higher and the buildings shrank, the Arc de Triomphe began to look like the sepulchres in Montparnasse, the Champs-Élysées and the wheel of the avenues spinning away from it like walkways for the curious and the bereaved to meander among the graves. The picture warped and juddered in the slipstream, and for a moment it looked as if the city was consuming itself in the haze. And then a blanket of grey spread beneath the winking green eye of the starboard wingtip and Paris was buried under the clouds.

I adjusted the Grach in the waistband of my jeans and

stretched out in the beige leather seat. The flight attendant who'd brought me a double Johnnie Walker Black before take-off returned with an ashtray. I unwrapped the packet of Gauloises I'd lifted from Lukov's corpse and lit the tobacco. The smoke was cool and soothing and I dragged it down deep into my lungs, holding it there for a long moment before exhaling and blurring the cabin with a blue-grey fog. That was the great thing about private jets: no security, and no *no-smoking* signs.

The other seven seats were empty. It took a day and a night of reasoning and bargaining, but in the end Baaz saw sense. Or at least he said he saw sense. At first I reminded him that Indians couldn't travel to Israel without a visa: a plausible argument, until he produced a British passport. Then I put the frighteners on: to which his only response was to make more tea. In the end I tried the oldest trick in the espionage handbook: flattery. I convinced him that he was more use to 'the operation' in Paris than he was in Tel Aviv – a secret, secure comms base that I could call on if the going got rough. What he got from me was the promise of teamwork – in spirit, if not in person. He sulked for a while, and then grudgingly accepted the wisdom of it. I knew the sting of disappointment would fade faster than that of a 9mm round.

What he didn't get was a guaranteed repayment plan. But like he said himself, while I waited for Ezra to send the car to the Best Western hotel at the southern end of Rue du Texel, 'It's all just Monopoly money, anyway.' He converted his 'winnings' – as he called them – into fiat: actual dollars, in an actual, numbered Swiss account, which he could spend as he liked. I asked him if a withdrawal could give away his identity to anyone inclined to investigate. He drummed the fingertips of his left and right hands together, frenetically. It wasn't *where* you banked that compromised your anonymity, he said, so much as where you were *from*.

'If you're American and you bank in Zurich,' he summed up, 'you're fucked. If you're Indian, you're sound.'

I was banking on a long shot: that when I found Rachel, she would believe me; believe *in* me. The thread that connected us as kids had unravelled across a lifetime of secrets and lies. I hoped it had not yet snapped. When I stripped away the uncertainties of the lethal money-go-round, all my mission amounted to was convincing Rachel that I hadn't killed Doc – and that whoever had might be after her next. At best, I was one day ahead of an enemy as tangible as a ghost.

I stubbed out the cigarette and closed my eyes and tried to calculate the size of the void in my knowledge that yawned in front of me. Colonel Ellard had trained us to measure the dimensions of the things we didn't know with reconnaissance and intelligence – narrowing the parameters of any operation as far as we could, remembering always that spooks could set you up and your eyes could deceive. But however much he tried to make us soldiers, he tried harder to make us gamblers – to accept that we would not, *could* not, ever know everything. 'In the end,' he told us, 'you will always roll the dice.' And no one – but no one – knew when they would throw a seven.

I surrendered to the rhythm of the engines and the Scotch worked its magic. I closed my eyes and felt myself slipping into sleep. But the darkness was confounded by a thousand fragments of wars gone by; of Frank leaving Doherty's pub in Ballina; and of my mother, sinking, as the faintest trace of a smile played about her lips.

As I went under, the Challenger reached cruising altitude, steady on a course set first towards the Alps, then over the heads of the bankers handling Baaz's profits – and then beyond, across the Balkans and the Aegean, above the eastern Mediterranean and onwards, until its tyres left a little rubber on the landing strip of the Promised Land.

20

The flight landed at half-past three in the afternoon, local time. Ezra's man was waiting for me airside: a security statue in dark glasses, suited and booted, arms folded across a barrel chest, standing stock-still on the apron. He took my passport, led me through security and drove me to the Hilton – a modern concrete block that loomed above the seafront, forty-five minutes' walk south-west of the main university campus. I checked in, went briefly up to the room – a well-appointed business box on the fifth floor paid for by Ezra's company – unmade the bed, dropped a towel on the bathroom floor and left immediately, hanging the *Do Not Disturb* sign on the door handle.

Then I walked north along the promenade – a narrow walkway sandwiched between the reddening sea and the winter-shabby dun of Independence Park. At least I knew my way around. I'd been in and out of Tel Aviv a dozen times or more over the last decade. I liked being there, the feeling that anything might happen – and that, when it did, it was never quite as advertised. It was an edgy but oddly relaxing place – foreign in almost every respect and yet, somehow, it always reminded me of Dublin: great bars and pretty girls and every shade of weapons-grade nutter on God's green earth.

I stopped for a moment and looked out across Metsitsim Beach. The sun was sinking like a fireship, setting the pale blue sky ablaze, lengthening the shadows of a gaggle of children jostling past me. A couple of surfers in wetsuits dragged themselves out of the waves and on to the darkening sand. It was an unseasonably warm afternoon, nearly twenty degrees; after the steel-grey cold of northern Europe it was good to feel the heat of the sun before it slid completely beneath the horizon.

Seventeen hundred.

I pressed on, and after a few minutes arrived at The Lemon Tree – a boutique four-star joint set back slightly from the sea, between the beach and the old port area. I paid for three nights in cash, in advance, and told the desk clerk I was not, under any circumstances, to receive visitors. Once in the room I checked the door and window locks – none of which would have stopped even the most inept of housebreakers – and plucked a sanitary bag from the dispenser in the bathroom. I untucked the Grach from the back of my jeans, dropped the magazine, ejected the round in the breech and checked and rechecked the mechanism. Thanks to a sticky can of 3-en-Un machine oil under Baaz's kitchen sink, the slide was smooth, the metalwork gleaming.

The Grach MP-443 was a good pistol – reliable and rugged enough to withstand the Russian military's most extreme postings. It wouldn't stand up to a SIG on the fifty-metre range. But I wasn't planning on target shooting. I wasn't planning on doing *any* shooting. I put the Grach's magazine back on, chambered a round and reset the hammer. Then I put the pistol into the sanitary bag, which I tied shut. I removed the top of the lavatory cistern and dropped the plastic-wrapped bundle into the water reservoir.

Walking around Tel Aviv with an unlicensed pistol was asking for trouble. Shopping centres, cafés, bars – not to mention official buildings – could all be protected by metal detectors. Avoiding them would hamstring my movements more than they were already. Bribery wouldn't help, either. The private security guards who operated the scanners and bag searches had skin and not just salary in the game: the first to get hit in an attack, they were the last people in whose interest it was not to do a thorough job. If I was found with a weapon and no licence I would be in a world of pain. Getting out of Paris after a firefight would look like a walk in the Champ de Mars compared to trying to flee Israel. I'd narrowly survived the attentions of the French Foreign Legion. I fancied my chances with the Israel Defence Forces even less.

Maintaining a low profile was a priority. I had no idea how widely circulated my photograph had been at an official level, or if I was publicly associated, visually, with the ambush in La Fée Verte. There was, though, one thing to take comfort from: unlike in Paris and London, CCTV coverage in Tel Aviv was at best patchy. Before I'd left France, Baaz had gone on his own special mission to replace my wardrobe. The ripped black kit I'd assembled before the dive into the tunnels had been replaced with new black jeans, black sneakers and a short black leather jacket. Baaz liked black. I liked Baaz.

I stuck my arm out, and hailed a cab to the university.

'Ken, ma bishvilkha?'

'*Shalom*,' I replied, trying not to sound annoyed. I'd been standing in the doorway, clearing my throat and tapping my foot, while the woman who I assumed was the faculty secretary finished a convoluted and – as far as my shaky Hebrew could make out – entirely personal phone call. 'I'm here to see Professor Levy.'

'Rachel?' I nodded. 'She isn't . . .' She stopped herself abruptly and sized me up. 'What is your name, please?' She spoke in careful American-accented English.

'Lazarus,' I replied. 'John Lazarus.' She looked at me, waiting for me to continue. 'From MIT,' I added – as if that explained everything. She pursed her lips and raised her finely plucked eyebrows.

'And did you, *do* you, have an appointment, Mr . . .'

'Doctor,' I corrected her.

'. . . *Doctor* Lazarus?'

'Yes,' I lied. 'I do.' I checked my watch ostentatiously. 'In five minutes, to be precise.' I gave her a quick smile. It wasn't reciprocated.

'I see.' She pivoted in her office chair, turning her back fully on the computer screen she'd been facing when I walked in. 'There is nothing in her diary,' she said. 'And your appointment is here, in the faculty?'

'Yes,' I said. 'My assistant called last week. I leave for Boston tomorrow.'

She turned around again and looked at me closely, as if making her mind up about something.

'Please wait.'

I didn't doubt she meant it. I looked around and saw an empty chair behind the door. I sat down. The secretary returned to her screen and tapped away at the keyboard before lifting the receiver on the office phone next to her. She spoke quickly, quietly, and the only words I could make out with any certainty were my assumed name and 'Rachel Levy'.

The Kolymsky School of Computer Sciences – part of the Faculty of Exact Sciences – was based in a low-rise four-storey building at the heart of the university campus.

It was the kind of place that should have inspired reverence and hushed tones, awe at the seemingly impossible problems being solved behind closed doors. All it inspired in me was an uncomfortable mixture of irritation and nervous expectation.

A young man stuck his head around the door, looked first at me and then at the secretary – who was deep in an interminable phone conversation that seemed mostly about *shakshouka*, and how not to cook it. He went to speak and then thought better of it, smiling at me conspiratorially as he backed out into the corridor. A student, most likely. I guessed she had cultivated a reputation that kept all but the most persistent enquirers at bay.

I rolled my shoulders, sat up straight and looked around the office, at the file-stacked shelves and coffee-cup laden filing cabinet and at the sheets of names and dates and events pinned to the walls. A photograph of the Red Sea hung in a cheap gilt frame above the secretary's desk; next to it a clock that I tried hard not to stare at. It didn't look like it from where I was sitting, but the Kolymsky School of Computer Sciences was one of the best in the world – or so Baaz had told me. How or why Rachel had ended up there, I had no idea: in the years since I'd lost sight of her, I'd never once looked her up. Where she was, what she was doing, who she'd become – they were possibilities my imagination rarely got to grips with.

In fact, until recently, I hadn't even thought of her that often. The memory of her – *any* memory of her – was so powerful, so visceral, that replaying the scenes we'd lived out gave me a physical jolt. More than one cup of coffee had been spilled when a stray thought of her tripped me up, unawares. But memory is an unreliable guide to the past. Ask any group of eyewitnesses to an event exactly what they saw and you're likely to have as many different answers as people you interrogate. My mother had told me once that when memories are remembered, they are delicate, fragile, vulnerable to being rewritten.

'Every recollection could be a fabrication, Max,' I could hear my mother say, not long after my father had said goodbye, taking off on his latest trip to Africa. 'Be careful you don't just end up with fantasies.'

A fortnight later they were both dead.

I screwed up my eyes at the thought of the lake water and concentrated instead on what Baaz had found out online in a series of encrypted internet searches – which wasn't much. The Kolymsky School of Computer Sciences was outstanding, but its supposed crowning glory – the Azriel Jacobs fellowship – barely featured online. Professor Rachel Levy was billed as a forty-four-year-old genius who, as Baaz explained with palpable excitement, had apparently spent her entire career wrestling with something called 'NP-complete decision problems in computational complexity theory'.

I'd nodded along with him, in utter ignorance, trying to keep my ad hoc researcher from going down an information technology rabbit hole. The only sums I was any good at were those that helped me acquire and kill targets. I used mathematics to judge range and angle; but the wisdom of the shot? There was no algorithm that could work that out for you. Autonomous weapons systems could tell you when to open fire, but not how to live with yourself once you had. For now, at least, someone always had to pull the trigger or press the button – and computers don't have nightmares about playing God.

Despite international plaudits it looked like Rachel had

published nothing in the four years she'd been at the university; she was camera-shy to the point of scopophobia and was, apparently, unmarried – a fact that did not pass unnoticed by Baaz. It took an effort of will to look at her faculty photograph – a low-resolution three-quarters-profile headshot – which was the only close-up image of her face we'd turned up. I'd last seen her a few days after her eighteenth birthday. She was in hospital, brought back from the brink first by me and then by Doc. The Rachel of my failing memory bore little resemblance to the confident professional staring out from that computer screen in Paris. But it was her for sure: olive skin, green eyes and a shock of black hair, shot through now with streaks of silver. I'd swallowed hard and realized my throat was dry.

'*You*,' Baaz had asked me in disbelief at the end of our joint investigations, 'know *her*?' I shrugged, feigning disinterest. 'But . . . she's brilliant. *And* she's hot.'

I opened my eyes again to find the faculty secretary standing over me. She was more smoking angry than smoking hot.

'*Koma revi'it, delet shlishit miyamin*,' she said. I frowned and she repeated tersely in English the directions to Rachel's office as she sat down again. I stood and thanked her, wincing as the wound in my shoulder flared up. I found the stairs she'd told me to take and climbed them slowly to the fourth floor, where the last flight emerged midway along a window-lined corridor. The sunset had faded but it wasn't dark yet. The sky was sapphire blue, punctured by white pinpricks of the brightest stars.

Despite Colonel Ellard's warnings to the contrary, I had done no recce, had precious little information and no means of processing what I did know into actionable intelligence. Ordinarily I wouldn't have gone anywhere near Rachel's office without first establishing a fireproof pattern of life. But the longer I waited, the more likely I was to be compromised. If I could be found in the Paris catacombs, I could be found anywhere. And so could she. An encrypted phone call made by Baaz from Paris to the university told me the one thing I needed to know: that she was in Tel Aviv. Any other enquiry risked tripping a wire, the consequences of which I could no more predict than I could control.

I turned right, counted three doors along and stopped. The cedar panelling was so highly polished that I could see my own face staring back at me around Rachel's name plaque.

It wasn't simply convincing her I hadn't murdered Doc that mattered to me. I needed to persuade her I could keep her safe – that she needed to be kept safe. But I knew now they weren't the only reasons I'd risked everything to be there. The shock of what I was about to do cleared my mind. For the first time I accepted what it meant to stand on the threshold of the last person on earth who could join my past to my present. I had come to her, not to plead my innocence, but to accept my guilt. When she had most needed me, I'd run away. Nearly three decades, a lifetime later, I'd come back to ask for absolution – not just for that act of abandonment but for all that I had become in its wake.

I took a deep breath and knocked, but there was no reply. I twisted the handle, pushed at the open door and crossed the Rubicon.

21

'Doctor Lazarus, I presume.'

I stepped fully into the office before I saw her. She sat facing away from me in a wide-backed chair behind a desk by the window, staring out over the city. Glossy black hair crested the headrest. A banker's lamp next to her laptop pooled light between us, the glare plunging the corners of the room into deep shadow. I held my breath, clung on to my words. Her accent was pure Israeli. No hint of Irish remained.

She spun the chair on its axis and faced the room. But her features were lost in the gloom above the green glass of the little lamp. It was only as I went to speak that I realized I had no idea what to say – and hadn't, for years. My throat closed around her name and there was silence between us. I let my hands hang by my sides and peered into the darkness, as if I might find there the words I was looking for.

But there is nothing to say to someone who thinks they are about to confront the man who murdered their father.

She leaned forward. My heart leapt in my chest. Her face suddenly illuminated: a disembodied, floating white mask. Lit from below, her cheekbones stood out as sharp as razors. And although her eyes were lost in shadow, I could see clearly enough to know, even after all these years, that I was not staring into the face of the girl I'd fallen in love with. I was looking into the eyes of a stranger.

But it wasn't simply that I didn't recognize her.

It wasn't *her* at all.

'Or should I call you "Max McLean"?' My right hand moved towards where the pistol would have sat in my belt. Her lips lifted at their corners. 'You are looking for this?'

She spoke clearly, slowly, and produced a white plastic bag as she did so – placing it on the desk in front of her with a metallic thud. She'd recovered the Grach from the cistern in the hotel bathroom.

The door clicked shut behind me. I turned my head. The woman I'd assumed was the faculty secretary had followed me into the room. She gripped a Glock 19 with both hands and held it close into her body, arms bent at the elbow – relaxed, but ready. She was too far away for me to take her down. I kept my hands still and visible, fingers spread.

'You can call me whatever you like,' I said, trying to suppress a rising anger. I felt foolish. Embarrassed. 'Seems you've got all the cards, anyway.'

'Far from it,' she replied. 'Take a seat.' I stayed where I was, trying and failing to size her up in the harsh light of the lamp. 'Please,' she said, motioning towards a leather chair to one side of the desk. 'If we wanted you dead . . .' she paused, as if trying to remember the right words, 'you would already be buried in Père Lachaise. *Ken?*'

'So, you're a friend of Lukov's?'

'*Lo,*' she laughed. '*Lo, lo, lo.* Lukov had no friends. Except maybe you. Please. Sit.'

That little fucker, I thought.

I relented and walked to the desk, drew the chair back and sat down, racking my brains to remember what – *exactly* what – I'd told him. *Never say anything, to anyone.* There were rules for a reason. Not that anyone seemed interested in playing by them any longer. The woman and I sat an arm's length apart, facing each other. Next to what I'd assumed was my

Grach she placed an open pack of Marlboros and a new book of matches.

'Help yourself.'

'To which?'

'As you like.'

I shook a smoke out of the pack and lit it. The woman did the same, reclining in her chair as she did so, vanishing back into the darkness. Then the sulphur flared and her face quickened in the void behind the lamplight, juddering for a moment.

The sky was black now. Beyond the windows Tel Aviv had flickered to life one street lamp at a time. The tip of her cigarette flitted across the city skyline like an orange firefly. I blew a thin cloud of smoke into the emptiness of Rachel's office. With the exception of a television screen on one wall and an oil painting of a chestnut hunter standing alone in a field, the room was almost completely bare. The Marlboro tasted good – familiar, reassuring. I smiled at the woman's shadow.

'You haven't killed me. And you haven't kidnapped me. And I don't think you're going to. But your woman there doesn't look like she's keen on me leaving, either.' I looked over my shoulder again. The guard had stepped to one side so that her superior was out of her line of fire. The Glock pointed towards me. 'So, what do you want with me? Am I under arrest, or what?'

'No, no. Not at all.' She leaned in again so I could see her face, spreading her arms as she did so as if to encompass our situation. 'In fact, this is quite, uh, the *opposite* of that. You are a free man.' She nodded towards the operator standing guard. '*Khaki ba'hutz*.'

I heard the door open and close behind me as she left the room. I guessed they wanted to show they trusted me. Or at least make me feel trusted. But I also guessed they'd unloaded the Grach. I would have.

'Better?'

'Yeah. Thanks.' I double-checked to make sure no one else had entered the room. 'I mean, this is all very interesting, but . . .'

'You came for Rachel?' she cut across me.

'Uh-huh.' I took another drag on the Marlboro.

'You aren't the only one. She is very popular, the professor. Surprisingly so.'

'I see,' I said. And this time I thought I did. 'Russian, by any chance?' She nodded. 'Small guy, light on his feet,' I added, 'leather shoes, tan portmanteau?' She nodded again. 'Fancies himself a doctor?'

'He *is* a doctor,' she replied. 'At least, he trained as one. Doctor Leonid Avilov. These days he is more interested in taking life than he is in saving it.'

'Well, he was doing his damnedest to keep me alive, that's for sure. What is he? *Bratva*? FSB?' I thought about the options. You never knew with the Russians. 'Both?'

She cleared her throat. 'He's GRU. Sixth Directorate, specializing in cryptography. His background is classic ex-KGB. He joined military intelligence in 2016, after GRU Director Sergun, uh, *died* in Lebanon. He's been in and out of Israel half a dozen times since. Apart from minor details, that is all we know.'

Or, I thought, *all you're going to admit to knowing.* 'Well that explains why he can't shoot straight, anyway.' I tilted my head and dragged on the cigarette. 'He's a bloody desk jockey.'

'So was Adolf Eichmann,' she said. 'Never underestimate, how do you call them, a "pen-pusher"?'

'Quite. Well, did Avilov find her? Rachel, I mean.'

'No. He was too late.' She rolled her cigarette butt between her thumb and forefinger, crushing it slightly. 'And so were we. Rachel has gone missing, Mr McLean. She was last seen more than two weeks ago. Just before the end of December. Avilov arrived the day *after* the last confirmed sighting of her in Israel.' Perhaps I looked incredulous, or maybe she doubted her English. Either way she added, 'She is not here, Mr McLean', just to make sure I understood her loud and clear. 'If she has left Israel – which is not certain – then she must have done so on a forged passport.' She weighed up the probability: 'Which we think is possible.'

'OK,' I said, 'but first things first.' I looked around the room. As far as I could tell we were alone, though I assumed every word was being listened to elsewhere. 'Who's "we", exactly?'

'My name is Talia,' she said. 'I'm with the Shabak.' She smoked her cigarette.

'Internal security. *Of course.* I bet you have a badge, too, that says, *Trust me, I'm a secret agent*, right?'

'Right.' She took a cell phone out of her jacket pocket and tapped in a string of digits. I heard the phone click at the other end as the call connected.

'*Hal-lo? Ken, rega.*'

She handed me the phone. I pressed it to my ear, and listened.

'Hi, buddy.' It was Ezra. Clear as a bell.

'Seriously?'

'Trust me. This lady will keep you alive. She's on the side of the angels.'

'Really?'

'*Really.* And why are you messing around with that bullshit Grach, eh? Ask her for something proper. That pistol's gonna get you fucked up.' He pronounced 'bullshit' *bool-sheet* which made him sound simultaneously sinister and slightly absurd. It was no coincidence he got on with the Glaswegian Jack Nazzar so well. Everything each of them said sounded like either a joke or a threat. I pitied the fool who couldn't work out which.

'OK,' I said. 'Thanks. I'll bear that in mind.'

'*Tov.* I have another surprise for you as well. It's a really good one. I promise you'll like it.'

'Oh . . . What's that?'

'You'll find out. Take care, buddy.'

The line went dead. I handed the phone back to my interlocutor.

'How exactly did Rachel go missing?'

'She vanished.' Talia took the phone from me and our fingers touched briefly. '*Exactly.*'

'But I called the faculty,' I said, 'and there was a newspaper report. She was quoted by *Haaretz* three days ago.' As soon as I'd said it, I realized how naive I sounded. Her face remained impassive. 'Ah,' the penny dropped. 'That was you, wasn't it?' She shrugged her shoulders. 'I'm guessing that was an Israeli in Paris, too. He cut quite a dash in that police uniform. I'm sorry about that.'

'If you say so.'

'Or maybe Mossad went for the AKs and keffiyehs, so you could blame it on your neighbours?'

'What the other departments do,' she said, tilting her head, 'or who they get to do it, is their affair.'

We sat in silence – breathing in the grey smoke, wondering if, when, to breathe out secrets. I counted a full minute and stubbed out the Marlboro in the heavy glass ashtray between us.

'Well, this is awkward.'

'But forgivable. You would not be the first operator to get in trouble for, uh, *personal* reasons. It happens.'

'Oh, no,' I said. 'It's not awkward for *me*. Not at all. Unfortunate, maybe. But not awkward.' I drew another cigarette from the pack. 'For you, though, this is a Grade A disaster.' I tore another match free of the little booklet, folded the yellow cover back on itself, pinched the matchhead between the cardboard and the striker and withdrew it smartly. It flared at my fingertips. 'A top Israeli scientist goes missing. Her father is assassinated. And the Shabak, the "Invisible Shield", the defender of the nation, is reduced to fishing, casting clickbait blind into the media?' I lit the tobacco, pulled down the smoke, and dropped the still-burning match into the ashtray. 'And all you've managed to catch is one pissed-off Paddy. *That's* awkward. No?'

She drew her lips tight across her teeth and then lit another cigarette herself.

'I thought *you* were the fisherman, Mr McLean,' she replied through the haze of smoke, 'with the hundred-dollar hook?' I shrugged. '*Lo*,' she waved her hand in front of her — dispersing both the smoke, and with it any suggestion the Israelis might be compromised. '*Lo*. What is, uh, *awkward*, is that the day before Professor Levy disappeared she sent her colleague — her closest, most trusted colleague — on an errand.' She paused to gauge my reaction. 'A routine errand that took him from Tel Aviv to Russia. But then, and most definitely on a forged passport, he travelled from Russia to the United Kingdom, where he arrived on the thirtieth of December.'

'Is that a fact?' I smiled at her. 'But really, now, wouldn't you say that was also your problem?'

'No,' she replied. 'I wouldn't.' She unlocked the cell phone I'd used to speak to Ezra and slid it back across the table towards me. 'I would say it was one hundred per cent *our* problem.'

I rested my cigarette on the edge of the ashtray and picked up the phone. A single photograph filled the screen. It was a mid-shot of a smiling man and woman, standing arms entwined, each holding in their free hand a slice of what looked like an apple. I separated my thumb and forefinger across the screen and zoomed in. Rachel stood on the left, eyes downcast above her smile, trying to avoid the lens. A length of black, silver-striped hair had fallen against her cheek. In the background, the unmistakable entrance to the building I was sitting in. The balding man on Rachel's right grinned at the camera, leaning forward as if sharing a joke with the photographer. Six-four, a hundred and seventy pounds and in good shape for his age. I recognized him immediately.

'The guy on the left,' I asked, 'who is he?'

'Stein. Amos Stein. Senior lecturer here in applied mathematics.'

'Israeli?'

'Of course. His father survived the Shoah. He's been with the faculty since the late seventies.'

The last – and only – time I'd seen him, his skin was turning black and the back of his head was missing. It was, without doubt, 'Chappie Connor' – who was, without doubt, not Chappie Connor. I looked at the date stamp: *20/09/2017* – *Rosh Hashanah* the year before.

'He is most definitely,' she concluded, '*not* Irish.'

I stared at her impassively. It was the first time I'd been debriefed by two different intelligence agencies for the assassination of a target I hadn't killed.

'I didn't kill him,' I said. 'I shot him, but I didn't kill him. He was already dead.'

'And why did you do that?'

'Because I was ordered to.'

The woman reached out and retrieved the cell phone from me.

'Who gave the order?'

'OK,' I said, lowering my voice, 'write this down.' She picked up the phone, poised to take dictation. 'Mike-India-Charlie-Kilo-Echo-Yankee,uh,Mike-Oscar-Uniform-Sierra-Echo.'

She put the phone down again. 'Tell me,' she sighed, 'was that the same rat who ordered you to shoot Jacob Levy?'

'Ah, you see, that's the problem with rats,' I said. 'I don't like them. But I don't want to fuck them, either.'

She was still angling for the connection between the hit in the cottage and Doc's murder. 'But you did kill him,' she continued. '*Ken?*'

I kept my mouth shut. Connecting me to Doc's death was pure speculation on her behalf. It had worked, too. There I was, after all. But as for *why* I was there? They weren't getting that for free. They couldn't know how I knew Rachel, and I wanted to keep it that way. I didn't know how Talia was getting her information. Maybe the Shabak had a tap on Lukov's phone. Maybe he'd sold her our conversation. Whatever the case, Talia had eased my conscience. According to her account, Rachel went missing *before* Doc Levy had been killed. His death hadn't put her at risk; unwittingly or not *she* might have endangered *him*.

'And the note?' Talia asked, breaking the silence. 'The hundred-dollar bill?'

'It's in a safe place,' I said. By which I meant that it was folded up in my jeans.

'We offer a very good rate against the shekel.'

'I'll bear that in mind.'

She crushed out her half-smoked cigarette and nudged the heavy white plastic bag an inch closer to me. I took the pistol out. It was a compact SIG M11-A1 with customized polymer grips and a fifteen-round magazine – a military version of the P229 I carried out of preference. Ezra had briefed her well. I eased the slide back a fraction. The chamber was clear. I dropped the clip: 9mm NATO ball.

'Take these, too,' she said, pushing the cigarettes towards me. 'I quit.'

I stuck the handgun in my belt, stuffed the Marlboros and matches into my pocket.

'How will I find you?' I asked. 'If I feel like ratfucking.'

'Look in the phone book,' she said. 'You'll find us under *S*.' I made to leave. 'Oh, one more thing, before you go. A word of advice, if I may?'

'Knock yourself out.'

'In this country, "following orders" is considered poor justification for murder.'

22

'Goldstar, please. Unfiltered.'

The barman nodded and tipped a frosted glass beneath a tap set high above the counter. I sat on the bar stool and stared at my hands. If it was true that you were only ever as good as your last job, I was screwed. I rolled my shoulders and stretched my thigh. The bullet wounds weren't improving. At least the bar was halfway decent – for a hotel joint, anyway. A gentle breeze was blowing. One of the three pairs of French windows leading to a decked terrace that overlooked the sea had been left open. Waiters serving guests who wanted to smoke traipsed in and out. Sodium-lit clouds peppered the sky beyond the glass. My bedroom window had the same view, one floor higher up.

I closed my eyes and tried to bring Rachel's face into focus, but all I could see was the half-smile of the Shabak agent. When I opened them again the glass of beer sat perspiring in front of me. I ran my index finger from the rim to the foot and then gripped it, gulping it down in one long draft.

Going up against the GRU was not good news. As far as intelligence agencies went, it was the envy of the Western world – blessed with an exceptional degree of autonomy and unquestioned, unbudgeted financing – but with this caveat: so powerful was it that not even the Russian president himself could ever really be sure if it prospered owing to his magnanimity, or he to its mercy.

So far it seemed that Avilov had tried hard not to kill me.

I couldn't count on that continuing. GRU operatives were masters of applying extreme, targeted violence in order to achieve their aims – even at their own personal cost. I wasn't unknown to them, either. Our paths had crossed on countless jobs in the past. So far I'd come off on top. And I wasn't keen on a grudge match.

'So what the fuck,' I said to myself out loud, after sucking the foam off my upper lip, 'are you going to do now?'

'Buy me a drink?' came the reply from directly behind me. I froze.

It's not possible.

I turned slowly on the stool, right hand drifting behind my back towards the SIG as I did so. But apparently it was all too possible. Standing before me was the irrepressible turbaned bundle of misplaced enthusiasm that was Bhavneet Singh. I had to give it to him, I had not seen that coming.

'Baaz,' I asked him, half-laughing despite myself, 'what are you doing here?' He smiled broadly. I was lost for words for a moment. '*How* are you even here?'

'I caught a plane from Charles de Gaulle after you left. EasyJet. Simple, really.'

'You followed me? Here? From Paris?'

'Of course. We're partners, right?'

'Yeah. No. But . . . we've been through this. In detail.'

There was a duffel bag at his feet and his skin had the sheen of someone sweating out the grease of a cheap airline meal. He must have just arrived from the airport. I rubbed my face and smelled the alcohol on my breath. I regretted the beer and immediately wanted another.

'But I mean *here*,' I repeated. 'Right *here*. How did you find me?'

'Talia,' he said. 'At the airport.'

It was unlikely that the operator who'd intercepted me at Rachel's office had also met Baaz at Ben Gurion – the times must almost certainly have overlapped. Either the Shabak had a better sense of humour than it was credited with, or that was how all its female agents introduced themselves.

'OK, well for God's sake sit down; we look like a right pair.' He drew up the bar stool next to me. 'Actually, no,' I said, changing my mind. 'Let's go outside.' And then to the barman: 'Another one of those please, and one for my friend here.'

'Tea, please,' Baaz corrected me. 'I don't drink.'

I raised my eyebrows at the barman in mock-exasperation and he smiled back, offering to bring the drinks to our table.

'And a Johnnie Walker Black, too,' I added. 'Actually, make it a double. Straight up.'

Outside, we settled into the linen-covered cushions that padded out the wooden patio furniture. Tel Aviv glimmered on either side of us – but dead ahead only sea and sky stretched to the horizon. Ships' lights swayed on the black tide. Above, inbound aircraft slipped blinking between glowing clouds. The marina south of the hotel was full of boats but empty of people.

'So,' I asked. 'Who is Talia?'

'I don't know, but she was hot,' he said so ingenuously that it was hard not to take him at face value. 'She was waiting for me at immigration,' he added. 'It was awesome. I didn't have to wait in line or anything. She just took my passport and waved me through. She even got me a taxi.'

'A taxi?'

'A *really* nice one, with leather seats and blacked-out windows.'

'I see. And the, uh, *taxi* driver brought you here?'

'Yes. I didn't even have to pay.'

'No,' I said, 'you wouldn't.'

'Was that,' he leaned in closer, 'all part of, you know, *government* work?'

Was it possible for anyone to be so brilliant and so stupid? Every alarm bell that nearly three decades of experience had hardwired into me was going off simultaneously. And yet here he was, clever, infuriating and – for all I could gauge – entirely genuine.

'We're just friends on holiday, OK?' I cautioned him.

He nodded. I looked around. The other guests looked like tourists and travellers. No self-respecting Israeli sits outside in January. A gay couple perched on the other side of the pool, talking discreetly over dinner. Two women shared a bottle of wine and a plate of *mezze* three tables to our left. A lone smoker sat by the railing, staring out to sea. He was clothed in an ill-fitting business suit and an air of regret. None of them looked like professional killers. But then we never do. And short of pulling the SIG on them, I was unlikely to find out if one, none or all of them worked for the Shabak, or whomever the two Talias took orders from – or guarded against.

The waiter put our drinks and a bowl of French fries glistening with salt flakes on the table between us. I turned back to Baaz.

'And if this Talia hadn't found you, how were you going to find me?'

'At the university,' he said. 'Obviously.'

'Of course,' I said. And then, raising my glass to him: 'Well, *sláinte*. Here's to you.'

'*Khush rho*,' he replied in Punjabi. '*Stay happy*.'

'Sure,' I said, 'I'll drink to that.' I downed the whisky and breathed out hard. 'So, Baaz . . .' He looked at me, wide-eyed, expectant. 'Partners work as a team. They look out for each other. Right?'

'Right.'

'And we talked about this, about you coming here. And you agreed not to. Right?'

'Right.'

'So, what changed?' I took a long swallow of beer. 'I need to understand this, Baaz, because I won't be able to protect you *at all* if you don't do as we agree.' He nodded again. 'And I am thankful,' I said quickly, 'for the money. I couldn't have done this – got here, I mean – without you. But . . .' The situation was so preposterous I didn't even know what to say. I took another long hit on the Goldstar.

'But you're scared I'm going to mess things up?'

'Yes. No. Fuck it, Baaz! I'm scared you're going to get killed. Or worse.'

'Worse?' He laughed and drummed his fingers in the air, plugging away at his invisible keyboard. 'There can't be anything worse than being killed.'

I gave him a hard stare.

'You have a family. You might not like them very much at the moment, but they're as much at risk as you are. How would you like to open the mail and find your auntie's head in a box? Or your little sister's fingers?' He looked away, ashamed. I pressed the point home. 'Baaz, I have no idea who is fucking with me – with *us* – or why, exactly. But trust me, of all the options on the table, you should be praying to your God to get you as far away from me as possible, not booking a one-way ticket to hell on bloody easyJet.' His hands were shaking. He looked resolutely at the table. 'OK, I'm sorry. That was harsh.' I didn't want to lie to him, but there was no other choice. I couldn't protect him from the Russians any more than I could protect him from myself. By following me, he'd given me an unenviable choice. 'We'll work it out. Don't worry. It'll be OK,' I lied. 'But you need to start doing as I say, as we agreed. As partners. All right?' I bent my head low and to the side, forcing him to look at me. 'Baaz?'

'OK,' he replied after a pause. 'Agreed.'

'Cool, now drink up. We've got a long day ahead of us tomorrow.' He brightened up at the thought of going on some damned fool mission and took a sip of the tea. 'Leave it,' I said. 'I'll order you dinner on room service.'

'Thank you.'

'Don't,' I said. 'You're paying, anyway.'

Zero two hundred. It had been five hours since I'd said good-night to Baaz. Before going upstairs to sleep, I'd made sure he was checked into the room next to mine, at the very end of the corridor. There was only the roof above us; below his room were the kitchen and the corridor to the bar. There was no sign of anyone occupying the rooms opposite. January was not the most popular month to visit Israel.

I sat on the edge of the bed with the lights off, and listened. Outside, from the beach below, the gentle rasp of surf on sand and, when the wind picked up, a faint pinging of halyards against masts in the marina. The TV set in the other room next to mine had died down after midnight. And from Baaz's room there was only silence. I concentrated on my breathing and cleared my mind.

There was only one thing to do.

I stood up and dressed fully and gathered up what few possessions I had. I tucked the SIG into the back of my jeans. Lightfoot, I stepped out into the hallway. Everything was still. No cameras. No staff except for the night porter downstairs. I slipped the spare key-card into the port on Baaz's door. The lock whirred and the LED shone green above the handle. I swung myself around the frame as quickly and quietly as I could, leaking as little light into his room as possible.

My eyes adjusted to the gloom. The windows were tight shut, the air rank with fried food and sweaty feet. Baaz had fallen asleep clutching his laptop. White light from the screen saver illuminated his face. Stretched out on his back, mouth open, snoring softly, he lay surrounded by sheets of hand-scrawled notes and strings of numbers. His hair was unfurled, masses of it, spilling over the pillow and keyboard. Next to him, on the bedside table, the remains of a half-eaten veggie burger. I stepped closer. He looked like a child.

Max, I thought, *he* is *a child*.

I drew the SIG carefully and cocked the hammer. I'd rather have had a .380. I'd rather not have to do it at all. I don't like the act of killing. And no professional likes collateral damage. But Baaz had made himself a player. And, I told myself, in comparison to what the Russians would do to him when – not *if* – they caught up with him, a bullet now would be a mercy. What I'd said about his auntie was harsh, but it was true. I was a single, isolated target. He was the node in a network of innocents. Anyone prepared to kill Lukov for that hundred-dollar bill wouldn't hesitate to wipe out Baaz's entire family if they thought it would get them closer to what they wanted.

I stood at Baaz's feet and lined the front sight up on the space between the tip of his chin and his Adam's apple. The shot would vaporize his cerebellum and sever his spinal cord.

Instant. Painless. The mattress and the thickly furnished room would absorb most of the noise. If anyone heard anything, it would be as unremarkable as a distant slammed door. By turning up in Tel Aviv, Baaz had ensured that I'd be unable to operate freely – and, consequently, Rachel would remain beyond help.

But it was more than that. For days I'd wondered if Baaz was really all he seemed. From the expert way he navigated the catacombs to the casual way he'd rocked up in Israel: naive, maybe; intelligence agent, possibly; inconvenience – definitely. Because I'd needed him, I hadn't interrogated him. A bullet to the brain would end the speculation. Permanently.

The Israelis would do nothing. A clean hit, no witnesses, their weapon. They knew I had the note, and needed me alive. The crook of my finger rested on the trigger. People who got in the way, people who didn't get out of the way: any operator too squeamish to tidy up was not long for this world.

But this wasn't a job. It was an obsession.

I heard my mother's voice then, a distorted hum at the back of my head, asking me exactly what I thought I had become.

Baaz stirred and muttered something in Punjabi. I kept very still and he started snoring again. It was justifiable; I could justify it. In the morning I knew I could look in the mirror and still see Max and not a monster.

Baaz slumbered on, four and a half pounds of pressure from the grave. I raised my left hand, palm out, behind the pistol to shield my eyes from any blood or bone blown back towards my face.

I felt the pressure of the trigger and looked aside.

Goddamn it, Max. Just do it.

On the bed beside him I saw the numbers he'd been writing out, over and over again. It was the same number – reversed, multiplied, factored, divided against itself. Rows and rows of tiny scrawled digits. Perhaps a hundred or more times he had returned to the same eight-digit number. My finger crept on the steel. I focused on the number.

The number. I knew that number. I'd been staring at it for days. Staring *through* it.

Fuck.

I dropped my palm and picked up one of the sheets of paper. I turned it over. On the reverse he'd written, simply, *Arkhangel!*

I switched the SIG to my left hand and worried the hundred-dollar bill out of my ticket pocket. I unfolded it one-handed, peering into the folds in the weak light afforded by the computer screen. I studied the serial number and Baaz's spidery digits. They matched exactly. Baaz had written it out with compulsive accuracy, working it into a series of equations and computations that I didn't even begin to understand. What I did know immediately, though, was that if I pulled the trigger I probably never would. I put the bill back in my pocket, thumbed the decocking lever on the 9mm and tucked it into my jeans.

And then I put my hand on Baaz's shoulder and rocked him gently back into the land of the living.

23

'I told you,' Baaz said, drumming the middle fingers of his right hand against his temple, 'it's bloody crowded in there.'

I was sitting on the edge of his bed now. He hadn't startled when I woke him, but he was clearly embarrassed by the situation, wrapping his hair up, struggling to make eye contact.

'Even if I'd wanted to, I couldn't have forgotten it. It's like . . .' He struggled for a simile. 'A worm! Just like a worm. You know when you hear a bit of a song and it goes round in your head, sometimes for *days*? Just like that.'

'The banknote, that number on that bill, is like a song?'

'Correct. But not just that number. All numbers. It's like they have a rhythm, a tune. Lots of people can remember songs. My auntie knows hundreds of them. Always singing. My mother, too. But my father is a numbers man. Just like me. He says numbers are like the hymns of the gurus. They have patterns. And patterns have meanings. And meanings have solutions.'

'And solutions . . . ?' Realization began to dawn on me. Baaz *had* figured something out. I felt a surge of adrenaline in my guts.

'Solutions have applications.' He pulled the covers up higher over his chest. 'But only,' he continued, 'if you know what the problem is.'

'OK.' I spoke calmly – as much to coax him as to relax

myself. It felt as if I was teetering on a cliff edge, about to find out whether or not I could fly. 'So . . . what's the answer?'

He looked at me blankly. 'What answer?'

I tried again, slowly, thinking how best to frame a question I had no idea how to formulate.

'What does it mean, Baaz? The number on the banknote. What does it . . . *signify*?'

'Oh!' he said. 'Oh, I don't know. Not yet, anyway.'

My shoulders sagged. He was exasperating. And I was a fool for imagining his night-time scrawling amounted to anything more than a distraction. There was no silver bullet. All he'd done was to buy himself more time. I breathed out hard and clenched my jaw, trying my best to smile through my disappointment.

'So, you came here *why*, exactly?' I asked.

'Because your friend told me to.'

'My friend? What friend?'

'The friend you spoke to from my flat in Paris.'

'What, Ezra? He called back?'

'No, I called him.'

'You called Ezra?' He was nothing if not unpredictable. 'Why did you do that, Baaz?'

I tried and failed to imagine how that conversation had played out. Ezra's promised 'surprise' had suddenly been realized.

'Because I needed to talk to you and you don't have a phone.'

'Right. And you needed to tell me what? That you really like that number, but you don't know what it means?'

He nodded.

'And you told that to Ezra and he spoke to, uh, *Talia*, and that's how you got here?'

'No, I got here on easyJet.' I stood up and slid open his wardrobe door. He looked at me warily. 'What are you doing?'

'Raiding your minibar.'

'What for?'

'A drink.'

I inspected the cabinet. Chivas Regal. *Shit*. I emptied one of the miniatures into his empty water glass, added some Evian from the fridge and swilled it across my teeth. It would do. I poured in a second miniature and pulled from my jeans the packet of Marlboros and book of matches that the Shabak agent had given me and shook out a smoke.

'Get up,' I said. 'We're going outside.'

I needed some air. *And besides*, I thought, *most likely the Talias can hear every word we say in here.*

'OK then, clever clogs. If you don't know what the number means, why bust a gut to find me? I need clear, simple answers. No "rhythms". No "hymns of the gurus". Just facts, all right?'

Three o'clock on a Wednesday morning and Tel Aviv was finally asleep. We were back on the terrace, sitting this time at a low table by the pool. The underwater lights had been switched off and the surface was inky black. It felt like we were at the edge of an abyss. Baaz had wound his hair up in a simple turban and looked more relaxed. I shifted on the cushions and felt the SIG dig into my spine. He'd come back unscathed from a journey he didn't even know he'd undertaken. Perhaps we'd both been saved. I tore a match out of the booklet and struck it and lit a cigarette. Baaz moved away from me slightly and cleared his throat. I exhaled and waited.

'The serial number,' he said, 'is *73939133*. That's obviously a prime number.'

'Obviously,' I nodded. I didn't know where he was going, but I was on safe ground. Prime numbers can be divided only by one and themselves. I'd at least learned that much in school.

'But it's a special prime number,' he continued. 'Because it's the largest right truncatable prime in base ten.'

'Right.' I dragged hard on the Marlboro. It had taken him less than thirty seconds to lose me. 'What does that mean?'

'It means,' he said, 'that if you remove the right-hand integer' – I cocked my head – 'uh, *number*, it's still prime. So *7393913*, *739391*, *73939*, and so on, they're all prime numbers, all the way down to *7*. It's really interesting because there are only eighty-three right truncatable primes in base ten, anyway.'

'Fascinating.' I blew a cloud of smoke up into the night sky. 'Tell me,' I asked, swallowing my pride, 'are we at the "patterns" stage here, or the "solutions" stage? Because I can tell you how many mils to correct a scoped target at a thousand metres uphill in a stiff breeze. But I'm not exactly sure I could tell you what "base ten" is.'

'Base ten is the . . .'

'*What*,' I interrupted, losing my patience, 'does it *mean*, Baaz? Why is the fact the number is a "right" *whatever* important?' I sucked on the cigarette. 'Man, you have risked a *lot* to be here. More than you know. Much more. So please, *please* tell me – for my sake as well as yours – that there is more to this than a quirk of the Federal Reserve's printing process.'

'That's it!' He stood up, his voice rising with excitement. 'You guessed! I knew you would!'

'Jesus Christ! Would you ever sit *down*?' I looked around.

Except for the night lights in the bar the joint was dead. He sat again, perched on the edge of his seat. 'Guessed what?' He was so excited now that his fingers drummed a constant tattoo in front of him.

'The Fed. That's it. Look. Look at the bill.'

'Sure. I will. Later, though.'

'No, now,' he urged. 'Let's look at it now. I can show you.'

With misgivings, I stubbed out the cigarette and removed the note from my pocket. Possession of the bill was, it seemed, both a death sentence and stay of execution. If we were being watched, the location of the note would be beyond doubt. But with the high wall of the hotel behind us and the sea in front we weren't directly overlooked and there was no obvious position for a snooper, or a sniper, to take up. I unfolded the bill and we sat closer. I struck another match and held it over the ragged slip of printed paper.

'OK, what am I looking at?'

'Here,' Baaz pointed. 'These two letters, before the serial number: *LL*. The first *L* is the series of the banknote. See, here at the bottom, *2009A*.'

'OK.'

'And the second *L* is the Federal Reserve Bank that printed it. There are loads of them, Dallas, New York, Virginia. *L* stands for San Francisco. You can see here, too, under the serial number, it says *L12*. So it's definitely the San Francisco Fed that printed it.' I dropped the match before it burned my fingers and the note dissolved back into the shadows. 'Except they didn't.'

'Didn't what?'

'Print it.'

'I don't understand.' It was hard to make out his expression, but the glow of the night lights in the bar caught in the corners of his eyes. 'How could you know that? Actually,' I lit another cigarette, 'how do you know any of this?'

'I asked a good friend of mine.'

'I see. And who is your friend?'

'Professor Google. He's, like, *totally* amazing. You can ask him anything.'

'Are you fucking with me?'

'No! You can check it yourself, Max, seriously. Did you see the other letter, *after* the serial number? It's a *J*. That series of bill was actually printed in 2013. Except that bill wasn't, couldn't have been, because the *LL J* notes end at *LL 44800000*.'

'So, the numbers and the letters don't match up?'

He peered at me with a look that mingled pity with incredulity. 'Correct.'

'And that, combined with the fact that the serial number is a right . . .' I searched for the term I'd already forgotten, '*prime* – this special number – made you get on a flight?'

'No.'

'No?'

'No. Ezra made me get on the flight. He wanted me to come and find you.'

'Ezra told *you* to find *me*?' It was a lot to take in. 'And why did he do that?'

'Because he has a message for you that I don't think he wants Talia or her friends to know about. He said I should tell only you.' He paused for a moment. 'Should I tell you now?'

'Yes, Baaz.' My own voice was rising, too. I took a deep breath. 'You should tell me now.'

'OK.' He cleared his throat, every inch the messenger arrived from Marathon with news of victory. 'Ezra told me to tell you that you must visit Moshe Mendel Katz in Mea She'arim.' He paused again, and then added, less formally: 'About the banknote, I mean. Ezra says he knows a lot about money.'

I pinched the sleep out of my eyes with my left thumb and index finger.

'And why didn't you mention this when you arrived?'

'I wanted to! But you started up with all your big man *bak-waas* about my auntie's head in a box. And I haven't even *got* a bloody sister! You think I'm a stupid kid, right? Well . . . *fine*. That's bloody fine. But I'm here and I did what I was asked and . . .' Tears welled up in the catchlights of his eyes. 'And I just wanted to help.' I put my hand on his arm and squeezed it lightly.

'OK, partner,' I said. 'I'm sorry.'

And I was.

24

'Good luck, brother.'

The taxi driver gave me a broad grin as we climbed out of the white cab. We might as well have been dropped into another world. Built just outside the walls of the Old City, Mea She'arim was one of the oldest Jewish neighbourhoods in Jerusalem. Getting there had been easy: a smooth hour-and-a-half drive south-east down Highway 1. It wasn't that hard to navigate the small, stone streets; but it was almost impossible for an outsider to understand the complexities of what it meant to live there. Sometimes maps hide more than they reveal.

Almost the entire quarter was populated by strictly Orthodox Haredi Jews. Men wearing wide-brimmed black fedoras and long black silk coats hurried about their business. Women sporting wigs and prim skirts bustled about beside them. The entrance to the district was presided over by a sign printed in red and black block capitals warning 'WOMEN AND GIRLS' visiting the enclave to cover up:

PLEASE DO NOT PASS

THROUGH OUR NEIGHBORHOOD IN

IMMODEST CLOTHES

Baaz and I looked each other over.

'It says, *No trousers*,' he pointed out nervously.

'Don't worry,' I reassured him. 'That's only for women. Besides, you look gorgeous.'

'I feel like a bloody Martian. Take me to your leader, *huna*.'

He was right. We looked entirely out of place. Blending in simply wasn't an option – though Baaz was making things worse by spinning three-sixty while taking in the strangeness of it all.

'This is *totally* crazy. Usually it's just me wearing the funny hat. But check out these guys.' He stared unceremoniously at the passers-by. But they ignored him, us, entirely.

'If only we were in East Jerusalem,' I muttered to myself. My Arabic was good; my Hebrew almost non-existent. I grabbed Baaz's arm and pointed him due west. 'We need to keep moving. Let's get this over with, then you can be on your way.' Although where he'd be on his way *to* was unclear. Even he must have suspected that going back to his flat in Paris was becoming increasingly unfeasible. 'Remind me,' I asked, 'what are we looking for?'

'It's on Hevrat Mishnayot,' he said. 'Like I said. Between Hevrat Shas Street and Ein Ya'akov Street. That's not how Ezra pronounced it, though. He also said it was a side street.'

'Yeah, I know *where* it is, but what's *on* Hevrat Mishnayot? Are we looking for a house, a business, a shop, or what?'

A few hours before, I'd been a fraction of a millimetre away from killing him. Now he was leading me across a city he'd never set foot in – a one-eyed king in a foreign land with a single blind subject. I had no choice but to go with it, with *him*, if I wanted to do anything other than stare out to sea at the hotel.

'I don't know,' he said. Anticipating my exasperation, he added quickly: 'He didn't say, OK? It's on a junction. With another street. Through the traitor's gate.'

'The what?'

He shrugged. 'That's what he said. "Through the traitor's gate."'

I stopped walking and put my hand on his shoulder. 'Is there anything else?' He looked at me blankly. 'Did Ezra say anything else to you? Anything at all?'

He shook his head.

We kept walking.

Whatever kind of 'traitor' we were going to meet, the fact that Ezra hadn't wanted the Israeli authorities – at least not the internal security team that had been put on our case – to know he'd introduced us would be significant. Either his source wasn't legit as far as the Shabak was concerned, or he was trying to protect Talia from blowback.

My reading of the meeting – interrogation, frankly – I'd had in Rachel's office was that I'd been given carte blanche to do whatever I needed in my search for their missing scientist. They knew I was there for her, and they'd done nothing to stop me. We were on the same side in that respect, after all – and no one gives a pistol to an assassin unless they're prepared for him to use it.

There would be limits, though. Step off the path and the consequences would be unpredictable. Contractor, consultant, mercenary: whatever Ezra called himself, I'd never known whom he really worked for. My best guess was military intelligence and the Mossad. And despite his faith in Talia, if the Mossad and the Shabak got on as well with each other in the Holy Land as MI6 and MI5 did back in Blighty, then Baaz and I would end up being the filling for a shit sandwich faster than you could say 'secret military tribunal' should we piss anyone off in Israel, apart from each other.

We headed north-west up Mea She'arim Street amid a stream of traditionally dressed Orthodox, past barred shopfronts and badly parked delivery trucks. The apartment buildings above were shabby, unloved. Everywhere walls fluttered with fly-posters printed in Hebrew, roofs bristled with scaffolding. Most of the buildings were either being renovated or looked like they ought to be. Wrought iron balconies peeling ancient paint over-hung the street; many were sealed off with plastic sheeting from the rooms inside. It was a couple of degrees cooler than the coast, and bright white candyfloss clouds piled up on the horizon. I was glad of the jacket Baaz had bought me in France.

I was glad, too, that the road signs were in English and Arabic as well as in Hebrew. Even though I'd memorized our route from a satellite image of the quarter that Baaz and I had recced that morning using a VPN on his laptop, the vis-ual check of the street names was reassuring. We turned left on to HaRav Shmuel Salant Street and then, at a huge and what looked like newly built synagogue on the corner, wheeled off north again up an alley that disgorged us both at the sharp elbow of a junction thirty metres off the main drag. We kept walking. I kept my head down and told Baaz to do the same. A hundred metres or so further on I swung us left down Hevrat Mishnayot.

It was an unkempt backstreet, lined with parked cars and graffiti-stained walls, and a dozen or so metal doors leading into buildings and passageways. Dead ahead a huge stone building loomed up – two massive storeys high and fifteen metres wide, with stone arches supporting a tier of impressive, ornate windows. It dwarfed the low-rise stone and stucco boxes that opened up into a sort of plaza in front of it. On either side the road divided. Baaz and I looked around, perplexed. If this was Ezra's idea of a joke, I struggled to see the funny side.

'And he didn't say anything else?' Baaz shook his head. 'Sure? I mean, *really* sure?'

The whole 'traitor's gate' revelation had come completely out of the blue. I shuddered to think what else Baaz had forgotten to mention. He rolled his eyes at me as if I was being unreasonable by asking again.

'Sure.'

I lit a cigarette and looked around.

The main entrance to the large building was framed by an archway three times my height. Above it, the only sign indicating what the purpose of the building might be had been obliterated with black spray paint. It looked like a synagogue, maybe, or a religious school – though it could just as easily have been an apartment block. Two young men in smart black hats chatted on the corner opposite. Long skeins of white wool dangled from their shirts, hanging down their thighs. Laundry strung out on the balconies above rippled in the breeze.

But of anything that could have been a traitor's gate, there was no obvious indication.

'These jokers love their spray paint. Shame you can't speak Hebrew,' Baaz said. 'All this graffiti might mean something.'

He had a point. I tried and failed to read the slogans daubed on practically every flat surface and marvelled at how anyone had managed to get up high enough to deface the upper storey.

'Like, what does *that* mean?' he asked.

'What?'

'You see there? On the far left-hand wall, on the other side of the main entrance.'

I followed Baaz's gaze. Stencilled on to the yellow stone wall between a metal gate and a wooden door were the black outlines of an oblong divided into three horizontal stripes. On the left-hand side a triangle cut into the middle stripe.

243

There was no colour, no tag line, no explanation – but the meaning was clear.

'Bingo.' Baaz furrowed his brow. I stubbed out the cigarette and savoured instead the momentary rush of unprofessional pleasure at having outsmarted him. 'That, clever clogs, is the outline of the Palestinian flag.' We walked over to it. The bolts of the metal gate to its left were secured by a small rusted padlock. The door to the right was fastened with a simple latch. 'And I'll bet you a hundred dollars that this,' I said, knuckles rapping on the painted metal, 'is the traitor's gate.'

Pigeons startled by the noise soared into the air and then settled on the gutter above. The men standing opposite called out to someone crossing the street further down and walked off. From inside there was nothing except the echo of my knocking in the void beyond.

I counted to ten and banged on the door again, harder this time, smacking the steel with the heel of my palm. After a few seconds I could hear movement within, and then voices.

'*Rega, ani ba.*'

Another pause. Then metal on metal. The door swung open a foot.

'*Rosh chidesh tov.*'

We were greeted by a strong smell of turpentine, and by a thickset man with a full grey beard, and a cautious expression framed by coils of messy *payot* – spring-like extensions of hair tumbling past his cheeks. Five-eight, two hundred pounds – and that was a lowball. A black waistcoat strained over his belly, decorated with what looked like the remnants of his breakfast egg. His face was flushed red with whatever exertions had brought him to the door. The sum of his parts added up to a heart attack about to happen.

A cigarette burned down almost to the stub was wedged

between the fingers of his right hand. They were stained a dark, nicotine yellow. Under his left palm, the close-cropped head of a small boy, no more than four or five years old.

'Max,' I said, extending my hand. 'I'm sorry, I don't speak Hebrew.'

'Ah, well,' he said, 'good first day of the month, to you!' His accent see-sawed with a Germanic twang. He dropped the cigarette and shook my hand.

'But it's the seventeenth already,' Baaz replied.

'*Rosh Chodesh Sh'vat,*' the man said, before I could apologize for Baaz's interruption. 'The first day of the month of Sh'vat of the year 5778.'

'My, uh, *colleague,*' I explained. 'Bhavneet Singh.'

'You can call me "Baaz", though,' Baaz piped up. 'Everyone else does. Even my auntie. And she's super-formal.'

He looked at Baaz, and then back to me.

'And you can call me *di Farreter,*' he said with a grin. 'Everyone does. Even *my* auntie. She's even more formal. Trust me.'

'What does that mean?' Baaz asked.

'It's Yiddish,' the man said. 'It means *the Traitor.*'

Baaz stepped closer. The child backed away and then scuttled off deeper into the room behind, no doubt spooked by the bizarre *goyim* at his door.

'My youngest grandson,' he explained, still holding my hand, though no longer shaking it. And then, by way of proper introduction: 'Moshe. Moshe Mendel Katz. At your service.'

'It's good to meet you, Mr Katz.' I stepped a fraction closer; my right hand still clasped in his. 'You were highly recommended.'

'Yes, well . . .' He let go of my hand and stepped back into the room behind him, opening the wide metal door enough for Baaz and I to follow. 'Please, close it behind you. Now, where's the switch?'

We stood in darkness for a moment and then Moshe hit the lights. Out of the darkness emerged an extraordinary store-room. Piled up in vertical stacks, on the floor, on shelves, in boxes and free standing in bunches of fives or tens rested dozens, hundreds of oil paintings. And above them, hanging properly, fully displayed canvases. Rembrandt. Dali. Turner. Klimt. Anything and everything. The face of Jesus beamed down from the far wall. Above us, Judith beheaded Holofernes. A white, eighteenth-century horse stood in a wide green field. I looked down. Narcissus fell into his own reflection at my feet. I guessed the room may once have been a garage. But now it resembled the overflow from the National Gallery and Hermitage combined.

'Wow.' Baaz blinked at the art around him. 'This is *totally* cool.'

We both took in the scene. It was as if an art avalanche had poured through the building and stopped at our toes. Baaz stepped towards a canvas of a burning candle and raised his hand, index finger outstretched, as if to touch it.

'Not that one,' Moshe cautioned him, urgently. And then, more relaxed, 'It's not dry yet.' Baaz dropped his hand and stared at it intently. I stared at Moshe, reappraising him. It wasn't egg on his waistcoat. It was yellow paint. And whether this was a shop or a studio, it most certainly wasn't legit.

'I didn't think all this was allowed,' I said, waving my hand at the walls, 'for the Haredim. Don't you have laws about painting people?' I racked my brain to no effect, trying to remember which of the Ten Commandments it violated.

246

'We do, and it isn't. Although, actually, the one that caught your friend's eye *is* permissible.'

'*You*,' Baaz asked, incredulously, 'painted all *these*?' Moshe dipped his head in humble agreement. 'They're beautiful,' Baaz continued, wide-eyed in admiration. 'But why do they call you "the Traitor"?'

'Well,' chuckled Moshe, 'the Haredim call me a "traitor" because I paint pictures of people; the Israelis, because I'm not a Zionist; our militants, because I don't support the Palestinians; the Defence Forces, because I didn't enlist; my family, because I smoke too much; my rabbi, well, my rabbi for a lot of reasons.'

Baaz turned back to the picture.

'I didn't just mean painting the pictures,' I said, taking the packet of Marlboros out of my jacket pocket. I shook two filter-tipped sticks clear and offered him a smoke. He thanked me and plucked one out. I did the same. He lit his and handed me the matches. 'I meant the forgery, too. "Thou shalt not steal", right?'

Baaz coughed. Moshe inhaled deeply to make sure the tobacco had caught and looked at me carefully. From around one of the piles of pictures the young boy reappeared, craning his neck to get a better look at us.

'Max,' Moshe said, exhaling the smoke between us as he spoke. '"Max" is a good name. I like the name "Max".' He looked over at Baaz. '"Baaz" is also good. But "Max",' he continued, looking at me again, 'is a strong name.' I smiled at him. He smiled back. I kept looking at him, but didn't speak. 'You said,' he resumed, filling the silence between us, 'that I was highly recommended. That is very kind. May I ask, *who* it was that recommended me?'

'A mutual friend,' I said. He raised his eyebrows and

pursed his lips as if to say, *So what?* I kept smiling. 'Ezra sent us,' I continued. 'Ezra Black.'

'Ah. So . . .' His face settled and he turned towards the boy. 'Binyomen,' he said softly, *'geyn tsu zen mame.'* The boy darted behind a rack of gilt frames. Seconds later his feet clumped up the stairs that rose from the rear right-hand corner of the studio towards his unseen mother. 'My apprentice,' he whispered. 'He's closer to me than my own shadow.' Once he was sure the boy was out of earshot, he continued. 'These,' he said, looking around, 'are not forgeries. They are interpretations. But I do not think that you are interested in my paintings, are you, Mr . . . ?'

'Just "Max" is fine. And on the contrary,' I said, 'there's a picture I'd like you to, uh, *interpret* for me.' Baaz cleared his throat. 'For *us*,' I corrected myself.

'I see. That's most . . .' he paused. 'Tell me, who is the painting of?' I dragged on the Marlboro and looked over at Baaz. Baaz stared at us, drumming the air with his fingers. 'One of Ezra's friends, perhaps?'

'Yes,' I said. 'You could say that. It's a portrait,' I gripped the cigarette between my teeth, took out the hundred-dollar bill and handed it to Moshe, 'of Benjamin Franklin.'

He took the bill and looked at it, his eyes darting between me and the money.

'A good man,' he said, 'by all accounts.' And then, turning the note over, 'But not, I think, an angel.'

I rubbed my face with my hands. It was past midday and I hadn't eaten. We'd been perched on two wooden stools in a small, stuffy space above the storeroom-cum-gallery with growing leg cramp and decreasing expectations. I probed the wounds in my shoulder and thigh with my forefinger to distract myself. They hurt – and the dressing on my collar-bone was leaking. At least the scratches I'd picked up on the beach in Kent had scabbed over, though the wire cut on my hands from the night run across the Mayo countryside to Doc's bled when I picked at it.

As soon as Moshe had gone to work, Baaz had slipped into trance-like reflection. When I'd asked him what he was thinking about, he'd replied, 'Factoring primes.'

I'd let him get on with it.

All the while that Moshe examined the banknote, he fed me with escapades from his past. Perhaps Ezra had con-tacted him. Maybe he'd called Ezra. Either way, he had decided to trust me, and to talk. Maybe he didn't get to speak English very often in Mea She'arim. Maybe Ezra had given him a green light to gab. Whatever the case, once he started talking, he couldn't stop: what started as a trickle ended up as a flood.

Painting, it turned out, was merely a profitable sideline for the Traitor. Moshe Mendel Katz's real vocation was money – specifically, the mass production of fake paper notes. In 1995, between the First and Second Intifadas, he told us, he'd been arrested, and then co-opted, by the secret services to help them pump an ocean of forged cash into the pockets and vaults of Israel's Arab neighbours. If he cut the plates, the Israeli government would cut him a deal. So, he did – and Special Forces smuggled them across the border, where they were installed in printing presses hidden in a network of caves north of Beirut. The operation was fronted by the Bul-garian mafia and run out of Tel Aviv.

Moshe never said as much, but it wasn't hard to guess how he and Ezra first met. And the Bulgarian connection might have been coincidental, but in a world as small as ours I doubted it. Seconds before he'd been shot, Lukov had told me that 'even the fucking Lebanese' were interested in the *Arkhangel* note. Maybe that was code. Maybe the gunmen wearing keffiyehs by the bakery *were* the Israelis. Indeed, Talia had all but confirmed it.

Whatever questions there were about what had just gone down in Paris, the results of Moshe's Middle Eastern enterprise were certain. So successful were his 1988-series bills – his plates had printed nearly a billion dollars' worth – that they didn't just destabilize the Lebanese economy, they became a global pariah. Once finally detected, they were shunned worldwide by corner exchange kiosks and central banks alike. But by then, of course, it was too late for anyone who'd bought them to give them back. The following year – Moshe recounted while he ran a chemical test on the ink on our note – the Federal Reserve had entirely redesigned the hundred-dollar bill.

'Because of me, Benjamin Franklin got a facelift. And the best of all?' he whispered. 'Iran got the blame.'

As far as a crook's curriculum vitae went, it was spectacular. I reckoned it must have been, all told, one of the most successful asymmetric attacks carried out before the internet weaponized the misplaced brilliance of boys like Baaz.

Moshe had left us with his history and a fresh glass of tea 'to check his files'. Baaz and I held on to the banknote. An hour later, Moshe reappeared. Cheeks flushed. Breath short. Brow moist. Whatever he'd discovered – or confirmed – had made him hurry to tell us. Baaz came to from his maths meditation. I sat up straight.

'Well?' I asked.

'It is absolutely genuine,' Moshe declared. 'And one hundred per cent fake news.'

'I don't understand.' It was Baaz who replied, but he spoke for both of us. 'How can it be a genuine fake? It has to be one thing or the other.'

'Well, yes . . .' Moshe ran his right hand across his forehead and drew up his own stool to the work bench where Baaz and I had sat waiting for the verdict, 'and no. It's both things at the same time.'

While he lit one of his own cigarettes, I finished the last mouthful of tea from my glass – long since stewed.

'You were right,' he said, speaking to Baaz, who smoothed the note out between us. 'The letters printed at either end of the serial number are inconsistent with the serial numbers of the bills known to be in circulation. So, in this respect, you could say that the note is a fake. It *looks* like . . . How to explain this?' He rested the cigarette in the ashtray and scratched his beard. 'An *impossible* note. But many bills get printed that are never meant to be circulated. Don't forget, you can put whatever numbers and letters you like on any plate – whether you work for the Bureau of Engraving' – he touched his chest lightly with fingertips of his right hand – 'or not.'

'But in every other respect the bill is genuine?' I asked.

'OK, there is always a margin of error. That, I admit. The tools I have, the software, the microscope . . . This old man's eyes! They are good, but I am not the Fed. If I was, I would photograph this bill and blow it up the size of a house and crawl across it on my hands and knees looking for clues. That's what they do. Really! Crazy, no?'

'How wide is the margin of error? How sure are you?'

'In this case,' he said, 'let us say that I am sure.' He smoothed his beard and picked up the bill. 'Why? Because I have seen this note before.' I went to speak, but he held his hand up. 'No! Not *this* one. But its twin. Exactly the same printing. Same series. Different numbers. And without, uh, "Arkhangel" written on the back, of course.'

'Where?' I asked him. 'Where did you see it?'

'Here,' he replied. 'Hundreds of them were found by our Special Forces, also in Lebanon,' he explained. 'During a raid. This time Israel got the blame, though. But it wasn't us. It was, how do you say . . . *quid pro quo*. Our mutual friend asked me to look at them. *Interpret* them, as you would say.'

'OK,' I nodded. 'But if you didn't forge them, who did? The Iranians?'

'No.' He handed the note back to me and retrieved his cigarette from the ashtray. 'The Russians, of course.'

He smoked his cigarette and we all considered what he'd said in silence. I lit another Marlboro and tucked the packet and matches back into my jacket.

Then he added: 'But you must pay attention to what I am saying. It is genuine. It is not a forgery. This is important. We *interpreters*, we like to add a signature, a deliberate error, a stamp – something that proves it was us, and proves it's not real. The plates I cut in ninety-five? The ones I told you about? I ran the *O* in *United States Of America* under the edge of the border that runs around the note so the top of it is hidden. That's not correct. The *O* should be complete. *That* is a forgery.'

'But why would you do that?' Baaz piped up indignantly. 'Why ruin something so . . . *perfect*?' Then he added, excitedly, 'Is it because only God is perfect? Is that why?'

Moshe burst out laughing.

'I'm not a Muslim rug weaver! No, we do it for the thrill of it. If an expert, a banker, passes a note I've forged with a deliberate error, then the victory is even sweeter. And anyway, printing a perfect dollar note is suicide. Economies would collapse. Presidents would fall. The Americans couldn't let it stand. And the Arabs,' he drew his index finger across his throat, 'the Arabs would hang you for it. No. No one would do it, *could* do it, unless they were protected. Otherwise not even your archangel could save you. And this note,' he waved the bill with a theatrical flourish, 'is perfect.'

'But you *were* protected,' I replied.

'Exactly,' he said. 'I *was*. And now?' He shrugged. 'The Haredim pray for all Jews. But not all Israel prays for us. In God we trust. But it doesn't hurt to have an insurance policy.'

'But,' I tried to find the words to crystallize his assessment, 'how can the Russians print genuine US hundred-dollar bills? How is that not automatically a forgery?'

'Because,' Baaz cut in, 'they used plates from the Federal Reserve. That's how they did it, isn't it?'

Moshe nodded.

'Your apprentice is very good. Very good indeed. Yes, this is exactly how they did it. With genuine plates.'

I narrowed my eyes at Baaz and took a mouthful of smoke down into my lungs.

'So, let me get this straight. This note was printed by the Russians on a US Federal Reserve plate, with a deliberately invalid serial number?'

'Yes,' Moshe nodded. 'A deliberately *uncirculated* number.'

'So, the Russians are working with the Americans?'

'No,' Moshe shook his head. I breathed out hard and rocked back in my chair. 'Look,' he explained, patiently, 'the CIA took plates to Afghanistan. They were used to print money for the Mujahedin. The Russians captured them. The same in Syria with the Syrian Democratic Forces, and probably with the Kurds in Iraq. The Americans, they are very consistent. The Russians, too.'

'The provenance?' I asked. 'Can you, could *anyone*, say where these notes originated?'

Moshe shook his head again.

'All you can be certain of,' he concluded, 'is that whatever route he has taken, your Mr Franklin here has been on an incredible journey.' He stubbed his cigarette out and leaned towards us. Baaz and I leaned in, too. 'But I think you already know,' he said, cocking his head to one side, 'that the real question is not *where* the bill was printed, but what it was printed *for*.'

25

'What now?'

Baaz and I stood at the south-east entrance to Mea She'arim, hands in our pockets.

'Food,' I said. 'I'm starving. The Old City is that way.' Baaz looked doubtful. 'You'll like it. Trust me.'

Five minutes later we passed underneath the pale stone arch of the Damascus Gate like a couple of jaded tourists and into the warren of narrow streets. Israel Defence Forces soldiers milled around. Elderly stallholders shouted out their wares in Palestinian Arabic. Tourist tat flooded the shop-fronts: nargilehs jostled for space alongside alabaster models of the Dome of the Rock, menorahs with crucifixes; Yasser Arafats rubbed shoulders with Jesuses of Nazareth. Brightly coloured cloths hung down above the covered walkways; beneath our feet the smooth stone blocks that paved the Via Dolorosa led us on deeper into the maze of alleyways.

Scruffy kids, delivery men and tourist touts shouted and growled, coughed and whispered around us and through us and to us. Hijabed women in elegant abayas picked their way through the chaos, seemingly oblivious to the street theatre unfolding around them. Here and there a blue and white Star of David draped against the stonework – but the black, red and green of the Palestinian flag was everywhere. We followed briefly in the footsteps of Christ before I showed Baaz into the Al-Quds Café – a decent joint that served strong coffee and good street food.

Outside, half a dozen American girls sat by the door giggling, juggling water pipes and fingers full of *kibbeh*. Inside, the waiter greeted us in English and showed us to a table at the back.

I ordered *mezze*. Before Baaz could speak, I added: 'Just the vegetarian stuff, please. No meat. And two glasses of fruit juice. Oh, and some extra hummus for my friend.'

Baaz relaxed.

The walls were hung with carpets, the tables topped with beaten metal. The food came quickly. We ate in silence. When he'd finished, Baaz gulped down the last of his juice and sat back in his chair. Crumbs of *lakhma* clung to the wisps of his beard. I pointed to the side of his mouth and he licked his lips like a cat.

'Thanks,' he said. 'But what *are* we going to do now?'

'Order coffee,' I said.

And think. Every minute I sat still was a minute lost looking for Rachel. And all those minutes added up could make the difference between reaching her or not; *rescuing* her or not. *If she even needs to be rescued*, I thought to myself. The fact that it might be me that needed her help was a possibility too hard to hold on to.

I put my cigarettes and matches on the table and the waiter brought over an ashtray. I offered to move outside, but he waved away my query with a flick of his hand.

'Please,' he said, setting an old metal dish between us. 'No problem.'

Baaz wrinkled his nose. He truly hated cigarette smoke. I should have truly hated him being there. But whether he'd been saved by the last gasp of my conscience or the diligence of his calculations, I was glad he was, all the same. The truth was that it was already too late to protect his family. He'd entered Israel on his own passport, made no attempt to hide his identity from anyone. As far as the Shabak – or anyone else – was concerned, he was up to his neck in it, whatever *it* was. In Paris he chose not to run; and that choice had consequences.

The waiter came back with our coffees – strong, spiced with cardamom and loaded with sugar – and pieces of sticky baklava.

'The number on the note,' I asked Baaz, as he sipped at the tiny cup, 'what do you think it means?'

'I don't know,' he said.

'But what's your gut instinct?'

'My computer science professor in Chandigarh told me that gut instincts are very bad. There is a right answer and a wrong answer. Correct solutions are arrived at with facts, not hunches.'

'What absolute bullshit, Baaz. Seriously.' I shook my head and slurped the thick black coffee carefully, so as not to get a mouthful of the grounds from the bottom of the cup. 'You're in the catacombs. There's been a cave-in. Or a flood. The route has changed. You use what you know to make an informed guess, right?' He pursed his lips. 'And don't tell me you don't, because I *know* you do. You're still alive. No one could spend as much time down there and still be in one piece if they weren't lucky – at least once.'

He shifted in his chair uncomfortably. I played with the packet of Marlboros.

'OK,' he relented, 'my hunch is that the serial number is too unusual to be a coincidence – especially if you consider that the number itself is from an uncirculated print run. Besides, this man – Moshe? He says that the printer can add any serial number they like to a plate. So maybe that prime has a purpose? As a prime, I mean.'

'How do you mean?'

'OK, well this is going to sound *totally* nuts, but there are lots of numbers on that bill, not just the serial number. The letters, they could represent values, too. And then,' he finished his own coffee, 'there is something special on the reverse. This is actually exciting. Let me show you.'

'What, here?'

'Yes, why not?'

'Because . . . Oh, fuck it.' I dug the note out of my pocket and unfolded it flat on its front. 'There aren't any numbers on the back – apart from *100*, of course.'

'No, you see,' he pointed to the blank white space on either side of the words 'IN GOD WE TRUST' cut in two by the spire of Independence Hall. 'There are ones and zeros written in yellow. Twenty-four of them on the left, twenty-one of them on the right.'

'Are you sure they're numbers,' I asked him, 'and not just marks?'

'There's no difference. A mark is a number, if you ascribe a value to it. I told you it was exciting.'

'If you say so.' I folded the note away again and picked up the cigarettes. 'Exciting *how*, anyway?'

'*How?*' His fingers drummed the table. 'It's like I told you in Paris. Ones and zeros. It's binary!'

'So . . . ?' He shook his head as if I was mentally incapacitated in some vital respect.

'So, Rachel is a computer scientist. Writing in binary values is what she does. One, zero. On, off. Yes, no.'

'Baaz?' He looked at me, eyes wide with unfathomable possibilities. 'There are billions of hundred-dollar bills out there in the world.' I pointed towards the window. 'And, you know, quite a few computer scientists, too. So . . .'

'But there are not billions of hundred-dollar bills out there with *that* serial number, connected to one of the world's *leading* computer scientists. What is the probability of that?'

'Small,' I admitted.

'Small? It's statistically *impossible*. And please don't tell me that she fancied you, because you are *totally* rubbish at mathematics.'

I let that go.

I wondered if his professor had also warned him of the dangers of looking for false positives.

'OK. Let's assume you're right. Back to my original question: what do you think it means?'

'Probably nothing.' He smiled at me and sat back in his chair. I made a strenuous effort to keep my hands on the table and not put them around his neck. 'But prime factorization is extremely important in cryptography,' he said, sensing my frustration.

'Cut me some slack, Baaz.'

'OK. You multiply one prime by another. The result is a semiprime, and that number secures the encryption. In order to break it, you'd need to know the numbers that were multiplied in the first place. It's very fast to multiply two large prime numbers and get the result. But it's *unbelievably* computer-intensive to do the reverse. Especially if you have a big prime.'

'How big?'

'The semiprime? Oh, up to 617 digits. Factoring them is an NP class problem.'

'A what?'

'Like I told you in Paris. A nondeterministic . . .' He cocked his head, patronizingly. 'A very complex problem that professors like Rachel can work on for their whole careers.'

'OK,' I said. 'Let's start at the beginning. How do *you* solve problems? Easy problems. One I could understand. Like . . .' I tried and failed to think of an easy maths question, 'a basic equation, or something.'

Baaz eyed me suspiciously. 'Simplify,' he replied. 'Get rid of all the clutter, so you can see exactly what the definites are. And then . . .' He paused.

I nodded at him. 'Go on.'

'And then you have to choose how you're going to do it – by brute force, trying every possible answer consecutively, or by using a shortcut, an algorithm.' He picked up another piece of the dessert. 'Why, how do you solve problems?'

'By eliminating their source.'

I stopped fiddling with the packet of Marlboros and pulled one out. I flipped open the book of matches that Talia had given me and tore a sulphur-tipped strip of card free of the base, and then looked again. There were only two other matches missing.

'That's strange,' I said under my breath, closing the cover. On the front was a black 7 logo stamped over a yellow flame. Probably some spook bar in Tel Aviv. I opened it again and pulled the matches away from the back cover. Printed in neat handwriting was an Israeli cell phone number. I put my hand into the jacket pocket I'd kept the cigarettes in. Empty. I tried the other one, and there it was: an identical book of matches, only with half the matches missing and no phone number – the book Talia had given me. I stood up and left a hundred-shekel note on the table.

'What's the matter?' Baaz asked, stuffing the last piece of baklava into his mouth.

'Nothing,' I said. 'Let's go.'

*

260

'*Ken, rega.*'

The bolts of the door scraped back again, the uncomfortable screech of metal dragging on metal. Moshe Mendel Katz's face appeared with a breath of turpentine in the opening; by his waist, the close-cropped head of little Binyomen.

'There was another question,' I said, 'that I wanted to ask.' I stepped forward and pushed the door. He stopped it with his foot.

'I'm sorry, but . . .'

I pushed harder and put my right shoulder into the door.

'Don't worry,' I said, 'it won't take long.' A shadow passed over the child's face. He backed away. Moshe caught his right arm by the wrist. As he did so, I shoved past them and back into the dark cavern of the studio warehouse. Baaz stepped forward, too, into the doorway, blocking the glare of the day outside. Moshe reached for the light switch. I reached for the SIG. He paused.

'OK,' I said, 'but keep your hands where I can see them.' I turned to Baaz, my palm wrapped around the grip of the pistol behind me, hidden from the boy. 'Come in and close the door,' I told him. He froze. 'Now!'

Baaz, startled, did as I said. He tripped the switch and the room flared to life. I turned back to Moshe. Under the unforgiving fluorescent strips he looked pale and scared. A film of sweat covered his face.

'Who is upstairs?'

'Please,' he said. 'The boy. I . . .'

'Who is upstairs?' I repeated more forcefully, cutting him off.

'His mother. Only his mother.'

'OK, Binyomen,' I said, 'be a good lad and go see Mummy. Grandpa and I have some business to discuss.'

'*Geyn,*' he said to the boy, letting go of his wrist. '*Ikh vel kumen bald.*'

The boy scampered off, across the storeroom and up the stairs, looking over his shoulder before he bolted through the door at the top. When he was out of sight, I brought the SIG around with my right hand. With my left, sandwiched between my first and second fingers, I produced the book of matches.

'Smoking is bad for your health, Moshe.'

'Max, what are you doing?' Baaz was standing to the side of us, slack-jawed. For the duration of the walk back to the traitor's gate, he'd been pestering me about what we were going to do. Now he knew.

'Solving an equation,' I replied. 'With brute force.'

I winked at him with my left eye, so Moshe couldn't see. I needed to relax him a little in advance of what was about to happen. I turned back to Moshe. I had a couple of minutes maximum before Binyomen and his mother and whoever else was really upstairs stuck their noses in.

'What was it you said? "In God we trust, but it doesn't hurt to have an insurance policy"?'

He put his hands up. I tucked the matches away. He'd given me a little gold, banking on it being enough to keep me at bay. It wasn't.

'Please, I . . .'

'You know her, don't you? You know Rachel Levy. That's why the Shabak was here. Isn't it?'

'The *Shabak*? No . . .' I moved towards him quickly, gun up, pushing his bulk against the wall with my left hand before he could finish his sentence. My shoulder flared with pain. We stared at each other. 'I don't know what you mean,' he coughed. 'I swear.'

I brought the pistol higher and placed the muzzle in front of his left eye. Then I leaned in, very close, and whispered into his ear.

'I'm not like them, Moshe. No rules. No laws. So, either you answer my questions, or your little apprentice will be watching *mame* sit *shiva* for his grandad.' I pinned him firmly with my left hand. 'I've come a long way. And believe me, I've got nothing left to lose.' He was breathing hard, rasping cigarette-scented breath into my face. 'Or maybe I should kill him instead. What do you think? You, or the boy?'

'No. Please.' He rasped. 'You don't understand. I can't . . .'

I pushed the muzzle into his eye socket. The metal split the skin by the bridge of his nose. He squealed with pain.

'Sure, you can. You know Rachel Levy, don't you?'

He began to cry. I pressed the SIG further into his eye.

'Baaz, go and get the kid.'

'Man, this is fucked up.'

'Just do it.'

Baaz stepped hesitantly away from us. I cocked the hammer of the SIG.

'OK, stop,' Moshe begged, barely able to get the words out. 'Please. Yes. Yes, I know her.'

I pulled the barrel clear of his skull and released my left hand. He collapsed on to his hand and knees, clutching his face. Deep sobs welled up inside him.

'And?'

'She asked me,' he said, 'to change that bill.'

'Why? Why did she ask that?'

'I don't know.'

'Look at me.' He kept his head low, hands on the floor. His body shook. 'Look at me, God damn you.' He raised his palms in supplication. Tears and snot matted his moustache and beard. Blood pooled in his eye and dripped along the side of his nose. 'Did you forge the notes?'

'No. I swear. It was the Russians. That's the truth. I told you the truth. I was trying to help you.'

'A lot of people are these days. *Which* Russians?'

'I don't know which Russians. *The* Russians. Those notes have been around for years. I only changed the number on that bill. That's all. I'm innocent, I swear.'

I brought the SIG to bear in the middle of his forehead. If you threaten someone with a weapon, there are only two rules: be sure they can't use it against you; and be sure you're prepared to use it. There was no way Moshe was going to wrestle the SIG away from me. And, by this point, pulling the trigger was just a formality. Colour and sound ebbed out of the world. My ears filled with the flat hum that comes just before a kill. My mind emptied, tethered to the bullet. Suddenly it was just me and him. Nothing, no one else existed. Of the many things Moshe might have been, *innocent* wasn't on the list.

'Why you? Why did she come to you?'

'She bought pictures from me. Horses. Always horses. She said they reminded her of home. The man who runs Gallery 7, the bar the matches come from. Avraham Landau. He buys from me. That's his number.'

'And he introduced you to Rachel?'

'Yes,' he nodded vigorously. 'We talked. I talked too much about the past. She came back last month, asked me to add the number to that bill. To remove the serial number on it and add that one. I don't know why. Please. I don't know any more. That's it. I swear.'

'Say your prayers,' I said, 'to your God.'

We locked eyes.

'Bad people,' he said. 'She told me the money, *that* money, came from bad people – people who wanted to kill her.'

'And that's why the Shabak was here?'

'No, I swear. They were never here. Never. Just Rachel. She was scared. Terrified. She said they would kill her. I gave her passports. Fake ones. So she and the old guy could get out. She was crazy. Insane. Nothing she said made any sense.'

'What, *exactly*,' I placed the tip of the barrel against the frown lines between his eyes, 'was she saying?'

'Please, Max. Please. They'll kill me.'

'So will I.' I adjusted my grip on the SIG. 'Keep talking.'

'She told me that . . .'

His shoulders slumped; his hands fell by his sides. He didn't seem to be able to get the words out. He was as frightened of telling me what she'd said as he was of having a gun in his face. Time was running out. I lowered the pistol.

'That what, Moshe?'

'That she had looked upon the Destroyer.'

'Who?' Baaz asked, incredulous.

I turned my head to look at him. He'd stopped walking towards the stairs once Moshe had started talking and was staring at both of us. He was in shock, overwhelmed by the violence, the weirdness of what was happening.

'The Destroyer,' Moshe said. 'The one Ha'Shem sent to kill the enemies of Israel.'

'You mean,' I said slowly, 'she told you that she had seen Death?'

'Yes,' he replied, wiping the blood out of his eye, 'that is exactly what I mean.'

'And she used that word? The "Destroyer"?'

'No,' he said. 'She used a Hebrew name, the folk name, from the Zohar. It means "the Helper of . . . Ha'Shem".'

'All right,' I said, tucking the SIG back into my jeans, 'and what folk name is that?'

He looked up at me. Tears and blood streamed from his eyes.

'Azrael,' he said. 'The archangel.'

26

'She was your girlfriend, wasn't she?'

I looked into the dregs of my beer and then up at Baaz. We were back on the terrace of The Lemon Tree hotel in Tel Aviv. He was sitting upright, hands outstretched, like a puppy waiting for a treat.

'Not exactly.'

'I knew it. And we're trying to save her.'

'No, Baaz. *I'm* trying to save her.'

He started to drum his fingers lightly on the table.

'You keep asking me what the number on that banknote means, like it has to mean something, like if it does mean something then you'll be able to help her. Right?'

'Right.' I put the glass to my lips and swallowed the last mouthful of Goldstar. 'And by the way, *you* said it meant something, not me.'

'OK, true. But this brute force business is bloody stressful. Do you want me to help you find a shortcut or are you going to point your gun at everyone we meet?'

'Pretty much. But sure, knock yourself out.'

'All right, but there's no "I" in "team". If you want me to help, then you have to level with me.'

'I have to what?'

'Level with me. You want to solve the equation? Then we have to balance it first. And I can't do the bloody sums if I don't know the bloody numbers.'

'But you do know the numbers.' I looked around for the waiter, impatient for another beer. 'You said you couldn't forget them if you tried.' I held up a single finger to the barman mixing a cocktail on the other side of the French windows. He nodded and I turned back to Baaz.

'Not the *numbers* numbers,' he said. 'I mean everything. You, her, the secret mission. That's the real equation.'

'Baaz, you're in enough trouble as it is. The more you know . . .' I paused as the waiter appeared with a small dish of roasted almonds, 'the worse it's going to get.'

'Who led you to the Traitor? Who bought you your bloody plane ride, anyway?' His voice was rising, scratchy and emotional. 'Just a kid, am I? A stupid kid you had to save in the catacombs, who's got in the way ever since? I don't think so.' His fingers fell still. And – unlike during his other outbursts – his eyes were dry, and looking directly into mine. 'So, what do you want to do?' he continued. 'Sit on your arse and drink beer all day or do some bloody work?'

'Fair enough,' I said. 'You've earned that.'

And he had. The catacombs had been a bloodbath. In the space of three days I'd saved his life, tried to lose him, tried to kill him, and then co-opted him. And in return he'd saved me in Paris, put everything at risk by following me to Israel, and applied himself with more success than I'd had to working out the possible meanings of the hundred-dollar bill. I'd taken him half into my confidence and my conscience – unsure whether he was an asset or a liability, a mate or a mark.

The wind was picking up. I pulled my jacket tighter across my shoulders. Out to sea the sun was slipping into the Med. On the terrace it was time for a potentially lethal dose of truth. When my beer arrived, I ordered a double Johnnie Walker Black chaser.

I was going to need it.

An hour later Baaz knew everything except my real, Irish, name. I'd been careful with my parents' details, too. But apart from that he knew more about me than anyone alive, except Rachel herself and, just maybe, Commander Frank Knight.

'This information,' I concluded with the same warning I'd begun with, 'is a death sentence. Best-case scenario when we get out of this – *if* we get out of it – you'll be given a new identity, a new life. Money, sure . . . but no more trips to see your auntie in London. No visiting your dad doing time in Chandigarh. No more trips to Chandigarh, *period*. Worst-case scenario, and I've been burned, permanently disconnected by London? That doesn't bear thinking about. You understand?'

'Yes,' he said. 'I understand.' He wrinkled his nose and picked up my glass of Johnnie Walker and sniffed the whisky. 'But what I don't understand is how you can drink this rubbish.' He grimaced. 'It's disgusting.'

'You and Commander Knight might get on, after all,' I said. 'Which is a terrifying prospect.'

I sat back in the chair, drained from unburdening myself, exhausted at the scale of the investigation ahead. Baaz, by comparison, was giddy, enthused with his new-found responsibilities. His mind was working overtime. His eyes flitted left and right, but no longer settled on mine. His fingers drummed the air again.

'There are,' he said at last, staring out at the darkened sea, 'three variables we need to assign values to.'

'That sounds optimistic.'

'Variables,' he said, emphatically, 'not unknowns. If we can assign a value to the variables, we can calculate the unknowns.' I raised my eyebrows. 'OK,' he conceded, '*probably* calculate them.'

'Go on, then.'

'Well,' he said, 'you need to know who released your passport photograph.'

'First of all,' I corrected him, '*we* need to know. We're a team now, remember? And second – that's not a variable. I already told you, no one but Frank Knight could have done that. So, the question isn't *who* did it, but why *Frank* did it.'

'No,' he said. 'That's not correct. You assume he did it, but you discount the possibility of unknown factors that might mean he didn't.'

'Baaz, if this is going to work – between us, I mean – you're just going to have to accept that there are some things I know that you don't. And one thing I know is that no one except Frank Knight could have connected that passport photograph to my name.'

'Totally . . .'

'Thank you,' I said, cutting him off.

'. . . incorrect. It wouldn't be an unknown if you knew it, would it? *Total* contradiction in terms. You said all that stuff – the photos, the passports – are stored online, at the passport office?'

'Yes, but . . .'

'Yes but, no but. If it's online, some tricky bugger will find it somehow. Trust me,' he said, smiling, 'I know.'

'OK, let's leave that one, shall we? What next?'

'*Arkhangel.* Totally crucial.'

'We agree on that, at least.'

'So, tell me . . .'

'Uh-huh?'

'Would you have kept the note if it hadn't had that word written on it?'

'No, I guess not.'

'Not "guess not". Of *course* not. It was completely crazy. There you are in this random cottage, and then *shabash*! You find something *totally* personal. It's like Benjamin Franklin bloody speaks to you. *Directly.*'

'Yeah, well that's how it felt. But . . . it's the wrong *Arkhangel*, isn't it? An actual angel, not the village. That's what Moshe was telling us.'

In truth I'd been trying *not* to think about some of what Moshe had told us, or what to make of it. Looking upon the Destroying Angel was not where I'd been expecting the interrogation to go. No matter which way I cut it, the most likely of all conclusions – and the worst – was that Moshe was right and Rachel had gone insane. The closer I got to her, the further she slipped away. I tried hard to block the image as it assembled in my head, but to no avail. There she was, lying in a crimson pool of her own blood. She'd been on the edge of madness then, as her arteries pumped the life out of her. I'd been crazy, too – running, only running. Stupid, scared Max, losing his lover and then his mother. And here I was, losing Rachel all over again.

But the word meant something. *Azrael.* I could see it, hear it, in an endless loop of almost-familiarity. The sound, the feeling of it, danced on the edge of my consciousness: a face in the crowd, a childhood memory – real but unreachable.

'Max?'

'Uh, sorry. What was that?'

'Cyrillic. It's written in Russian. In Cyrillic.' He paused, as if summoning up the courage to say something.

'Go on. Spit it out. What is it?'

'Does Rachel speak Russian?'

'No, at least not when I knew her. Her father couldn't speak it, either. His parents refused to teach him.'

'Exactly!' he said, triumphant. 'You see, it doesn't have to mean one thing or the other. It can mean both at the same time. *Totally* quantum. Tell me,' he said, 'your mother and this Doctor Levy, Rachel's father . . .'

'Easy, sunshine.' I fixed him with a stern look.

'No! No . . . It's just, well . . . Would it . . .' he chose his words more carefully, 'have meant anything to *him*? The place where your mother was born, that is.'

I looked out to sea. I saw my mother at home, laying her hand lightly on Doc's arm. During my father's long absences they would sit together, side by side in the gathering Wicklow dusk, saying little, sharing a drink. And then, out of nowhere, that peal of laughter, light and bright and full of joy, bringing her to life.

'Yes,' I said. 'I think it would.'

'OK. So, let's assume Rachel wrote it on the banknote. Maybe not insane, after all then, hmm?' He left that idea and moved on, aware enough, at least, of the effect of his questioning on my mood. 'That just leaves Moshe,' he said. 'He was right about the money.'

'What about the money?'

'About what it's being used for. Its purpose. Not just your note, though. You said there was more money?'

'Uh-huh. A *lot* more.'

In the 1980s, the Lebanese plates had printed over a billion dollars of forged fiat. Frank Knight would have known that, and most likely used the size of Moshe's run to calculate the numbers he'd quoted in Doherty's pub. If the Israelis had printed that quantity of fakes then, there was no reason to doubt that the Russians could do the same – or more – now.

'OK, so we follow it. That's what they say, isn't it? "Follow the money." It's *so* Hollywood, *huna*? Who do you think will play me in the movie?' Baaz burst out laughing.

'Jesus, Mary and Joseph. What did I do to deserve this?'

'Heaven knows, but right now you're guilty of starving a poor Punjabi boy half to death. I could eat a horse.' Then he looked worried, and added: 'If I wasn't a vegetarian, of course.'

Baaz was right. I was hungry again, too. I stood up to fetch a menu, and looked out across the city for a moment, considering what he'd said. It seemed to me there were far more than the three variables he had lit upon. Chief among them was whether or not Frank Knight had known that it was Rachel's colleague Amos Stein, and not Chappie Connor, waiting for me in the cottage. And finding out what Stein was doing there in the first place didn't seem likely while I was stuck in the Middle East.

'I'd give my kingdom for a bloody horse, never mind eating one,' I said under my breath. 'Anything to get out of here.'

And then a window opened in my mind and through it I looked back into the Traitor's studio. And then another, through which I saw Rachel's office. The images began to run together. Doc patching my shoulder, me turning a quick circle around the corpse in the cottage. There it was. Mane flowing, nostrils flaring, the pale mare galloping across the Irish countryside. There *they* were.

'That's it!' I said out loud. 'Baaz, that's fucking it!'

'That's what?' He looked nervous – worried, probably, that I was about to do something violent or unpredictable.

'Go and get your laptop. We're going to do some bloody work sitting on our arses.'

'OK, what are we looking for?'

Baaz sat poised over his screen, veggie burger in one hand, fruit juice in the other. Although it was chilly on the terrace, it made a good office. I'd ordered a steak and another Scotch.

'Title deeds. Is there any way you can see who owns the cottage in Donegal?'

'Probably. Let's see . . .' He bit a mouthful out of the burger and started typing.

'Anonymously.'

'Thank goodness you reminded me. I was totally going to post this on Facebook,' Baaz sighed. I ignored that and he tapped away. 'OK, Citizens Information . . .' He paused and clicked his tongue. 'Property deeds . . .' Another pause. 'Land registry. OK. Here we go. What's the address?'

'It doesn't have one; not an official one, anyway.' I leaned in next to him and looked at the map he'd loaded. 'Zoom in here, to Gortnalughoge. That's where I did the recce from, the holiday park. Go east across the bay. Stop. There.' I pointed at the screen. 'That's it.'

Baaz clicked on the oblong outline of the old cottage.

'The property isn't registered,' he said. He chomped on the burger again and mumbled, 'What next?' But before I could answer, he'd loaded a new page. 'Hang on.' He typed and then swallowed. 'This is going to cost five euros.'

'Anonymous, remember?'

He gave me a sideways glance.

'Right. No, nothing on the house. It's going to be tricky to determine ownership.'

'Great.' I sat back and chewed a mouthful of steak. 'It's never bloody easy, is it?'

'But the land it's on,' he continued, a grin spreading across his face, '*is* registered.' He paused dramatically. 'Drum roll, please.'

'For fuck's sake.'

'OK! Registered . . . in the name of one Jacob Benjamin Israel Levy.'

'Fuck.'

'But you knew!' For once he looked genuinely impressed. 'How?'

'The horses. Moshe said he met Rachel because she bought paintings from him, paintings of horses that reminded her of home. There was one on Moshe's wall, in the storeroom. There's one on her office wall, too. And another in Doc's house, in the room where he stitched me up.'

'And there was one in the cottage, too?'

'Yeah, there was. And that's not all. The painting, there,' I pointed at his laptop, as if it were a magic portal back home, 'the fourth horse. It was of a pale mare.'

'So?'

'So, look it up, clever clogs.' He did, and his face dropped. 'Let me see.'

He turned the laptop towards me. The screen was filled with the image of a painting by Viktor Vasnetsov, a Russian artist, reproductions of whose pictures my mother had adorned our house in Ireland with. In it the Four Horsemen of the Apocalypse ran amok. They were led by a white horse and its mounted archer; a swordsman followed on a brown steed; and in the hands of a third horseman, astride a black stallion,

275

a set of scales dipped menacingly. But at the back, slightly distant from the others and carrying a spear, a fourth figure rode a sickly, pale mare: staring down over the land he'd laid waste to, sat the shroud-wrapped skeleton of Death himself.

Baaz closed the screen.

'Man,' he said, blowing out hard through puffed cheeks, 'you Christians are, like, *totally* nuts.'

27

'More coffee, please.'

It was a bright, breezy morning – already nearly twenty degrees. There was a stiff wind from the south that cut across the hotel terrace, carrying with it the harsh, flinty taste of the city. In Jerusalem it always felt as if I was on the edge, caught between the ideal of the city and the reality of the desert that surrounded it. I preferred Tel Aviv. The sea was constant, the horizon fixed. *Just like home*, I thought to myself. But the truth was that home, like the Holy City, was just an idea. It could mean anything you wanted it to. The waitress cleared away the remains of breakfast.

'And for your friend?'

I shrugged. There was no sign of Baaz. She smiled and headed back inside. There was no sign, either, that shaking down Moshe had stirred up trouble. I looked at the date on the copy of *Haaretz* I'd brought with me from my room. Thursday 18 January.

Shit.

Ten days ago I'd blown the top of Amos Stein's head off. He might have lived as a mathematician, but he'd died as a courier. I worked backwards and pieced the dates together. His run from Tel Aviv to Donegal had taken him two days, via Moscow. Ellard was right: *A rabbit never bolts straight for the burrow* – Stein included. If Avilov was on to him, then Stein's forged passport slowed his pursuit. If Baaz and I could work out that Doc Levy owned the cottage, so could

Avilov – too late to intercept Stein at the cottage, but in time to intercept me by the shore of Lough Conn. Talia said Stein had arrived in the UK on the thirtieth, so he must have left Israel on the twenty-eighth. That put him in the cottage two days before I showed up to do the recce – which tallied with the date Frank had given me.

Stein had also left Israel a full twenty-four hours before Rachel had gone missing. It was possible that his departure had triggered her disappearance; and possible, given how terrified Moshe said she'd been, that she'd known something was going to happen to her. Perhaps she'd sent Stein and his message back home while she still could – as a failsafe, an *insurance policy* in Moshe's words. But against what?

'Sorry I'm late.'

Baaz sat down in the chair next to me and set his laptop on the table. It was as if he was connected to its shiny silver case by an umbilical cord; a digital witch's-familiar for the twenty-first century. He'd switched his simple black turban for a crimson one and marshalled what passed for his beard into a neat series of wisps. I ran the back of my hand over my chin and made a mental note to ask housekeeping for a razor.

'I've been thinking about the dates,' he said, 'and about that Russian joker, too, who you said turned up in Paris, in the catacombs.' Baaz sipped from my untouched glass of orange juice. 'The boss man.'

'Who, Avilov?'

'Yeah. By my calculation, he arrived here in Israel a couple of days before you started the stakeout, at the cottage.'

'Reconnaissance. We do reconnaissance, not stakeouts.

But yeah, that's correct – assuming Talia isn't spinning us a line.'

Which was always possible, of course. Ezra had said that she was on the side of the angels – though from where I was standing that was no longer necessarily a good thing. The fact she had that book of matches meant she'd definitely known more than she was letting on. It seemed unlikely that she'd given them to me in Rachel's office by accident.

'OK, whatever. But then he pops up again on that ship in the English Channel, where he's trying to keep you alive – sort of. That's when you first meet him, right?' Baaz was speaking fast now. I got the feeling sometimes that if he could entirely dispense with words and just use numbers, he would.

I nodded. 'So?'

'So that means he's behind the curve. Don't you see? He's trying to solve a problem, too. He's got his own equation and the reason he, or whatever boss-Russian he works for, wants you alive is because they think you can solve it for them – just like the Israelis, probably.'

'OK. But why not just take the banknote? He had me strung up by my ankles – and what, his goons didn't even think to search my pockets? Any amateur would have done that. It doesn't make sense.'

'Variables. Your equation has variables. His equation has variables. *Unknown* variables. Same–same. You're both in the dark. And then, *boom*!'

'There have been a lot of *booms* so far, Baaz. Which one is going off now?'

'Bloody Paris, Max! Before you meet this – what did

you call him, "bad Bulgarian"? – no one knows you've even *got* the banknote. And then you tell . . . Ah, what *is* his name?'

'Lukov, Sergei Lukov.'

'Right. You tell Lukov, and he tells bloody everyone, and the next thing you know Bob's your bloody uncle: the whole city's a war zone, and some Russian bastard is trying to drown me in the catacombs.'

He had a point. Until Lukov started the auction, the only people who'd known I'd laid hands on the hundred-dollar bill were Frank and the shooter in the cottage. I'd told Frank I'd lost it, and the shooter had no way of knowing whether I'd managed to hang on to it in the surf. Prior to Lukov going public, my connection to the note rested on whether Frank bought my lies – or, maybe, whether the shooter had survived.

The waitress arrived with more drinks. We both fell silent and looked awkwardly out to sea while she refilled my coffee cup and poured tea for Baaz.

'So,' I said quietly, 'Rachel uses her colleague Amos Stein to send a message to her father. But nobody, not even Moshe, *knew* she had. Maybe not even Doc knew it. To everyone else it would just look like she was sending him cash. Like you do, to your auntie.'

'*Will* do,' he corrected me, blushing. '*Totally* unremarkable.'

'Exactly,' I said. 'The gunman in the cottage was waiting for some*one*, not some*thing*. Otherwise why stick around?'

'Well done, Maximilian. Professor Bhavneet Singh awards you an A-minus for effort.'

'Yeah, but who the hell was he?'

'That,' replied Baaz, 'is one hundred per cent your department. But from what you're saying, he can't have been a

Russian. The dates don't work, do they?' He looked around for the waitress again. 'I wonder if they have bagels? I mean, it's Israel. They've got to have bagels, right?'

He was right. The shooter in the cottage couldn't have been one of Avilov's men. The dates didn't tally. Until my name and face had popped up in *The Times*, Avilov hadn't even known what to call me – at least, he hadn't spoken my name in the ship's hold.

The same couldn't be said of Doc. He *could* have been killed on Avilov's orders – though my money was on one gunman, with that signature shot to the heart. Most terribly of all, if the shooter in the cottage had survived, and then killed Doc, I'd led him straight to my oldest friend's door, after all.

It was heartbreaking and infuriating in equal measure. As soon as one question was answered, another presented itself. But we *were* getting somewhere. While Doc had worked on my wounds, he'd told me that I'd been lucky to find him, that he'd had a shooting trip planned. And there's good shooting in Donegal in January – snipe and woodcock, particularly. The more I looked at everything, the more it seemed Doc must have been the intended recipient – even if he might not have known he was, or what the banknote signified. But as soon as he'd spotted the name of my mother's birthplace, he – like me – would have understood it meant something important. But if Doc *had* known what was going on, or if he'd had the means to work it out, then that knowledge was gone, too – incinerated in the remains of his eccentric mansion.

Trying to work out what it all added up to didn't make me feel like an A-grade student. It made me feel sick to my stomach. No matter how hard I tried to wash it off, Doctor

Jacob Levy's blood still clung to my hands. I went back over every detail of the firefight in the cottage, sieving my memory for anything that might help point to the path ahead.

Discovering the banknote and then deciphering its significance had been woven inextricably into my own personal quest to find Rachel. Seeing my photograph in the paper had forced me to run. Sure, it had shrunk the world around me. But as much as it had made life more complicated, it had also released me. The press reports were like a knife, cutting the bonds that tied me to process and procedure. However difficult it was operating beyond orders, I was free to do what I liked, how I liked. There were no rules, and no one to answer to except myself.

I didn't know if Rachel had made a run for it or had been abducted. I didn't even know if she was still alive. But if Avilov was as much in the dark about her whereabouts as I was, I might still get to her first.

'Well,' I said, 'we've only got one lead left, so we may as well use it.'

'What's that?' Baaz asked.

I put Moshe's book of matches face up on the table. The black 7 logo danced on its yellow flame. Then I opened the book and pulled the matchheads forward to reveal the hidden cell phone number scrawled on the cardboard backing. Baaz half rose out of his seat in excitement.

'You're going to call it?'

'Not yet.' He sat down again, disappointed. 'Let's scope out this Gallery 7 online first. Look nationwide, not just in Tel Aviv.'

Baaz opened the case to his digital demon and clicked away at the keys.

'It's definitely a gallery.' He typed some more. 'A gallery *bar*. Art and cocktails. "The most relaxed VIP vibe in Tel Aviv."' He looked over the screen at me. 'It's a few blocks south of here, in the centre of town.'

'I wonder,' I said, finishing my coffee, 'if the punters know they're buying Moshe's *interpretations*?'

28

Baaz and I got out of the taxi simultaneously and cut north, across Rothschild Boulevard, up Allenby Street. I'd assumed we'd be followed. So, as a precaution, we'd changed car three times, splitting up for an hour and then rejoining for the final, short drive. I couldn't discount the possibility that Talia had given me her book of matches by accident – but equally I'd never seen or heard the Israelis do anything that wasn't deliberate. Whatever the case, even the slimmest edge of surprise counted for something.

There were any number of ways the visit to Gallery 7 could play out. In anticipation of it going wildly wrong – which wasn't unlikely – I'd spent the rest of the morning familiarizing Baaz with the SIG semi-auto. By the time we left the hotel he could strip, reassemble and load it, make ready and make safe. He said he'd never even picked up a gun before, but after an initial bout of unease his fingers moved confidently around the steel frame. The point at which Baaz needed to use my pistol was the point at which it probably didn't matter whether he managed to successfully or not. But instructing him gave us something to talk about other than endless unanswerable questions and intractable equations.

We went through the basics of what to do if the shit hit the fan (if he forgot everything else, just get small, fast), and then I'd broached the delicate issue of concealment: there was no way I was walking to the bar unarmed, and no way I could risk trying to conceal a weapon from the inevitable security search at the entrance.

'No!' he'd said at first, so vehemently that I was physically taken aback. 'Impossible. I'm not a bloody Nihang warrior. It's *manha*. Forbidden. *Totally* out of the question.'

It had taken an afternoon of persuasion and perseverance, but eventually he agreed – on the condition that he did it himself, entirely alone and without me looking, never mind helping. I consented. And forty-five minutes later Baaz had emerged from the bathroom resplendent in his now over-sized, tightly wrapped crimson turban – this time concealing not just his hair but also the compact frame of the SIG 9mm.

'OK,' I'd said, 'now you have to practise walking and talking. Back straight, no nodding. Think of it like spy finishing school.' He didn't laugh.

By the time we'd climbed – carefully – into the taxi at The Lemon Tree he was so slick that, if I hadn't known, I'd never have guessed he was carrying. In the security line outside the bar he was quiet and concentrated – a dignified ramrod try-ing and failing to make small talk.

'This,' he said, still unsmiling, 'is absurd.' His voice wavered with nerves. His fingers drummed the air by his sides.

'It's OK,' I tried to reassure him.

'I can't do it,' he blurted out. 'Max, really . . .'

I put my hand on his shoulder, and gripped him tight. The couple in front of us turned to stare at him. I smiled and they looked the other way.

'Five minutes,' I hissed in his ear, 'and we're in. And then it's off. It's done.'

'But . . .'

'Baaz?' I stepped back a fraction and looked him straight

in the eye. He stared at the pavement. 'Be cool, OK? You can do it. It's all good. Everything's going to be fine.'

He breathed out slowly. When his fingers stopped drumming, I saw that his hands were shaking.

'OK,' he said. 'It's OK. I'm OK.' Then he turned around and his fingers resumed their silent dance.

The entrance was on the ground floor of an uninspiring modern block, fringed by a line of evergreens. The faint thumping of electronic bass trickled out into the street. Above the door a black 7 was embossed on to a bright yellow flame; in front of the door a thickset bouncer with an ear-piece and a bulging suit waved down would-be punters with a handheld metal detector. The crowd was well-heeled and had a few years on the bright young party things we'd seen queuing up elsewhere from the taxi windows. The security check was so second nature it didn't even interrupt conversation.

Baaz went first.

'*Ma kore*,' he greeted the doorman in Hebrew. *Good evening.* His nervousness manifested as arrogance. He fitted right in.

The bouncer's reply was inaudible, but within another couple of minutes we were both inside the building.

'Since when could you speak Hebrew?'

'The waitress at the hotel. She's been teaching me. Easier than French.' He winked. 'Good accent, eh?'

I stepped in front of him, parted a velvet curtain on the far side of the coat-check and walked into the bar first. The electronic beats that had seeped outside deepened and expanded, filling the cavernous low-lit joint with a disconcerting, undulating rhythm. Centre stage was an island bar, orbited by beautiful women and older, manicured men. The walls were lined with paintings – all the same size, all

286

reworkings of the same drowning-man motif in different shades of red and blue, pink and white. Limbs twisted. Mouths gulped. Silent screams engulfed in a horror-kitsch art-aquarium. Above them, at the far end of the room, a glass staircase led to a mezzanine. Short skirts flashed above the parapet. A DJ kept the beats going on a set of turntables behind them. It was busy, but not crowded – the atmosphere fine-tuned to make men in their forties feel as young as their girlfriends. There's nothing quite so effective as the promise of eternal youth to part men from their money.

'You find the bathroom; I'm going to get a drink. Remember what I said about how to do this?'

'Yes,' he replied, but he looked suddenly unsure of himself.

'Don't worry. You'll be grand.'

He headed off, back straight, avoiding the clusters of drinkers orbiting the bar. I took my time and spiralled around the perimeter, checking out the paintings and the people who might purchase them, eventually winding up at the far end of the bar, where there were no tables and no punters to hem me in. After pretending not to see me for an almost-but-not-quite unprofessional moment, the barman drifted over and jerked his head towards me. He looked like he should have been shaking down customers out the back, not shaking cocktails for them behind the bar. Blond hair. Blue eyes. Six-four, two-twenty pounds and ripped. It was like looking at a hologram of my younger, fitter self. I rolled my shoulders and felt the wound left by the shooter in the cottage pulling at itself. I remembered, again, that I needed a shave. Right then I didn't feel even forty-two, never mind twenty-two.

'Johnnie Walker Black on the rocks. A double. And, hey,

is it OK if I use the house phone? I left my cell in the cab. Pain in the arse.'

He looked at me in such a way as to leave no doubt that I was, leaned over and handed me the receiver from a wireless landline docked beside the till. As he did so, his shirt gaped open at the neck. Hanging there on a gold chain was a traditional three-barred Russian cross. I thanked him, squinting over his shoulder at the expensive bottles lined up behind him. Individual labels drew into focus: vodka. A *lot* of vodka.

I looked around for Baaz, but there was no sign of him in the crowd on the other side of the room. While blondie poured the Scotch, I dialled the number in the book of matches and counted the rings. On the sixth tone the line clicked. Coming back to me, in a distorted reverb, was the fractionally delayed *thump-thump-thump* of the music smothering the bar. Avraham Landau was on the premises.

'What the fucking shit do you want, Yossi? I told you not to disturb me.' Pure foul-mouthed mother-tongue Russian. I took a deep breath.

'I've got a problem,' I said, also in Russian. 'At the bar.'

'Then fucking deal with it,' came the reply.

'*Nyet*,' I said. 'It's a big problem. Shabak.'

'Fuck. OK. Offer them a drink on the house. I'll come down.'

I hung up and exchanged the handset for a heavy tumbler of whisky. As I did so, Baaz sidled up beside me. The plan was a simple one: he would remove the SIG from his turban in the bathroom, retie it and then hide the pistol in his folded jacket – which he would then pass to me in the dimly lit jostle of the bar. He stood next to me, nervously swaying from one foot to the other, out of time with the music.

I stepped back from the bar to give a lone, black-eyed

woman with an elaborate hairdo and an expensive smile a shot at getting served.

'OK, let me have it.' I was looking over Baaz's shoulder, scanning the room for any response to my call. He didn't move. 'Baaz?' I faced him properly. He was rooted to the spot. He was still wearing his jacket.

'I'm sorry,' he said. 'There was a . . . a problem.'

'What, in the bathroom?'

He nodded. I looked around. A short guy with a black ponytail, wearing a red shirt and a deep frown, bounced down the stairs. Avraham Landau. I watched him skirt around the customers and rock up to the bar. The frown evaporated into a shit-eating grin.

'Yossi,' I saw him mouth at the barman in Russian. 'Where are our friends?'

The barman shrugged, kicking off the inevitable 'you said, he said' exchange.

'Baaz, I need it now. Is it in the bathroom?' He nodded, eyes downcast. Landau put his hands on his hips and looked up at the ceiling. The barman was looking for me. 'Fuck it. Which stall is it in?'

'It's in . . .'

'Where, Baaz? Where is it?'

He looked up at me, eyes pleading. 'It's in the hotel. I couldn't do it. It's not . . . It's forbidden.' Tears welled up in his eyes. 'I'm sorry.'

The barman clocked me and turned to his boss.

Fuck.

I gave Baaz my whisky glass and headed straight towards them. The barman's hands went under the countertop.

Two metres.

The black-eyed woman who'd been served after me turned

on her heels, martini glass in hand, the DJ's rhythm moving her hips, smile dancing on her lips.

'Hey,' I said, wrapping around her, 'you look great.'

I drew her close to me. She froze, rigid, the movement of the music draining out of her. Our cheeks touched. My fingers found the back of her head and slid up her neck, withdrawing the long, forked silver slide holding her hair in place. With my left arm I swept her away from me, gently. Her glass fell and smashed. Vodka evaporated into the barroom night. She stumbled and I heard her gasp. My right hand kept moving, arcing forward and then down, hard. The barman's fist was wrapped around the grip of a Jericho 9mm. I drove the pointed metal tongues between his knuckles, trapping his trigger finger beneath the steel of the guard and the wooden countertop.

I twisted the hairpin and brought my wrist across his face, striking his left temple. He reeled backwards, gun hand relaxing. I wrenched the barrel of the pistol up and out, snapping his index finger, the limp digit still caught in the guard. Then I brought the Jericho to bear on him at point blank. His left hand came around, gripping the neck of a vodka bottle. I leaned in, ramming the muzzle into his sternum. I put my thumb on the back of the slide and fired. The 9mm round tore a wound channel straight through his chest, severing his spine – the noise of the shot absorbed by his lungs and the unopened breech. He dropped. Six seconds from grabbing his gun to hitting the deck.

The bass rumble of the music thundered on, overwritten by the bright notes of an electronic crescendo shifting from one turntable to another. I'd blocked the line of sight of the black-eyed woman I'd robbed, and there wasn't anything more unusual to hear than the vodka bottle hitting the ground.

No one turned around. If they had, all they'd have seen was an unattended bar. I racked the Jericho. The spent cartridge case leapt out, clattering like a brass ice cube into a tumbler on the bar. The only other person who knew what was happening was Landau.

He started to run but ploughed into a couple dancing. Entwined in hair and limbs, he stumbled. The pissed-off dancing partner pushed him back towards me and I caught him by the wrist, twisting it up into a lock behind his back.

'*Prostite*,' I said in Russian to the dancers. *Sorry*. 'Too much vodka.' They shrugged it off and wrapped their arms around each other. I dug the Jericho into Landau's ribs, hard enough to bruise them.

'Move. Your office. Now. Keep smiling or I'll kill you here. *Ponyal?*' He told me he understood. I turned to Baaz as we moved off towards the stairs. 'Don't go to the hotel. I'll meet you on the beach, by the marina. OK?' He nodded. 'And ditch the turban.' He nodded again and we went our separate ways.

'Kneel down.'

He was trembling, sweat glossed his face. Close up, in the brighter light of his office, I could see him clearly for what he was: a mid-fifties, art-dealing, mafioso arsehole. I turned my head.

'You too.'

The skinny brunette standing next to him got on her knees as well, high heels splayed out behind her, miniskirt halfway up her waist. She'd been bent over when we walked in, snorting a line of white powder off the desk. Now she was sobbing, eyes red and wet, begging me in hoarse, tear-soaked Russian whispers not to hurt her. She was pretty and still in her teens, and as high as a kite.

'Listen,' he pleaded in Russian. 'You're not the Shabak, so who are you? We can cut a deal. Is it money? I've got money. You can have money. My name is Avi, OK? Avi Landau. Everyone knows I have money. Sveta, show him where the safe is, honey. Give him the money.'

Sveta looked at me. I looked at Sveta and then behind her at what I guessed was a door to a walk-in closet.

'Is the safe in there?'

She nodded. More sobbing. She buried her face in her hands, gagging on the phlegm clogging her nose and throat.

'OK, get up and get in and lock the door. Don't come out till the police tell you to.' She looked at Avi for permission. 'Move!'

She stood and then lurched forward, grabbing at the desk to steady herself. Keeping her back to me, she ran her fingers across the remnants of the powder, rubbing it into her gums, before stepping through the doorway. I turned back to Avi.

'I got your number from a mutual friend. I'd like to do some business.' His eyes widened. 'I've got one hundred dollars,' I continued in Russian. 'It's an unusual bill. A very sought-after issue. I'd like to know what I can buy with it.'

He dropped his hands slightly and held them out towards me, palms up.

'OK, man, I don't know who your friend is, but you got the wrong guy. You understand? If you want money, or a painting, we can talk, but . . .'

I cut him off with a round through the left hand. His thumb, forefinger detached. Blood splattered his face. Sveta screamed through the door. He doubled over, groaning through gritted teeth, forehead scraping the floor. Outside, the music throbbed and pulsed, louder and louder.

'What can I buy with my hundred dollars, Avi?'

'Fuck you.'

'No,' I said, 'fuck *you*.' I swept my left leg around, catching him on the left ear with my foot. He fell sideways, and looked up at me.

'Do you know who the fuck I am?'

Right foot thrust kick to the ribcage.

I felt bone crack under the force of the blow. Old-school punishment beating: underrated and surprisingly effective. PIRA had taught us a trick or two. Avi balled up on his side, the remains of his bloodied hand clamped over his shattered ribs, knees drawn up to his chest. Saliva pooled on the floor beneath his cheek. I kicked him again in the same spot and felt more bones snap. He was in trouble now. Blood bubbled around his mouth; his breathing had become shallow and fast. In all likelihood I'd punctured his lung. I squatted down and pushed the tip of the Jericho into the back of his left knee.

'Tell me about the money.'

'I swear I . . .'

I shot out his kneecap.

Avi roared a deep, tearing scream. He writhed and begged and brought both his hands down to the wound. The knee had imploded; lead, bone and shredded clothing blown out through the joint. I kicked his hands away and put the muzzle of the pistol against the back of his right knee. Sveta stopped screaming. I took out the hundred-dollar bill and held it in front of his face.

'What,' I said, 'does this money buy?'

'Please God, no. Please. *Please.*'

'What did it buy Rachel?' I pushed the barrel of the Jericho deep into the soft flesh below his thigh.

'*Arkhangel,*' he hissed through gritted teeth.

'What the fuck is *Arkhangel*?'

'Her work, man. Her project. The money paid for everything. Understand? Everything. Please, help me now. Please.'

'Who sends it?'

He was crying wildly now, the pain crushing the sense out of him. The main door to the office swung open. The doorman from downstairs had replaced his metal detector with a Mossberg pump-action. As he raised the barrel, I put two rounds in his chest. He collapsed backwards into the corridor. I walked over to him. There was no one else in sight – just the illuminated emergency exit sign at the far end of the corridor. And then the music stopped.

Screaming. Heels clicking on stone.

Motorcycle cops would arrive within seconds of the barman's body being dialled in. I dragged the bouncer into the office by his ankle and closed the door. Breath rattled in his chest. I shot him again, and then turned the pistol on Avi.

'This is it, Avi. This is what all their money gets you. Shit paintings and a bullet to the head.' He crossed himself right to left, the Orthodox way. 'Who sends it?' I asked again.

'*Moskva*,' he gurgled through the blood and pain. 'The Akvarium.'

29

'You killed Landau, didn't you?'

I found Baaz slumped on the beach where we'd agreed to meet, just south of the marina. He was balled up against the cold, shivering. Leaving the bar immediately the fight broke out, he'd swapped the crimson turban for a plain, black wrap. I hoped he'd walked the long way around. It was quiet, just a couple of kids drinking beer and making out by the promenade. Further off, a string of joggers pounded along by the sea.

'Don't worry about it,' I said, squatting down beside him. 'What's done is done.'

It had taken me well over an hour to get to him, ducking down side streets and back alleys. It was a relief to escape the blue light shed by the police cars. The cops had made it into the bar while I was still upstairs. I'd forced a window and scaled a drainpipe, before taking off over the roofs and dropping down into a private garden. The Shabak would put two and two together almost immediately – if it hadn't had someone in place in the joint all along. I hoped Sveta had stayed put until the cops covered the bodies. To them it would just look like a gangland shootout.

'No,' he said. 'I messed up.' His voice cracked. Tears fell on to the already wet sand between his bent knees. He was shaking – though whether from nerves or the cold I couldn't tell. 'If I'd done like you said and hidden the gun, you wouldn't have had to kill the barman.' His shoulders heaved.

A light breeze from inland carried his sobs off over the sea. 'I knew how important it was. I know how much trouble we're in. And now it's my fault he's dead.'

'Hey . . .' I put my hand on his shoulder. We were too exposed. The city was no longer safe – if it ever had been. 'It's OK. I asked too much of you, that's all. It wasn't your fault. If he hadn't drawn on me, he'd be mixing Moscow mules right now.' I could see how he was pinned. I'd been hanging from the same hook for days. I wanted to tell him that at least the barman hadn't been his oldest, only friend. 'We create our own Angel of Death, Baaz. He made his. That's all there is to it.'

He wiped the snot out of his moustache with the back of his sleeve.

'And I've made mine by coming here, haven't I?'

'I'm not going to tell you anything that isn't true. This is dirty work and we're up against it, that's for sure. All hell's going to break loose in the morning. Let's hope Ezra was right about Talia keeping us alive.'

'Yeah, but which Talia?' He managed a weak laugh at his own joke.

'Best to stand up, shake it off. We'll look less conspicuous if we're walking.'

I hauled him to his feet and then washed my hands and face in the sticky salt water lapping the sand by his feet. My clothes were still fouled with blood, but the black fabric hid most of the gore. We headed north, keeping the sea to our left.

'Listen, Baaz. I need to ask you something. You have to concentrate, all right?' I took his silence for agreement and pressed on. 'The Azriel Jacobs fellowship. Have you ever heard of it?'

'The what?'

'The Azriel Jacobs research fellowship at the Kolymsky School of Computer Sciences. Here in Tel Aviv. Had you heard of it? Before we met, I mean.'

'No, I hadn't. Are we going back to the hotel? I'm freezing.'

'Yes,' I said. 'We are. But right now I need you to think hard. Are you sure? It didn't mean anything to you, nothing at all?'

'I don't . . .' He looked around, eyes wide, hands shaking. 'When I read it in the paper online. In *Haaretz*. That's the first time I saw it.'

'OK. You're sure? When you were researching where to study, applying to university, looking for funding: you never heard it mentioned anywhere else?'

'No,' he said, wrinkling his brow. 'No, I didn't.'

'Think about it,' I said, quickening the pace. 'Az*riel*. Az*rael*. It's the same name. Azriel pays her. She looked upon the face of her paymaster and her paymaster is the Destroyer.' Baaz looked at me, dumbfounded. 'And it terrified her. Moshe said she was scared, that the money came from bad people.'

'So, what?' he stopped abruptly. 'She's being paid by the Devil?'

'Yeah,' I said. 'She is. *Was.* Avi Landau, the guy whose number is in this book of matches' – I took them out of my pocket and lit a cigarette – 'he didn't just run the gallery. He ran cash to her. He said it paid for Rachel's work, her project.' I looked around. We were completely alone now. 'Her programme is called *Arkhangel*. It's the third variable.'

'Follow the money, right?' Baaz's fingers began to dance in the air in front of him.

Follow the money. Everyone else certainly was, Frank included. *Round and round the money goes, but where it starts only a Russian knows.* Except now I did, too.

'It comes from the Akvarium,' I said. 'In Moscow.'

'Now you're speaking Punjabi. What even is "the Akvarium"?'

I took a long drag on my cigarette.

'It's the headquarters of the GRU,' I said. 'Russian military intelligence.'

We continued towards the hotel in silence. I tried to ignore the chill in the air, struggling to work out what all the slaughter amounted to. Baaz's fingers drummed the air beside him as he walked. Whatever was going through his mind didn't make it to his lips. Speaking slowed him down. Numbers energized him. I made my own calculations, too.

Whatever Rachel was working on was being underwritten by the GRU, lubricated with a slick of untraceable filthy lucre.

The visit to Gallery 7 answered the question I'd asked Moshe: I now knew which Russians were supplying the cash. But if Rachel hadn't simply absconded, Moscow could still have been responsible for her disappearance. Just because the doctor and his goons were behind the curve didn't mean the Russians were out of the picture. If Leonid Avilov had exceeded his orders as far as I'd exceeded mine, he could be a long way off-piste – and as out in the cold as I was.

I considered that carefully. It was a real possibility: my father – every inch the Ministry of Defence loyalist as well as a brilliant scientist – had once told me that 'London is not a monolith'. Thames House competed with, and loathed, Vauxhall Cross; MI5 and MI6 agents outplayed each other for grace and favour, ego and advancement; government undermined the military; the Foreign Office undermined everyone else. They all played their own games for their own ends – ends which sometimes, but not always, excused the means. There was no reason to expect that Moscow was any different, and every reason to suspect it wasn't.

In the catacombs Avilov had told me that I was a hard man to help. Maybe he wasn't the enemy. Or maybe that was the point: there were no enemies, because there were no friends. Whoever held the banknote held the cards. Perhaps Rachel knew she'd been dealt a dead man's hand and folded. The more I looked at it, the more that hundred-dollar bill looked like aces backed with eights – with the queen of hearts in the hole. I thought of Doc's last words to me: *She'tamut*. To death. It was a game that had already seen the end of a better gambler than me.

The closer we got to the hotel, the clearer it became: there was only one way to protect Baaz. Rachel had unburdened herself. It was suddenly inevitable I'd have to do the same. We drew up alongside Independence Park, deserted in the winter night.

'Stop a minute,' I said. 'I've something for you. Give me your hand.'

Baaz hesitated and then stretched out his palm, his fingers finally stilled. On to it I pressed the folded banknote.

'Don't you need it?'

'No. I've memorized the numbers.' Baaz raised his eyebrows as he pocketed the bill. 'I'll never work out what they mean, though – assuming there is anything to work out.' We stood close, barely more than a foot apart. 'You have my pistol, at the hotel. Leave it there. And don't, under any circumstances, fuck with Talia.' We both smiled.

'Why are you giving me this? We're a team, right?'

'Right. And that's *why* I'm trusting you. It's why I told you everything. I doubt very much I'm going to make it up the steps to the hotel, which is why you're going to turn around now and keep clear till dawn. Photograph both sides of the note, and then hide it. Send it to yourself encrypted, and then throw your phone in the sea. Once the Shabak has picked me up, Talia will find you and interrogate you. If you're clean, she'll probably just deport you.'

The alternatives to not being deported didn't bear thinking about.

'Well then, don't walk up the bloody hotel steps. Problem solved.'

'Trust me, Baaz. There's no other way.'

I was expecting an argument. This time I held out my hand. He hesitated and then took it with a force that surprised me. His eyes had filled with tears.

'How will I find you if I work out what the numbers mean? You don't even have a phone.'

'I'll check in with our mutual friend in Sierra Leone. If you leave a message with him, I'll get it. Eventually.'

'*Kushkismat*,' he said. 'Good luck.'

I turned around to take a last look at him as he was walking away. After a few paces he stopped and turned, too.

'Max,' he said, cheeks wet, but with a strong voice, 'I have to know. In the hotel . . . if you hadn't, you know, seen the numbers. Would you have killed me?'

My shoulders slumped and I squinted at him through the gloom. I knew then that he'd be OK. He was a smart kid, canny. And though he had the frame of a boy, he was wiry and lean: a man, no mistake – however unlike me in the making. I'd trusted him with everything else. There was no point lying now.

'Yes,' I said, pulling my jacket tight to my chest. 'I would have.'

He held my gaze for an instant and then set off, head down, towards the city. That was the trouble with the truth: once it starts, it's hard to stop.

There was no police car waiting for me, no snatch squad; and if there was a sniper watching, he was sitting tight. I made it up the stairs and pushed open the doors to the hotel, treading carefully across the marble floor. Only the night manager's lamp lit the lobby. He was asleep in his chair, neck crooked at an impossible angle. I looked at his thorax. Breathing. I cleared my throat and he roused himself, tightening the tie under his creased white collar.

'*Shalom*,' I said. And then in English: 'Room 101, please. Has anyone asked after me?'

He composed himself and leaned forward, looking at me, through me. His mouth opened, but the reply came from behind.

'No, they haven't.' The harsh syllables rang with a seductive edge. I splayed my fingers out, hands wide of my sides, and turned: black hair, pale face, cheekbones like knives.

'Hello, Talia.'

'Good morning, Mr McLean. Quite the holiday you're having.'

'It's been enlightening, shall we say.' She stood staring at me, right hand in her coat pocket. Left hand holding a cell phone. 'Nine millimetre,' I said, 'in the back of my jeans. Just so there are no misunderstandings.'

She nodded and I extracted the Jericho with my thumb and forefinger from my Levi's. I crouched and put it on the floor at arm's length and then stood up straight again. The night manager circled around me, Glock 19 at the ready. They had the place locked down. She told me to kick the Jericho to him and I did. He picked it up and moved behind me again, out of sight.

'I guess it's over between us, then.'

Her lips lifted into a half-smile. 'On the contrary. It's not me I'm worried about getting shot. This is just – how shall we say – an *insurance policy.*'

'Sure. How is Moshe, by the way?'

'Dead. We found him this afternoon. Shot through the heart with a police pistol.'

She turned and held the street door open for me. That he'd been killed was not surprising; how he'd been killed was profoundly alarming.

'I see,' I said, trying not to take the bait. 'Tell me, why "the Traitor"? He served you well in Lebanon.'

'Why? I will tell you why. The Palestinians. The Iranians. Even the Russians. They are our enemies.' She stood close to me. I could feel her breath on my lips, smell the musk of a long day clinging to her clothes. 'They want Israel to fall. All this,' she looked around the lobby as if it encompassed the extent of her aspirations, 'gone.' She clicked her tongue against the back of her teeth. 'But an enemy is just an enemy. A traitor was once a friend. Even so, don't blame us, Mr McLean. Moshe Mendel Katz had many enemies of his own.'

I brushed past her on to the steps outside. A black Chevrolet Suburban pulled up – tinted windows, diplomatic plates, off-road tyres.

'It's no longer safe for you to stay in Israel, Mr McLean. I made a promise to our mutual friend. But questions are being asked. Questions I cannot avoid any longer. No one will miss

Avraham Landau. But the girl, Sveta? That was, uh, *unfortunate.*' The rear nearside passenger door opened.

'But I didn't . . .'

'Please, Mr McLean.'

'OK,' I said. 'But go easy on Baaz. He's an innocent. Just send him home.'

'Of course.'

I scanned the rooftops as best I could, but it was pointless. If I ran, I was dead – if not right there, then eventually. It had ever been thus.

'Thanks,' I said. 'I appreciate it.'

I turned my back to her and walked towards the Chevy, bent slightly at the waist, straining my eyes to no avail to make out any detail in the darkness inside. I stepped up on to the running board and turned around.

'Tell me, were you and Ezra in the field together?'

'No. We weren't.' She moved back into the doorway. 'Ezra Black was my husband.' I swung myself into the SUV. 'Please, Mr McLean. If you find Rachel, bring her home.'

'Which home is that, Talia?'

I gave her a mock salute. She smiled and disappeared into the lobby, and I was alone in the back of the car with only the driver up front for company. I pulled the door to. He hit the gas and together we sped into the city.

'Where are we going?' I asked.

He looked over his shoulder, eyes wrapped with Ray-Bans despite the dimness of the sodium-lit streets outside.

'Moscow.'

30

The cold bit like a knife.

Minus eight. Air dry as steel. Skies grey as lead. It had been snowing all night – fresh drifts of powder set solid as the temperature dived. It was a hard, unforgiving cold, offering no mercy to the city frozen in its grip. I thrust my hands into my pockets and kept my head down, and waited in line impatiently for the taxi that would take me into town.

I needed to get into cover. Fast. Every second I was in the open, in public, risked detection. The express train was too exposed. Moscow was littered with CCTV cameras which, MI6 had briefed us at Raven Hill before I went AWOL, were linked to an increasingly sophisticated facial recognition system. A taxi at least kept me off the streets. Talia had loaded a black daysack for me with winter clothes, a washbag, a few rubles, a wad of dollars – and a fake Russian passport.

'Sorry,' the Israeli driver had said with a grin as I'd surrendered the Greek papers I'd got from Lukov. 'The boss doesn't trust Bulgarians.'

For the first time in my life I'd entered Russia as a Russian citizen – on an Aeroflot flight from Ben Gurion direct to Sheremetyevo International. The Shabak had taken care of formalities in Israel. Speaking with what I hoped was a Russian accent unmuddied by growing up in the West, I'd been propelled through immigration in less than fifteen minutes. Maybe I'd got lucky. Maybe Avilov and the GRU were running their own show, outside the scope of internal security.

Or maybe they were watching to see what I'd do next – namely, buy a sandwich and a sharpie and change some dollars to rubles.

In the arrivals hall the cashier had examined the hundred-dollar bills carefully and passed them under an ultraviolet scanner. It had crossed my mind for a moment that Talia might have equipped me with a stash of Moshe's interpretations. I'd craned my neck to see what happened when the note passed under the light, but the only thing obvious was that the plastic strip beside Benjamin Franklin's face glowed pink. The woman behind the window had seemed happy enough, and passed me a stack of crisp local notes.

Then I'd found a bathroom and locked myself in a stall. From the wad of leftover dollars I'd extracted a C-note and on the reverse written *Архангел* in thick, black Cyrillic letters. I'd folded it up and put it in my jeans ticket pocket and emerged into the first Russian winter I'd experienced for five years.

Just as a cab was within touching distance a babushka with sharp elbows and ageing furs barged me out of the way from behind and bundled herself into the back seat. The cabbie emerged, shrugging his shoulders as he opened the boot for her bags.

'*Dobro pozhalovat v Moskvu!*' he said. *Welcome to Moscow.* Damned straight. In the politeness stakes the Russians gave even the Israelis a run for their money.

Another car pulled up behind and I climbed in. I had no hold luggage, just Talia's daysack, in which I had also discovered a guidebook – designed, I supposed, to make me look like a tourist out to have fun and not a spook on the run. I'd changed my wound dressing, had breakfast in departures and a shave thirty thousand feet over the Black Sea. I felt good.

'*K Bolshomy*,' I said. *To the Bolshoi*. From there I'd easily pick up another cab. And another. Eventually ending up in the Kuzminki area, a messy, down-at-heel neighbourhood in the south-east of Moscow, which was about as far away in feel as it was possible to get from the slick city centre. From there I'd plan my next move. The driver was sealed off from the rear passenger seats by a glass screen – an innovation since my last visit. An intercom allowed us to speak.

'Just like New York,' I said in Russian, tapping the partition. From behind the wheel his eyes caught mine in the rear-view mirror.

'*Da*,' he nodded, and carried on his conversation through a hands-free rig with someone I guessed was either his wife or his girlfriend.

I also had a phone. Talia had left me a burner with a clean Russian SIM and one number in the address book: hers. As soon as we'd got airborne, I'd switched it off and taken the battery out. Carrying it *at all* was like being tethered to a personal locator beacon. But so far Talia had been good to Ezra's word: I was still alive.

But sending me to Moscow wasn't just a cute way of getting me out of her hair. Her personal imperatives notwithstanding, either I'd manage to unravel what had happened to the Israelis' disappeared scientist or Russian intelligence would take grateful delivery of their number one suspect. Whatever the case, Talia would emerge smelling of roses. Less so me. Once the GRU found out I'd sent its money man to meet his maker, then Talia's motives would be the least of my concerns.

I thought about Moshe, and about Avi's girl, Sveta. Despite the drugs and the fear, she'd have to be able to identify me and had probably listened to her sugar daddy spilling the beans. Even if I'd become an increasingly reluctant executioner, someone was taking care of business behind me. But who? The signature heart-shot that had done for Moshe was chilling. If the same assassin had dispatched Sveta, too, then I wasn't a day ahead of anyone: he'd had the drop on me all along.

I recalled what old Colonel Ellard had said at Raven Hill once, after a job had unravelled on me: 'There's no use worrying about things over which you have no control.' I stretched the flight out of my legs and tried to relax. Cars crept past the tinted passenger windows. Long gone were the old Volgas and Ladas – now it was all SUVs and foreign imports. A smart new Range Rover inched past: Moscow mafia chic. Few traces, if any, of my mother's city remained. Although the roads were clear of snow, progress was slow. We ground on south-east down the M-11, crossing the Moscow Canal and then over the sprawling intersection with the Central Ring Road towards the Marfino district, before dropping due south, bound for the city centre.

And then what?

There was, as usual, no plan and very few possibilities. Cut off, and without comms to London, I had no way of contacting anyone in the GRU, except for the receptionist at its headquarters on Grizodubovoi Street. And walking into the Akvarium was as good an idea as jumping into the Moscow River. But the GRU's operators would track me down, all right. The trick was making sure the crisis was forced at the place and time of my choosing. It was high risk: I just hoped that whatever Rachel's project meant to them was heady enough to trip them up in its pursuit. And I prayed, too, that wherever Rachel had ended up, she thought it had been worth it all – because, as far as I could see, its most significant outcome for her had been to lay her father in his grave.

We passed Dmitrovskaya Metro station. The traffic slowed even further as we hit Sushchevskiy Val Street.

'Detour,' the taxi driver said in Russian through the intercom. 'Too much traffic.' His accent was hard to place. From Georgia, maybe. I was about to ask him where, exactly, but he was trying to reconnect a dropped call, fiddling about with the hands-free set which was draped around an icon on the dashboard. We headed west. And then after a couple of klicks swung on to the junction with Leningradsky Avenue. But instead of heading south-east again, the driver stayed in the outside lane and took the slip road north-west.

'Hey.' I leaned forward and tapped the glass. 'Wrong way. The Bolshoi theatre, remember?'

'Shortcut,' he grunted. 'Faster.'

Larger fare, more like. I looked at the meter. It was still set to zero. I went to rap on the glass again, but stopped myself, and thanked him instead.

Something wasn't right.

We passed the Dinamo Metro station and then came off the main highway, driving parallel to the bare trees rising up out of the frozen white ground of Petrovsky Park. Then we cut across the busy road we'd just left, over a wide bridge that formed a junction for cars turning left. We came to a stop in the middle of the filter lane. Another taxi pulled up to our left. The woman in the back was chatting away to the driver. She leaned forward to show him something on her phone. There was no security screen. No partition. I saw my driver's eyes dart back to mine in the mirror. He cut the intercom and began speaking rapidly into his cell phone.

I looked right: another cab – again, with no screen. I tried to get my bearings. We were in the Aeroport district, close to the inner-city Khodinka airfield.

Shit.

In my mind I brought back into as sharp a focus as I could manage a set of intelligence maps we'd been shown of Moscow in 2009. We'd been given them for good reason: to help familiarize ourselves with the location and construction of a brick and glass monstrosity that was an almost straight rip-off of the MI6 building at Vauxhall Cross on the Thames. Not two kilometres from where we sat waiting at a red light was the one building in Moscow I wanted most to avoid. Rising up on the south side of the airfield – and home to all manner of spies and sharks – was the now fully operational headquarters of the GRU. There was no doubt about it. We were heading straight for the Akvarium.

I was sitting on the right side of the vehicle. I curled my fingers around the door-release but to no avail. I looked at the safety screen more closely. Half-inch bullet-resistant plexiglass recessed into the chassis. I looked at the passenger windows, too: also reinforced. I was trapped. I guessed I'd enter the Akvarium the same way I was always taken into Vauxhall Cross: via an underground tunnel that emerged in a secure area. I would have no opportunity to run – because there would be nowhere to run to.

In a couple of minutes I would be swallowed, lost. The Akvarium was rumoured to be so labyrinthine, and internal access so heavily restricted, that whole sections of it remained mysterious even to the people who lived and worked there. It was an entirely self-contained and self-sustaining state within a state: water, electricity, food, living quarters, weapons, manpower – and even, General King had said, one of Russia's three *cheget* nuclear briefcases, a key command and control component of the Kremlin's Strategic Nuclear Forces. Once I was inside the Akvarium, it would be the GRU calling the shots, and no one else.

I ran my hands through the daysack. I needed a miracle. I felt for anything I could use as a weapon or to force a lock. My right hand closed around a small can of aerosol deodorant in the washbag, my left around the barrel of a plastic lighter. I thrust them both into my jacket pockets.

The traffic cutting across us from south-east-bound Leningradsky Avenue stopped. The lights turned green. But before we could move, the front passenger door opened and a heavily built man with a buzz cut climbed in and sat next to the driver. He turned and smiled through the reinforced glass. I looked around. The Range Rover had pulled in behind us. They must have been waiting to see where I was heading. Now they'd decided to spring the trap.

We inched forward. I looked at the driver and then past him, out the left-hand window, scanning the road for signs of more operators. The car lurched. And then my ears filled with the slip-shunt bang-crack of metal colliding, crunching, smashing.

The taxi next to us began to move, veering across the intersection. It was rolling, lifting. My head tilted. The winter sky slipped away. I could see the cab's ceiling. Then the right-hand window. A child waiting to cross the road was standing on his head, screaming, but his feet were on the ground. Then the grey clouds were underneath us. The driver was turning, his phone suspended, dancing in front of him. My face against the plexiglass.

We were rolling.

Silence.

And then a deafening wrench-roar of hard energy compressed into a decelerated *pop* of pulverized glass imploding around me. Blood in my mouth. My eyes. The world snapped out of slow motion and spun in crazy corkscrew spirals until my head found asphalt and the white winter sun turned black.

Shouting.

Pain.

And then white light and focus.

I was lying on my back in the middle of the intersection. I turned my head and spat the remains of a tooth on the frozen ground. I sat up. The world rocked, faded. I braced, elbows on the ground, and the darkness ebbed away. I was half in the taxi, half on the road. The car was upturned, turtle-like. There was no smoke. There had been no blast. I pushed myself clear of the wreckage and on to all fours. The driver was dead, neck snapped, nose flattened in a red smear across his face. The goon next to him hung from his seat belt, unresponsive.

The woman who'd been in the taxi next to mine weaved across the road, holding her hands to her head. A brand-new Mercedes, bonnet wrecked, steam pouring from the engine, had come to a halt in front of her; its driver clambered clear of the airbags and jumped out of the passenger side away from me – five-eleven, athletic, head down and sprinting for safety. The Merc had run the red light and ploughed straight into my cab. I hadn't been blown up: I'd been T-boned.

I tried to stand. My right leg was injured. The bullet wounds in my thigh and shoulder had torn. As I found my feet, the Range Rover swerved around me. The doors opened. Two men stepped out – dressed in black fatigues and respirators, AKS carbines in their shoulders. I moved back, gripped with pain, nausea. Another Range Rover screeched to a halt, spilling more men on to the street. I retreated further. The front passenger of the second Range Rover stepped into view. Leather shoes, black wool coat, light build – and a gash splayed across his right temple: Doctor Leonid Avilov, the GRU officer who'd hounded me from the ship, through the tunnels and all the way to Moscow.

He moved towards me, fast. I staggered backwards, covered on both sides by shooters.

'I didn't expect to find you in Paris,' he said, closing on me.

I tried to take another step back, but I was stopped by the low stone parapet guarding against the steep drop on to the highway below. He drew a syringe from his coat. I put my hands into my pockets and glanced over the side, counting under my breath, calculating speed, distance. He was close enough now that I could smell his aftershave.

'You see, I always thought we would meet here in Moscow.' He removed the cap from the needle.

Now.

With one movement I brought both my hands up to his face, right thumb on the aerosol, left thumb sparking the flint of the lighter. A short burst of yellow-blue flame expanded into his eyes. He dropped the syringe, screaming. I bent over backwards, grabbing his wrist as I went, and let my feet go from under me. My spine arced over the wall, skimmed by a volley of shots. Avilov's hip caught on the parapet. I held fast. The wound in my shoulder ripped further, the black coat billowed out above me. I let go.

One sickening second of freefall freedom.

And then the relief of contact as I slammed down, starfish-like, on to the stretched-out tarpaulin of a passing truck. A moment too late, Leonid Avilov fell clear of the bridge. I heard the dull thud of him hitting the asphalt and then the wet crunch of his skull flattening beneath the tyres of the truck behind.

My driver carried on, unchecked, and took a left on the Garden Ring. We were heading east. On the Eurostar platform in Kent I'd imagined a life in the mountains – a life of solitude and peace. I'd imagined I could escape. But I'd been alone and on the run since I was sixteen. I could disappear into the Eurasian steppe or the Great Northern Forest as easily and perfectly as a pebble would vanish into the Pacific. But I would never outrun myself. I knew then, as the wind lashed my face, that Rachel had been lost to me the moment I'd turned my back on who I really was. As I hung on to the truck, I let go of the idea of her – and understood, finally, that it was not Rachel that I'd been trying to save all along, but myself.

And I knew then that there was only one place left for me to go.

Home.

31

'What do you want?'

The old lady spoke in a barely audible whisper behind the thick panels of a heavy wooden door. It was difficult to make out what she was saying. I looked around. It was snowing hard now. Large silent flakes filled the air, burying deeper the steps that climbed up to the entrance of my mother's old house. I put my ear to the lock and raised my voice.

'My name is Maksimilian,' I said. There was no reply. 'Maksimilian Ivanovich,' I tried again, remembering to use my patronymic. 'Anastasia's son.'

Anastasia's son. They were words I had not spoken since she died. I straightened up and rolled my shoulders and prayed for the old lady inside to let me in. Blood dripped from my fingers, spotting the white blanket that carpeted the porch. My clothes were filthy – covered in salt and dirt. I looked over my shoulder again. There was nothing behind me but darkness.

'Who?'

'Anastasia,' I said, shouting at the still-shut door. 'Olga Milova's daughter.'

There was a long pause, and then the scraping of wood on wood. The snib sprang loose and the door inched open, throwing a wedge of light on to the snow. The woman looked as if she was in her eighties – at least: a jumble of bones and leathery skin and fine white hair that fell down to her shoulders. Her eyes were brilliant, though. Blue and piercing, searching mine like Doc's had less than a fortnight before. An eddy of snow blew into the old cabin. She drew a black shawl around her shoulders and thrust her face towards mine.

'Olga Milova doesn't live here,' she said. 'She's dead.'

'I know,' I said. 'I . . .'

'This is *my* house. Polina Yurievna's house. Not hers.' She paused, and then added: 'Or yours.'

'I know, that's not . . . Polina Yurievna, may I come inside?' She looked at me, at my fouled jacket, squinted at the red snow by my feet. The temperature was dropping further. My mouth still tasted of iron – tongue, teeth still bleeding from the impact in the taxi. 'Please.'

'Why?' she asked. 'Are you in trouble, Maksimilian Ivanovich?'

'No,' I lied.

A wry, unexpected smile spread across her face.

'Rubbish,' she cackled. 'I've never known anyone from your family that wasn't.'

She pulled the door open further and stepped aside, and for the first time ever I walked into my mother's house, cupping my left hand with my right so as not to spoil the floor with blood. Once I was inside, the old woman gazed at me intently, looking, perhaps, for proof – some trace of my mother in my face, eyes.

'These are strange times,' she said. 'One day to the next you don't know whom you'll meet. And always,' she said, leading me deeper into her home, 'without warning. Everyone always wants something.'

'I'm sorry,' I said. 'I didn't . . .'

'How did you get here?' she interrupted – though whether from impatience or deafness I couldn't tell. 'The roads are blocked. It's been snowing all week.'

'Yes,' I said. 'They are blocked. But only once you leave the highway. A farmer out clearing snow gave me a lift on his tractor from Koptevo.'

I spared her the details of the rest of the journey from Moscow – the majority of which I'd made hidden in the grit box of a truck heading north-east to Ivanovo, the oblast capital. I'd climbed out when the driver stopped to refuel, shivering in a culvert until the coast was clear. From there I'd hitchhiked – a series of short lifts repaid with a few hundred-ruble notes – then taken the tractor. I'd walked the last mile – with difficulty. The car crash and fall from the bridge hadn't only knocked out one of my teeth – they had badly bruised my ribs, and sprained my left knee, as well as reopening my bullet wounds. I'd made good time, all things considered.

We stood in silence for a moment, her eyes continuing to explore my face until she made up her mind.

'I have an old sheet,' she said, pausing again to clear her throat, 'for bandages. Hot water, too.' She waved her hand towards the stove. 'And *pokhlyobka* for your belly.'

I looked around. On a shelf in the far corner, an ancient, gilded icon of St Michael presided over her proud, searing poverty. We were standing by the dining table – a solid wooden platform more like a butcher's block. Years of elbow grease and pork fat had rubbed into it a deep, burnished patina. By the door where I'd come in, a woodfired range warmed a large pan of soup. On the far side of the table sat a metal-framed bed covered with an acrylic blanket. A bucket with soaking soiled clothes lurked in the corner. There was no TV, no radio – no luxuries at all, nothing that wasn't entirely necessary to sustain another day of life – St Michael included.

There was a flight of stairs – open wood planks with no banister – leading to an upper level, which, Polina said, her legs could no longer manage.

'I'm sorry to have disturbed you,' I said. 'I didn't realize how late it was.'

'There's no harm done,' she replied, waving her hand at me. 'I don't sleep much, anyway.' She patted her thigh. 'Restless legs.' Then she laid her hand on the table, skin tight across her knuckles. 'Are you really Anastasia's son?' I nodded. 'Well, this is where it happened, you know.'

I took off my jacket, and began to ease myself out of my sweater. Talia had dressed me in black – guessing, perhaps, I'd need to be camouflaged against gore as I had been in Tel Aviv. She hadn't figured I'd spend five hours up to my neck in rock salt. The wound in my left shoulder felt as fresh as the day I'd been shot in the cottage. The furrow in my right thigh had split open again, too.

'Where what happened, Polina Yurievna?'

'Your grandmother, Maksimilian Ivanovich. Where she crossed into the next life. And where your mother came into this one.' She stroked the table.

'And how,' I asked, 'would you know that?'

'Because I was here when it happened, Maksimilian Ivanovich. Right here.' She turned to look at me, pale blue eyes lingering on mine in the lamplight. 'I delivered your mother, on this very table.'

I scraped the last of the soup from the bowl.

Polina had helped to dress my wounds before we ate. While she'd wrapped my shoulder, I'd told her that my mother was dead, too – a fact that she had received with the sign of the cross.

317

'Her first breath was your grandmother's last,' she'd said.

We'd broken bread after that. When Polina finished eating, she got up from the table and fetched two small glasses, which she filled to the brim with colourless liquid from an unlabelled glass bottle balanced on the stairs.

'Let's drink to Anastasia, may God rest her soul.'

We drank in silence, without touching glasses. Then she stood up again and shuffled off towards the bed. From under it she produced a scuffed tin box tied shut with a length of twine. She unpicked the knot and, back turned to me, riffled through what sounded like a stack of papers. Finally she returned the box to its place and turned around, a piece of card in one hand, and a knife in the other.

'These are for you,' she said.

The piece of card revealed itself to be a black and white photograph. The image showed a young girl, laughing, blonde hair wound up in the glowing crown of a tight basket-braid.

'It's Anastasia. Your mother.'

I looked on the reverse. There was nothing except the date: *1959*. She would have been seven or eight years old. Decades of certainty crumbled on the lips of that bleached-white almost-smile. I'd thought, when I ran away aged sixteen, that her past had evaporated – and mine with it; I'd imagined that Doc beamed the last rays of light shed by a star that had died long ago. It wasn't so. My mother had made me an orphan. But I had chosen exile.

I sat with my hands on the table, feet on the floor, trapped in the space between the competing stories of who I was.

'And the knife?'

'It was your grandfather's,' Polina said, sitting down again. 'He said it killed many fascists in the Great Patriotic War.' She winked at me. 'But Olga said he just whittled wood with it.'

I drew it from its home-stitched leather sheath. It was an old Red Army scout's knife – with a pitted six-inch blade and battered, black wooden handle. It had an inverted S-guard, designed for holding it with the cutting edge upwards, and a needle-sharp clip point. It was rudimentary, but oiled and well balanced.

'Thank you,' I said, slipping it into the makeshift scabbard and then tucking it away in the back of my jeans. It sat comfortably in the spot where I usually carried my pistol.

I turned back to the image of the enigmatic little girl playing behind the rusted pelmet of the Iron Curtain. It was the only photograph of her I had.

'She kept that smile her whole life, you know. I never could tell what she was thinking.'

'They said she was a spy. Is that true?'

I zipped the photograph into my inside jacket pocket. 'Who,' I asked, 'said that?'

'Everyone. After she went to England.'

'Ireland,' I corrected her.

'Yes, there. Everyone said she must have been a British spy. How else could she have . . .' She looked around the room, at the worn wood panelling and sparse old-fashioned furniture, searching for the right word, 'escaped?'

'My mother wasn't a British spy,' I reassured her. 'Of that, I am one hundred per cent certain.'

'The woman who came here at Christmas said the same thing.' She poured two more glasses of vodka.

'*This* Christmas?' I asked. 'In December?'

She looked at me as if I was a simpleton.

'Anastasia brought you up speaking Russian, but she didn't bring you up in the Church, did she?' I shook my head. 'January the seventh. *Our* Christmas.'

'But that was less than two weeks ago.'

'No, it was the sixth. I remember, because Aleksandr Denisovich brought me some fresh logs in his new car . . . or . . . No, *that* was the day before. It's very nice, his car. His brother bought it . . .'

'Polina Yurievna,' I interrupted her, 'what woman?'

'Rakhil,' she said. 'It's a lovely name, isn't it? And so unusual.'

My pulse quickened. I swallowed hard.

'What did she look like, this "Rakhil"?' Inside my chest my heart banged against bruised, burning ribs.

'Black hair and green eyes.' She looked at me and smiled. 'And so beautiful. Are you sure you're not in trouble, Maksimilian Ivanovich?' She chuckled to herself and added: 'Or that she's not?'

Rakhil. It was as if she'd shot me between the eyes. Rachel. In Arkhangel. It was inconceivable.

'And she's here, still here, in *this* village?'

'Yes,' she said. 'In *your* village.' She smiled and held her arthritic fingers up for inspection. 'I'm old, but I could still deliver one more of Arkhangel's sons.'

I reached over and took her hands in mine, rubbing my thumb gently across her knuckles.

'Trust me, Polina Yurievna,' I said, struggling to keep my voice steady. 'You already have.'

I steered clear of the path.

It was barely a hundred and fifty metres to the church of St Michael the Archangel, but the snow was thigh deep between the trees. Fresh flurries piled it even thicker. It must have been minus fifteen. There was no moon visible, no street lamps. Away from the glow of Polina's windows the night absorbed me, sucking me into the void of the winter landscape.

Polina told me that Rachel had declined her offer of hospitality and said that she would be staying at the priest's house next to the church instead. And what was the harm in that? It was nice to see young people moving back to the village again. Polina had also confirmed – to the point of irritation at how many times I asked – that no one else had visited Arkhangel immediately before, or since, Rachel had arrived.

I put one foot after the other, and tried to fathom why, of all the places she could have bolted to – whether she was running from something or towards it – she had come here. Was it me? Or my mother? Or perhaps it was closer to home than that. In my mind's eye I saw Doc dead in his drawing room, slumped in front of the fire. For better or worse, he linked us all. Our pasts and our presents all spun around him. The thought of what might happen if – when – they collided made me shudder.

On the way to my mother's old family house I'd avoided the road and persevered along an old cart track that had taken me to the west of the church, but not past it. The birch trees on the approach were thick enough to give good cover against infrared, though if anyone nearby had thermal imaging I'd be lit up like a Christmas tree. Despite Polina's protestations about no one else having come to the village, an entire detachment of Special Forces could have deployed without her suspecting a thing. I was about to find out for certain if the GRU had connected Arkhangel the place to *Arkhangel* the project. My cheeks burned. There was just enough time for a simple recce. Ideally, I'd have watched the churchyard all night – but without the proper kit, minus fifteen will kill you. I didn't have the proper kit. I didn't have *any* kit – and I was injured.

I tried to empty my mind of Rachel, of the uncertainty of what meeting her might beget, and filled it instead with the specifics of safely crossing the short distance to the churchyard.

I looped around the other painted wooden cabins neighbouring Polina Yurievna's. There couldn't have been more than ten houses in total – smallholdings, mainly, and all separated from each other by fields and trees. At the front of the third plot along stood a snow-covered Lada Niva, tyres unworn, snow around it undisturbed: Aleksandr Denisovich's new car, in which he'd brought Polina the logs for her Christmas fire. I watched the house. The silhouette of a man passed in front of the downstairs window and then vanished behind the woodpile. Five-eleven, maybe, and wrapped up against the cold. I heard a door shut, and then the lights went out. I listened carefully, but the night was silent again, all sound muffled by the snow: no wolves, no planes, no car engines. I crept around the offside of the four-by-four and pulled gently at the door handle. It was unlocked, keys in the ignition.

I crossed the road at a crouch. The church itself was a dilapidated nineteenth-century two-storey white box – topped by a short spire and onion dome supporting a silver Orthodox cross. At the west end there was a lower extension – where the congregation would have entered and bought candles. It had been a long time since I'd been inside an Orthodox church. In Ireland my mother had taken communion with my father in the Roman Catholic church of Sts Mary and Peter in Arklow – although there were parts of the service she always refused to say out loud.

I wished I'd paid more attention.

Snow worked its way into my pockets, boots. The wind

picked up a little and cut through my jeans, stinging my ears. I was chilled and getting colder. Whatever the risks it was time to get back inside. The church itself, Polina Yurievna had told me, had been closed for years – another victim of the Soviet era which had never recovered. The St Michael that hung on her wall had been rescued three days before the doors had been shut for good. More recently, by the looks of it, a large metal grille had been bolted over the north entrance – though who, or what, it was meant to deter out here was anyone's guess.

The priest's house was set in the south-west corner of the churchyard – a ramshackle wood cabin that looked as if it might have been used more recently for livestock than clergy. I slipped through the remains of an old picket fence, the tops of which crested the drifting snow like the masts of a sunken clipper, and threaded my way between the frosted branches of ancient apple trees to the back of the house.

Smoke leaked from the chimney. A light flickered in the window, but the panes were smeared with grime and impossible to see through. I circled around to the front door and stamped the snow off my boots. I breathed deeply, sending a column of silent white mist into the air. Since I'd fled the burning cottage in Donegal, all roads had led me here. Led me home.

Whatever happened next, I knew Rachel would at least want to know how her father had really died. In Tel Aviv I'd braced myself to be confronted, hoping all the while to be forgiven. I'd thought I'd been prepared. But as soon as I'd stepped into her office, I'd been swamped with uncertainty. I still was, but with this difference: I no longer knew which of us was guilty, or of what. I thought that I had come to assuage her. But I hadn't. I'd come to accuse her. What followed might lead to revenge. Or atonement. Either way, I told myself, I'd be ready.

Midnight in Arkhangel and all was quiet.

I raised my fist to strike the door, but as I did so I saw that it was already open. I pushed it gently, and stepped through the looking glass.

32

Rachel was facing away from me, sitting on the floor in the middle of the room, knees drawn up to her chin, arms locked around her shins. Her hair hung long, falling down the back of her tunic in a jumble of black tresses.

Three candles – arranged neatly in a line – burned on an old dresser pushed up against the far wall. Wax spilled on to the bare floorboards. The remains of a fire glowed in the stove. I closed the cabin door quietly and stood still, letting my eyes adjust. The ceiling was fouled with lamp soot, the walls covered with crazy patterns scored into them by years of decay.

Before I could speak, she said: '*Ner tamid.*'

She turned and looked hopefully at me over her shoulder. She was both Rachel and a stranger – familiar and yet disarmingly different. Her face was set with worry; a hard journey etched in her eyes.

'I'm sorry,' I said. 'I don't understand.'

'Eternal light,' she replied, pointing to the taller candle in the middle. 'God's gift to us who live in darkness.'

I took a step closer. I looked at her, at the room. Light pooled above the candles. The marks that at first had looked like random patterns in the cracked wooden panels took shape. The whole back wall was covered in an organized explosion of mathematical calculations. Dead centre, repeated in dozens of permutations, the serial number of the hundred-dollar bill: *73939133.*

I trod the ten feet between us. I tried to squat down beside her, but my knee gave way. I grunted with pain as I sprawled on the floor, leaning on my right hand with one leg folded beneath me. I could feel fresh blood leaking into Polina's bandages.

'I knew you'd come,' she said, 'after I saw your photograph in the paper. You want to convince me that you didn't kill him.'

'That's right,' I said.

We were a foot apart. Her accent was harsh and unfamiliar, pulled between Ireland and Israel, edged with fear.

'But you did, didn't you?'

'I don't know where to start,' I said.

I looked at the candles, at the few personal effects scattered around the room: a sleeping bag by the stove, a half-eaten loaf of bread, a plate and a bowl. But I could find no anchor to steady me; see no compass to navigate by. It felt both unremarkable to see her again and deeply disorientating.

'Yes, you do, Max. Where all stories start,' she said. 'At the beginning. Remember?'

She looked down and rested her chin on her knees. Her hands were dirty, nails blackened. Then I saw on the floor next to her a burned stub of kindling, sharpened to a point. I studied the wall again. She'd been using firewood to write with, her hands as an eraser.

'Rachel,' I said, feeling the weight of the syllables fill my mouth, 'this time you have to tell me the story.' I opened my left hand and gestured towards her calculations. 'I don't understand what any of this means.'

'It means,' she said, slowly and deliberately, 'the eyes to read every word, the ears to hear every whisper.' She smiled at me. 'It means the triumph of light, Max, and the defeat of darkness. At least that's what I thought it meant.'

'I see,' I said, looking for some way, *any* way back into the mind, the soul, of the person I'd cherished as a teenager.

'Do you?' She stood up abruptly in one strong, fluid movement and moved away from me. She wrenched the centre candle free of its wax fixings and brought the flame to bear on the charcoal scrawl. '*Do* you see? *Do* you understand?' I looked up at her and pursed my lips.

'What do you think death looks like, Max? A skeleton on a horse? The Grim Reaper? A fantasy to scare children with?' She turned around to face me, holding her arms and the candle aloft. 'Well?' The sleeves of her tunic fell back, revealing the thick, angry scars that ran from her wrists to her elbows. I bowed my head. 'Look at me, Max. Look at me!' she shouted. 'Look at *them*!'

'I've seen them already,' I said, still staring at the floor. 'Remember?'

'Remember? How did you think I could forget? I wanted to disappear, Max, to slip away quietly without bothering anyone. To vanish. I didn't want to *be* any more. And then . . .' her voice calmed again, 'and then you brought me back.'

I looked up at her.

'Of course I did. Of course I saved you. What else could I have done? Doc loved you. *I* loved you. We were kids, Rachel, and you were out of your mind with . . .'

'Saved me? *Mamash, mamash lo*, Max. No. *Really* no. You *condemned* me.'

'Condemned you to what, exactly?'

She was quiet for a moment, making the space for what she needed to say, making sure I would hear her words. I kept my eyes fixed on hers, glowing green in the half-light.

327

'*Náire shíoraí*,' she said at last, in Irish. *Eternal shame.* 'You brought me back and then you ran. You vanished and left me to burn in the heat of my own humiliation. And do you know why, Max?' I struggled to my feet. Blood ran down my arm. 'Because you *are* a coward. Whoever put those words in my mouth in the paper knows you better than you know yourself. You were too scared to let me die. Too scared to keep me alive. Too craven even to spare the life of an old man who loved you. But I survived, Max. And I survived for a reason. Everyone always does.'

'Stop!' I blurted out with unexpected force. 'Please.'

I reached for her, but she recoiled, her face flickering in the chaos of shadows thrown up by the candles.

'I asked you a question, Max Mac Ghill'ean. But I'll give you the answer. Death is beautiful. They say the angel Azrael is covered with eyes, millions upon millions of eyes – beautiful, piercing eyes whose gaze no one can avoid. That no one has *ever* avoided. That is what is written.' She jutted her jaw towards me, resolute, her own eyes catching the light again, filled with the certainty of belief. 'And that is the truth. Do you know how it happens, Max? Do you know how Azrael takes your soul?'

'No,' I said, struggling to find anything to help me calm the storm I knew could drown us both.

'You look into those eyes, those million, million eyes, and you fall in love. That's how. There's no escape. There's nowhere to run. You can't hide. He sees everything, all the time, from one end of the world to the other. And as you open your mouth to tell this angel, this wonder, that you love him, that your heart has broken, he lets fall a drop of gall between your lips, and then you cease to be, putrefied by your own passion. *That* is the Helper of Ha'Shem. *That* is the Destroyer. And *I* have seen him.' She pivoted abruptly and threw the candle at the wall with all her might. Wax exploded across the giant calculation laid out before her. 'And *this* is what he looks like.'

Everyone has a breaking point. I had one. Rachel had reached hers. Moshe had been right: she had gone insane. She stood facing the wall, shaking. I peered into the corners of the room, glanced at the ceiling, and then over my shoulder towards the door. She kept her back to me and composed herself.

'I know who you are, Max Mac Ghill'ean, or McLean, or whatever you call yourself now. I know who you are. And I know *what* you are.'

'And what's that?'

'A murderer.' She turned around. 'My father told me everything. About how he helped you to join the army. About how you ran away. And do you know what? He was *glad*, Max. Glad I got away from you, glad I was free of you. He loved you. But, by God, how he despised what you became. That's why he drank. Not because of your mother. Because of you.'

'That's not true, that's . . .'

'There is only one reason that you're here, and that's because you've got the banknote. It's the only reason you *could* be here. The only person *Arkhangel* means anything to, apart from him, is you.'

'And you? What does it mean to you? Why name your project after it? Why write it on the note? Why send it to him? Why come here at all? Why run? There's nowhere to go from here. You're trapped.'

'I didn't come here to escape, Max. I came here to do something I should have done a long time ago. I came here for the same reason you did.' She took a step towards me. 'To understand.'

329

'But I don't . . . I don't understand.'

Yet in my guts I began to feel the truth unfurling like the Devil's banner.

'You don't think they sat up all night just talking about Russia, do you? Your mother and my father?'

'Rachel, don't.'

'Don't? Don't what? They were lovers, Max. For years. And you know they were. While we were fucking in my bed, they were fucking in hers. Oh, don't look so shocked. You've always known, whether you wanted to admit it or not. Your mother changed my father's life, Max. She changed *our* lives. She showed him what it meant to love. And she taught me what it meant to serve.'

'Serve whom? Men like Avilov?'

'Not who, but *what*. She loved this place, these people. She thought they were special. She thought *I* was special. *Ty moi volchonok*, she called me. Remember? *My little wolf.* She was obsessed with the idea of Russia. The beauty of it. The promise of it. Her work, her vision, was brilliant. One of the best, brightest scientists of her generation. That's what they said when she died, wasn't it? That was what I clung to after she drowned, Max, after you ran away. I escaped to Israel to serve an idea. I clung to faith, and to science – just as she had done. My father assimilated. I never could. Your mother thought that one day Russia would be her saviour, all our saviours.'

'And so you came here to do what? Understand my mother?'

She shook her head. 'No, Max. I came here to understand how she could have been so wrong. So completely and utterly wrong. My work, Max. It's bigger than Russia. Bigger than anything you can imagine.'

330

'But you knew that the money came from the Akvarium, didn't you? You knew that the GRU was funding you, funding *Arkhangel*.'

Now she looked down, hair falling in front of her face. 'Of course.'

'You worked for them, for Avilov.'

'No. I worked for the beauty of it, the promise of perfection. I imagined a world without shadows, a world without secrets, a perfect future where everyone is equal because nothing can be hidden.' She lifted her head. Tears flowed down her cheeks, matting wild strands of black and silver hair. 'No one else would fund me. No one. They thought I was crazy – some whacko who'd tried to kill herself.' She began to cry harder, her body swaying in the flame-light. 'All anyone ever saw were the scars. No one could ever see past them. But Avilov did. He found me. He saw *me*. He saw what I could do, what I could create. I know what you think, but I'm not crazy, Max. I saw the Destroyer, the Helper of Ha'shem, and Leonid Avilov was the only person who believed me, believed *in* me. And then he betrayed me.'

I moved closer to her. Only a couple of feet separated us now. 'I believed in you, Rachel. And I still do.'

'No. You betrayed me, too. You ran, and you kept running, and now you've come full circle. I thought I would be spared. I thought the angel would pass over me. But he hasn't, has he? That's why you're here.'

'I'm not going to hurt you, Rachel. That's not why I'm here. I didn't kill Doc. I didn't kill Amos. Whatever that means,' I pointed at the wall, 'that's what murdered them. Not me. Whoever gunned them down was looking for it, for you.'

She collapsed to her knees, and then sank to the floor, hair spilling about her head in a ragged black halo at my feet.

I reached down and took her by the bicep, and for the first time we touched. I pulled her to her feet and tried to think straight, through the pain and exhaustion.

'Listen. Listen to me. What was on the note? What does it really mean? You have to tell me.'

She wrested her arm loose and unstuck the hair from her face. She wiped her eyes with her fingers and sucked the tears from her lips.

'It's everything,' she said. She was looking directly at me, eyes wet and wide. 'All my work. It's all written there, in the numbers and letters. It's a key.'

'What does it unlock?'

'An algorithm. One *simple* algorithm.' I thought of Baaz, our conversation in Paris. I hoped that he was safe, that the banknote was safe; that Talia had come through for him.

'It's for a quantum computer, isn't it?'

She nodded. 'It's the ghost in the machine.'

'And you've given this to the Russians? This algorithm?'

She shook her head. 'Moshe hid it from them on the note. It would take a genius to crack it. Amos took it to the only person I could trust.'

'But you did this *for* the Russians?'

'No. It's not like that. You wouldn't understand. I did it because . . . because I *had* to. People dream of revolution, of the Second Coming, of *Aharit Hayamim*, of . . . whatever.'

All the bombs, I thought. *People dream of all the bombs.*

'It's everything,' she said, 'and I did it for everyone. It's beautiful and invulnerable. No cryptosystem could withstand it. And the Russians paid the price.'

'No,' I said. 'Doc paid the price. Amos, too. And Moshe. Shot through the heart because of that hundred-dollar bill. I didn't pull the trigger. Not me. Not this time. All this – all this blood – for what? An equation? It's madness. And it's over. We've all paid. Them, you, me. Now let's get out of here while we can.'

'You still don't understand, do you? It's too late, Max.' She laid her hand on my chest. 'The money they sent to me, they used it for hardware, too. That's why I stopped. That's why I left. Amos found out what they were doing, what it was really for.'

'And what, exactly,' I asked her, 'was that?'

'A computer. The Russians are building a computer, a working, powerful, *true* quantum computer. The Americans, the British, the Israelis, the Chinese – even the Indians – *everyone* has been trying. It was always just an impossible idea, a dream that no one really thought would ever come true, not like this, not for decades. But the Russians are doing it, Max. Soon it won't be a dream any more. They lied to me and they used me. Used my vision. My faith.'

I looked at the mad marks on the wall with fresh eyes and saw, finally, what she had seen all along. She followed my eyes as I read the signs and symbols.

'You asked what it means, Max. It means absolute power. It isn't a dream any more. It's a nightmare.'

33

Zero zero thirty hours.

Outside, the church of St Michael, patron saint of soldiers, loomed over me in the night. The snow had stopped falling and the clouds had opened enough to see stars here and there. But there was no moon and the road beyond the village dissolved into darkness. Under different circumstances it would have been beautiful. But then and there it looked, felt lethal.

We had around seven hours until first light. It was a twenty-two-hour, twelve-hundred-kilometre drive first north and then west across frozen-hard tank country to Estonia and the nearest friendly border that bypassed Moscow. I had no decent cold kit, no intel and no meds. I did have half a dozen bruised ribs, a badly sprained knee and two bullet wounds. But thanks to Aleksandr Denisovich I also had the keys to a car – or soon would. And Baaz? He had the keys to the kingdom, if only he knew it. He'd never get the credit for bringing back the algorithm – but I'd make sure that he was compensated handsomely. The 'Bhavneet Singh School of Quantum Computing' had a satisfying ring to it.

I put the battery into Talia's cell phone and switched it on. The screen was cracked, smashed from the dive on to the truck in Moscow. But the processor was undamaged and it came to life. One bar of service cut in and out. I moved further from the house, opened Signal and typed:

Mobile to Värska by road. RV 2300HRS. Likely have Red Forces
in pursuit. Please have welcoming committee ready.
Tea and Medals. Out.

I pressed send and waited for the double ticks to appear by
the message. Talia had given me her contact details. But I
didn't need them. The phone number of the only person I
could count on had been seared into my memory for twenty
years. Frank Knight might have been unresponsive, but Sergeant Major Jack Nazzar never was. Somewhere on the other
side of Europe a very grumpy Scotsman was about to live up
to his nickname.

Whoever had released my photograph had known exactly
what they were doing. After I'd been exposed in the press,
asking for Nazzar's help again had become impossible. It
would have compromised him unacceptably in the eyes of
the Crown he'd sworn to serve. As far as Whitehall was concerned, Jack wasn't off the books: he was on the cover.
Besides, there was little, if anything, he could have done that
would not, ultimately, have made things worse – for me, and
for Rachel.

Calling on him now wouldn't just do me a favour – it
would help him out as well. He couldn't refuse my request
for evacuation – and London wouldn't want him to. However things stood between me and Frank, no matter what
apoplexies General King had been sent into, and irrespective of what Nazzar personally made of my run and subsequent
about-turn – it was a fair bet that the only thing uniting us all
was an urgent desire to see me, and the intelligence I'd col-
lected, back in Britain as quickly as possible. Nazzar and I
had both crossed a line when we'd spoken via Doctor Rose
from the hospital in Ashford. His bringing me in would set

the record straight – for him, at least. By keeping me close, he'd tell them, he'd kept me on side, *inside*. What happened then was neither his prerogative nor his problem. But there was no question at all that he'd be the one they'd send to get me.

I didn't know what would be waiting for me and Rachel on the road ahead. Mystery gunmen were uncannily good at tracking me down. But Avilov was dead, and Arkhangel village apparently hadn't figured in his equation. I was banking on the GRU having no more idea where I was than Frank did. They would have better luck looking for a needle in a haystack than a Lada in north-west Russia.

I didn't know what was waiting for us back in London, either. But we had tabs on the banknote and that was all the security we needed. It had kept Baaz, Rachel and me alive this long; and our funerals would be Frank's failure if he didn't gain possession of the bill first. Killing us – or allowing us to be killed – lost him everything. In that respect, if nothing else, Commander Frank Knight and Doctor Leonid Avilov had a great deal in common.

I went back into the priest's house. Rachel had sat down again, huddled on the floor, fixated trance-like on the candles. I raised the phone and took a photograph of the calculations scrawled across the wall. Then I removed the battery and put the phone back in my pocket. Moshe would have approved: it doesn't hurt to have insurance. I walked over to her and touched her gently on the shoulder.

'It's time to go.' She shook her head and kept her back turned to me. 'Rachel, please. We need to leave now.'

I circled around and stood in front of her.

'I can't,' she said, looking up at me.

'We can make it, Rachel. We can get over the border. My people will meet us, they'll help us. It's a long drive, but we can do it. We can give them the algorithm. You can continue your work.' Her eyes widened. 'It will be a memorial to Doc, to Amos. Finish what you started. You can do it. *We* can do it. But first we have to leave.'

She scuttled away from me, terrified.

'No.'

'Rachel, please. Trust me. Everything's going to be all right.'

'You can't give it to them, Max. You can't. It has to be destroyed. You can't give it to anyone.'

'It's OK, I promise. I won't.'

She backed away further, fingernails clawing at the wooden floorboards.

'I don't believe you. You *did* kill my father. That's why you're here. You've got the algorithm, and once you understand it you'll get rid of me. You and Avilov. You're the same. You're all the same.'

I bridled at the thought of it. But she was right. Frank Knight and Leonid Avilov had something else in common, too: an individual – *any* individual – would always be expendable in the face of their ambition, whether that be serving the interests of national security or their own personal advancement.

'Avilov is dead,' I said.

'It doesn't matter. The Russians have the computer.'

'Let them build it. Without you it will only be a dream. No ghost for their machine, hey?' I fished the fake *Arkhangel* bill from my pocket. I unfolded it and then opened the stove door. The embers inside flared with the rush of air. I held the note up so she could see it, see my near-perfect interpretation of her sloppy, Cyrillic script on the reverse. 'Forget London. We'll go east, deep into the forest. Not even your angel will be able to find us. We'll survive. Thrive. You and me.' And then I held the note over the grate and let the flames take it. 'There,' I lied. 'It's over.' I walked back to the candles, to the wall she'd used as a blackboard. 'And this is the algorithm, too?'

'Yes,' she nodded. 'Part of it. The final part.'

'How do you mean?'

'The banknote wasn't complete,' she said, turning to look at the calculations writ large behind her. 'It took coming here finally to see it, to finish it.'

'So, this is the conclusion?'

She nodded again.

'It gives Azrael the eyes to see.'

'The hundred-dollar bill and this,' I pointed at the wall, 'are, were, the only copies?'

'Yes, but . . .'

I paced back to the stove and picked up her sleeping bag.

'And Amos, could he have told anyone?'

'No. He didn't know how close I was to solving it.'

'And Doc, what did Doc know?'

'He knew I'd made a breakthrough, but . . . Max, what are you doing?'

She watched me as I picked up a candle and held it under the sleeping bag. The nylon sacking caught almost immediately. I swung the growing ball of fire under the dresser. The old varnish cracked and blistered. Small blue flames licked up its sides and took hold of the legs. Within seconds the wood was alight, the room filling with smoke. I stepped back and covered my face as a rush of flame leapt up. Whatever had been stored inside the cabinet had accelerated the burn into a roaring blaze. Soon the floorboards would catch, then the wall and ceiling. The roof would go up and the house would come down – by which time we would be on our way.

I took her by the wrist, but she twisted free.

'No,' she shouted above the hiss of the fire, stepping backwards towards the flames. 'You're not listening. You haven't understood anything. It isn't the note that needs to be destroyed.'

I went after her, arms outstretched, lungs already straining from the smoke and heat.

'Please, Rachel.' She was choking now, struggling to draw breath as the oxygen burned out of the room. She hesitated and then let me embrace her. I held her close to my chest as the blaze began to spread across the floor. 'It's OK,' I said.

She flattened her hands against my back and I readied myself to take her weight. My shoulder, ribs throbbed. She buried her face into my chest. With one hand she gripped my waist; with the other the back of my neck.

'Just relax.'

A brilliant mind; an infuriating, captivating lover; a revolutionary – whatever she once had been was consumed then and there by madness. Perhaps completing the algorithm had sent her over the edge; perhaps it had taken the descent into insanity finally to scc thc answer she'd devoted a lifetime to looking for. She had spent years fighting her demons, without ever imagining that she would create one, become one. She had gazed into the abyss; and the abyss had gazed into her.

I could feel the fire singeing my hair, clothes, burning the skin on the backs of my hands. But as I braced myself to lift her, she pulled away from me again, even closer to the fire. Her hand was still at my neck, so that our heads touched, but her body, legs were clear of mine.

'Rachel ...' I moved forward again and felt her fist clenched between us. I looked down and saw the scout's knife, drawn from behind my back: blade up, old steel reflecting red in the fire-glow.

'I'm sorry, Max,' she said, pressing her mouth to my ear.

Then she drew her head back, eyes fixed on mine, and thrust. I brought my hand around, down, but I was too slow. The cutting edge ran across my fingers, slicing to the bone. The point went in hard. She gasped with the effort of it and then smiled, pushing herself on to me, forcing the steel in and up. I felt the blade lodge home, felt the blood pumping on to her stomach and mine. I closed my fist around the grip and we clung to each other. I saw my mother and Doc, laughing, happy; I saw Rachel on the bedroom floor, the life pouring out of her; I saw her in the forest, the wind in her hair, laughing, free. And then all I could see were her eyes, flashing green in the firelight. She raised her hands, red with gore, and laid them on my cheeks.

'God forgive me,' she whispered in Irish. 'It is finished.'

I let her go and she stepped back, pulling herself free of the knife. Then she looked up, and her legs gave way, and she fell into the flames – and it was.

34

Zero one hundred.

The glow of the fire threw a halo around the village. I ran to Aleksandr Denisovich's house and didn't look back.

I headed east and then north, and within a few minutes the red glow in the rear-view mirror vanished and there was no sign that anything had happened at all. The Lada ground on through the darkness to Vologda. Hunched over the wheel, the heating cranked to the maximum, I strained my eyes into the bright beams thrown by the four-by-four's headlights. The sides of the road were piled with snow. Fresh ice formed on the asphalt as new flurries froze between the tyre treads. My hands were stained red with my blood and hers.

I wanted to turn around. I wanted to rub my face with ashes and scream at the sky. I wanted to do, say something, anything, that would change what was. The road pulled me onwards. I repeated the words we'd said. I imagined a life in which I had not run; in which she was not dead. But what's gone is gone. And you can never go back. Trying to has cost many a man his head, his soul. Mine nearly included. The consequences of survival would be something I lived with for ever.

I flexed my fingers gripping the steering wheel through makeshift dressings I'd torn from my shirt. Only when I tasted the salt on my lips did I realize I was crying. I blinked hard and kept on keeping on. It was all I could think to do.

But it was slow going.

The further north I drove, the harder the snow fell. I esti-mated the drive at sixteen hours in decent conditions, adding four hours to account for the winter weather and another two on top to be safe. If I stayed in-country any longer than twenty-four hours, getting out would become almost impos-sible: no matter how ineffectual the Russian police were, a day was the most I'd have before they caught up with me. Steal more cars, and I risked tripping a wire where it counted. If the FSB got involved and joined the dots with the GRU, I'd be lucky to make it halfway to the Estonian border.

Even if Aleksandr Denisovich had already reported his car stolen, I doubted the police would make visiting him a priority. And it was unlikely that he or anyone else would bother to call the emergency services about the fire: the dilapidated priest's house had been consumed entirely and there was no one to call an ambulance for – even if one was available to send. No, the real variable was old Polina Yurievna. I couldn't count on it, but I'd have bet my last hun-dred rubles that she'd send the authorities on a wild goose chase. I was near enough kin. And Russians take blood very seriously indeed.

I kept my speed steady and my driving unremarkable. I didn't want to give the police any excuse to pull me over. It wasn't only a case of being identified: even a successfully negotiated routine stop would slow me down. Although there were hours of driving ahead, I knew that, in the end, every minute would count.

Timing my escape was a fine balance, though: if I'd given Jack Nazzar much less than twenty-four hours, he wouldn't have time to get an extraction team on location. Sometimes he'd use local Special Forces for exfiltration. But for this job I knew he'd insist on running the whole show with his own men from the Revolutionary Warfare Wing. Deploying the SAS in Estonia was a political minefield, but I doubted the pro-NATO government in Tallinn would object – always revelling in any opportunity to stick two fingers up at Moscow.

But the entire plan – if sending one message and then driving halfway across Europe to find out if it had been acted on could be called a plan – might be tipped into failure by even the slightest margin of error. A flat tyre, worsening weather . . . It would take very little to defeat me.

Zero five hundred.

I arrived in Vologda two hours before first light and refuelled. Then I fished Talia's cracked-screen cell phone out of my jacket pocket and weighed up whether or not to create a backup of the photograph I'd taken of Rachel's final calculations. I could send it to myself by Signal – but it was too much of a risk. I had to assume that the handset would be loaded with spyware, and, just as Baaz had cautioned in Paris, even if the messaging application was fireproof, it would be straightforward for Talia to capture the photo before the data was encrypted and sent. Besides, as soon as I switched the phone on, Talia would see exactly where I was again.

In Israel she'd been good to her word. But as soon as she knew that Rachel was gone there was no reason for her to keep me alive. On the contrary. I was a witness, the only witness, to the Shabak's absolute failure to protect someone who'd turned out to be one of Israel's most valuable human assets. It was an unsettling thought – but whatever happened in the hours that followed would owe as much to the quality of Talia's relationship with Ezra as it did to the quality of mine with Frank.

As far as the Shabak was concerned, though, the clock was on my side: even if Talia wanted to, she simply didn't have enough time to take direct action. And given everything, it seemed unlikely she'd enlist the help of the Russians. Although that was a gamble, too; if she was monitoring the phone, then she knew I was heading for Värska from Arkhangel. But if anyone was following me, they couldn't be sure where I'd approach the border – and cordoning off half of Russia simply wasn't practical.

I wrapped the phone tightly in a plastic bag I'd found in the glovebox of the stolen Lada and buried it deep inside my jacket with my Russian passport and the photograph of my mother. I restarted the engine and pushed the gearstick into first. But as my foot hovered over the gas pedal, I heard my own voice come back to me.

Forget London. We'll go east, deep into the forest. Not even your angel will be able to find us.

I didn't have to make a run for the border. Turn east, and I could disappear – for ever, if I liked. I put my foot back on the brake and thought about that. I was beyond orders. No one could compel me to do anything. I'd been on the run for days. And now, finally, came the chance – perhaps the final chance – to escape.

But Rachel's angel was real all right, and I knew I'd never shake it off in the trees. No matter how deep I went, the damned thing would be on my tail until the day it finally caught up with me. I could outrun any man sent to hunt me. But not even riding the fastest horse east from Arkhangel could I escape my fate.

It would be disastrous if the Russians intercepted the phone and the photograph of Rachel's calculations. But destroying her Destroyer wouldn't solve anything. Eventually another mind, perhaps even more brilliant – and more unhinged – than Rachel's, would rediscover what had been lost. And then we would be at *their* mercy, enslaved to the interests of some unforeseen tyranny.

No. Getting out of Russia wasn't merely a case of ensuring my own survival, or even of sabotaging the Russians. I had to stick with the plan, and make certain that what Rachel had brought into being was either used for the greater good – or never used at all – and I could only guarantee that from London. Rachel had been blinded by the brilliance of her creation, warped into madness by the power of it. Perhaps I would be, too. Perhaps *Arkhangel*'s promise of absolute authority would always prove impossible to protect against.

But there was someone I trusted to see clearly enough to navigate the landscape that Rachel's angel would reform – and yet Baaz had only one part of the algorithm. Without the photograph of the writing on the wall neither of us could unlock the secrets that had driven Rachel to her death.

It didn't matter whose side Commander Frank Knight was on. Good or bad, he was just one man – and Grumpy Jock would make sure I got to Blighty in one piece. But only by returning would I ever know why I'd been sent out in the first place. The death knell might have sounded, but this watchman was still alive.

I hit the gas, and turned west.

A hundred and fifty klicks further on and an hour behind schedule and the sky began to lighten. Mezga, Trukhino, Khvoynaya . . . the towns and villages of north-west Russia hid behind the snowflakes blowing constantly around the car. Saturday traffic was light; the local cops more concerned with keeping their feet warm and cars moving than shaking down drivers. No roadblocks. No sirens. No one in pursuit. No one I could see, anyway.

Sixteen hundred.

I pulled into Veliky Novgorod with an hour of daylight left and refuelled for the third time. I bought food, too – a barely edible snack wrapped in plastic – and coffee. I kept my head down, covered with Aleksandr Denisovich's driving cap, said the bare minimum to the teller and paid in cash. Then I parked up in a quiet side street and swallowed a mouthful of the insipid, brown liquid. At least it was hot.

While I ate, I mapped out the rest of the journey in my mind. If conditions remained the same, the drive to the border would take another five hours. That would put me at the RV at nine o'clock – with two hours to spare before Jack Nazzar and the Wing were expecting me. Where, *exactly*, they were supposed to expect me, I hadn't said. But I was hoping that one look at a map of the border would leave Jack in no doubt.

Five years before, I'd trained on Russian Hind helicopter gunships in Poland with A-Squadron SAS. Jack had come along for the ride, never happier than when he was airborne. As part of one of the exercises he'd devised with MI6, we'd studied every possible exfiltration method and route out of Russia imaginable: commercial flights with operators using false IDs; border-hopping light aircraft flown by Romanian pilots; RIBs manned by the SBS collecting personnel on the Baltic coast and then taking them to a submarine rendezvous offshore; vehicle extraction by road in both summer and winter across the land borders with the Ukraine, Finland and Latvia – and various combinations of all of them. But it was escaping via Estonia that had stuck in my mind as the most feasible, achievable plan. I hoped Jack had been similarly impressed.

South-east of the Estonian village of Värska, Highway 178 – a single-lane road fringed by forest and farmland – slipped out of the Baltic state and into Russia. It continued across sovereign Russian soil for just over a kilometre before crossing back into Estonia again. It was a geographical oddity, a cartographer's hiccup called 'the Saatse Boot'. And because the road led nowhere, except from one part of Estonia to another, the border crossings were open to local traffic and almost completely unguarded. To the south-east, the highway connected a small patchwork of villages virtually cut off from the rest of the country by poor roads and a vast expanse of forest. But to the north-west there would be easy and inconspicuous access for Jack and what I hoped would be his rescue mob.

Halfway along the 178's course inside Russia there was a junction with a forest path – which cut through the trees for two klicks from the Russian village of Gorodishche on the east. As far as low-profile easy-access exfil went, it was the only option. The track was too narrow for vehicles. But I was prepared to gamble that on foot, and with two hours to spare, I could make it down the track, along the road and over the north-west frontier of the 'hiccup' to freedom.

It was time to go.

I nosed back out on to the highway, pointing towards the backwater city of Pskov and the border a short drive beyond.

Twenty-one hundred.

I was close now. The frontier with Estonia was only eight klicks away as the crow flies. But the point at which I'd have to ditch the Lada was another twenty klicks by road. I turned off the highway and parked up in the village of Molochkovo-Dubenets – a bitterly cold clutch of houses that clung to the southern shore of Lake Peipus, two massive bodies of water, connected by a narrow sound, which were cut vertically in two by the border. Its frozen wastes stretched away to the north for a hundred and forty kilometres – not that I could see more than a few metres of the lake itself, even with the headlights aiming directly at it. The weather had closed in dramatically since the last of the daylight had bled out of the sky hours earlier. Thick squalls of snowflakes now filled the air, spun into great white gyres whirling away from the headlights.

I'd planned to hug the lakeside northwards along a winding rural road before cutting west to the jumping-off point, where I'd continue on foot. But the route ahead was already impassable. I was going to have to double back on myself and take a larger road that ran parallel to the lake, inland.

I killed the lights and closed my eyes in the darkness. I went to sleep immediately, and then woke abruptly as my head fell forward. I was exhausted, injured and overwhelmed by the blood-tide Frank's mission had unleashed. I pinched my eyes and rubbed my face. I was losing time. Two hours until RV – assuming there was anyone to RV with. The last stretch could take an hour to drive – after which I'd have to make two klicks on foot in the dark, thigh deep in snow. And that was assuming I could even remember the way. I was pushing it. If I hit one more dead end, it would all be over, anyway.

I switched the lights on again and turned the Lada around, retracing the short drive towards the main road. It only took a couple of minutes to reach the junction where I'd turned off. I emerged cautiously on to a triangle of snow-buried asphalt. And then the air lit up.

On the other side of the road the flashing warning lights

of a Russian police four-by-four blitzed me with a red and blue strobe. An officer was already out of the vehicle, walking towards me, left hand outstretched, waving a light baton. The headlights of both our cars lit up his electric-yellow hi-vis vest in the torrent of snowflakes between us. If I dropped the clutch and punched the gas, I'd hit him hard enough to put him down. But there would almost certainly be another officer in the vehicle. If I was going to drop him, it had to be clean. I left the motor running and opened the window. The blast of air sharpened my senses. The officer touched the brim of his fur hat and smiled.

'*Dobriy vecher!*' he greeted me through the open window.

I wished him a good evening, too, and looked at the logo on the arm of his blue overalls: DPS – Russian traffic police. Five-ten; hundred and forty pounds. Clean shaven. Nose like a hawk's bill. A misdemeanour cop in a felony world.

'You're a long way from home,' he said. 'You must be lost.'

'Oh no,' I said. 'Not at all. Thanks for asking, though. Hell of a night, isn't it?'

The headlights of the police vehicle opposite brightened to main beam, filling the junction with a powerful wash of white light. There were at least two of them, then.

'*Da,*' he said. '*Takaya kholodina.*' *Bloody cold.* The cop peered into the Lada, checking out the empty passenger seats. 'It's just that I saw you take the turn to Molochkovo-Dubenets. And five minutes later, here you are again.'

He laughed.

I laughed.

He must have clocked the Lada's out-of-area number plates. If he was crooked, he'd try for a bribe before calling me in. If he wasn't, and he had already asked for backup, he was playing it cool.

'No,' I said, raising my voice over the mounting hiss of the gale, 'it's just that the road to Pesok looks a bit sticky, that's all.' I jerked my head towards the lake. 'I'm going to head up to Krupp and see if I can get round that way instead.'

A gust of wind hit the side of the Lada, blowing snow into my face.

'Pesok?'

I nodded.

'OK then. No problem.' He stepped back and raised his voice. 'I'll just check your licence and insurance and you can be on your way,' he continued. 'Wouldn't want you out-of-towners to think we didn't do our job right, would we?'

'Of course not, officer. It's in my wallet.' I looked at him, still smiling. 'May I?'

He nodded and I moved my right hand slowly behind me, putting my fingers into my jeans back pocket and producing a folded hundred-dollar bill. Benjamin Franklin had been getting me in and out of trouble for days now. He was worth a final shot, either way. I straightened the note and held it out, so the policeman could see how much I was offering.

'Here you go.'

He snatched the note immediately and folded it, palming it out of sight with a flick of the wrist so practised he could have performed on stage.

'And your insurance, Mr . . . ?'

'Ivanovich,' I replied. And then, producing another hundred-dollar bill: 'My pleasure, officer.'

The second bill followed the first into his top pocket.

'It's fortunate your paperwork was in order, Mr Ivanovich.' He wrinkled his blade of a nose. 'Have a good night.'

He turned and walked back towards his vehicle, signalling to his partner through the windscreen with a flick of the baton to kill the flashing top lights. I put the Lada into gear. I could do it now and eliminate any uncertainty. But I didn't want to kill Russian cops any more than I did Irish or French ones. Corrupt or not, they weren't the enemy. And anyway, knocking a traffic patrol out could cause more problems than it might solve. As soon as they failed to respond to their HQ's first radio call, someone somewhere would know something was up. Much better that everyone went home happy.

The patrolman opened the passenger door of his DPS Niva. I let out the clutch. My tyres rolled forward, biting into the freshly fallen powder. But instead of climbing in, the cop hesitated for a moment, half covered by the open door, before turning around to face me. His right hand dropped to his side, degloved, struggling with the cover flap on his white leather holster.

His partner must have run the stolen Lada's plate.

I floored the gas. The cop looked down at the holster trapping the pistol he couldn't free, and then up again into my headlights. Mouth open, screaming, he put his left hand across his face, as if blocking out the glare would shield him from the impact.

It didn't.

The Lada struck the passenger door dead centre – hard enough to pin him between my front bumper and his chassis, but not hard enough to fire the airbags. He coughed a spray of blood on to my windscreen. From deep in his throat came a dreadful shrieking, cutting through the howl of the wind and the throb of the engine.

I opened my door and fell to the road, rolling clear on the frozen ground as the second cop stumbled out into the snow, little Makarov pistol in hand. He spun around and fired high, sending three shots whining well clear of my head.

There were five metres between us. I found my feet and kept low, thrusting forward, hitting him in the guts with my shoulder. His boots slid from under him and he came down on his back, gun arm up, sending more shots into the sky above us. I rolled away and grabbed his right wrist with my left hand, twisting it backwards. Another shot rang out. The awful screaming from the police car stopped abruptly.

I rotated his arm and chopped down with the inside of my right palm. His elbow snapped inward. The pistol fell into the snow, tethered to his belt by an expanding coil of white safety wire. I unclipped it from the butt of the semi-auto and stood up. The policeman was on his knees, left hand scrabbling at the road, right arm dragging limp behind him. He was half begging, half crying, pleading with me not to kill him. I let him go and went back to the patrol car. Through the shattered side window I could see the policeman I'd bribed hanging lifeless. The last stray shot had passed through the Niva's door frame and hit him in the side of the head. The Makarov's steel-core rounds punch way above their weight.

I needed to move on, and fast.

I leaned in and removed the keys from the ignition and threw them into the trees beside the junction. Then I fired a shot into the radio receiver. Lying in the passenger footwell was a metal flashlight. I reached in and took it, and then circled around to the nearside. Brain matter and blood clots patterned the snow-covered highway. Though my fingers were slowing with the cold, I did what the cop had failed to do and opened the flap of his holster. I extracted a fully loaded magazine and stuffed it into my pocket with the Makarov I'd already picked up.

My Lada hadn't been damaged beyond smashed sidelights. I got in and cranked the engine and reversed, sweeping the beams of the headlights across the surviving patrolman. He was sitting up now, staring at me, clutching his shattered arm. Tears sparkled on his cheeks, glistening in the halogen glare. He'd lit a fuse that threatened to blow up the border in my face. Russia's western sector was one of the most highly militarized on earth. His radio call could pull the combined weight of two entire divisions down on me – five thousand troops or more of which were within rapid striking distance of that area alone. Even if the local commanders didn't know who I was, all that would matter to them was that they were hunting a cop-killer.

As I drove, I dropped the magazine out of the Makarov. Empty. But there was a round in the breech. I juggled the steering wheel and the pistol and put on the replacement clip. Nine bullets in total. Then I felt inside my jacket to make sure the Angel of Death hadn't taken flight. It hadn't. Talia's cell phone and the photograph of Rachel's calculations were secure, pressed tight to my chest next to the snapshot of my mother.

I checked my watch. Twenty-one thirty. I had ninety minutes to get to the RV before the Russians likely sealed it off for good.

35

I drove north until I reached Krupp. There the road struck out west, through forest. Frozen birch trees inched past the window – silver statues glowing by the verges. Snowflakes the size of moths careered into the windscreen, as if pulled towards the car by the traction of the headlights. I checked the rear-view mirror obsessively, looking for any sign of unwelcome company – but there wasn't another car on the road.

I was losing time.

I cursed the cops, the delays, the weather. Then I crossed what felt like a small stone bridge. I hit the brakes and slid to a halt and jumped out, running back to check. I shone the police flashlight at the side of the road. It was buried in snow, but I'd driven over the tiny, frozen Piusa River. I got back in and turned left down the next farm track.

I drove cautiously, but the way had been cleared. This was horse country. Most likely tractors were keeping the roads open for supplies to the farms and stables whose lights dotted the clearings between the trees. After a few hundred metres the lane looped back on itself. I crept forward in second gear, searching beyond the white veil clinging to the windscreen for the switchback on to the forest path I hoped would take me to the border. Ten metres, twenty, thirty . . . I stopped.

Nothing.

I closed my eyes again, willing the image of the old satellite maps I'd spent so many hours poring over to reassemble in my mind. But all I could see were Rachel's eyes staring back at me through the inferno in Arkhangel. I blinked. And there in the rear-view mirror, illuminated in the red glow of my tail lights, was the snow-fouled opening of the shortcut through the trees. The entrance to the track was hidden at ground level by a bank of frozen snow, piled up in the wake of a plough. I shoved the gearstick into reverse and rolled backwards, taking the car off the road.

I switched off the engine and looked at my watch again.

Twenty-two thirty.

It had taken an hour to drive eighteen klicks, and the thought of the upcoming trek across country filled me with foreboding. My legs cramped, my shoulder burned, every time I flexed my hands the cuts at the base of my fingers opened and stung. But then, just as I killed the headlights, the outline of what looked like a man flitted across the road in front of me, heading away from the track. I squinted into the snow-swirls and scoured the darkness for any sign of him.

Nothing.

To my right, through the trees, what might have been the porch light of a farmhouse flickered weakly through the snow. Whoever it was must have been heading home. If I'd really seen anyone at all. I was almost hallucinating from tiredness, and I knew it. There was no time – and no point – in chasing ghosts now. Perhaps there never had been.

Come on, Max, keep it together.

I stepped out into the blizzard and stuck the torch into my belt.

The base temperature had risen a few degrees, but the wind chill made it feel like minus twenty. I pulled Aleksandr Denisovich's cap down and blinked into the white storm swirling unseen in the blackness between the trees. But as much as the weather blinded me, it also blinded anyone trying to follow me. It would be impossible to get a drone or chopper up, and a satellite would be useless. And although a thermal imaging scope would pick me up as easily here as it would have done in Arkhangel, they'd need to get close enough to identify me, not just detect me. At six hundred metres the glow given off by one man looks the same as any other. I hoped not even Russian officers would want to start shooting up their own troops.

Their night vision kit was going to be of limited use, too. It was so dark there was almost no image to intensify, and I was crowded by trees. I'd taken the torch for signalling, not navigation. Switch it on, though, and even in those conditions I'd be painting myself a bright green target.

There was no hiding the car. But snow was falling thick and fast enough that my footprints disappeared almost immediately – not, at this point, that there would any longer be much doubt where I was going. I looked up. For the first time in hours a smudge of light in the sky silhouetted the tops of the trees. I stepped forward and counted twenty paces – pistol at the ready – running my hand along the ice bank for balance until I found the break in the branches that marked the opening to the track.

Thirty minutes to RV.

I stopped, momentarily overwhelmed by the cold and the darkness. And then I heard my mother's voice, clear against the white-whistle of the storm-song, whispering 'Bayu Bayushki Bayu', warning me to be careful lest the grey wolf snatch me away into the woods.

The wind dropped a little. I mouthed a pointless *thank you* and sniffed the air. The intensity of the snowfall softened. High above, the blanket of cloud was beginning to fray.

Here and there moonlight bled through the rents in fleeting flashes of silver, pooling for a second or two on the forest floor.

It was a straight shot for another kilometre until I hit Highway 178. It was doable. I could do it.

Just walk, Max.

I stumbled immediately, falling as my boot found a rabbit hole. I cursed as my already bruised ribs crunched on the ground. I picked myself up and listened. But I could hear nothing except the wind ebbing and flowing and my mother's voice, steel-sharp in my brain, singing lullabies to her wicked son. I willed myself westwards. My hands, cheeks began to sting. Frozen beads of ice clogged my eyes. I took another step. And another. My legs moved like lumps, weaving me in an uncertain path between the birches. After what felt like a few minutes, I checked the time again. I'd been out of the car for quarter of an hour.

Fuck.

I pressed on. And then the path stopped abruptly. Trees on three sides. The scattered moonlight that had got me this far was swallowed by the forest. I groped in the dark, squinting obliquely along what I thought was the trail, using any faint scrap of light to see the way. I cracked my shin on frozen deadfall. In my mind's eye I saw the satellite map I'd memorized in Poland – lush green in the spring photographs, almost useless in the winter darkness. The track should have veered sharp right, but now I was trapped. I must have disorientated myself when I fell. I turned a silent circle. And then another, spinning myself inside the vortex of the dying storm.

And then I stopped still, and breathed out, and accepted the deeply inconvenient truth that I was profoundly lost.

I listened intently for my mother's voice, racked my brain for any solution that did not involve retracing my steps. But I was blind and deaf and out of options.

I was almost out of time, too.

If Jack Nazzar had assembled a team on the border he wouldn't, couldn't, keep them there indefinitely, however much he might want to. And whatever it turned out that Frank really wanted, I could guarantee it wasn't a land war on NATO's eastern border. The wind dropped to a stand-still. I bowed my head and listened again.

Above the gentle whisper of snow falling on snow, I heard the unmistakable sound of a man cough. I held my breath. Ten seconds. Twenty. And then again, muffled this time, as if the mouth had been smothered by a hand. Six to eight feet away. Low down. Directly in front. Unmistakable. A man for sure. I extended my right arm, aiming the Makarov down into the darkness.

The wind picked up again. Clouds scudded overhead. Moonlight flitted across the clearing. It took a heartbeat for the landscape to take form. When it did, the ground in front of my feet seemed to turn in on itself, churning shadows into the snow, whipping a branch towards me. But it wasn't a branch. It was the barrel of a rifle. No one was trying to follow me. They were already here. A soldier in winter camouflage, lying prone on the forest floor, was turning to engage his target: me.

I fired first.

Two shots centre mass. The sniper's white ghillie snow-suit turned him into an amorphous, abominable snowman. He fell back but not down. The muzzle of his rifle dipped. I couldn't see my sights, but at that distance I didn't need to. I fired again into his white balaclava as the moon hid itself again. He disappeared into the shadows. I was on him in an instant, firing another shot into his torso at point blank. But he was already dead.

The round from the Makarov had obliterated the mouthpiece of his comms set. I pocketed the pistol and pulled the headset free, holding it to my ear. An operator was asking him in Russian to confirm his position, confirm contact. I dropped the radio and picked up his weapon: an SV-98 – a standard-issue Russian sniper rifle fitted with a tactical suppressor, and a thermal scope mounted in-line with the optics. Good enough.

I brought the scope to my eye and scanned the treeline. The silver-dark of the birch forest morphed into a black and white thermogram. It was like looking at a video shot in photographic negative. Heat gave off a bright, white signature; cold showed up as inky-black. As I swept the optics across the black snow around me, white outlines darted between the trees at two and three hundred metres on either side of my position. And if I could see their heat trace, they could see mine.

But unlike them, I could positively identify my enemy.

Either they'd been waiting for me, or I'd stumbled into a border exercise. I wasn't planning on asking them which. The man I'd just killed had been lying down, facing away from me. No sniper would do that in those conditions unless he was covering a choke point and expecting his target – imminently. It was a sure bet that the path I'd been looking for unwound in front of him. Getting lost had almost certainly saved my life.

If I ran now, they'd know to shoot me. If I stayed put, I risked not being able to outpace them when they caught up with me. The safety on the rifle was off. I eased the bolt back and checked the breech. Bullet brass glinted in the moonlight. I set the scope magnification to times six and dialled in one hundred metres. Weapons free.

I stood up.

Deep breath. Long exhale. Stop. Settle. Squeeze.

The first outline dropped into the black snow-sea at his feet. I pivoted. Cheek on the stock. Eye to the scope. Right hand working the bolt.

Acquire.

Fire.

Two more dead men in the snow – and more soldiers to come than I had shots left in the rifle's magazine. I racked the bolt and checked the trees again. On either side and forward of my position men were scuttling through the undergrowth. From the way they were spread out, it looked as if I'd walked into the back of a cordon stretching north and south along the road. Whomever they'd been expecting, they'd assumed their target would come up Highway 178 itself – which was less than two hundred metres distant through the trees as the crow flies. It looked like they'd fanned out along it.

I squirmed down next to the rapidly cooling corpse of the sniper I'd shot in the face and considered my options. It was a further six hundred metres along forest track to where it joined the highway. From there it was another seven hundred metres along the road to the north-western Estonian border post. I couldn't risk cutting back the three hundred metres to the southerly crossing: there was even less of a guarantee that Jack would have his men in place there – and if they weren't, the odds were that the Russians would take a gamble and keep up their pursuit. The corner of Estonia that lay to the south-east was effectively cut off, and my chances of getting more than a gunshot ahead of the enemy were bleak.

The wind started to bite again. Snow fell from the branches overhead. Through the scope I could see that the cover up ahead was patchy. If they had men on the other side of the road I'd be a sitting duck at the crossing point. The pain from whatever I'd done to my knee falling off the bridge in Moscow made it impossible to maintain a steady kneeling position. I sat instead, locking my ankles, bracing my elbows against the inside of my thighs.

I studied the white traces of the men closing in on me, slipping like ghosts through the undergrowth. The nearest had got to within a hundred metres. Putting them down would telegraph my identity to anyone else with a thermal scope within half a kilometre or more. I looked at the luminous hands of my watch. Ten minutes to RV. I adjusted the scope and took the soldier to the right of me with a single shot to the chest. But as I swung round looking for the next target, the air filled with the *zip-crack* of incoming high-velocity rounds. I rolled sideways and flattened myself into the snow, squirming down behind the body of the dead sniper and a tangle of fallen branches. Everyone within range opened up simultaneously. Chips of ice, bark and bone blew into my face. Whatever cover I had left was being shredded around me, the dead-body barricade included.

I rolled right and got myself back on the gun. I could see the left side of the nearest shooter, who'd taken cover behind a skinny birch. He stepped sideways to fire. My steel-core 7.62 cut his legs out from under him. I worked the bolt, sending spent brass spinning into the night. A bullet clipped my left boot heel. I moved the rifle up and to the right. His wingman was seventy metres further out – crouching, firing. My fingers were freezing, my breath erratic, and all the while my body was leaching heat into the frozen ground. If I didn't run soon, I wouldn't be able to run at all. The wingman stood up. I fired. He toppled sideways into a bank of snow.

I took more suppressing fire from my right. It was working. I was pinned down in a game of full-contact murder in the dark. I needed to take out the shooters directly ahead of me – and then split. If I made it to Highway 178, and then kept tight to the treeline, there was a slim chance I could outmanoeuvre them. It was a gamble, but the snow was falling so thickly again that it might cover me enough to reach the frontier. But however fast and loose the Russians might play it, there was no way Jack Nazzar or the Wing would cross the border itself; if he was waiting, though, he'd know for sure by now what was going on.

I turned a tight circle and raised myself up to take a shot. A bullet clipped my left shoulder. Another passed between the inside of my left arm and ribcage, punching through the jacket, grazing skin. I pulled the trigger and felled one of the shooters as another round scored a line above my temple.

Go. Now.

But as I got ready to run, the snow in front of me lifted, filling the air with a thick white curtain. A deep, resonant *boom* filled my lungs. Shock waves expanded under me – flipping me into the air, twisting me on to my side. I clawed the ground, coughed blood into the blackness. My ears rang, chest heaved. Then another eruption, behind this time, knocked me forward, sprawling me headlong between the trees. White-hot shards of steel peppered the snow. A splinter of shrapnel gouged my back. Another tore at my left bicep.

Rifle grenades.

Deep snow had absorbed the impact of the blasts. As soon as one hit a tree I'd be in trouble.

I pushed up on to my elbows. More rifle shots zipped between the trees, the usual *snap*, *crackle* and *pop* of incoming rounds muted by the snow. I reached for the SV-98 but dropped it smartly as the stock split, cracked by a direct hit.

Moving forward was impossible. I hauled myself up and lurched back along the trail, head down. Every footfall was like driving a knife blade under my kneecap. I dodged around the trees as best I could, pursued by a stream of copper-coated steel. I was slow, snowbound. Fragments of ice blown from a tree-trunk ricochet blinded me momentarily. A round nicked my right calf; another, my left wrist. I stumbled on, twisting, ducking, zigzagging my way back to the Lada. However I was going to get to the border, it wasn't going to be on foot – and it had to be fast.

I emerged back into the lane as the clouds pulled apart enough to wash the landscape with moonlight. Dead ahead, eighty metres away through the trees, was the light I'd seen when I'd pulled up – a porch lamp, perhaps, or a security light for a barn or an outhouse. I was in a crook on the lane, the point where it looped back on itself, and I could only see a few metres in either direction. Behind me: shouts. I turned and faced the Lada and took a step towards it. And then the moonlight was overpowered by a bright white flash.

For a fraction of a second it looked as if the four-by-four had been lit from the inside by a bolt of lightning. And then the windows buckled and exploded outwards. The chassis jumped clear of the ground, lurching sideways. The *kaboom* of the blast ripped down the lane. Metal twisted around metal. Razor-sharp cubes of glass cut my face, neck. I dived flat as the gas tank went up, sending a pall of oily orange flame up into the treetops.

After the explosion, shots. Electric green tracer lit up the night sky like lasers.

I crossed the track and ran towards the farm buildings ahead. My legs buckled. I grabbed a branch and levered myself forward. More shots. The soldiers reached the road, distracted by the burning Lada. I limped free of the trees and into a frozen meadow.

I was well met by the moonlight reflected from the snow in the air and on the ground. Out of the silver-white night a row of wooden buildings emerged. The lamp I'd seen was suspended on a pole over a smaller, enclosed field. The individual houses also had lights over the doors, but they shone too weakly to have been seen from the road. From one of the doorways a man stepped out, torch in hand. He fixed me with the beam.

'*Stoi!*'

But I wasn't going to stop. I drew the Makarov and levelled it at him.

'Drop it,' I shouted in Russian, 'or I shoot.'

'Don't,' he blurted out. 'You'll hurt them.'

The torch tumbled to the ground and then I was on him, left hand at his throat. He wasn't a man, but a boy: fifteen at most. Moments before, he'd been defending the family home. Now he was shaking with fear. In the woods behind me firing started again. Tracer arced over us. I looked at the boy, at the buildings. Above the chaos of shots and shouts, I could hear another sound, too – wild and free, an echo from my deepest childhood memories. They weren't houses, and he wasn't protecting his family. He was a stable boy, protecting his horses. I spun him around and shoved him forward.

'Davai!'

He walked quickly towards the nearest stable block, hands up, breathing hard, and went in first. I followed. An intense, heady tang of dung and hay and sweat and leather rolled over us. Half a dozen stalls were lit by dim tungsten lamps. In the nearest, a sixteen-hand Akhal-Teke stallion nodded over a half-door, his palomino coat glowing a deep gold under the orange lights. He was, simply, stunning. I stepped away from the boy, still clutching the pistol.

'Tack him up.'

Tears ran down his face.

'Please,' he said. 'Not him. Any other one, but not him. Please, mister.'

'Just do it,' I said. 'And be quick. He'll be OK,' I added. 'I promise.'

He went to work and I went to the door and pushed it to, trying to keep beyond the reach of thermal scopes. I pressed my eye briefly to a tiny gap in the door jamb. Despite the scattering cloud, gusts of fresh snow still swept across the open ground. It was impossible to see more than a few metres. I peered into the darkness around the halo cast by the outside lamp. Shadows moved at its edge. Then, dead ahead, a white-clad trooper stepped into view, assault rifle in his shoulder. Then to his left, another. And another.

I stepped back. The Akhal-Teke whinnied. I turned to the boy and placed my index finger to my lips, urging silence. He'd got the tack on – English saddle and a simple snaffle bridle. I beckoned and he led the horse out of the stall. I pressed my eye to the door again. Outside, the soldiers edged closer – forming and vanishing as the wind picked up, sweeping flurries of snowflakes across them.

Fifteen metres.

I turned to the boy again.

'Hold him steady,' I whispered. He nodded, eyes still wet with tears. 'What's his name?'

'Boynou.'

'Is he fast?'

'As an arrow.'

I stepped carefully back to the door.

Ten metres.

Close enough.

From the adjacent stall I led a grey Don mare by her head collar. The two horses touched noses. I handed the Don's lead rope to the boy and took the Akhal-Teke reins in my left hand and the pommel in my right, still holding the pistol. I put my left foot into the stirrup and pushed up, pulling myself over, into the saddle, gritting my teeth at the pain in my knee. I found the other stirrup, and cocked the Makarov.

'Let go of the lead and open the door,' I said in a stage whisper. 'And then get down.' He put his hand on the wooden catch. 'Now.'

He pushed down and the door swung open. As a blast of frigid air ripped into the stable, I slapped the unsaddled grey on her rump and she bolted into the night. I dropped low on Boynou's shoulder, leg on, and squeezed hard.

'*Nu!*' I yelled. *Go on!*

The stallion gave a buck and surged ahead, leading with his left leg, neck straining forward. The first soldier was within touching distance of the door. The Don mare had flung him backwards. He swung his rifle towards me but overbalanced, falling sideways into the snow, loosing a shot above my shoulder. The second soldier – a barely visible ghost crouching in the winter whirlwind – brought his barrel to bear on me as I raised mine to him. But he was too slow, too far behind me. I fired. The bullet went high and hit him in the throat. The third soldier had been knocked flat on his back. Flailing in the snow, grasping for his weapon, he was out of sight within seconds.

I cantered north-east towards the lights of another farm, coming out on the lane a few hundred metres beyond the burning Lada. Although Boynou took the snow in his stride, hacking straight across country was a no-go: one buried rabbit hole and we'd both come a cropper. I'd have to stick to paths and ride like *Fear na gCrúb* – the Man with the Hooves himself. The stirrups were too long, and I couldn't get my heels down, but Boynou carried me lightfoot across the fresh powder. I shortened the rein and sat hard in the saddle, slowing him to a trot and then to a walk around the houses. Tactical torches flicked fingers of light into the falling flakes to my left. I patted Boynou's golden flank.

'Easy, boy.'

We stood in the shadows of a frozen yard, steam streaming from his nostrils, front hooves pawing the ground.

If I turned on to the lane, whoever was behind those torches was going to have a clear shot: one round in Boynou was all it would take. But straight ahead, at right angles to the lane, there was another path leading back into the woods. It was clear enough of snow to try it. The stallion started to step sideways, tossing his head. I tightened the reins, bunching them in my left hand, threading them between my fingers. I squeezed gently, and clicked my tongue, urging him to walk on. We edged around a barn and then I dropped my hand forward and pressed my heels into his ribs. My shoulder met his, unbalancing me for a moment. Then he leapt out, into the road. Two strides and we were across, following the trail between the trees. The shooting started again immediately. Streams of tracer fire fanned out, first along the road and then through the trees. Branches cracked. Burning bullets ricocheted off tree trunks, zapping this way and that, filling the woods with a lethal green cat's cradle. After a hundred metres I took a sharp right. The path ended. Boynou picked his way through the snow, cautious, lifting his hooves high, shaking his head.

We moved clear of the firing. The original RV was blown, but Nazzar would be able to follow the radio traffic – at least between the ground units. With any luck the chatter would lead him to me. I'd have to find my own way across the border, though. We threaded our way north. Even in the moonlight it was hard to see more than a few strides ahead. I kept inside the trees, parallel to a cleared path, and then stopped at the point where it converged with the main, Russian, road that had taken me from Krupp to Gorodishche. The route continued north-east for six klicks to the village of Kulisko at the mouth of a narrow inlet to Lake Peipus. The Estonian border was on the far side of what I hoped was a frozen solid expanse of fresh water.

I leaned down and slipped the fingers of my left hand under Boynou's girth. Too loose. I pocketed the Makarov and swung my right foot forward. I lifted the saddle flap and pulled the girth straps a notch tighter in their buckles. There was no time to shorten the stirrup leathers properly. I put two twists into each and stood up. It would do. It would have to do.

Akhal-Tekes are bred for speed and stamina. I'd dreamed of riding one since I was a boy. But if Boynou wasn't shod in iceshoes, it would be a stunningly short gallop. I broke a switch of birch from a branch beside me and nudged him out of the trees. The road ran ahead of us – a silver, snow-blighted ribbon of highway glinting under a recalcitrant moon. I listened hard, but heard only the beating of my heart and the deep nasal rasp of horse breaths in the frozen air. Snow fell. I checked the Makarov was secure and held the reins tight in both hands. I closed my fingers around the makeshift crop. They were stiff and painful, unresponsive from the cold, still bleeding from the cuts my grandfather's knife had scored across them.

Leg on, heels down, back straight. Boynou went from a walk through a couple of strides of a sitting trot and then into a canter. The road beneath held his sure-footed hooves. I urged him on, touching his shoulder with the birch. I shifted my weight and rose in the saddle, dropping my hands either side of his withers, moving my arms forward to give him his head while keeping the rein short enough to control him.

He didn't gallop.

He flew.

I hung on tight with my calves like a solo eventer riding the White Turf at St Moritz. The road dissolved into a blur, a continuous frozen stream of white-water rapids. I looked up and over Boynou's ears, focused on the way ahead. But I could see almost nothing. Snow spattered my face, filled my eyes. I blinked and was blinded, wind lashing my cheeks. I moved the crop and the reins to my left hand, and wiped the ice from my vision. As I opened my eyes, the village lights of Yachmenevo sped past to the right. The frontier with Estonia was only thirteen hundred metres to my left – but there was no path through the thick forest and I knew I couldn't make it that way. I pressed Boynou onwards, as far out of the saddle as I dared, my head sheltering behind his neck, my shoulders just above his. The trees on either side of us slipped past in the darkness – a white-crusted mass of shadows that flanked the road, giving it shape, form.

I twisted in the saddle and looked behind me. If anyone was on our tail, they were engulfed in the pale veil of snow kicked up by Boynou's hooves. And then as I turned back around: headlights – dead ahead. Distance was impossible to gauge exactly. I kept going. It was too late to stop, and there was nowhere else to go. A third light appeared above the first two – brighter, cutting a focused beam towards me. Boynou galloped another two strides.

Snap. Snap. Snap.

Tracer fire arced out of the spotlight towards me, past me. Then more. A lot more. Bright green rounds whipped through the snow, streaming either side of Boynou's head, zooming into the void behind. I dropped as low as I could, all the way down on to his right flank – every tracer chased by four invisible high-velocity rounds. I dug into my jacket pocket, frozen fingers fumbling for the Makarov. Then I saw them clearly.

Ten metres ahead, two soldiers manned an all-terrain vehicle. They were stationary. The driver was leaning into a PKM. Spent brass from the belt concealed in its magazine box spewed into the night. A bullet nicked Boynou's neck. His blood sprayed across me. But the gunner had opened up too late, too high. He struggled to get his barrel around far enough, fast enough.

I pulled the pistol clear of my pocket and swung my arm up. The first trigger pull was heavy, cocking the semi-automatic as well as dropping the hammer. The pressure, the gallop, the cold – everything was against me. The shot went wide. I drew parallel and fired again. And again. The third shot hit home and the tracer leapt into the sky, sending a stream of green bullets into the ether. The ATV disappeared behind me in Boynou's white wake.

It was another six minutes to the inlet. Now everyone knew exactly where I was and where I was heading. If there weren't already Russian troops by the inlet at Kulisko, there soon would be. I rode hard, head down. For a minute I was in the clear. Then more electric green ribbons unwound themselves past me – this time from behind. I looked over my right shoulder. The ATV was back in service. I cracked the birch crop on Boynou's flank and thrust my hands further forward, giving him the rein to run as fast as he could. Ahead of me the road curved sharply to the right. I leaned into the bend as the driver behind me loosed another burst of 7.62. But he was firing one-handed, at speed, and his aim was way off, spitting the barium-bright bullets into the snow around us.

We took the corner fast and I sat back in the saddle. A soldier stood in front of me, chainsaw in hand, turning towards the noise of Boynou's hooves thundering on the road. I passed him at arm's length, firing point blank into his chest as his snowsuit brushed the end of the Makarov's barrel. He twisted and fell, the saw biting into him as he hit the ground. The semi-auto's top slide locked back. Out of ammo. I dropped the pistol and took the reins in both hands. As the lights of the ATV swung around behind me, I saw what the soldier had been doing. The road was cut, logs felled across it. Then I saw muzzle flashes – but they couldn't get a line on me without shooting up the ATV on my heels. I pulled back twice on the reins, hard, to slow Boynou's pace, and then released them, squeezing with my calves as I came up out of the saddle.

He jumped. The logs passed beneath us. Soldiers dived

371

for cover. Silence. And then a terrific *crunch* as the driver ploughed headlong into the barricade behind. The halogen headlight beams swivelled crazily in the snow-filled air. And then the only light was the weak silver sheen cast by the moon as it struggled to break through the reforming clouds. The road forked. I bore left. Boynou's hooves skidded on the ice. He stumbled, back legs faltering. But he steadied himself and carried on, sinews straining, nostrils flared, streaming sweat and steam and blood into the cold night air.

Kulisko swarmed with sweeping headlights. I pulled Boynou off the road and into a field. His canter slowed to a trot, bouncing his way through the freshly settled snow.

Two hundred and fifty metres to the lakeside.

Searchlights combed the landscape around us, but their beams struggled to cut through the still-falling flakes. I brought Boynou to a walk with a low whistle and patted his flank, soothing him. The wound in his neck was superficial, the bleeding light, and he seemed hardly affected by the gallop.

A small creek opened up ahead of us. He stepped down one hoof at a time. The ice held. Four paces and then we were out again, on to the lake shore. I turned us left and rode west for another three hundred metres at a sitting trot, picking my way as carefully as I could along the edge of the frozen water. The land bulged into the lake.

Another two hundred metres and that was it: the point of maximum vulnerability.

Estonia was quarter of a klick to the west; Kulisko five hundred metres to the east – and there was nothing between me and either side except a flat, white sheet of ice. I stood up in the stirrups and faced Boynou towards the border. I prayed that Jack Nazzar was waiting on the other side and stepped out on to the ice.

I didn't hear the launch charges go off.

But I heard the mortars land. First one, then another. The bombs fell on to the ice, fifty metres wide of us, detonating with a deep *thud*. Hard as iron, the ice topping the frozen lake absorbed none of the blast. Instead, shrapnel spread out from each explosion unhindered, spewing thousands of searing-hot, razor-sharp shards well beyond the usual kill radius.

A third round fell, closer. Boynou spooked and reared. I leaned in and tried to calm him. It was a short, deadly sprint to freedom. I looked back towards Kulisko. More incoming. Not bombs, but bright white flashes that popped and burned on the ice. Five, ten, fifteen of them. Within seconds the inlet was on fire.

Flares. Fuck.

It was too windy to launch them over me, so they were firing them directly at the lake. The entire southern shore was burning with blinding white magnesium.

'*No, poshel!*' I shouted at Boynou. '*Yah!*'

His pent-up power unleashed itself into a massive leap forward. We rode out on to the ice, dangerously silhouetted by the flaming Schermulys. Another mortar round landed, spattering the ice with spiked steel. Boynou galloped on, legs, flanks cut by needle-fine splinters of shrapnel. The wind drove into my face. We were in the middle of the inlet now. I lashed Boynou on with the birch switch. As I did so, a mortar bomb landed in front of us, filling the air with a hissing swarm of killer metal. I felt a punch in my chest. I gasped as the impact winded me. My jacket was torn open, ripped by shrapnel.

Boynou rose up.

A heartbeat.

Then pain.

I lost my grip on the reins and tumbled backwards, falling free of the saddle but not the stirrups. My left boot caught fast as Boynou bolted. My head, hands hit the ice. I twisted on to my back. I put my palm to my sternum and burned my fingers on the steel stuck there. I'd taken a direct hit to the chest. Boynou dragged me, his hooves pounding inches from my head. I flexed my foot, but I was wedged tight.

I squinted at the snow-blurred sky. I was beginning to lose consciousness. All around me the lake whited out. I thought for a moment it was snow powder, whipped up by the wind, but it was too dense. All shape, substance dissolved. Above, the night sky disappeared beneath the white wings of an angel swooping down to engulf me. The wounds in my chest, arms, shoulder, thigh tore apart.

This is how it ended – dragged through a world stripped bare of everything I held dear, from Ireland to Arkhangel. Doc Levy shot in his chair; Rachel consumed by fire; all the dead laid out behind me – engulfed by an inferno of my own creation. I strained and looked up into the fog, searching in vain for Jacob's Ladder. But there was nothing to see except an infinite emptiness. It was too late to ask for mercy. Whatever happened next, I had it coming. My eyes dimmed.

'I'm ready,' I said.

But my words were swallowed by the tattoo beaten out by the bombs and Boynou thundering across the ice. And then the strength went out of me and the bright white world went black.

36

'I have to hand it to you, McLean. It was a brilliant story.'

Major General Sir Kristóf King, Director Special Forces, leaned over and charged two glasses with red wine from a lead crystal decanter.

'Convincing that Bulgarian chap I'd sent you on some damned fool mission to shoot a terrorist who was already dead. Quite the ruse. No one gets hanged for killing a ghost, what? Least of all you or I.'

'Thank you, sir.'

'*L'Chaim.*' King raised his glass in a toast. 'That's what the Jews say, isn't it? *To life.*'

'I believe so, sir.'

I nodded at him and drank deeply. He sipped from his own glass and set it down on the old oak table that separated us.

'Château Musar, 1988. So hard to get the genuine stuff from the Lebanon these days. I remembered how much you liked it.'

'Thank you, sir.'

We were sitting in General King's private dining room in Whitehall, all polished wood and oil paintings. His reflection glinted off the tabletop, white skin taut across his skull, black eyes lost in the beeswax shine. It was dark outside. The room was lit by a single chandelier.

It paid to be cautious with King. He was as much an outsider as I was, and his upper-class affectations just that: an act. Hungarian by birth, ruthless by nature: not even the

Chief of the Secret Intelligence Service could outplay him. Never mind aces and eights – to play at King's table, and survive, you needed a fistful of jokers. One slip with him and you'd vanish without trace. I kept my mouth shut and my ears open.

Boynou had unseated me fifty metres from the Estonian frontier, and then dragged me to the NATO front line. I came to in the helicopter, oxygen mask over my mouth, medics working on my chest. Then I understood that it had not been Azrael swooping down on me, but an altogether grumpier angel. Jack Nazzar had received my message and tracked my progress. The dense fog shrouding the final moments of my escape was not the wings of the Destroyer come to get me, but smoke pouring from canisters dropped inside NATO territory by the Wing.

The wind had carried a solid white blanket out across the ice long enough to get me clear. In the end Nazzar's complaint wasn't that I'd interrupted his weekend but that he'd not managed to 'slot any Russkies'. His Revolutionary Warfare mob hadn't fired a single shot.

On the Special Duties flight back to Brize Norton I'd given him a rundown of what had happened – and asked a favour: it was a straightforward breach of protocol, but I wanted to be taken directly to see King.

'I don't fancy my chances in Ulster right now, Jack,' I'd explained.

I didn't have to spell it out. Nazzar knew better than anyone the parlous state of my relationship with Frank. He knew, too, that General King's displeasure cut both ways. If he was not against you, he was for you: the blessing of Director Special Forces, however hard won, was a literal lifesaver.

'Aye, all right, son,' he'd agreed. 'But your lifesaver's right here, no' in bloody Whitehall.'

'I'm sorry,' I said. 'I owe you.'

'Aye, that too. But I'm no talkin' about me, ya daft prick. I'm talkin' about *this*.'

He'd handed me Talia's cell phone. I propped myself up on the stretcher and stared at it in the dim glow of the C130's cabin lights. It was pierced through by a piece of shrapnel – a two-inch chunk of steel, sides sharp as razors. The tip of it had broken the metal casing on the back of the phone, tearing a hole through my passport and gouging a lump out of my chest. But I'd been spared what otherwise would have been a fatal wound to the heart.

'I saw it once before,' he said. 'In Bosnia. Some glaikit cameraman's wallet stopped an AK round.'

'There was stuff on it. Stuff I need. Data.' I slumped back down. '*Shit*.'

'Christ, son. There's no pleasin' you, eh? Tech says he can save whatever's on the drive. But I wouldnae try callin' yer burd wi' it.' He dropped the phone on to my stomach. 'Luck o' the Irish, ya Paddy bastard.'

I finished my wine.

'Commander Knight thought I'd be furious about that phosphorus grenade.' General King brought his face closer to mine and winked. 'Not a bit of it. Burned all the evidence *and* got those New IRA yahoos in trouble. Two birds with one stone, eh? Best not make a habit of it, though. Scares Downing Street half to death.'

He refilled my glass and stared at me, tilting his head to appraise me as one might an animal before slaughter. Where to put the knife? How deep to thrust it? I'd been back in

London for twelve hours. My wounds were as raw as the day they'd been cut.

'I'm glad we have this, ah, opportunity, to clear up any outstanding *personal* matters. Tell me, McLean. Is there anything in *particular* I can help you with?'

He was good. I gave him that much. I thought about all the questions that still remained, but decided instead to ask him the one I knew he'd answer; one that would determine all that followed.

'How did you know, sir?' I said, nursing the wine. He kept still, close, watching me. 'How did Frank – Commander Knight, I mean – how did he know to send me to the cottage in Donegal in the first place?'

'The devil,' he said, sitting back in the dining chair, 'is always in the detail. But if it's all the same with you, I'll let Commander Knight delve into the specifics.' He reached for his wine, crossing his legs under the table as he did so. He paused, calculating, I supposed, the cost of continuing. 'What I will say, though, is that it's a bloody good job Doctor Levy didn't have a telephone. Never mind a computer.' And then a broad grin spread across his face. 'Apparently Commander Knight had been watching him for years. And then his daughter wrote him a letter. A bloody *letter*. Can you imagine?' He turned the glass in his hand, first examining the wine, and then my reaction. 'She was unstable by all accounts. Tried to kill herself once before. Looks like this time she followed through. Shame she didn't survive, though. She'd have made a good gift for the Americans. God knows we could do with some credit at the White House, what?' He sipped the wine. There was a knock on the dining room door as it began to open. 'And talking of the Devil, that will be him now.'

378

King's batman put his head into the room and cleared his throat.

'Commander Knight, sir. Shall I . . . ?'

'Yes, do.' The door opened wider. 'Ah, Frank. Come in. We were just finishing up, weren't we, McLean?' We both stood. I rolled my shoulders and braced myself, though for what, exactly, I wasn't sure. Frank Knight stepped into the room. 'I'll leave you two Irishmen to it,' he continued. 'But before I do, and seeing as we're all here together, there was just one thing I wanted to double-check.' He looked at Frank, and then at me, working out, perhaps, which one of us would lie least effectively. I was both flattered and appalled that he settled on me. 'This Punjabi chap, the one who turned up in Tel Aviv.'

'Baaz,' I said. 'Bhavneet Singh. What about him?'

'Are you sure,' he turned his attention to Frank, 'are you *both* sure, that was his name?'

'Yes,' I said, also turning to Frank. 'I've already been through this with Jack Nazzar on the evac from Tallinn.'

'I see,' said King, shooting his cuffs and adjusting his tie. 'Or rather, I don't see. See him, that is.'

'I don't follow.'

'Neither does anyone else, McLean. The address in Paris you gave for him? On Rue du Texel.' I nodded. 'It's leased in the name of one "Pierre Shor".' I went to speak but he cut me off with a raised hand. 'And there is no one – of either name – enrolled in Saclay University.'

'I . . .'

'And the Indian Ministry of Home Affairs,' he continued forcefully, 'could neither locate anyone in jail in Chandigarh who might be his father nor find any academic who might plausibly have been his professor.'

My mind raced. Sweat broke across my back. The centre of my chest throbbed with pain as my heart rate climbed.

'An auntie. He said he had an auntie in London. I told Nazzar about her, too.'

'I'm sure you will forgive our colleagues in the Security Service if it takes them a little longer than twenty-four hours to pinpoint that *particular* Mrs Kaur.'

In my mind's eye I saw Baaz walking away from me in Tel Aviv and the scales fell from my eyes. Frank shook his head at me like a dissatisfied schoolmaster.

'Fortunately, if somewhat embarrassingly,' King continued, 'the Israelis have found him for us.'

From a pocket inside his uniform jacket he produced a folded piece of paper. He smoothed it out and handed it to Frank, who passed it to me. He wasn't wearing a turban, but it was Baaz all right, caught in three-quarter profile from above by a security camera – rucksack over his right shoulder, ball cap and upturned collar hiding his hair.

'Haifa?' Frank asked.

'No. Ashdod,' Knight replied. 'Your man here is queuing to board a cruise ship bound for Piraeus. His ticket was booked last Wednesday.' The date stamp on the video grab read *07:00:06 19-01-2018*. Friday morning. 'According to the ship's manifest he was due to disembark at Alexandria on Saturday morning.'

'And then what?' I asked.

'And then he vanished, McLean. No one has seen or heard anything of Bhavneet Singh since.'

That beautiful, brilliant boy had stepped out of the shit-storm, pocketing the one thing we'd all wanted. Whatever his motivations, it was a stunning achievement. That much I had to admit. It would have been a coup as magnificent as it was monstrous – were it not for one defining fact: he'd jumped ship too soon. Unless his mind proved equal to Rachel's, without her final calculations all he'd escaped with was precisely one hundred United States dollars. King took the printout from me and walked towards the door.

'He's all yours, Frank. The best of bloody luck to both of you.'

General King stalked out of the dining room, swatting away the attentions of the lance corporal whose undesirable job it was to wait on him. Frank and I stood staring at the floor, waiting for their footsteps to recede. When the only sound left was the distant hum of traffic creeping along Whitehall, Frank looked up at me.

'Well done. Not often you see the old bugger lost for words.'

'Well done?'

'The cottage was burned out and all the evidence destroyed. All anyone on the circuit abroad knows is that Her Majesty's Government wanted you to kill a dead man – and I don't need to tell you, of all people, how easy it is to lead the press. As usual, the great British public will believe exactly what we want them to: 77th Brigade has been on it for days. All things considered, I think it went rather well.'

'But the banknote. The . . .'

'What banknote?' Frank interrupted me. 'There is no banknote. It washed out to sea. Remember?' I opened my mouth to contradict him, but thought better of it.

'There was a shooter, Frank. There was a gunman waiting in the bloody cottage.'

'If you say so, Max. Though as things stand, you might want to think twice before putting that to King. But I did take the precaution of doing as you suggested and checking the sat feed. You were right. We'd have seen a runner clear as day.' He helped himself to a glass of King's wine. 'There wasn't one. Goldilocks must have fried.'

'Show me, Frank. Show me the satellite images.'

'As you well know,' he said, 'those images are classified. So I'll say it again, Max. All the evidence has been destroyed. You vaporized it.' He turned to face me squarely. 'I expect exactly what happened in Donegal will remain permanently, uh, how shall we put it? Unknown.'

'And Avilov, Doctor Leonid Avilov? His GRU goons picked me up in-country, in Mayo.'

'Ah, yes. The good doctor. He didn't survive, either. A traffic accident, it seems. The Kremlin has issued a statement. Thrown from a bridge in Moscow during a collision. He was court-martialled a month ago, apparently. They're denying all official knowledge of his excursions to the Holy Land and our Emerald Isle.' I flexed the fingers of my right hand. 'So, uh, all's quiet on the Eastern Front.'

But there was one thing he hadn't considered.

'The computer, Frank. The Russians have built a computer.'

'Yes.' He nodded slowly. 'As far as we can tell – and it's hard to be certain – that does indeed seem to be the case.' He took a long draft of the wine, and put the empty glass back on the silver tray, next to the decanter. 'But then again,' he smiled, 'so have we.'

'Does it work?'

'No, it doesn't. Not now, anyway. And you know,' he said, taking a step closer to me, 'perhaps that's for the best. After all, if it did, you and I would be out of a job, wouldn't we?' He put his hands in his pockets and went to leave. 'The general's batman will show you out.'

We both knew that I could kill him right then and there.

The fact that I wouldn't was perhaps the last guarantee of survival I had. Standing on the train platform in Ashford, I'd thought all bets were off. They weren't. Frank had never even dealt me in. He'd manipulated me so perfectly that I'd believed all along that I'd been the one in charge.

'You played me, Frank.'

He hesitated in the doorway; his back still turned to me.

'No, Max. You played yourself.'

Epilogue: Appointment in Arklow

Saturday 27 January 2018

I pressed my face to the railings. The old Regency pile sat at the far end of the drive, grey beneath a damp Wicklow sky, windows full of clouds. It had rained earlier and the ground was wet, just as it had been twenty-seven years ago. On her eighteenth birthday Rachel had already been teetering on the edge of madness, greatness. All I'd had were stories.

And of all the stories I'd told, the most enduring had been the one I told myself: that the gates to our family house had guarded a prison I'd been lucky to escape. But I'd known, sitting at Polina Yurievna's table – my mother's table – that I'd ended up on the wrong side of them.

Hand over hand I hauled myself up over the old ironwork, fingers still smarting, chest and shoulder burning, and dropped down on to home ground.

I walked to the front door and tried the handle, but it was locked. Then I skirted around the house, past the library, and under the shadow of the clock tower. The formal gardens fell away and there, landscaped into the edge of the woodland that rolled on for miles towards Croghan Mountain, was the lake that had taken my mother's life.

I sat down on the bench my father had carved for her before his last trip to Africa, and unfolded the old photograph that Polina had given to me.

Rock-a-bye baby, don't lie on the edge, or the little grey wolf will bite your side . . .

I couldn't say she hadn't warned me.

Frank would never admit it, because he didn't need to: there was only one person who could have released my passport photograph, and only one person who could have called me at Doc's – the same person who tipped off the Gardaí: him. Almost the only thing I'd got right was that we'd been equally suspicious of each other. The moment I'd hung on to the hundred-dollar bill had been the moment he'd cut me loose – not to discard me, but to force me towards the conclusion he'd gambled I'd reach, propelling me onwards at every turn. He didn't trust me. But he'd needed me to help him unravel a mission that he didn't fully understand himself. He knew the only way I would do the job – the only way I could do it – was if I didn't think I was doing it at all. I would have chased anyone on earth to their death for him.

But not her.

I suspected it as I'd watched her pyre burn, but hadn't wanted to face it. The lean, wiry man running away from Doc's; the BMW motorbike rider in Paris; the athletic Mercedes driver escaping the crash in Moscow; maybe even the figure in Aleksandr Denisovich's front yard: all five-eleven, all the same build. Whoever he was, it was possible he'd dogged me all the way to Arkhangel. And if I was right, he'd saved me in Moscow, too. My father didn't believe in coincidences. And neither did I. Frank's operators were as unknown to me as they were to each other. Maybe I'd imagined it, or maybe I'd had a guardian angel after all – or a guardian knight. And maybe, just maybe, his name was Bhavneet Singh.

One way or another, I was sure I'd be seeing him in the future. To survive in the tunnels like that takes more than intuition; it takes training. And to vanish into thin air like that takes more than courage; it takes connections. Perhaps

I'd imagined it. Perhaps I was looking for patterns that weren't there. But whoever or whatever Baaz was, a child prodigy from the Punjab simply didn't cover it. Being photographed on the quayside wasn't proof he'd boarded his ship. And Frank and I had both fiddled enough passenger manifests to know they weren't worth the paper they were written on. The drive from Ashdod to Ben Gurion airport takes less than an hour: perhaps it wasn't the line at the port the Israelis should have been looking at, but the queue of people checking into my flight to Moscow – assuming, of course, that Talia even wanted to find him.

The only real mystery left was why in the end I'd been spared at all. But as Frank had said himself: neither of us was out of a job yet.

I'd started the drive that last night in Russia with the road lit by firelight, turning my back on the forests that would have swallowed Rachel and me. I'd thought I was coming back home, but bricks and water were nothing to come back for. She'd known all along that there was nowhere left for her to go. Not so me. I'd had a choice. And despite everything, I'd chosen to come in from the cold. Frank had sent a ghost to kill a devil. I watched the world, compelled towards my own completion – looking out over the still water, unable to let go.

Rachel had set honour in one eye and death in the other. It had blinded her until she'd died. In the gathering gloom I asked myself what I might possibly be owed from the cost of all that bloodletting. Out of the flames I tried to conjure her face. But all that remained was the memory of those eyes flashing in the inferno; and the reality of me, alone, holding on to nothing but a name. I thought I had known my own mind. But I no longer even knew for sure which one of us had gone insane.

Then from inside my jacket I removed the stricken cell phone, wrapped tight in waterproof bindings, and hurled it into the lake. It had saved my life once. The image in its circuits might one day do so again.

When the ripples reached the shore, I heard footsteps and then a man wearing a black uniform appeared beside me. A security guard, watching for trespassers, face hidden by the peak of his cap. He cleared his throat.

'You shouldn't be here, you know,' he said.

'Yes,' I replied. 'I know.'

I put away the photograph of my mother and stood up. Turning my back on the lake, I let the lights of the town guide me to the sea. I had survived for a reason.

Everyone always does.